PRAISE FOR

"... *Abnormal Ends* is a must-read for lovers of science fiction novels blended with spine-chilling horror and nerve-wracking action, all based on a gripping tale of sacrifices, manipulation, tough choices, murder, running, egotistic sleuths, and opportunistic workmates."
– READERS' FAVORITE BOOK REVIEW of *Abnormal Ends*
– 5 out of 5 stars.

"Futuristic and thrilling—Abnormal Ends brings a new, horrifying perspective to machines fighting back."
– INDEPENDENT BOOK REVIEW on *Abnormal Ends*.

"Descriptive, enthralling, and offers a vision of the future both frightening and believable. There are hints here of Philip K. Dick, Neal Stephenson, and William Gibson. This work is sure to delight and entertain fans of the genre."
– US REVIEW OF BOOKS on *Abnormal Ends* – Recommended.

"Mystery fans and tech-savvy readers will find this multilayered combination of an SF novel, a suspense yarn, and a technothriller to be a cut above others of its ilk.
  A visionary, futuristic police procedural that buzzes with imagination and intrigue."
– KIRKUS REVIEWS on *Abnormal Ends*.

PRAISE FOR *AFTERWORLD*

"*Afterworld* establishes itself as a dark fantasy that is not to be missed, with its original and deadly world, exciting and dynamic tale of fighting for survival, and deep characterization of its protagonist."
– READERS' FAVORITE BOOK REVIEW on *Afterworld*
– 5 out of 5 stars.

"The writing in this novel is phenomenal."
– INDEPENDENT BOOK REVIEW on *Afterworld*.

"A nuanced and thrilling take on a bellicose future."
– KIRKUS REVIEWS on *Afterworld*.

"The plotting is tight and tension relentless. However, McBee's greatest strength is in narrative voice: he renders the grim situation with laser precision."
— BOOKVIEW REVIEW on *Afterworld* – 5 out of 5 stars.

"[The] tale has shades of *Fahrenheit 451*, *The Planet of the Apes*, and *1984*. All are stories about civilizations that have collapsed and been replaced either by totalitarian structures or other societies in which humans are marginalized or enslaved."
— THE US REVIEW OF BOOKS on *Afterworld*.

PRAISE FOR *VECTOR ZERO*

"Distrust and deceit throw soldiers and civilians into a tailspin in this gripping tale."
— KIRKUS REVIEWS on *Vector Zero*.

"This tale of ever-increasing contagion and the manhunt to run down the original source of the virulent killer is heavily dosed with science, suspense, and action ..."
— PACIFIC BOOK REVIEW on *Vector Zero*.

"A rip-roaring work of fiction with plenty of suspense, surprises, action, and dread to offer readers."
— READERS' FAVORITE BOOK REVIEW of *Vector Zero*
– 5 out of 5 stars.

"One of those rare thrillers that perfectly paces through the events and switching perspectives in a way that instantly sucks you in, all while not leaning too heavily on cheap tricks."
— Margaret Carmel for the *Idaho Press Tribune*.

"His characterizations of their past influences, present challenges, and unknowable futures infuse his narrative with empathy, immediacy, and anxiety, respectively. McBee has indeed penned a page-turner for today and a cautionary tale for tomorrow."
— The US Review of Books on *Vector Zero*.

BRYAN McBEE

FROM GREAT HEIGHTS

A NOVEL

atmosphere press

© 2024 Bryan McBee

Published by Atmosphere Press

Cover design by Matthew Fielder

No part of this book may be reproduced without permission from the author except in brief quotations and in reviews. This is a work of fiction, and any resemblance to real places, persons, or events is entirely coincidental.

Atmospherepress.com

Dedicated to the men of Bravo Battery 2/3 FA 1/1AD, whom I served with from 2009 to 2014. Brothers always: STRIKE HARD

"Any sufficiently advanced technology is indistinguishable from magic."
– Arthur C. Clark

ALSO BY BRYAN MCBEE:

Vector Zero
Afterworld
Abnormal Ends

To Kylie,
Never stop believing in
Magic!

31 May 2025

FROM

GREAT

HEIGHTS

CHAPTER 1

RANCE

The gris-gris man came to town the day after the storm blew down from the southern mountains and hit the village of Windmill's Watch for three long days and nights, knocking down the ancient, dilapidated hilltop windmill. It had been a hard year, and some residents took the windmill's collapse as an omen of bad tidings to come. A wall of dust enveloped the village, blown by gale-force winds. Stunted trees, weakened by summer droughts, were ripped from the ground and tossed about like kindling. Needle hail plowed into and, in some cases, through battered roofs and thin walls, injuring several people and even killing a newborn sleeping soundly in his crib. The temperature dropped so suddenly that pipes burst in the few houses with indoor plumbing. While most people were lucky enough to make it to shelter, the sudden arrival of the storms always caught an unprepared few, carrying them away, never to be seen again.

It was late in the year, before the snow but after the harvest. Nobody knew where the gris-gris man came from, why he had come to their small town, or even his real name. He was just the gris-gris man, a practitioner of the old magic. One of the enigmatic wanderers traveling the countryside offering their skills and knowledge in trade.

He had seen dozens of hardscrabble towns like Windmill's Watch in his travels. The rutted dirt streets that turned to glue when it rained. The careworn boardwalks skirting each storefront and home. The washed-out, dreary clapboard buildings. Windmill's Watch was a town that fought mightily each day of the year to survive to see the next.

Evidence of humanity's tenacious nature never failed to make him smile. The human will to survive was one thing that could always be counted upon.

As he passed the tumbled-down windmill, the gris-gris man glanced up at the beige murkiness above. *I miss blue skies*, he thought. The sun was hiding behind a cloud bank, but according to his chronometer, it was just past six in the evening as he walked down the main street with the assured stride of a man who knew exactly where he was going. Glancing neither right nor left at the people gawping at him, he strode directly to the mayor's house without once asking for directions.

Mayor Selma McChaze answered his knock and was immediately taken aback. She knew what he was even before he opened his mouth in greeting.

"Good day, Mayor McChaze," the gris-gris man said before she could introduce herself.

He looked like an old vagabond and had a voice like rustling paper, but there was something in his bearing that conveyed power and authority. His skin was tan but smooth, and his wild white hair sprang from his scalp in all directions. His smile displayed a mouth full of perfectly set, healthy teeth. It was his eyes that struck her. Deep penetrating jade stones that seemed to see everything at once.

McChaze worked up her courage to speak. There were many tall tales about the wandering wizards. She figured most of them were bullshit. All the same, she did not want to risk this stranger's anger. "Good day to you, sir," she said in a halting voice. "What can I do for you? We're a peaceful town and don't want no trouble."

The gris-gris man smiled and nodded. After so many years and so many towns, he was used to this sort of greeting.

"Madam, you know me for what I am; therefore, I think we

can dispense with some of the obligatory back and forth. I've been on the road all day, you see, and I'm quite tired. I'm not here to bring trouble to you or your neighbors, Selma. I merely seek a room to rent and your permission to ply my trade."

McChaze nodded as if that was the answer she expected to hear. "Talk to Peter Lopez. He's got a shack he might be able to rent out. You should be able to stay there as long as you've got coin. As for your trade, most folks 'round here don't care much for magic and hokey-pocus. You might have a tough time of it."

"My thanks," he said. "I'm sure there are some who would listen to an old man. If that turns out to not be the case, I'll say my goodbyes and be on my way." He bid her a good day and then stepped back into the street, headed straight for Lopez's small farm, again without asking for directions.

Over the following days, the gris-gris man became a common sight around town. Most people even stopped staring or crossing themselves whenever he came near. To most of the residents of Windmill's Watch, the gris-gris man was just a batty, albeit harmless, old man. He could be seen aimlessly wandering the streets in his threadbare coat, muttering to himself. Some of the old timers claimed they could recollect him visiting years before. If asked, they would swear it was the very same one then and now, though he didn't look a day older.

Occasionally, he would stop someone to offer cryptic advice.

To Suzanne Owanapi, he said, "Look beneath the floorboards beneath your washtub. That's where you'll find it."

He told Mikhail Giovanni, "If you give her snow tulips, she will kiss you. Kill the beast attacking her livestock, and she will marry you and be yours forever."

When Suzanne pulled up her floorboards, she was astonished to find the locket her mother had worn and lost years ago. Mikhail killed the stinglynx harassing the Widow Emily

De Soto, and they married come the spring thaw.

Others actively sought him out for advice, healing, to purchase the good luck charms he fashioned, or simply to stare in wonder at the living relic.

This was how the gris-gris man got by during his time in Windmill's Watch. Food, clothing, and even a bit of coin gratefully given in repayment for his services. Everyone knew he had the nan in him. There was no other way he could possibly see all he saw or know all he knew. This notion made many people in town fearful. For all the goodwill he engendered, there was an equal and opposite measure of mistrust and dislike provoked by his presence. Fear of the old magic was still great, and there were those who wanted nothing to do with it or with the gris-gris man.

Winter arrived like a hammer fall. It was long, and it was cruel. Through it all, the gris-gris man preached and taught and helped those who called upon him. He spoke to anyone who would listen about a diverse range of subjects: three-field crop rotation techniques, insulation techniques to keep a home warm in winter and cool in summer, sanitation procedures to prevent illness, improved food preservation techniques, and so on. There seemed to be no end to his knowledge. He pointed out three places where wells could be dug, and come the thaw, there was water where he predicted. He gave the town doctor tips and tricks for healing various maladies and injuries common to the region. For Mayor McChaze, he drew up diagrams and instructions for rebuilding the wind turbine to bring it back to life and provide electricity for the town.

On one especially frosty night during the darkest months of the winter, he felt his alarms chime, telling him Celia Pittman's six-year-old son, Christopher, burned in the grip of a fever.

For three days, Celia had tried everything she could to nurse her son back to health. Nothing worked. She was alone, her husband having died the year before after being stung by a rockwasp. He had lain screaming in agony for four days before finally succumbing to the wasp's venom. Now, snow fell thick and hard. Most stayed indoors, where it was warm and safe. To protect what remained of her family, Celia threw her cloak over her shoulders and got ready to brave the snow to reach the doctor. She didn't want to leave Christopher alone but saw no other choice. She was just about to leave when there came a knock at her door. The gris-gris man had walked through the freezing snow from the other side of town and arrived unbidden on her doorstep. His heart ached at the sight of the bedraggled widow who opened the door.

The air outside caused Celia's teeth to chatter. But the gris-gris man, wrapped in his worn, patched traveling coat, gave it no notice at all. In fact, despite the heavy sheets of fluffy falling snow, he was completely dry. It looked to her eye as though the snowflakes evaporated an instant before touching him.

"I am here to help you, Widow Pittman," he said, gently pushing open the door and entering her home. "If you do what I say, I promise Christopher will survive this night and live to play again tomorrow."

At Christopher's bedside, he placed his hands on the little boy's chest, closed his eyes, and began chanting under his breath.

He paused and opened his eyes. "I need you to place a kettle of clean water over the fire, please." Then he closed his eyes and resumed chanting and remained in that position until the first rays of dawn peeked through her windows.

Celia had fallen asleep in a chair across the room from them and snapped awake at the sound of laughter. The storm had passed, and chilly morning light streamed through her son's bedroom window. On the table next to her chair sat the kettle and teacups, ready for a morning brew. She saw Christopher sitting up in bed, giggling merrily at the simple magic tricks the gris-gris man performed. A disappearing coin reappeared behind his ear, a handkerchief mouse skittered up his arm, and a butterfly made of rainbow smoke danced a halo above his head. There was no sign at all that the boy had been on the verge of death only hours before as he laughed and clapped his hands. Celia immediately swept her son into her arms and held him tightly.

With tears in her eyes, she turned to thank the gris-gris man and found him already gone.

He spent much of his time that winter healing and helping. He would arrive unannounced exactly where he was needed, exactly when he was needed. Some perceived his actions to be divine providence, while others saw them as proof of the Devil's hand working and claimed he was trying to bring the town under his thrall. One thing was certain, though; the people who attended his lectures regularly and followed his advice almost immediately became healthier and happier. This incensed those who mistrusted and feared the gris-gris man and made them hate him even more.

The loudest among them was Marjory Beckham, the owner of the cleaner of Windmill's Watch's two saloons and the richest woman in town.

"He ain't nothin' but trouble," she hollered to a full barroom. "He's got the old magic, and he'll take us all to hell with him. You mark my words." Most simply chuckled drunkenly at her rant, but some listened and took her words to heart.

"He's just a kindly old coot what likes to help folks, Marj," someone from the far side of her bar called out. "You need to calm yourself."

"And you need watch yer fuckin' mouth if you want to keep drinking, Carter Trammel. I know you think that Devil bastard speaks with God's words; I saw you talking with him just last week. Selling your soul for a pittance."

"I ain't sold shit!" Carter yelled back. "I wasn't even looking to talk to him. He just walks up to me outside Macy's store and tells me and my wife our baby will be a healthy girl. Then he hands me a basket of vegetables he says are high in iron and advised Alisa to eat 'em regular for the baby."

The man standing next to Carter turned to him, saying, "I didn't know you was havin' a baby, Cart."

"I didn't neither, but Alisa went to Doc Stanley's straightaway, and sure as shit, she's pregnant. Baby be born middle of spring, he says."

There were several shouts of congratulations, and someone offered to buy Carter his next beer. Determined to see the gris-gris man run out of town on a rail, Marj wouldn't let this happy news deter her.

She gave the father-to-be a few mocking claps of her hands. "So, you knocked your little wife up. Congratulations to you, Carter. That doesn't change the fact that he is evil. Evil to his very core. And if you all let him have his way, he will destroy our town. Our home. He ain't one of us and never will be. You mark me well; nothing good will come of his bein' here. The sooner he's gone, the better. Or else our town will end up like the Ashlands."

The bar became a sea of bobbing heads. Everyone knew of the Ashlands. A patch of land said to be poisoned by magic, so nothing could grow there. Anyone who entered fell ill. Anyone who didn't immediately leave died.

Feeling the drunken adoration of the crowd, Marjory continued, "That man is the Devil's own servant, and he freely walks our streets like he owns 'em. Just like he were a proper king. Well, here's what I have to say to that." She turned her head and hocked a large brown wad of phlegm into the trash bin behind the bar.

Her customers responded with an uproar of cheers, clinking steins, and clapping hands. The few who disagreed remained quiet and slowly slunk to the fringes of the crowd.

"What we need are a few men who ain't too yellow to do what needs doing. Men who ain't too cowardly to stand up to him, take him down a peg or two. Brave men who will tell him his welcome in our town is worn out and that it would be in his own best interest to move along. If he wants to stay above ground and breathing, that is. Are there any men like that among you?"

The chorus of "Yes, ma'am," "Hell yeah!" and "You're Goddamned tooting!" made her smile.

Tomorrow, when they sobered up, these men and women wouldn't be nearly as brave. For most of them, the moment was already past, and they started to disperse to their tables to finish their drinks. Most, but not all. There were a few in whom Marg's words had ignited a righteous fire.

The gris-gris man's time in Windmill's Watch was coming to an end.

Something big tripped the gris-gris man's sensors while he slept, awakening him.

He had been expecting this for some time. It was always the same story in the end. Fear and superstition overrode any good-intentioned help he provided. It had happened so many times, in fact, that he could set his chronometer to it.

He confirmed what his sensors were telling him. *Four of them*, he thought with a shrug. *With that many, I'll be able to perform a complete rebuild and make it to the Convocation without any trouble.*

They would have weapons. Guns, maybe, but certainly clubs, axes, and pitchforks. Not that these implements would help them. Nothing would. Not tonight. These four had made their choice. Silent as a shadow, he rose from his cot and went outside to greet his would-be attackers.

They had stopped in the darkness, unsure whether to continue or not. He could have enhanced his hearing to pick up every word of their hushed argument, but chose not to. He'd heard it a hundred times before. Besides, he didn't want to know who was out there.

Ten feet from the shack, it was nearly impossible to see in the blackness. Only people who knew the area well dared travel by night. He accessed his night-vision application and adjusted his eyes. The countryside around him appeared before him, bathed in sharp green and gray light. He had been using the nanotech applications and enhanced abilities for so long he hardly remembered what it would be like without them. Forgotten what it was to be as mundane as the people he helped.

The gris-gris man accessed his defense and armament menus, hardened his skin into armored plate, and charged his weapons.

In the black of the night, they never saw him coming.

He hated this part. But there was no other option, which did nothing to make him feel better.

They made their choice, he thought again.

He snuck up and snapped the first one's neck from behind before the others even knew he was there. The biggest of them felt the hair on his arms stand up as the gris-gris man pointed, and a bolt of harsh white lightning erupted from his fingertips, slammed into the big man's chest, and knocked him to the ground like a ragdoll. The last two were blinded by the flash and tried running away, tripping and stumbling blindly in the dark. The gris-gris man quickly ran down the closest and stopped his heart with another electric jolt.

The last one surprised him by turning to fight. He must have caught a hint of movement because he raised the ax he carried and swung it sideways, catching the gris-gris man squarely in the cheek. The clang of the steel on his skin reverberated in the dark. Yelping in surprise, the inebriated attacker dropped his ax and ran. The gris-gris man caught him and crushed his skull in one hand.

Without looking at their faces, he lined the bodies up behind the shack and went to work. Haste was imperative to harvest. Dead tissue wasn't as nourishing as living tissue. He placed his right hand upon the forehead of the first corpse and his left over the heart. Then he probed with his nanites, activated the dormant nanites in the corpse, and began harvesting healthy cells from the rapidly cooling dead man in much the same way as he had drawn the sickness from Christopher Pittman. He also ran a diagnostic scan on the corpse's nanites, looking for any latent applications or interesting bits of code he could harvest and incorporate into his own systems before they died, too.

Once he had what he needed, he repeated the process with the other three.

Finished, he stood, raised his palms, and incinerated the desiccated corpses with a focused and intense beam of fire until all that remained were four vaguely human-shaped scorch marks in the dirt. It was as if they had never been there at all. Between the four of them, he had harvested enough to facilitate the re-morph he had in mind.

The only consolation he could take from this ordeal was that it would be at least another fifty years before he would need to glut himself like that again. He had never wanted the life of a wandering wizard. The role had been thrust upon him and those like him. Their work, it seemed, was never-ending. Too much to be fixed overnight.

Decades ago, in another life, he had been Terrance Rance, a researcher at a major corporation dealing in nanotech and climate restoration. Back then, nanotech was everywhere; even the poorest person had applications built in, connecting them to everyone else in the world. Science had been the answer to all of life's problems and big questions.

After the Break-Down, Rance and others like him, survivors of the catastrophe, set out to fix what had gone wrong. They built an order dedicated to the preservation of humankind and the continued restoration of the planet. Daunting tasks both. He had lost track of exactly how long ago that was.

He could easily bring up his calendar application and find out. But he didn't want to know. It was just too depressing. Better deal to with the world in front of him.

He hurried to pack his meager belongings. Though Lopez's farm was on the outskirts of town, the commotion might have drawn some attention. There might be people from town about, looking for their friends and loved ones, and he didn't want to kill anyone else if he didn't have to. Even though he couldn't linger, there was one more stop he wanted to make before leaving Windmill's Watch behind.

Long after the doors were locked and the windows shuttered, Marj was still behind the bar, clearing away the collection of mugs and cleaning up the various messes left behind.

A coughing fit doubled her over the basin behind the bar, interrupting her chores. Once she could breathe again, she looked at the bloody, black chunk she'd spat into the sink. Clearing her throat, she rinsed her mouth with cold water. The cough was getting worse every day. Gripping the rim of the sink, she closed her eyes and whispered a prayer. Then she lit a hand-rolled cigarette.

"Good evening," a voice said behind her.

She whipped around to find the gris-gris man smiling at her. "How the hell did you get in here? Get out! I'm closed. We don't serve your kind here." She blew smoke in his direction.

The gris-gris man continued smiling. "Then it is fortunate for you I'm not here for watered-down whisky or stale beer."

The glass she had been cleaning with a bar rag shook in her hands as Marj turned red with rage. Few people could speak to her like that and escape unbruised. In the saloon she had built, the business that was her own personal fiefdom, such words would certainly draw blood.

"The fuck'd you say to me?"

"I'm not here for libations, Marjory Beckham; I'm here for you."

"How dare—" Marj started, but the gris-gris man interrupted her with a raised hand.

"I do not want to fight or to cause you trouble. I can see you're sick. I'm here to help you because Doctor Stanley cannot. He does the best he can with what he's got. It's not like he has an X-ray, an MRI, or a Holographic Diagnostic Scanner at his disposal. I suspect, being the proud woman you are, you haven't even gone to see him."

"I don't want none of your help, devil man. You can leave my bar and go straight back to hell where you come from."

The gris-gris man slowly shook his head. "You're afraid now, aren't you? It's becoming harder to breathe, you're coughing all the time, and you're tired and weak when you wake in the morning and drop into bed exhausted every night. You've recently started coughing blood, haven't you?"

"You can't know that!"

The gris-gris man shrugged. "Maybe so. But it does not change the fact I do know it. You know what the black lung does to people. How they waste away, suffocating, drowning in the open air. You remember what happened to your dear Walter, your sweetheart, with whom you built this establishment. You remember his final agonizing days, and you are afraid."

Tears welled up in Marj's eyes. Her rage had dissipated, replaced by sudden fear. "Get out!"

The gris-gris man stepped forward, close enough he could reach out and touch her. Marj shied away, terrified of what would happen if he laid hands on her.

"I can take the tumors away. I can heal your battered body and make you whole again. One touch is all it will take, and you will live out the rest of your days in good health and peace."

"No." She shook her head violently. "Don't you touch me. I won't let you use your black magic on me."

The gris-gris man moved fast. In a blink, he was around

the solid oak bar top and standing beside her.

"Let me help you." He raised his hands and gently placed one on her right shoulder and the other on her chest. She was still shaking her head but had lost the will to resist.

The gris-gris man closed his eyes. His brow furrowed in concentration. He could see it now. She had lung cancer, alright, non-small cell lung cancer, probably stage-IV Adenocarcinoma. Bad, too. When he first saw her, he could tell she was sick. Now that he had linked with her, he could see just how sick she really was. Not impossible to cure, but not easy either. She was right, after all; he had the nan in him. Then again, so did she. So did everyone in Windmill's Watch. It was how he knew where to tell Suzanne Owanapi where to look for her mother's lost locket, how he knew about the stinglynx attacking the widow De Soto's animals, and how he knew Carter Trammel's wife was with child. He'd tagged and tracked each of the four hundred and thirteen residents of Windmill's Watch upon first entering the little town. They had all been born with it, passed down through the generations.

But only he, and others like him, could use it.

Marj's cancer was deep-rooted and stubborn. He had to activate an extra dose of her nanites to work in concert with his to dislodge it and draw it out. Once it was moving, however, the process went quickly and was over in a minute. The gris-gris man deactivated her nanites, withdrew his, and opened his eyes. She was cleansed now. The murderous tumors were trapped inside his body, contained behind walls of nanites that tore each cancer cell apart down to its RNA and remade them. The process was one he had used with young Christopher and was completed just as quickly. He had merely stayed the night with the boy to add a bit of theatricality and allow Celia a chance to get some much-needed sleep.

When he removed his hands from her, Marj slumped. Then she blinked and straightened up. She took a deep, astonished breath, looked right into his eyes, and nearly smiled in ecstasy. He could even see the "Thank you" forming on her lips. Then her expression darkened, and the familiar scowl her face usually wore returned.

"How dare you?" she hissed. "How dare you touch me? Devil man. You've tainted me with your evil magics and, and—"

Her body gave out from the ordeal, and she collapsed into his arms. Effortlessly, he hoisted her and carried her to her bedroom on the second floor.

On his way out, he stopped at the sink behind the bar, then dipped his fingers into the fibrous black mass Marj had coughed up. It was almost an inch in diameter and slimy with phlegm and blood. He pinched it between his thumb and forefingers, popped it into his mouth, and swallowed without chewing.

On the way out of town, the gris-gris man wondered whether healing Marge had been the right choice. She would never become an ally, no matter what he did. But he hoped by healing her, she might at least stop actively inciting the town against him and the things he had taught. It was a gamble. One that had the potential to undo everything he had worked for during the long, frigid winter. This deep in the amber zone, people needed all the help they could get.

"What's done is done," he muttered as he hitched his pack up on his shoulders.

No one saw as he skulked down the western road.

A few miles away from Windmill's Watch, the landscape west of town was dotted with clumps of hills and sparse, sickly-looking trees. In the east, the sun was rising on another day, bringing light to the poisoned earth. A dozen meters south of the road, he got a small fire going, laid out his crockery, and set his bed roll, then sat on a shriveled log to watch the rising sun. The sky was layered with colors cast by the fading light. Nearest the sun were blue and green, while above them, purple and red clouds swirled, and directly overhead was a black so dark even the stars couldn't shine through. During the day, the sky was a murky quagmire of pale gray light. Only sunrise and sunset brought a brief respite from the gloom.

Off in the distance, he heard a wraith-cat stalking prey. It wouldn't come near him; the nanite wards would see to that. His security applications could set both a warning net and a defensive perimeter if he desired; for the time being, he just used camouflage to conceal his camp. Security in place, he settled down on his bed roll, activated all his nanites, and began reshaping his body.

Within him, micron-sized robots had finished the process of reconstructing Marj's cancer into healthy viable cells and incorporated them into the tissues harvested from his would-be attackers, as well as the rest of the tissues he had siphoned from those he encountered during his stay in Windmill's Watch. These cells were used straightaway, replacing and reconstructing the old, worn-out cells within him. The nanites cocooned him while they worked to complete the metamorphosis the gris-gris man desired.

Nineteen hours later, the operation was complete. He emerged young and strong and vital. He stood taller, his bones were thicker, and his muscles had taken on greater mass and definition. His wild white hair had regained its fullness and taken on the burnt bark color of his youth.

It's good to see you again, Terry, he thought as he examined his rejuvenated face in a looking glass and smiled.

As he packed up his camp, he whistled under his breath and thought about the town he had left behind. He hoped he had done enough for Windmill's Watch and lamented how things had ended. When he rejoined the road heading east, he murmured a quick prayer for the small town. Without a backward glance, he walked through the pitch-dark night and long into the pallid, sickly day.

The Convocation was still months and miles away. There

was a whole lot of good he could do between now and then. While he walked, Rance started whistling a jaunty tune from his youth.

CHAPTER 2

KINNEY

Kuridian was a smallish rocky planet, second in orbit around its star, four thousand one hundred and sixteen meters in diameter, tilted twenty-two degrees on its axis. Though small, it possessed a dense iron core, giving it a strong magnetic field enclosing a thick atmosphere comprised primarily of carbon dioxide, methane, and other trace elements, with an average temperature range between 23 and 82 degrees Fahrenheit and mild seasonal shifts. Gravity was a close ninety-seven percent of Earth's at the equator. All these facts, plus the discovery of liquid water on the planet's surface, made Kuridian ideal for human habitation after a complete terraforming.

HelixCom won the bid to reshape Kuridian into an Earth-like world where human beings could live. It was a grand experiment. Twenty years earlier, four Earth-like planets had been discovered, and colonies were established on two of them, with some cosmetic adjustments required to make them more ideal for habitation. The other two were deemed prohibitively distant for colonization. In the two decades since, no other planets had been discovered that so closely matched Earth. The focus, therefore, shifted to near-Earth-like planets. The thinking then was to take these unsuitable worlds and make them suitable.

The scope of the project was immense. Once a suitable target planet was identified, in this case, Kuridian, capsules containing payloads of programable matter were launched into space at near-light speeds. Once these capsules reached their destination, Stage One began with the nanites inside awakening and beginning construction on the long-range transceiver array in orbit using programable matter, as well as constructing labs and habitation areas. Once the orbital array was online, pathfinder technicians were transmitted along the entangled transceiver, waking in new bodies printed for them via nanites. Next came the orbital transfer and receiving stations, where the personnel overseeing further construction both in orbit and on the surface were installed. This painstaking process was hurried along until the ground was prepared enough to erect the permanent structures where the next phase of terraforming would be undertaken. During Stage Two, surface facilities were completed, and the crews slated to work in them were transmitted and installed in bodies printed from their DNA templates. The last piece of the puzzle put in place before the actual terraforming could commence was a skylift. This space elevator was built in reverse, with the counterweight hung in geosynchronous orbit first, then the "tether" lowered into the atmosphere and connected to the enormous pyramidal ground station, one thousand meters in height and one thousand five hundred and seventy-two meters wide on each of its four sides. The skylift base complex was also constructed using nanites and programable matter dropped to the surface in capsules. Once operational, Stage Three could begin, with the workers overseeing the actual terraforming riding the skylift down to the surface.

 From start to finish, the first stage of the program took five years. The second stage, converting the atmosphere and biosphere into something hospitable for people, would take another five years. The final stage, terraforming, colony construction, and inhabitation, would last a mere fifty years.

 If successful, the Kuridian Project would usher in an era where humanity was not confined to the worlds where nature set up a convenient niche for them. From here on out, humanity, not nature, would dictate where they settled.

FROM GREAT HEIGHTS

*

Jerry Kinney woke and sat up feeling refreshed and alert. The mattress registered his absence and began the process of making itself ready for Kinney's return during his next allotted sleep period: first microbe removal, then the bed smoothed and fluffed itself and pulled the thin but surprisingly heavy top cover taut before disassembling itself into the floor and going dormant until required. The bed had been programmed to meet its owner's tastes and comfort parameters. Over the months it had been occupied by Kinney, it had further customized itself to his needs and would continue to do so for as long as Jerry Kinney was registered as its primary occupant.

On the way to the water closet for a steam shower, he set the kitchenette to start fixing his usual morning repast: toast, buttered and slightly burnt; one egg, sunny side up; and seven hundred milliliters of strong black coffee. While he ate, Kinney watched the central feed to catch up on the events of the previous shift. On a good day, the feed was boring, filled with mundane entries meant to record the minutia of the different shifts for examination by the home office. On a bad one, some minor catastrophe or other would fill the feed. If the problem was bad enough, then the other shifts would be brought in to help correct it.

Feeling refreshed and finally alive, he dressed, his dark gray coveralls immediately adjusting to fit his body perfectly. It was zero-five-hundred; he had one hour to report to his station for work. He collected his access badge from the cubby in the corner of his room. Why they required them to carry the stupid things was beyond him. Everyone in the facility transmitted an identity code that tracked them throughout the facility. There was little actual on-site surveillance because the applications built into each of them projected their presence for Central to monitor and log. It was how they tracked work productivity, leisure time abuses, medical issues, and a number of other things. All that biometric tracking made him roll his eyes every time he clipped the badge to the top pocket of his uniform.

He glanced around his living space to make sure everything was picked up and tidy before leaving. Kinney was expecting to receive good news today. News that meant he wouldn't be living in this small, bland closet for much longer.

Ever since he had become Joined, he knew big things were in store for him. The smooth, cream-colored walls were featureless except for the three porthole windows. The water closet and kitchenette had folded away just like the bed had. The only permanent fixtures were an armchair with a side table, upon which rested his personal tablet, and a set of cubbies for personal items. Otherwise, the five-by-three-meter space was completely open and devoid of personality. Lighting came from recessed soffits along the walls near the floor and ceiling. Kinney counted himself lucky that his position on-site warranted him getting an exterior room with windows.

Not that the view through the windows was anything to boast about. The landscape around Site 2 was drab and unremarkable. A few low hills covered with scrub lichen. The outlines of foundations and roads were being marked off in preparation for colony construction. Site 2, in addition to its primary mission, was also going to be home to the first city in the region. If all went according to plan, they would start growing the habitats by the end of the year. Kinney had seen the designs and thought the place looked beautiful. Once all the infrastructure was implanted, they were going to use the same experimental methods to build the city that had been used to construct Site 2. Nanites, feeding on raw materials from slag heaps, would swarm and assemble the various buildings and structures.

The idea was to save costs and reduce waste. Site 1 had been built from prefabricated components and joined together in place. Once online, Site 2 was touted as a major success of automation and remote engineering. The first facility of its kind grown entirely with nanites and programable matter. The ribbon cutting heralded a new era of industrial construction and automation.

The creation of nanite-controlled programable matter had been a milestone in the evolution of human technology, on par with harnessing fire, the discovery of the wheel, the invention of the printing press, the development of the steam engine, and the proliferation of the internet. Each of those milestones demarked a significant leap forward in human knowledge and capability, paving the way for further incremental advances.

Nanotechnology truly was a blessed gift from Aion.

As a species, the human race always sought to create the ideal environment in which to settle and call home. Clearing forests, damming rivers, and mining resources. In their infantile steps away from the cradle of civilization, people had spread to inhabit every landmass on their home planet, bringing the scars of civilization with them. Often with detrimental and even disastrous consequences for the indigenous flora and fauna. Still, the search for the perfect place to call home continued. From the trough of the lowest valley to the peak of the highest mountain, the depths of the oceans to the farthest reaches of the solar system. Humanity's search for elbow room was never-ending.

Programable matter had allowed the human race to finally realize the dream of attaining full mastery over their domain. This new product of materials science had put an end to strip mining, oil drilling, and other environmentally hazardous ventures. Almost overnight, recycling had gone from an unprofitable exercise with limited utility to being transformed into a primary method by which new materials were created. Nanites were able to break down used materials to their most basic molecular components and rebuild them into programable matter that could be commanded to take on any shape and characteristic required.

It was nothing short of miraculous.

Among themselves, the nanites created a cloud network that operated as a rudimentary intelligence. These networks possessed intelligence greater than that of viruses or bacteria but less than that of insects like the common housefly. Yet, there were some who felt these cloud networks could be trained to work in concert with other clouds to create even greater distributed intelligence networks. This notion gave the most forward-thinking humans something to work towards. Computer-generated artificial intelligence had failed to live up to the expectations and, in some cases, the fears of its proponents and detractors. At its best, AI was a simulacrum of true intelligence. Capable of fooling the casual observer interacting with it, but incapable of true independent creative thought. The fears of a robot uprising, instilled in human workers since the dawn of the Industrial Revolution, when their jobs had been taken over by machines, proved to be the stuff of mere fiction.

Nanites, on the other hand, demonstrated a clear ability to creatively problem-solve and even plan for the future. Not only that, but the cloud nodes shared knowledge with the others they encountered, creating a knowledge base and expanding upon it with every new interaction. Humanity had finally realized the dream of creating life beyond its own biological progeny.

Nanite-controlled programable matter was the miracle that had granted humanity the stars.

From orbit around Earth, human beings once again explored and spread into every available nook and cranny they could find. Their telescopes informed them of the first major problem: hospitable planets, like their own green and warm Earth, were few in number, whereas rocky planets closer in relation to their satellite, the Moon, were far more common. As were gas giants like Jupiter and Saturn. This was a vexing problem. In order to leave the stellar cradle, humanity first needed someplace to go.

Enter the planet-builders. Companies dedicated to terraforming new worlds for humanity to inhabit and call their own. To date, there had only been two successfully terraformed planets. HelixCom hoped to plant its flag and become the first company to build a planet from the ground up, bring it to market, and sell it.

Kinney swiped his door open and then swiped the lock once he was through. Time to go see what the previous shifts hadn't done throughout the night. He managed a four-person team on A-shift, from 06:00 to 16:00. The twenty-eight-hour day took some getting used to, but it wasn't so bad.

The walls of the corridor were nearly as smooth and featureless as his room. There was a ridge running along the length of the ceiling, which hid the cables, pipes, and conduits connecting one section of the site to another. There were also periodic bulges in the wall, usually near doors or intersections, that marked maintenance access points. Each intersection was labeled to make navigating the warren of corridors and tunnels easier. Different colored lights could also mark a path for newcomers still learning their way around. Kinney had worked there for nearly a year and hadn't needed the light path to get around for most of that time. Some people took months to get used to the uniform sameness of Site 2, but Kinney had known his way around in three weeks.

Site 2 was the newest and best. Incorporating cutting-edge tech and aesthetics to make the workspace as user-friendly and pleasant as possible for the two hundred people who had to live and work there for years at a time. Extra attention had been paid to providing sufficient entertainment and relaxation amenities. There was a well-equipped gym with a pool, a theater, and a library full of actual physical books. That last was surprisingly popular among Site 2 staff, such that the stock of books had been expanded several times with new titles.

Last but certainly not least, the entire place smelled faintly of lilac. Not overwhelmingly so, but just enough to make the air fragrant and fresh. It was one of the things Kinney liked best about Site 2. Even the bad days seemed to melt away as time went on. That was in part due to the care put into the site's design but also due to the cocktail of calming drugs pumped into the air in vapor form. Chlorafednate-7 was chief among these and the source of the pleasant floral aroma.

Change-over with C-Shift took six minutes. Kinney's counterpart was smart and capable, but she didn't have the greatest work ethic. No drive to do anything beyond what was prescribed in her job description or outside the parameters of whatever protocol she was finishing up or babysitting. She was there to fill her seat, collect her pay, and rotate back home at the end of the tour. In short, she was pretty much like the other denizens of the nighttime shifts.

"Hey, Jer. I finished up the amino audit you started yesterday," she said, shrugging into her jacket. The entire site was climate controlled, the temperature a constant and comfortable twenty-three degrees, yet she felt the need to wear an extra jacket everywhere. "The levels are within tolerances. I think we might be ready to start the run up for introducing the next level of producers."

Kinney already knew that. They'd been ready for a few weeks now, but it was protocol to double- and triple-check before each step. With trillions of dollars of development credit on the line, such thorough measures made sense.

"That's good," he said. "As soon as we finish the audits and prep, we should be ready for stage two. Pending approval from Central, of course."

"Exciting times," she said, stifling a yawn. "You need anything else from me?"

Kinney gave their crossover on the feed another quick once-over. "I don't think so. Is there anything else I need to know?" She shook her head. "Then have a good sleep. I'll see you tomorrow."

*

Just after lunch, Kinney was summoned to his area manager's office. He'd just sat back down at his station to begin verifying the next round of sims when the message flashed, summoning him. Not one to keep the boss waiting, Kinney paused the batch and locked his station.

"I have an opportunity for you, Kinney, my man," the manager said once Kinney sat down. "I'm sending you to Site 1."

"What the hell for?" Kinney demanded. "What did I do? We're getting ready to roll out stage-two upgrades. You need me here for that."

"Which is precisely why I am sending you." His supervisor, a long-time company man named Arun Mehta, gave him a level look and pursed his lips.

Looking at him each day was disconcerting. He didn't have the aura he'd come to expect from someone who'd become Joined with Aion. Kinney had been the first on-site to experience connection with Aion, nearly a year ago. Since then, many of the ground staffers, including everyone working under him, and several of the midlevel managers had become Joined. But not everyone. Not yet. Though Aion's flock grew by the day, it would be some time before everyone had accepted his sacrament into their lives.

"They've been having difficulties reaching their benchmarks this quarter," Mehta continued. "If they can't, then the next phase of Stage Three will be delayed across the board. We advance together, or we are all held back together."

"I understand that. But why me? I've got my hands full here managing my team and keeping up on the other two shifts' work." Kinney had been expecting news. Aion had promised a wonderful opportunity would come today. This was not what he'd expected.

"Your record here proves you're the perfect person for the job. They need someone to whip them into shape over there.

Your team boasts the best numbers here. You've achieved your benchmarks, and maintained them, faster than any of the other teams."

"So, what you're telling me is that I'm being rewarded for all my hard work with more. Thanks a lot." He thought back to the last time he had to travel to Site 1 a few months ago. He hadn't enjoyed the experience. "Some opportunity."

"I supposed that's one way of looking at it," Mehta admitted. "Or you could view this transfer as a major stepping stone to promotion." This got Kinney's attention. "That's the opportunity. Do a good job over there, whip those lumps into shape, and there'll be a section supervisor position waiting for you when you return."

That was a big promotion, which was exactly what Aion had promised.

"Look, Jerry," Metah said, leaning forward, his expression serious. "I'm going to level with you. Corporate thinks something is going on over there. They've been behind on nearly every benchmark for the last two years. Ever since the last crew change-over, in fact. The number of on-site accidents and incident reports has gone up by over eighty percent. Additionally, MirrTech's own research has advanced by leaps and bounds during that same time period. They've started growing their own starships. Something Analytics says they shouldn't have been able to do for another three years."

MirrTech was HelixCom's biggest competitor. Though they were close to matching HelixCom's capabilities, they were still years behind on nanotech. HelixCom had developed or purchased nearly all the patents related to nanotech and its constituent technologies. They doled out a few licenses a year to prevent anti-trust litigation and overt government oversight. MirrTech catching up so quickly implied some underhanded business practices were in play.

"Are you saying you want me to go to Site 1 to investigate industrial espionage? Don't we have specialists for that?"

"We do. But that's only part of the reason you're being sent. Officially, you'll be there to nursemaid them and bring them back on track. Fix their safety issues and such. That's your primary tasking. Unofficially, yes, you are going there to snoop around and see if you can uncover any industrial espionage."

"But Site 1 is leaky, and it smells bad," he said. The protest was half-hearted. He already knew he was going to do it. So did Mehta, who gave him a small, placating smile in response. "When do I leave?"

"The day after tomorrow."

Two days later, Kinney stepped off the transport tube car and into the station and immediately frowned in displeasure.

It was as bad as he remembered. No, actually, it was worse.

The platform was cold, damp, and poorly lit. The walls were lined with exposed conduits and piping. A loose electrical wire dangled above a backlit poster featuring a smiling woman in a lab coat. Her exaggerated expression was meant to imply the utter joy she felt in her work, but it made Kinney wonder what kinds of drugs she was on. The background of the image was brightly lit, almost sunny, and clean. A stark contrast to the damp, dim platform where he found himself.

He looked around, expecting to see someone waiting to greet him. But the station was empty.

Even though there were over seven hundred people occupying Site 1, there was no evidence of them anywhere around. This shouldn't have surprised him. The tram station wasn't directly connected to the facility. Because it had been constructed a decade after Site 1 came online, around the time Site 2 began construction, it was separated by a hundred meters. The tube station at Site 2 had been integrated into the design from the outset.

Shaking his head, Kinney picked up his duffle and carried

it over to the wall terminal next to the poster of the manically happy, possibly stoned lab tech. He punched in his ID number on the physical keypad, and the system responded by informing him that he was not authorized to access the system.

In an annoyed huff, he found a floorplan diagram on the opposite wall of the platform. He held up a hand over it to illuminate the simple map and committed it to memory. If he was reading it correctly, getting to the Ops wing wouldn't take too long, but it would be a hike. His destination was up three levels on the far side of the facility. Shouldering his duffle, he sighed and left the station platform.

He already hated it there. He just wanted to finish the job he was given and go back to where he belonged. Why had Aion sent him here? This was not the place for a rising star.

The walkway was just as dim and dank as the platform had been. Everything looked well-maintained but old and worn. Old, like everything else at Site 1. Through the wide aluminum oxynitride windows set in reinforced tungsten frames, Kinney watched the landscape outside as he walked. Though two hundred kilometers stretched between the two terraforming sites, it looked basically the same as the area around Site 2, though there was less construction and more weak greenery. Site 1 had been in place working for a little over twenty years, and the land around it had been reconstituted to the point where it was almost healthy. It would be a long while yet before the land around Site 2 showed the same progress. One look through the thick armored windows proved they were making a difference. Soon, the climate transformation would become largely automated, with the biome they'd set in place doing most of the work for them.

At the far end of the tunnel stood a pressure door. Kinney spun the locking wheel to release and open it. The air was fresher inside, but only slightly. He grimaced as he closed and locked the door again, sealing himself in Site 1 until his mission was complete. After taking a moment to rest, he checked the map again and started making his way up to the site manager's office.

This level of the complex was less industrial than the rest. The floor was covered with grimy traffic-worn carpeting, with the walls shod with office dividers to make it more comfortable for the people tasked with administering the site.

They couldn't do anything about the smell, though. Despite the attempts to cover it with artificial floral fragrances, the stink of old engine oil and damp canvas and ozone permeated the air. Each time he thought he had finally become nose-blind to it, he turned a corner, and a new concentration punched him in the sinuses. Kinney shook his head and tried breathing through his mouth.

Slightly winded and more than a little annoyed, Kinney pressed a button next to a door made of flimsy prefab plastic and heard a soft chime inside. It was sturdy enough to enforce privacy but not to hold out against anyone determined to get inside.

Sixty days.

That was what Mehta had promised him. Kinney didn't think he could stand being here any longer. The fixes he was here to implement and oversee should only take sixty days. If he was quick and thorough, then his investigation should be wrapped up by then as well. In all honesty, he thought Mehta and his corporate watchdogs were just being paranoid. But this was the path Aion had set him on, and Kinney would do his absolute best to implement His will.

He was about to ring the bell again when he heard rustling sounds from the other side of the door, indicating Director Waler, his boss while on this temporary assignment, was inside. Kinney figured the director was making him wait to express his displeasure at outside interference. No one liked it when outsiders were sent in to fix things. He also assumed it was why nobody had met him at the tube station.

The door opened, revealing a tall, balding man in his late

forties. He had a narrow, almost pinched face, with small, close-set eyes and a long, hooked nose.

"Mr. Waler," Kinney said, inserting as much deference into his tone as he could. "I'm Jerry Kinney. I've been reassigned here."

"I know who you are, Kinney," Waler said, and he looked Kinney up and down a moment longer before stepping aside. "Come in and have a seat."

The inside of the office was just as shabby as the rest of the floor. It was a small space, barely large enough to accommodate a desk and three chairs.

Waler dropped into his chair and swiped open a screen between them. "It says here you are a nanotech particulate engineer. You graduated in eighteen and were hired by the company right out of college. You worked on the Sinai Project before signing up to come here. You were promoted to line supervisor pretty much right away. You elected to remain, signing for another year-long tour. By all accounts, you are professional, hardworking, and efficient."

Kinney could sense a "but" coming. However, Waler said nothing. The silence stretched uncomfortably long, and then Kinney cleared his throat. "I was given to understand you were having issues with certain nano-processes."

"We aren't having issues," Waler said flatly. "Things are proceeding within the schedule on our end. Our site is just old. Especially compared to the cushy little playground you come from. Sometimes things take a little longer here, that's all. We can't help where the company chooses to spend its money. Why buy us a new pressure regulation system for the gas scrubbers when they can just accuse us of going too slow and send someone over to crack the whip?" He sighed and shrugged. "Nothing to be done about it. You are clearly qualified and will make an excellent addition to our family here at Site 1. I'm sorry I didn't have someone at the station to meet you and begin your orientation. That was an oversight on my part. If you'll follow me, I'll set you up with one of our best envirotechs to show you around."

Waler rose and escorted him out of the tiny office, back to the stairwell, and down two levels. He led Kinney into a large room partitioned into a cluster of smaller lab spaces. The partition he stopped at was occupied by a single woman hunched over a workbench. Her dark hair was a frazzled mess, precariously held atop her head by a single clip. The lab coat she wore was worn and faded to gray. There was a pop and fizzle from the bench in front of her that caused her to recoil.

"Fuck!" She slapped the device in her hand down on the bench surface. "Damnit. You stupid piece of—" She broke off when she saw Waler, her eyes narrowing suspiciously.

For his part, Waler seemed not to notice as he beamed brightly at the swearing woman. "Astrid, I'd like to introduce Jerry Kinney, your new boss. He's the nano-construct engineer sent to us from Site 2. Kinney, this is Astrid Free, my chief environmental engineer."

"Pleasure to meet you," Kinney said, extending his hand. She ignored it, her eyes never leaving Waler.

"What the hell am I supposed to do with him?"

Sensing more than a little animosity between them, Kinney let his hand fall and took a half step back.

"I want you to orientate him. Give him the tour. I've forwarded all the details. You need to set him up with access, take him to HR, show him his workstation and quarters and such."

"I'm a tour guide now? Waler, I don't have the time to deal with FNG bullshit. I'm in the middle of something kind of important here."

"It looks to me like you've reached a good place to pause."

She rolled her eyes and continued scowling at him. "Fine. I'll show the FNG where the bathrooms are. But I need to get back to work as soon as possible. This is all time-sensitive. If it takes too long, then I'll lose all the data and have to start over."

Waler's smile widened. "That's all I ask. Thank you, Astrid."

Without another word, Waler turned and walked out the way he came in.

Astrid Free turned gave Kinney one look, then scoffed. "Come on, newbie, the shitters are this way."

The tour was short. Astrid led him along at a brisk pace, showing him the mess hall, his sleeping berth, his lab space, and the lavatories. She ended her tour at the Human Resources office.

"Here's where we part ways, newbie. HR will set you up with access to the system, provide you with the station map so you can't get lost, and give you your timecard and everything else you need. They can also send someone with you on a more complete tour if you need it."

"If HR does all that, why did Waler leave me with you?" Kinney asked, confused.

"Because he's an asshole. He did it to fuck with me and waste my time."

Such a waste of resources would never have happened at Site 2. It was unthinkable.

"I'm sorry. If I had known, I would have brought myself to HR without bothering you."

She gave him a little smile, the first he'd seen during their brief time together. "I appreciate that, newbie." Then he raised a knuckle to her forehead in mock salute. "Good luck, boss. And welcome to Site 1. Sorry it had to be you."

The HR bureaucrat barely looked up from his screen while Kinney was in his cubicle. "I've just uploaded the necessary transfer paperwork to your drive. Be sure to fill it out and send it back before the end of the week. Here is your badge." He passed Kinney a plastic rectangle with a bad picture of him on it. "I'm sure I don't need to tell you to keep it on you at all times. Wait here a moment while I find someone to give you a tour."

"Oh, that's not necessary," Kinney said, trying to be helpful and away from this unpleasant bureaucratic monkey and his red tape as quickly as possible. "I've already been given a tour."

The HR bureaucrat gave him a deeply suspicious look. "By who?"

"Mr. Waler had Astrid Free show me around before she brought me here."

The HR bureaucrat threw his head back and gave an altogether unpleasant, short, loud, barking laugh.

"Why is that funny?" Kinney asked. He wasn't sure he wanted to know, but curiosity and a desire to know about any potential pitfalls demanded he find out.

"Oh, I just love Waler's sense of humor," the HR bureaucrat said and had another short chuckle, then seeing Kinney's confusion, went on. "Astrid Free was in line to be promoted into the position you slid into. I guess Waler thought it would be a good joke to have her escort you since she's been such an unpleasant pain in his ass. Anywho, good luck, and welcome to Site 1."

He didn't offer to shake Kinney's hand. Even if he had, Kinney wouldn't have taken it.

He'd hoped to avoid pissing off anyone when he got here. But because Waler's management style seemed to rely completely upon the toxic treatment of the people beneath him, he had already upset at least one person, and who knew how many more, just by coming here.

As the door slid closed behind him, he sighed. "This is going to be fun," he said with a groan.

CHAPTER 3
REGALINE

Regaline Lager accepted a cup of water from a frail-looking woman while the husband eyed her suspiciously. They were seated in the front room of the clapboard shack that served as their home. Regaline could feel a draft coming through the ill-fitting walls.

"What do you want with our boy?" the woman, named Kata, said. She spoke in a halting manner, her voice barely audible. It was like she was afraid to draw attention to herself with her words.

"I've been in your little town a few days now," Regaline said, "helping your friends and neighbors where I can. In that time, I've noticed your son has displayed some remarkable abilities."

This wasn't precisely true. During the most recent survey, two signals were identified, indicating two people who not only showed increased capacity to use nan but were already actively using it. Due to the difficulty in explaining their abilities, self-taught individuals were often at odds with their communities. This town was on the edge of a green zone. Just a few kilometers outside of town, the landscape was practically barren. This close to the far edge of the amber zone, little grew and people led hard lives. They had little time for anything mysterious, no matter how beneficial.

Regaline had already collected the two she'd been sent for. In doing so, she'd been alerted to the possibility of another individual displaying the traits she was looking for. So, with her new charges in tow, she'd detoured to this small, unnamed hamlet to collect a third.

"Told you we shouldn't have let the boy outside once it started happening," the husband said quietly enough she could pretend she hadn't heard. He hadn't given her his name, though she knew it was Domen. He was definitely afraid of something. Most likely her. That was the way it went whenever she came to a new town. It took a while before the locals warmed up to her. If they did at all. Some superstitions were hard to overcome.

Kata pretended not to hear her husband. "Did he do something wrong, ma'am? Are you here to punish him?"

Regaline turned on her best smile. "No, ma'am. Your son didn't do anything wrong. On the contrary. I would like your permission to take him with me when I leave tonight."

The couple shared a look. The emotions that passed between them were varied, but chief among them was relief.

"Where you takin' him?" Domen said.

"I intend to take him for training. So he may make the most use of his abilities."

"And he'll never come back here?"

"I can't say for certain what he will do once his training is complete. He will go where he is needed most. He may choose to return. He may not. But that won't be for several years at least."

The couple visibly relaxed. They were clearly afraid of their son and were desperate for her to take him off their hands. It was a common story here in the outlands. Education was sparse and superstition rampant. The people they referred to as gris-gris men, and women, were objects of awe and fear. Anyone who manifested abilities in nan was often ostracized and cast out because of it. Hearing he would be gone for several years at the least seemed to shift some weight from their shoulders. Domen smiled for the first time since Regaline had entered their home, and Kata finally allowed herself to look somewhere other than the floor in front of her toes. They were being rid of a problem, and they didn't have to do anything but thank their lucky stars.

This was why she was there. She'd ventured from Hillcrest on a mission to find two special wild nan casters and had chanced upon a third. Their son was a bonus. In these uncertain times, nan casters were more vital than ever before. The ruling council of Hillcrest maintained a standing mission to gather wilders who were objects of fear and derision and remove them before the worst happened. Finding a prize like this before the zealots from Interland was fortunate indeed. Like the gris-gris men of old, their agents ventured to the settlements, towns, and farmsteads throughout the green zone, amber zone, and even the far-away red zone to provide aid and ensure their success and prosperity.

"Taeg!" the father shouted, making Kata jump in her seat. "Taeg, get out here, boy. There's someone here for you."

There was some rustling from the back of the house, followed by the sound of footsteps approaching. She performed a quick scan of him: Taeg was nineteen, almost twenty, tall and stocky, and in good health. He stooped as he walked, as though constantly ducking the hit coming at him. He stood before his father, his eyes downcast and his hands clasped before him. "Yes, sir?"

"This woman's going to take you," Domen said. "Go pack your things." He waved a hand, and Taeg theatrically flinched before hurrying back down the hall to do as he was told.

A few awkward and silent minutes later, Taeg returned wearing a traveling coat and rucksack. Kata and Domen saw them to the door, where she embraced him in a stiff, reluctant hug. "Goodbye, my sweet baby boy. Always remember, I love you." Domen stood with his arms crossed, wearing a scowl, and said nothing.

"I'll take good care of him," Regaline assured them. But

they were already closing the door.

She shook her head slightly. Ignorant people always got under her skin. Once they were safely outside town, Regaline stopped them to get a good look at her find.

"Stand up straight," she said. "And look me in the eyes. That's better." She reached out with her nan. She could see he was already very capable. He'd been using nan for years, it seemed. It was just a matter of expanding his capabilities and building on what he already knew.

"Come, let's go meet the others. We have a long way to travel and a lot of work to do along the way."

The gossamer cloud hovered against the breeze blowing gently in a northwesterly direction. The tiny motes, scarcely visible to the eye, swirled and spun above the wilted tree husk hunched on the cracked bank of a muddy trickle. The tree was misshapen, twisted by disease and thirst, and covered in blotchy gray-and-blackened bark that crumbled to the touch. The creek from which the tree drew nourishment had long since dried. The waters that once flowed along its bed had reduced to a trickle, consigning the tree to a long, slow death.

Which made it the perfect test.

Regaline brushed an errant wisp of steel-colored hair from her brow as she watched the adept weaving the nanite cloud above the dead tree. He was attempting, without much success, to revive and rejuvenate the tree. Even ten meters away, she could tell the boy, Houston Diaz, was struggling to control his cloud. He'd been at it for nearly ten minutes, and his only progress was the sweat pouring down his cheeks and soaking his underarms. Though the nan cloud swirled and undulated above and about it, the tree remained unchanged.

"That's enough, Houston. Draw them back and come sit down." The cloud formation immediately collapsed upon itself. The swirling dust scattered like a swarm of angry bees, then rematerialized itself into a tight funnel that wound itself into Houston's outstretched hands, disappearing into his body. Once the nan was recovered, he slumped and stumbled over to where Regaline and the others waited, grumbling under his breath about the stupidity of the task.

"A good attempt," she said, trying her best to sound encouraging. However, she was no teacher and found it difficult to articulate the hows and whys of using nan. It was just something she innately knew, and she'd been doing it so long that she never thought about how it did what she wanted anymore. But here she was, trying to explain the basics of nan casting to people with the technical background of the dead tree she had Houston trying to revive. Neither of the boys had much in the way of formal education. The girl, Kayah Handler, was at least better off. She was seventeen and had grown up in a township that held school for children up to what would have been the fifth grade, so she could read and perform basic arithmetic. Regaline felt she had at least to teach them the basics before they returned to Hillcrest. Otherwise, they would be a danger to themselves as well as others. She looked each of them over and worried whether she was up to the challenge of teaching them. To say Regaline was feeling the pressure would have been an understatement.

Taeg was the oldest of the three and the least naturally capable. Houston, at thirteen, was the youngest and by far the most difficult of them, and Kayah was the most willing to learn. Taeg plodded through her lessons with slow determination. Houston, who had learned to use fire early on, was only interested in learning how to make things burn. However, when she could get him to pay attention to her, Houston seemed quick to pick up the skills she was trying to impart. Kayah was by far the best of the three of them. Patient and eager. Even if she wasn't the strongest, Regaline thought she might turn out to be the most capable of them.

"That's enough for today," she said, with a clap of her

hands. "Let's return to camp and prepare dinner."

They all got up and trudged away from the dry creek bed.

She had to figure out a way to instruct them. She could access the ancient technical manuals and even transfer them to her adepts. The first problem would be teaching them how to access and open the files. The next, for all but Kayah, would have to teach them how to read the files, and even Kayah would probably drown in the jargon contained therein. When she'd advocated for this course of action, she hadn't accounted for how ignorant people had become since the Break-Down. Even in the green zone, the struggle to stay alive took precedence over book learning. She found herself slipping into a dark mood and saw it reflected in her adepts.

To cheer them up, she decided they would play a game.

"Houston," she said. "Build us a fire, please, and I'll cook the rabbits we caught earlier." By force of habit, Houston reached into the satchel hanging by his hip. "With your nan, if you would be so kind."

She saw his eyes light up. He was better with fire than the others. Things had a habit of smoldering and spontaneously combusting around him. She wanted him to practice with what he already knew and to make using his nan second nature.

"Thanks, Reggie," he said. She stopped herself from rolling her eyes. He'd given her the nickname; he'd given them all nicknames—Kayah was Twigs, most likely because she was skinny and all awkward elbows and knees, and Taeg he dubbed Rocky because he was big and slow and immovable like a rock—which seemed to be how Houston made himself feel at ease with people. He also insisted everyone call him Drak, which he said was short for dragon. It was appropriate, she supposed. He did so love to set things on fire. Over the past few days, ever since she uprooted him from hearth and home, he had jumped at any chance to use his natural talent.

Regaline stewed the rabbits they had caught earlier with

some roots and edible plants she'd hunted up. The result was filling, if not exactly satisfying.

"Time for a game," she said as they finished up. "I want you three to spread around the fire, equal space between you. Good. Now, I want you to focus on the flames and relax. Let your mind drift as you watch the flames." She glanced around. "No sleeping, Houston!"

He immediately snapped up and gave his head a little shake.

Regaline followed her own instructions, letting her mind wander.

"Now, I want you to reach down within and take hold of your nan in whatever way you know how. Once you've got it, I want you to manipulate the flames. Like this."

She used her nanites to begin moving the air in and around the fire. Creating slight changes in the air pressure. Feeding and drawing off oxygen to make the fire expand and contract and dance. She introduced wisps of different gases to create new colors of flame. Her nanites created localized air currents to make the fire swell and sway to a rhythm she set.

After a few minutes of showing off, she withdrew her nan. The fire quieted back to its original size and intensity.

"Your turn, Kayah."

The young woman glanced at the others around the circle, then tucked her dark hair behind her ears, took a deep breath, and focused. Her performance wasn't as smooth as Regaline's. The fire seemed to jump and stutter with each change Kayah introduced. It was impressive, nonetheless. Kayah managed to copy every move Regaline had made conducting the flames. The girl was a natural.

"Excellent. Now, Houston."

"I already told you; it's Drak," he said. Then he rolled his shoulders and began. Being more skillful than either of the others, his performance was smoother, and rather than simply copying what Regaline had done, he improvised to provide a good spectacle. At one point, though, he seemed to lose control, and the fire swelled blue almost beyond the rocks that ringed it, but he managed to rein it in before she had to intercede.

Last up was Taeg.

The fire barely twitched for him.

He is going to be the most difficult to train, she thought. *Too much emotional baggage. It's almost like he's afraid to even try.* Kayah and Houston were both still children. Young enough to bounce back from their childhood strictures.

"Very good attempt," she said.

"No, it wasn't," Houston said. "He didn't even do anything."

"Houston—"

"I told you; I'm Drak! As in Dra-Gon! Call me Drak."

"Shut up, Drak," Kayah said. "You're being a brat."

"You shut up, Twigs! Just because you're in love with Rocky doesn't mean you need to show off. Kiss-ass."

The color that rose in Kayah's cheeks could have been embarrassment or anger. It was difficult to tell by the firelight.

"That's enough," Regaline said, but neither of them heard.

"Better to be a kiss-ass than a dumb-ass," Kayah fired back. "And at least I can do more than light a stupid match." She was referring to the fact that she'd been the only one of them to get the tree to bloom.

"Maybe I don't want to do more. Who needs to change the leaves on a dead tree when I can just burn it and you if I want?"

"You are such a stupid child."

Neither of them noticed Regaline rise to her feet and extend her hands.

"I said, enough!" She gestured and shut them up with a brief sonic blast. "Drak," she said in a placating tone. He smiled at the use of his preferred name. "We all learn at different rates. Taeg just needs to figure out how to access and take control of his nan, and it will handle the rest. So it will be for all of you. The more you handle it, the easier it will become. I can't teach you how to handle or use it any more than I can teach you how to breathe or make your heartbeat. All I can do is show you the path and how to safely walk it."

"I'm sorry I said I would burn you, Twigs," he said, eyes downcast. "And I'm sorry I made fun of you, Rocky."

"It's okay," Kayah said. "I'm sorry I called you a stupid child." She crossed her arms and bowed her head as if to make herself smaller and less noticeable.

Taeg muttered something that might have been an apology acceptance.

Regaline nodded her approval.

"It's time for bed."

Long after her adepts lay down and began snoring their cares away, Regaline lay awake, trying to figure out a way for them to access more nan. According to the elders, it had been easier in the old days. Well, not actually easier. They'd built the applications from the ground up. In that regard, it was easier to know what to do and how to do it when you knew the system inside and out.

She was just about to give up and go to sleep when a thought occurred to her. Before the Breakdown, one of their forebearers had wanted to make the applications accessible to children. From what Regaline could remember, she'd gone on and on about how they were going to revolutionize education systems with this technology. Regaline was sure she remembered something about a pilot tutorial program designed for kids.

She closed her eyes and delved into her archives. It didn't take long to locate the memo. Though the language was professional, there was a boastful undertone to the letter. Once she finished reading, she opened the applications archive. Voilà. A tutorial program had indeed been completed. Smiling, Regaline finally relaxed.

She'd start them on the program tomorrow.

*

The anthropomorphic circus seal named Wally balanced atop a beach ball on its nose and juggling bowling pins with its tail flippers was just finishing up its discourse on how and why Kayah was special.

"So, you see, Kayah"—she found it mildly disconcerting that it called her by name— "these tiny, microscopic robots have attached themselves to the DNA in your body. They can help you heal, prevent you from getting sick, and give you a ton of abilities you didn't have before. Not the ability to fly. I know that's the first thing you want to try out. But there's lots of other cool stuff they can do for you. And best of all, if you start to run low, your body will just make more of them. They are powered by the food you eat and the water you drink and the air you breathe."

Despite the slightly condescending nature of the lecture, as it was written for someone younger than Drak, after all, not an adult like her, Kayah was fascinated. She knew there was so much more than this simple program was telling her. Regaline had told them as much when she guided them to find and open it. Now, she was impatient for these kiddie lessons to be done so she could get to know her abilities for real.

"This is the end of the introduction," Wally said, in a voice designed to be pleasant, almost soothing, but which grated on her ears. "Would you like to move on to the first lesson?"

Finally.

Kayah used the gesture Regaline had shown her for selecting and rejecting options in the program and selected yes as fast as she could.

"Very good, Kayah. Sit back and pay attention." Wally hoped on a bicycle—somehow, she knew it was a bicycle, even though she'd never seen one before—and motioned for her to follow along. "We are going deep into your body to learn how to play with the different abilities you've unlocked."

Kayah grinned greedily. *Yes, Wally. Show me more, please.*

*

Though he would never admit it to Twigs or the others, Wally the Seal delighted Drak. The cartoon seal's antics were so funny that he barely paid attention to the lesson. He made it through the first section by simply choosing "continue" every time the option appeared. He didn't care why he had nan or how it worked; he just wanted to know how to use it. He liked burning stuff but felt there were other things that might be just as fun to learn.

Wally the Seal turned and faced him, his expression solemn. "Now, I want you to take a deep breath, Drak." At least Wally got his name right. "Close your eyes. Good. Now, think of your heart. Feel it beating in your chest. Concentrate on that rhythm."

Drak did so. It was another stupid exercise. Just like the others, Reggie tried to get him to do. He was hungry. When would they have lunch? Sitting here with his eyes closed was stupid.

"I know you think this is a waste of your time, Drak," Wally said. "But I mean it when I tell you this is necessary."

Drak's eyes snapped open to find the seal giving him the same look his mother had given when she had wanted to guilt him into doing his chores. Hunger forgotten, he felt suddenly ridiculously small and just a little scared at the rebuke. Drak closed his eyes again and listened to his heart.

"Thank you. Now, I want you to picture your heart in your mind. See it grow and shrink as it pumps your blood. Can you see a faint glow around it?"

Drak nodded.

"Very good. Now, I want you to reach out and touch your glowing heart."

Drak did so. The moment he grasped the heart, he felt something shift inside of him. He felt energized in a way he'd never felt before. Eyes still closed, he lifted his head and panned from left to right. He could see a perfect image of his surroundings. The sensory information bombarding him was almost overwhelming. He saw Reggie watching him, could almost taste the pride swelling within her. To his right, Twigs was looking around the same as he was; he could hear the synapses in her mind firing as they forged new connections. Even Rocky, sitting on his left, smelled of awe and possibilities. They were all experiencing the same wonder he was.

"Very good, Drak!" Wally the Seal said. "I'm so proud of you!" The imagery faded and winked out altogether, leaving him longing for its return! "Are you ready for the next lesson?"

Regaline couldn't have been happier. In just a few hours, they were already proficient at grasping and handling their nan. Even Taeg was making progress, though still slower than the other two.

As she marked their progress, she thought about what she wanted to teach them first and decided upon the medical kit. These were uncertain times, after all. Interland was on the march, and there were ominous readings coming from the Tower. Tidings of troubled times on the way.

CHAPTER 4
RANCE

Feeling young and virile again, Terrance Rance, the gris-gris man, made his way home. Working in the amber zone always took a lot out of him. However, they were in the most need of help. Places like Windmill's Watch, barely clinging to life, were all too common. He truly hoped his efforts there would have an impact on those people. With any luck, the altercation as he departed wouldn't have a significant negative impact.

Nothing he could do about it now. They were on their own till he, or another Watcher, traveled out their way again.

The change in the landscape as he walked was remarkable. True to its name, the closer he came to the green zone, the more living greenery he saw. This close to the Tower and the center of their efforts, the climate could even be called verdant. There was still much to do to fulfill the ancient mandate to improve the land, to reclaim and establish a healthy climate for people to thrive. The progress was slow but steady. Healthy, disease-free wildlife. Farms capable of feeding the people working the land. Trees were still sparse, but here, they weren't as sickly and even bore leaves of green. The farther one traveled towards the center, the more hospitable the land became. The area immediately surrounding the Tower was fertile and veritably teaming with life.

Since crossing from the amber into the green zone, he began receiving communiques from others in the Order. Signal reception was spotty and sometimes nonexistent the farther they traveled from the Tower. There was a lot of chatter back and forth concerning the upcoming Convocation. He ignored all that and looked for any missives directed at him and smiled when he didn't find any. They could argue politics all they wanted; his only desire was to do his job and enjoy the life he'd built.

The home he'd made for himself was located near the edge of the green zone to the east of the Watch Tower. In two days, at his current pace, he would see it again. The thought of sleeping in a bed under a roof put a spring in his step. When he set up camp at dusk, he lay on his back gazing into the hazy night sky at the pinprick stars beyond and eagerly thought of home. The thought of being somewhere where he wasn't feared and suspected of evil doings brought a smile to his lips.

How long had he been away this time? He consulted his calendar application and found, to his mild surprise, that he'd been away for nearly two years. Being essentially ageless, time truly slipped away from him. Though he loved his work, helping people and improving their lives, he deeply missed being home. It was where he felt he'd made the greatest difference.

He went to sleep thinking of his return and how happy it would be.

Two days later, he reached the summit of a tall hill and Hillcrest came into view. Looking down upon the collection of buildings, he swelled with joy.

I created this, he thought.

Rance had been working with the people of Hillcrest for going on thirty years now. At the time, it had been an unremarkable little settlement, just like hundreds of others. The same hardships, the same failures, and scant successes. He remembered what it had been like during the first year. It took a while, but he eventually managed to root out and extinguish the superstitions and ignorance plaguing the townsfolk, replacing them with logic and enlightenment. He'd started with the necessities: clean running water and electricity. From there, he built up their education in medicine, farming, and engineering.

The changes he found every time he returned were simply remarkable. Dirt streets had been paved. Clapboard buildings replaced with more permanent structures. They even had enough water to run a small fountain in front of the town hall. Hillcrest was a testament to the willingness of people to accept change and progress. The town was laid out like a wagon wheel, with a plaza in the central hub with the town hall and eight wide, cobbled streets radiating out like spokes. Each main street was connected to another on either side by five narrow avenues. The edge of town was clearly marked by a line of eight watch towers facing outward.

There were a dozen farmsteads arranged around the town proper. They grew the food Hillcrest ate and received goods and services in trade. Everyone worked together for the benefit of the community.

That was the part that continually amazed him. These were human beings who did their best to coexist and resolve conflicts peacefully. Which was not to say there weren't conflicts. There certainly were, but when you could read your neighbors' intentions as easily as your own, duplicity was difficult.

This was his great experiment. His big reason to avoid returning to the Watch Tower. And it was working. These people were thriving in his absence. Not only thriving, but they were starting to teach the neighboring towns and settlements what they knew. When he founded this town thirty years earlier, he'd brought together a scraggly bunch of emaciated dirt farmers and given them a purpose, to build and maintain a home. He'd activated the nan living within his people and taught them to use it. Some were more adept than others. But everyone had access to the basic applications that made their lives easier. Rance had worked with them for a decade, making sure their town wouldn't collapse in his absence. Then, he'd had to leave to carry on with his work elsewhere. Not only had his people thrived without him, but they had begun actively improving the lands in and around Hillcrest.

Rane felt a swelling of pride. He'd accomplished in thirty years what all the Watchers combined hadn't in a little over a hundred. A feat unrivaled in the century since the Breakdown.

However, he had to keep it secret. There were strict rules preventing the sharing of nan abilities with outsiders. He had not just disregarded those rules; he had outright broken them, ground them underfoot, and spit on them. If other members of the Order discovered Hillcrest and connected it to him, he would be in deep trouble.

Looking at his creation, he knew it was worth it.

The sentries in the watchtowers were the first to see him. Though bandits weren't unheard of in these parts, the main reason for the towers was to keep a weather eye out for approaching storm fronts. A task especially important during the long winter months. The woman in the southeastern tower rang her bell, three long, three short, signaling that a visitor approached. Rance was still too far away yet to be identified, and he wondered if they would even recognize him. It had been two years, after all, when he'd left, he'd been an old man.

A few parlor tricks to jog their memories might be in order.

Though there was no protective wall, many of the outermost houses had built high fences. He saw a delegation gathered to meet him at the end of B & O Street. He'd named the four major streets after railroads in his favorite game: Short Line ran north to south, Reading east to west, Pennsylvania northeast to southwest, and B & O ran northwest to southeast. These streets connected to roads leading in and out of town. The four lesser streets were dead ends that didn't connect with the land outside of town. These he'd named Mediterranean Avenue, Baltic, Boardwalk, and Park Place. The avenues running between them were numbered on the west side of town and lettered on the east side. His people had no idea where his inspiration for their street names came from, and he had no way of showing them, as there hadn't been a physical version of Monopoly created in over a hundred years. Still, the whimsy reminded him of better times in better days.

As he came close, Sheriff Marc Tassmaker started walking to meet him, followed by Mayor Enid Folger and a deputy. He thought that might be cute little Antonio Rustikov, all grown up and wearing a badge.

When they were separated by a few meters, the sheriff called out to him, "Hellooo there, stranger. Welcome to Hillcrest. Gonna stop right there. We need to have a look see at'cha. Make sure ya ain't a dangerous type."

Rance loved the old sheriff. The man looked almost as old as he himself was. Had to be nearing retirement soon. He'd been the lawman for the settlement atop which Rance had built his city.

"Well met, Sheriff Tassmaker, Mayor Folger." He smiled at each of them in turn. "It's almost as nice to see you as it is to be back."

The trio shared a look.

"Back, you say?" Sheriff Tassmaker said, his brow knit with skepticism. He took in the gris-gris man's ratty clothing, weathered, travel-dirty continence, and youthful appearance and smirked. "Don't recognize ya. But I am getting on in years. Memory ain't what it used to be. Why don't ya tell me yer name? See if that rings a bell or three."

"Gladly. I'm Terrance Rance."

The old sheriff's eyes went wide, and the mayor clapped her hands together. Behind them, little Deputy Rustikov gasped and staggered back a step, saying, "The Founder."

"I'm so sorry, sir," Tassmaker said quickly. "If I'd knowed it was you, I wouldn't'a stopped ya like this."

Rance stepped forward and placed a hand on his shoulder. "Please don't worry yourself about it. You were doing your job. If you hadn't, I would have been worried and maybe a little upset. You're keeping our home safe. Now, let's get inside and find some cold drinks. I'm tired from traveling and would like to sit."

Thirty minutes later, they were all seated around the mayor's dining table, drinking ice-cold lemonade. All three town representatives had joined them. With them, the sheriff, and the mayor, the entire governing body of the city was seated around the comfortable dining room.

"This is my specialty," the mayor confided. "I also use it to make the ice in the glasses. I'm honored to have you in my home, Founder."

"There's no need for honorifics, Enid," Rance said after taking a sip. It was good. Just what he needed. "How have things been in my absence?"

"Things have been pretty good, actually," Enid said. "The crop yields from the harvest were greater than expected. We have more than enough food to get us through the winter."

"Animal attacks are on the rise, though," one of the representatives, a man named Harwick, said. "No deaths yet, but we've lost some livestock. And just last week, poor Riku's daughter was mauled pretty badly by a stinglynx. Her healing nan had already done much of the work keeping her alive. Fortunately, we found her quickly enough to apply more advanced healing, so she won't bear too many scars."

"Good to hear," Rance said. He turned to the sheriff, asking, "What are you doing about these incidents?"

"We tried the usual deterrents," Tassmaker said. "This critter don't care. It leaves the bait boxes and avoids the snares and goes right for the meat on the farmsteads. It's against yer policy to kill an animal without first checking the biome. We doin' that check now. If it's all good, then I'm gonna lead a huntin' party to tranq and move the beast. If it comes back, I'm going to take the same folks out and kill it."

Rance nodded thoughtfully. That was about as reasonable

as he could expect. "Good. Let me know when the investigation is complete; I'd like to accompany the hunting party."

Tassmaker touched his forehead, saying, "My honor."

They discussed other town issues and news for another hour or so before Rance stood and called the meeting to a close. "Thank you all for bringing me up to speed. You are doing a remarkable job, and I am unbelievably proud of you. Now, if you don't mind, I'm going to find somewhere to take a nap."

"You can use my spare room," the mayor quickly offered.

"You are too kind."

Once everyone had said their farewells and departed, Enid showed him through the house to the back room where he'd be staying. Even though Enid was the mayor, her home wasn't any bigger or more ostentatious than her neighbors. The house was a classic square-frame frontier structure. More rough and rustic than Rance had grown up with but was clean and well-maintained, unlike many of the hovels he'd seen during his travels. There were two ground-level bedrooms and a bathroom, kitchen, dining room, living room and laundry area. The two larger bedrooms, a bathroom, and an office area occupied the second floor. Rance had made sure there were at least twelve different floor plans when he was designing the town, though he encouraged some customization to suit each owner.

All the buildings in Hillcrest were built with an eye toward simplicity and longevity. Which wasn't to say they weren't beautiful. Raising a new house was a community event. Everyone participated, adding little touches here and there to make each building unique and special. Rance spied ornately carved animals in the roof support beams: an eagle, a lion, a beaver, a deer. None of these animals existed around here, but he'd made sure the townsfolk had access to his encyclopedias. Someone must have found the wildlife files in the communal database and had a heyday with them. He made sure his people had access to in-depth medical, horticultural, and construction knowledge, as well as art, film, and literature.

"Here you go, Founder."

He looked at the down mattress Enid had led him to and smiled. "Enid. What did I tell you? It's Rance. Please, just Rance."

"Of course, sir. Do you require anything further ... Rance?"

"Not at all."

"Then sleep well. I'll wake you for dinner."

The sky was black and starless and cool and damp. The sun barely a hint on the horizon. The hunting party gathered in the central plaza had been up for hours, getting ready to run down the troublesome stinglynx. There were eight people, nine counting Rance, making their final preparations. Sheriff Tassmaker and his chief deputy, M'Benga, were in charge. The other six were a motley collection of people with hunting and tracking skills. Even with nan to aid them, such skill sets required practice to use effectively.

"Ready to go whenever you are, Sheriff," Emily Lager said. Her breath visibly puffed in the cool morning air.

"We good to go here, hun," Tassmaker said. "Lead the way."

Emily nodded, turned, and started walking into the dark. They took Pennsylvania Street past the last row of buildings, and thirty minutes later, they passed the farthest farm. Everyone activated their night eyes to navigate the dark as they entered the hills southwest of Hillcrest, where they suspected the stinglynx nested. With the exception of Rance himself, everyone in the group was armed. Six carried compressed-air rifles loaded with tranquilizer darts. Tassmaker and M'Benga carried firearms in case they got in more trouble than the air rifles could handle. The weapons applications were among the few Rance was reluctant to permit his people access to, though he did grant them many of the defensive applications. Even the most trustworthy person could have an accident or a moment of thoughtless rage. Limiting access to those applications limited the number of living weapons walking around town. Only the sheriff's office had access to physical weapons, like shotguns and rifles, further reducing the chances of accidental maimings or killings.

However, this was a special exception. A stinglynx was an especially dangerous animal. It was fast, strong, and highly intelligent. Rance and others had cursed that damned fool Mario when he created them in his monster lab and had nearly executed him when he released a breeding pair to the wild. They hadn't released enough predator animals, or so was the justification he'd given, and without them, the more docile prey species would overpopulate and crowd out the food sources. By way of a remedy, Mario had created his own super-predators to cull the other animal populations to keep them in check and the biome in balance. The arrogant idiot had had no idea his progeny would come to threaten the fragile human populations barely gaining a foothold after the Breakdown. He had shouted his defense to anyone who would listen, even as the Order banished him to the lands beyond the red zone.

Thankfully, stinglynxes were solitary creatures, gathering only to mate and briefly raise their young. Also thankfully, a mating pair only produced a single offspring. Most female stinglynxes would sire no more than three pups over the course of their lives. This had made it easy, in the beginning, to track and control their expansion and growth. Once, they'd been a nuisance; now, stinglynxes were becoming a genuine hazard.

The hunting party trekked into the hills well past sunup, Emily Lager in the lead, taking them through gulleys and around hollows, wherever the stinglynx tracks lead. Approaching noon, they stopped to rest and eat.

Rance noticed Emily sitting alone on a rock with a clear view of the area around them.

"How goes the tracking?" he asked.

"Slow," she said. "The bastard's been roving all over this area. Makes it hard to tell which tracks are fresh and which are old. There's a game trail not too far away; I was thinking about taking us to it. See if we can spot fresher sign there."

"Will that work?" He had often hunted small game to eat while on the trail. But he rarely attempted hunting something as smart and dangerous as a stinglynx. Even with nan to protect him, it was dangerous to attempt alone.

"Not sure," she admitted. "But we need to try something. We're fast running out of daylight."

"Is there anything I can do to help?"

"Not really. Unless you have a way to make the thing's tracks more clear."

Rance thought a moment. Then held out his hand. "Give me your hand, please."

Without hesitation, she clapped her palm to his. The link was established the moment they made skin contact. He quickly browsed her current applications. Those she'd learned to access on her own, as well as the access he had granted everyone in Hillcrest, and was surprised to find how advanced she was. She had pressed her abilities right up to the lockouts he'd put in place and explored nearly everything else. No wonder she was the town's best hunter. She was on her way to becoming a self-taught Watcher.

He smiled. Even though she'd learned as much as she could, far more than anyone else he'd ever seen in Hillcrest, she hadn't fine-tuned much. Something he could help with.

It didn't take long at all to adjust her scanner settings. Now, her eyes would be capable of magnification, viewing the IR and UV end of the spectrum. He also tweaked her hearing. No point in allowing something dangerous to sneak on her.

He opened his eyes and released her hand. The adjustment

had barely taken a second.

"There," Rance said. "Take a look at the tracks we've been following and see if you can see any difference."

Wearing a dubious expression, Emily hopped off her rock and sauntered back to the trail they'd been following. She stood a moment staring at the ground, gave a quiet whoop, and came back to him.

"I can distinguish which sets of tracks are newer now."

"Good. Glad I could help. Do you know which way to go now?"

"I think so." She turned to the others. "Chew, choke, and swallow. We're back on the trail in five."

Moving with greater confidence, Emily practically charged through the countryside, following tracks that only she and Rance could see, leaving the rest of them to keep up or catch up. Occasionally, she paused to read the trail more closely and allow the others to regroup. The excitement in the group was palpable. The weariness of the morning was gone, replaced with a heady sense of anticipation that they were going to return having rid the town of a dangerous menace.

There were still a few hours of daylight left when she paused again. The track she'd been following led them into a small depression between two rocky hills. Her pace slowed until she stopped altogether. Rance stopped beside her and found her frowning at the ground.

"What's the matter?"

"The tracks disappeared."

"You mean you lost them?"

"No," she said, not bothering to keep the annoyance from her voice. "I mean they completely disappeared."

He was about to respond when an alarm sounded in his head, the danger indicator flashing to his left. He quickly turned to face the threat, with his weapons and armor charged and ready, and unconsciously placed himself in front of Emily.

Before it leapt, Rance got a good look at the creature.

Its mane and scaly skin were pigmented to blend in with the background of the sun-bleached sand and rocks. As it moved, its colors shifted slightly to mimic the surrounding terrain, where it sat coiled like a cat about to pounce. Its enormous red reptilian eyes bore into him.

The stinglynx was basically cat-shaped. Measuring one and a half meters tall at the shoulder when on all fours, nearly three meters when upright on its hind legs, and weighing in at nearly four hundred kilograms. Thick, coarse fur grew into a mane around the serpent-like hood, fanning out from its head and tapering down its short neck to its shoulders. The fur sprouted in uniform patches around the rest of its body: a bib running from neck to navel, all four massive paws and forelimbs, and its twin tails. Where there was no hair, a scaly, thick hide showed through. Its slender, forked tongue whipped out of its maw, tasting the air for prey. Four of the humanlike fingers of each paw ended with laser-sharp, retractable, sickle-shaped claws, the longest of which, on the middle finger, measured fourteen centimeters. The opposable thumb didn't have a claw. Instead, it bore a retractable stinger capable of delivering up to three hundred milligrams of venom in a single strike.

The stinglynx shifted its weight, gathering itself to strike, while Rance stood mesmerized. The chimera's huge, unblinking eyes locked on his, freezing him in place for what seemed like an eternity.

The spell was broken by the percussive blast of Tassmaker's rifle. The bullet grazed the beast's back. Its roar was equal parts wolf howl, mountain lion shriek, and banshee wail.

In an instant, it fluidly pivoted and leapt, landing among the hunters gathered in a knot three meters behind Rance and Emily. The sounds of gunfire and shouts of terror filled the air in the little gully.

Rance saw Tassmaker on the ground, covered in blood, while his deputy and the other three hunters stood together to fight off the nightmare bearing down on them. A hail of darts flew through the air like gnats. Two protruded from the skin on the beast's flanks, a third dangled impotently, tangled in its mane. Behind him, Emily dashed to the left, putting some distance between her and the beast. She crouched atop an outcropping on the opposite wall of the gully, raised her rifle, and squeezed off a shot that went wide. The stinglynx whipped around and began stalking toward her.

Rance's trance broke. Moving by instinct and muscle memory, he raised his hands and hit the stinglynx as it coiled for another jump. The blast of super-heated ionized air took it in the side and threw it three meters back.

It was on its feet and sprinting at him so quickly that Rance barely had time to think. Once again, he let his body do the reacting for him. As the stinglynx leapt, he threw out both hands. Thin ribbons of red-gold light erupted from each of his fingertips, slicing the stinglynx open down the length of its abdomen. He threw himself into a diving roll to his left, out of the path of the monster. Coming out of the roll into a crouch, he turned and backhanded the stinglynx with another blast.

It got back to its feet and came for him again, though more slowly this time. Blood and entrails trailing behind, it swiped at him with a massive paw.

Rance ducked and gave it another blast, point blank, right in the center of its face.

The stinglynx's head flew back. More blood, along with bits of singed fur and bone and cartilage, arched upward with the motion.

Though catastrophically wounded, the stinglynx still had some fight left in it and tried once again to get to its feet. Rance stepped in close and cupped his hands on either side of its head. More red-gold light, this time a ball of incandescent brilliance, engulfed the monster's entire head. When he put it out, the stinglynx's body ended in a charred stump atop its shoulders.

He stepped back, staring wide-eyed at what he'd done, his hands shaking with fury. Fury at Mario for creating and then releasing these monsters. Fury at the dead beast before him for not staying in the outlands where it belonged. But most of all, fury at himself for allowing it to take him by surprise.

He knew better than to underestimate these things. Their intelligence made them nearly impossible to eradicate.

Shouting from his right grabbed his attention.

The hunting party was all gathered around the fallen sheriff. They were trying everything they could to save their fallen leader. Rance joined them, to no avail. The stinglynx had slashed him from groin to neck, and Rance could see where the creature's stinger had punctured the skin around his neck. There was nothing any of them could do except take him back home for a funeral pyre.

Rance was struck by how aggressive the stinglynx had been. They were apex predators, sure, but even creatures that hunted humans regularly wouldn't attack so brazenly. What had triggered this one to do so? He reached out with his senses and found his answer almost immediately.

Emily was standing next to him, watching intently.

"Stay here," he said before stalking further into the gully.

Twenty meters from where Sheriff Tassmaker lay, rapidly cooling, Rance found a small cleft between the rocks. A small burrow had been dug out beneath the cleft, and in the depression, a mewling pup writhed in its nest. It was blind, hairless, and pale, making hungry newborn noises.

Without hesitation, Rance reduced the nest and its occupant to cinders.

The funeral had the atmosphere of a morbid picnic. Hillcrest didn't adhere to a strict religion. Rance had made sure of that. Instead of being a spiritual affair, funerals were a celebration of the deceased's life and accomplishments.

Once news of Sheriff Tassmaker's death became public knowledge, the ceremony was arranged. His body was dressed in his best clothes, shrouded in white cloth, and set atop a dais in the public room of town hall. His family and close friends were seated to the immediate left of the dais. A podium was placed to the right. One by one, the citizens of Hillcrest stepped up to the podium where they could see their dear one a final time and share fond remembrances of the beloved sheriff. Tassmaker had been in office for twenty years. Unlike most public officials, he was both good at his job and well-liked by the people; therefore, nearly the whole town attended his funeral.

Rance stood in the shadows near the back of the room, watching until the crowd inside was noticeably thinner than it had been. Only a few waited on their turn at the podium, among them the mayor and other town officials. This allowed the people who truly knew and cared about the deceased to speak before the politicians.

Figuring now was as good a time as any, Rance ducked out and joined the festivities outside.

The feast held in the sheriff's honor was an ample culinary delight. At a typical funeral, only those close to the deceased and their family were expected to attend, cook, and eat. Once again, due to Tassmaker's popularity, the entire town had turned out for the picnic. The smells of roasting meat, freshly baked bread, simmering stews, and more assaulted Rance's nose and set his mouth watering. He realized he hadn't eaten since lunch the day before and was famished. He joined a serving line, intending to pile a plate high and return to the line for seconds once his plate was clean.

A shadow fell across his plate as he was mopping it clean with a roll. He popped the last bit of bread into his mouth before looking up to find Emily Lager standing over him.

"It's impolite to hover," he said.

"I'm sorry," she said, a flush rising in her cheeks.

"Have you eaten yet? I was just about to go for another round. Care to join me?"

She nodded, and they rejoined the serving line. By now, the remembrances were finished, and a few barrels of beer and honey wine had been opened. Never much of a drinker, Rance nevertheless accepted the mug offered at the end of the buffet table. Emily took one, too, though he noticed her plate was mostly empty.

From somewhere in the plaza, he heard an eruption of raucous laughter. Someone had started early, by the sound of it. He smiled as they found another table.

"How are you feeling, Emily?"

She stared off into the middle distance, lost in thought. Unsure if she heard him, he was about to repeat his question when she looked at him.

"I'm not sure," she said. "The sheriff was a good man. He taught me how to hunt and track."

"You were close to him?"

"My family was. He came over a lot for lunches and barbeques and stuff. He and his wife brought over games, and we would all play and have a fun time." She'd been one of the few who hadn't stood at the podium and given a remembrance in front of the town. Rance hadn't thought anything of it at the time. In truth, he hadn't even noticed. Now, here she was, giving her remembrance to him. He said nothing. Merely listened and watched as tears welled up in her eyes.

"After my parents died, he and his wife kind of stepped in and filled the void. I was seventeen, not really a child, but it felt good to know I wasn't alone. That someone still cared for me."

"He was a good man. Everyone seemed to really love him."

Emily nodded and took a drink from her mug.

They shared a moment of companionable silence, listening to the sounds of grieving merriment around them.

Rance set his chicken leg on his plate and pushed his plate away.

"Want to get away from here," he said.

"I really do," she said, nodding rapidly.

A few minutes later, they were strolling around the outskirts of Hillcrest. The sun was sinking swiftly, laying twilight across the land.

"You are an amazing tracker," he said, wanting to change the subject to something happier. "I've seen a lot of hunters over the years. Few have been as good as you are."

"That's kind of you to say," she said, shaking her head. "But we both know I was flagging at the end. The son of a bitch had tripped me up. If I'd been better, then maybe it wouldn't have gotten the drop on us."

"That's bullshit. Remember, I was there too. Stinglynxes are smart and dangerous, even to my kind. They are ideally suited to their environment. It snuck up on me, too, you know. You did everything you could, which was more than most people under the circumstances."

"I lost its trail. If it weren't for you and whatever the hell you did to me, I doubt I would have been able to lead us to its nest. What the hell did you do, by be way?"

Rance grinned sheepishly in the waning light. It wasn't against the laws of the Order to discuss nan with mundanes, but it was heavily frowned upon.

To hell with it, he thought. *Keeping the rest of the world in the dark about nan for the last hundred years hasn't worked. These people have proved that being more open with our knowledge works. Giving her a direct explanation won't hurt anything.*

"You know what nan is, right?" She nodded her head. While he hadn't kept the knowledge from his people, up to that point, he hadn't provided anyone with any in-depth information about it either. "And you are aware it resides within you as much as it does in me, right?"

They'd stopped walking and were standing beneath one of the watchtowers.

"It would take a lifetime to teach you everything you

would need to know to completely understand exactly what nanites are and how they work. Even I don't know everything. But I can tell you a little something. You think the nan is a form of magic. It's not. It's actually just tiny machines in our bodies that allow us to interact with the environment in different ways. Everyone has them; that's the way we designed the system. These machines allow us, me and my order, to monitor people like you when we get close enough. There are many things these machines can do. They can protect, they can create, they can kill. I accessed the nanites you were already innately using and gave you increased access to them."

"There are little machines inside me? How come I've never noticed them before?"

"They are too small for you to see with your eyes. They live everywhere in your body: your skin, your blood, your organs. I can show you how to use them and control them. I can only stay here a few more days, but in that time, I'll tell you all I can."

"Why? What makes me so special?"

"You've already figured out a lot on your own. It might be a while before I return. I think I would like to leave somebody in my place to watch over Hillcrest in my absence. I'd like that person to be you."

Emily didn't respond, though her face took on a pensive cast.

Without speaking, they started walking back to the plaza. It was dark now, and the funeral was nearly over. What remained of the crowd was gathered in a semi-circle around an orderly pile of wood and combustibles, atop which lay Sheriff Tassmaker. Mayor Folger was saying a few final words to the crowd. A final farewell was bid to the honored dead. Less than half of the people who had attended the viewing and the feast were present at the pyre, and most of those left were swaying visibly. At Enid Folger's signal, a flaming brand lit the kindling beneath the corpse, and the body was returned to the earth.

Watching the flames grow and consume the wood and body, Rance felt Emily's hand slip into his as she leaned in, pressing herself close to him.

Rance came awake in the dark, and for the briefest moment, he wasn't quite sure where he was. Soft sheets, down comforter, slender arms draped across his chest. Then it came back to him. He smiled and relaxed. He was in Hillcrest, lying in Emily Lager's bed. Though content to lay next to her for the rest of the night, he felt the call of nature. Even a gris-gris man had to piss. He gently extricated himself from her embrace and padded down the hall to the toilet. Once he was done, he dressed and went to the kitchen, where he flipped on the light and started gathering ingredients for cooking breakfast.

Now, with Emily, he was embarking on a new phase of the experiment. Giving them greater access to their nan, someone to teach and guide them. If it went as well as he hoped, then in a few years, these people should be completely self-sufficient and as capable as anyone in his order.

This is progress, he thought as he padded around the kitchen and started making breakfast.

As he whisked eggs, he heard a floorboard creak and didn't need to scan to know Emily was awake. The last six days with her had been magical. When they weren't making love, she was engrossed in his lessons about nanites and the capabilities they provided. She listened without interruption, and her questions were well-considered and intelligent. In short order, she was becoming an expert nan caster. Knowing he had to leave today filled Rance with mixed emotions. On the one hand, he was proud of her and felt assured that Hillcrest would be safe. On the other, he dreaded leaving her. They'd been together less than a week, but he already thought of her as an indispensable part of his life.

Her arms enfolded him from behind. "How long have you

been awake?" Her voice had the dreamy quality of someone still half asleep.

"Only a minute or two before you, love," he said. "Thought I'd make us breakfast."

She released him and stepped around next to him, her left arm still resting across his shoulders.

"You don't have to do that," she said.

"But I want to spoil you."

"You spoiled me plenty last night. And the night before that. And, come to think of it, the night before that, too." She gave him a coy smile, then leaned in for a kiss.

After breakfast, he dressed, gathered his few belongings, and went outside. Looking around, he was reminded of how limited his successes in other towns had been and frowned slightly. He'd been visiting and helping more than fifty other towns and villages, and none had made the progress Hillcrest had made.

"You're leaving tonight?" Emily asked, breaking his reverie.

He turned to find her smiling at him from her doorway. He reached out to gather her in his arms and gently kissed her.

"I think so. It's time for me to leave," he said. "There is so much work to be done elsewhere. I must go where I'm needed." He lifted her chin and looked into her sad eyes. "Don't be sad, love. I'll be back before you know it."

She nodded and gave him another final kiss, then without a word, she went back inside her house. After a moment, Rance followed and gathered his belongings. As much as he would have liked to stay, he couldn't. He'd been there too long already. There was still much to do and many miles to travel if he was going to make it to the Convocation in time.

The people of Hillcrest seemed to sense he was departing. As he walked, the streets lined with people waving hands and blowing kisses, all gathered to see their founder one more time. By the time he reached the edge of town, the crowd had swelled to include every woman, man, and child, cheering and singing to him. He turned and they hushed.

"You are the best of my children," he said. He looked for Emily in the crowd but couldn't spot her. "I am proud of all you have accomplished and all you will yet accomplish. Farewell. I will return." Then he gave them a smile and a wave and turned to go. Better to keep it brief.

This was his last stop before the Convocation. His proof of what needed to be done. He had empowered these people, and they would flourish long after he was gone. Maybe even carry on his work. Though long-lived, he and his ilk were far from immortal. Many of those who had survived the Breakdown with him were gone now. There weren't many. In fact, as far as he knew, there were less than fifty. Like him, most of them wandered the outlands. It was the covenant they made long ago. To heal the land and its people, to improve their lives, to find a way to fix what had been broken. Soon, they would all meet in a great convocation. The first in a long time.

I hope everyone makes it this year, he thought.

The trials of wandering the land, dealing with the hostile distrust of the people they sought to help had taken the lives of so many companions. The biggest killer of all, however, was simple despair. The task before them was simply too big, the damage done too invasive. The few who remained were the strongest of them.

Even the strong eventually break.

CHAPTER 5
KINNEY

Kinney woke with a kink in his neck. Bleary-eyed, he groaned and rolled out of bed. He'd been up late the night before and was definitely feeling the lack of sleep today.

He missed his bed back at Site 2. His bed, the food, the clean, well-lit corridors, the smell.

The rack he'd been assigned here barely qualified as a bed. It was a narrow, short alcove built into the wall of his quarters. Which itself was also narrow and short. He had just enough room to stand up, turn around, and shuffle from side to side a few steps. There was an office hutch with a fold-out table and stool and cubbies, a small safe for anything of value, and a wall locker for his clothes. The lighting came from dull panels recessed into the floorboards and overhead ceiling trim. At least the room was clean, and there were no bedbugs—the parasites hadn't been introduced. However, the bed was thin and lumpy and smelly. There was simply no way to get comfortable on it.

Miserably, he rolled out and placed his bare feet on the cold metal floor decking. Time for work. Site 1 hadn't been infused with nanites, so he was forced to prepare his showers and breakfasts manually. The only concession to modern amenities here was remote access to the intranet. This allowed him to get up to speed while he got ready.

The problems at Site 1 hadn't been immediately apparent at first. Because the structures had been assembled, rather than nanite-printed, the whole place was more mechanical in nature. He'd spent the last three days reviewing maintenance logs and double-checking the more obvious points of failure. It was slow work, requiring him to physically inspect anything he wanted to check on. Like yesterday, when he'd been forced to crawl along a half mile of maintenance crawlspaces just to reach a pipe fitting that looked completely fine. The whole time, he bemoaned his luck and wondered whether his promised reward was worth enduring such discomfort.

To make matters worse, everyone here treated him like a pariah. Nobody spoke to him when they didn't have to. When they did, it was in short, clipped sentences that were often unhelpful or even outright hostile. As far as they knew, he was there to help them reach their quarterly goals and get their bonuses. Helping him do his job was in their best interest. But they didn't see it that way. He was an outsider. Brought in to do their jobs for them because corporate didn't think they were capable enough. They were blissfully unaware of his other mission there. If they knew he was conducting a covert investigation to uncover industrial espionage and possible sabotage, then no one would ever talk to him.

Kinney stepped into the hot, humid air of the corridor and locked his door behind him. He was one of the few who rated a single room, another point against him.

At his workstation, he logged in and brought up the next item on his list. Waler had assigned him a space across from Astrid Free, who made no pretense about how she felt about him. Another great joke from the eminent humorist, who Kinney suspected was the source of much of Site 1's current woes. He couldn't believe someone like Waler had risen to such a position of authority. With such a huge investment, HelixCom worked hard to weed out toxicity in their managers. A happy workforce was an efficient workforce. To that end, the company spent a lot of credits to ensure its managers and leaders were well-trained, professional, and even compassionate. There was simply too much money on the line to do otherwise.

He glanced over. Astrid hadn't arrived yet today. In the two weeks he'd been here, he had never once observed her being late to work. She was a dedicated workaholic who came in early, stayed late, and cut her breaks short in favor of her projects. He checked the time; he was only a few minutes early. Which meant she was already several minutes late.

"First time for everything," he murmured and turned back to his own station.

Kinney logged in and opened the reports he'd been reading through. He hoped to find something pointing the way to the deficiencies Site 1 was experiencing. From everything he could see, there was nothing amiss with the work output from the people working here. Their procedures were up to date, even if their equipment was old. There was room for improvement nearly everywhere. But nothing truly detrimental was hindering Site 1, just a lot of inefficiencies in need of correction.

Site 1 had been built upon a low-rising plateau. The site had been chosen as the anchor point for the whole colony. Flat steppes stretched out below it to the west. To the east rose a series of rolling hills that continually climbed until they touched a mountain range. This was to be the edge marker of the colony for the first several decades. If all went well with the initial settlement, then plans were already in place to occupy another of a dozen pre-selected sites that had been scouted for suitable expansion. That was still many, many years in the future, but the plans for them were continually updated to keep them current.

Kinney tried and failed to stifle a yawn. Pulling double duty like this was going to be the death of him. He'd received an encrypted message the night before containing instructions and then spent the next five hours carrying them out. He glanced again at Astrid's desk. Still empty. Where was she?

He could understand her animosity towards him. She'd been tasked with the same job he was officially sent here to do. When she didn't provide answers or solutions fast enough, corporate sent him to do her job for her. Promoting him over her. That would gall him as surely as it infuriated her. In that light, he didn't blame her at all for hating him. However, her personal grudge was no reason to slack off on her work.

He returned his attention to his work. There was a definite problem with the carbon balancing systems. The underlying cause of this was still a mystery. He foresaw a trip to the gas exchangers in his near future.

Both sites had been established to correct the climate, reverse the greenhouse effects in the atmosphere, and make the planet livable. Site 1 was dedicated to the initial phase of atmosphere processing. Site 2 was the crown jewel of the project here in Kuridian. The state-of-the-art facility was brought online near the western coast and tasked with enriching the soil and sparse oceans to support life, establishing an active biosphere. Site 2 also housed a database of colonists ready to be printed. The first wave of human life populating the planet would be indentured to the corporation for their short lives, laying the groundwork for the live-born to settle the land for themselves.

Due to the trillions of credits invested in this planet, the corporation was not tolerant of disruptions to their timetable.

Once the atmosphere was the correct composition of oxygen and nitrogen for Earth life, Site 1 would be converted into a fusion reactor. Air maintenance would always be a secondary application of the facility, but once plant and animal life took hold, the facility would be primarily a backup, much like the massive air scrubbers back home. The natural cycle set in motion by Site 2 should handle air replenishment automatically.

In preparation for the next stage, Site 1 was being prepared for conversion into a power plant for the future colony.

The conversion process was not going smoothly. The facility's reactor was operating normally, but for some reason that Kinney couldn't identify, it wasn't generating power anywhere near the levels it should be. Certainly not enough to power the planned city in the cradle between the three sites. Which brought to mind his secondary task: uncovering anyone working against the interests of HelixCom here at Site 1.

Though he'd only been there a couple weeks, Kinney had already developed a list of people to investigate more closely. Many held positions in the key areas that had been experiencing the most setbacks. He hadn't had the time to search more thoroughly, just identifying and cataloging the problems around Site 1 had taken up much of his time since he arrived. He also didn't want to draw any unwanted attention to himself for snooping around.

A small pang of hunger twisted in his stomach, and he checked his watch. He'd skipped breakfast to get an early start on the day. He frowned when he saw there were still four hours until lunch and thought about sneaking away for a quick snack.

Across the aisle, Astrid's station was still empty.

Very odd, he thought.

He stood and looked around, thinking she might be at someone else's desk in conversation. But she was nowhere to be seen. Curious, Kinney walked across to her desk and opened her computer link. She would berate him harshly if she found him using her equipment. She already hated him, and he didn't want to anger her further. But he couldn't let go of the fact that it was twenty minutes past the start of shift and Astrid wasn't there. He hadn't beaten her to work once in weeks. The closest he'd come was two days ago when they'd arrived at the same time. He'd given her a friendly good morning, which she'd pointedly ignored.

Strange. Her station listed her as logged in at zero-five-forty-eight. She wasn't late; she'd been incredibly early. Kinney thought she must be out on the floor diagnosing or repairing something she'd found. But when he checked, he didn't see any error messages or flash alerts. That, in itself, wasn't concerning. But now he wondered what she'd seen that dragged her away from her desk. Using his supervisor's access, he linked with her desk to see what she was working on. It didn't take long to locate her in the crawlspaces above the reactor.

Oh shit, he thought.

Kinney locked his desk and left in search of Astrid.

The farther he went away from the living areas, administration, and work sections, the more cramped the corridors became. By the time he reached the reactor building, the hall was only wide enough for a single person to pass comfortably. Much of the work in this building was done via drone or robot. The designers hadn't thought there would be much need for a person to physically be in this part of the building. As a result, the hallways were long, claustrophobic, and poorly lit, with few junctions or doors leading to other areas. There were periodic sensor contact points installed in the floor, walls, and ceiling. These oriented the drones and robots as they raced down the dim halls. Instead of full-sized corridors, numerous crawlways branched off the main routes, designed for the automatons and barely big enough for a human to pass comfortably.

What was Astrid up to, coming down here? Without an error in the site event log, there seemed to be no reason for her to venture this deep into the station's automated sectors.

What are you doing down here, Astrid? he thought as he followed her deeper into the bowels of Site 1.

When he reached the correct junction, Kinney took a breath before activating his sensor suite. He wasn't crazy about enclosed spaces. Tight confines didn't send him into a full-blown panic attack; they just mildly nauseated him. The sensors helped, though. By feeding him constant updates about air quality, atmospheric pressure, and background radiation levels, they provided him with something he could see and use to convince himself everything was alright.

One more deep breath, then he dropped to his knees and ducked into the tunnel.

Since drones were the most frequent users of these paths, almost black inside. Kinney adjusted his vision until he could clearly make out the details of the tunnel in the dark.

"That's better," he muttered.

According to her desk, Astrid's last known location was three junctions up and four over, a little over five hundred meters distant.

The heat in the tunnel was stiffening. Sweat trickled down his forehead into his eyes and dripped off the end of his nose. He had to pause every few meters to wipe his forehead with his sleeve. The floor grates were roughly textured to afford the robots and drones a better grip as they sped along. After a hundred meters, his palms had been scraped raw. After two hundred, every time he placed them on the floor, pain like fire shot up his arms. Panting, he paused around the halfway point to rest.

While seated and cradling his hands, he checked the maintenance schedule for this section of tunnels. The robots were furnished with high-power sensors that told them to stop when they met any obstructions in the tunnels, and the drones had human operators moving them. Therefore, he was theoretically in no danger of being run down while shambling about in there. Still, he couldn't shake the worry as he bent forward to start crawling again.

In addition to the drones and robots, there were also the trollies that techs used to ferry tools, parts, and anything else they needed through the tunnels to worksites. The trollies were low and flat. Like the other automatons, there was no room in the tunnels to pass when one was coming from the other direction. Fortunately, the web of passageways was extensive, and it was easy enough to make a detour to avoid a collision or jam up.

A cyclic infrasonic thrumming echoed in the tunnel and hammered his eardrums, making him woozy and disoriented. He tipped his head back, closed his eyes, and took a few more deep breaths. Focusing on the data his sensors fed him, he tried not to think about how close the walls were and how far he still had to go before he was out of the tunnel.

This is the last time I go in here, Kinney told himself. *Never again. Next time, send a fucking drone.* Then he got moving again.

He passed the seventh junction. According to the internal display map, Astrid Free was located in the chamber just ahead. He didn't give a damn if she hated him or not; once he got there, he planned on giving her a sharp reprimand before getting her the hell out of there.

That was another thing bothering him. Why was she here in person? Why not send a drone?

He hadn't considered her when compiling his initial list of suspects. But there in the tunnel, she seemed a most likely saboteur. She had sneaked away from her workstation without telling anyone and ventured into the deepest parts of the station by herself. She often worked alone. At first, Kinney had thought she was just a loner, but now he could imagine more sinister reasons for her behavior. Could she be the one he had been sent to expose? A spy and saboteur. Why else would she be down here? He barely knew her, but Astrid seemed like a hardcore company woman. Dedicated to her work and the end goal it strived toward. She was rough around the edges, but everyone seemed to like and respect her. And they thought he had stolen her promotion from her. In that light, their shunning of him was completely understandable. They hated him and loved her. What better person to implant as an agent provocateur? Given her popularity, convincing everyone else would be difficult.

The exit was in sight now. The heat exchanger room was one of the tallest chambers on site. It housed a dozen massive heat sinks that regulated the temperature of the reactor. God only knew why she'd decided to crawl all the way out here.

At last, he was out.

Gasping, Kinney rolled out of the crawlspace and lay flat on his back for a moment, breathing the thick, stifling air. It felt good. So relieved was he to be out of that hellish, cramped tunnel that it took a moment for him to hear and acknowledge the warning alarms screaming at him. He sat up and swiped open the alarm window, which immediately informed him he was currently being exposed to five hundred and sixty-seven rads, and his watchdog systems were demanding he exit the area and seek immediate medical attention.

Yellow emergency lights high on the walls flashed in their glass casements. Now that his pulse wasn't pounding in his ears and he'd silenced his internal alarms, he could hear the emergency siren as well. A high-pitched hissing drowned out the claxons, and the chamber itself was filled with a dense, wet mist that occluded the flashers.

"What the hell is going on in here?" he said aloud.

Refusing to panic, Kinney set his nanites to begin a scrub and purge of his internal organs and to act in place of his white blood cells. Then he interfaced with the local diagnostic node to see just what the hell was the matter.

The first thing he detected was a faulty sensor, which explained why an alarm hadn't been logged either at his station or in operations. The next thing he saw was a small rupture in a conduit running along the manifold that transferred heat from the reactor cooling systems to the massive sinks protruding up from the floor. High-pressure, intensely hot steam spewed from the tiny hole, contaminating everything in the room.

Approaching the rupture, he saw Astrid Free lying on the floor beyond the jet of super-hot vapor.

After activating a heat shield and ducking beneath the spume, he knelt beside her unconscious body to assess her condition. Every employee was given a basic first aid and medical evaluation kit when they awoke in orbit. Being a supervisor, his programs were a little more advanced; however, it was far from adequate for dealing with the injuries he was seeing.

First, there were the steam burns on her face and the exposed skin of her neck and hands. She must have been standing right in front of the manifold when it ruptured. Then, there was the acute radiation sickness. Kinney himself was already burning red hot from exposure, and she'd been lying there for at least an hour.

He did his best to stabilize her and then called the infirmary.

"Site 1 Medical," a bored operator answered, "how may I direct your call?"

Kinney gave his name and ID number, then said, "I have a medical emergency. Two people with severe radiation exposure, one with extensive steam burns. She's been unconscious in a category-five radiation zone for at least an hour."

He could almost hear the boredom evaporate. "What is your location?" Kinney gave it to him. "We don't have a way to get in there with radiation suits. You're going to have to bring her out and meet the response team at Junction Twelve-C."

"Understood," Kinney said. He'd been afraid of that. The thought of dragging Astrid five hundred meters down crawlways almost made him despair.

"There's no way we are going to survive that," he said to himself. It had been tough enough making his own way there. The radiation exposure was already starting to sap his strength and was burning out his nanites at an alarming rate. "I'm not going to die in here."

Before he could move her, he needed to deal with the rupture. If the heat exchanger failed, then the entire system would fail with catastrophic results. He directed more of his dwindling nanite reserve to the heat shield and approached the hole. Even through the shield, he could feel the heat of the steam as it soaked his face and body. His nanites filtered out the steam from his vision so he could see. A hairline crack less than three centimeters long was the issue. The metal around the failure glowed white-hot under his thermal view. Another check of the diagnostic node told him the manifold was approaching critical failure. If that happened, it wouldn't matter if they got out of there and to the infirmary. The entire site and everyone in it would be dead in a flash.

He placed both hands on either side of the fissure and infused the metal with nanites. He couldn't spare them, but there was no other choice. They burrowed into the pipe and immediately executed a repair protocol, wielding the fissure shut and cutting off the steam.

It was only a patch job. Not meant to last. This whole section needed to be taken offline and thoroughly inspected and repaired. For now, it was safe enough to leave. He shot the reactor control center a message warning them about the weakened state of the manifold and advised them to reduce the heat load in this sector.

Finished, Kinney hooked his arms under Astrid's armpits and hefted her over his shoulder to carry her to the access tunnel. He worried briefly that the manifold would rupture again. But there was nothing else he could do about it, so he ignored it. Instead, he focused on getting them both out of there alive. While debating whether it would be better to push her in front of him or pull her behind him, he noticed a small utility trolly beside the tunnel entrance. In his relief to be free of the crawl space, followed by the immediate danger of the situation he found himself in, he'd been too distracted and hadn't noticed it.

"Aion be blessed! That must be how you got here," he said. He immediately felt foolish for not having thought of it himself. Of course she would use one. Kinney was new and didn't think of it because he hadn't had to use the tunnels much yet.

With a sigh of relief and a thankful prayer to whatever was looking out for them, he draped Astrid over the trolley, set its destination to Junction Twelve-C, and got it moving.

Then he climbed into the darkened tunnel.

Kinney tried to read, but found it hard to concentrate. It had been two weeks since the accident. Astrid was going to be released today, and he wanted to be there when she was. His efforts at distracting himself until the time came were wasted, though. He simply couldn't stop watching the clock, which seemed to slow time to a crawl.

The EMTs took possession of Astrid the moment they cleared the tunnel exit, placed her on an auto-doc gurney, and hooked her up to it. Moving quickly, they immediately administered anti-radiation meds, as well as an additional cocktail of drugs to stabilize her while the gurney transported her to the infirmary. He'd overheard one of them saying nearly all her nanites were expended and dead, and she was lucky to be alive at all.

Then, she was whisked away as fast as the gurney could fly.

For Kinney, they'd moved at a far more sedate pace. His condition, while still urgent, was not nearly as critical as Astrid's. They took their time triaging him and made sure he was comfortable before he, too, was shuttled off to the hospital. In fact, he had already begun feeling better by the time his gurney docked at the infirmary.

After treating him, the doctors decided to keep him under observation for three days in case a new or previously hidden trauma appeared. Upon his release, he was ordered to take an additional three days to rest and recuperate. As a part of his treatment, he'd been given a fresh infusion of nanites. Which always made him feel antsy. They were essentially identical to his own, but because his body hadn't manufactured them, the new nanites felt foreign and uncomfortable. The feeling would pass once they were fully integrated. Until then, however, he found himself unable to sit still. Fortunately, they hadn't looked too closely at the nanites already native to his body.

With a few hours still before Astrid was set to be released, Kinney gave up, exited the book he wasn't reading, and went for a walk.

The air in the corridor felt warmer and more humid than usual. Until the damage to the heat exchanger was completely assessed and repaired, the facility was running without air conditioning. In fact, the entire site was operating on minimal power. Kinney's team estimated the repair job should only take a couple of days, provided more problems didn't crop up. All other on-site work was on hold till then. Which did not sit well with corporate. An atmosphere processor that didn't process the atmosphere was a credit drain. To make matters worse, it held up progress at the other site as well. Kinney imagined corporate breathing down Waler's neck. The thought of him twisting in the wind made Kinney smile.

By this stage of the project, both facilities were dependent upon each other's applications. While each site provided something vital to the terraforming effort, Site 1 manufactured the gases that formed a breathable atmosphere. Which made it more vital during the early phases of terraforming. Site 1, situated as it was near the coast, was built to process the liquid oceans, to make them potable for life. This, in turn, would support the atmosphere provided by Site 2 and vice versa. If all went according to schedule, then Kuridian would have a permanent Earth-quality environment, capable of supporting human life. Site 2, the newer climate processor, had two missions: First, now that the air on Kuridian was mostly breathable and the water nearly drinkable, Site 2 had begun testing the various simple plants and animals to be printed and introduced in carefully controlled batches to create a biome and fix the manufactured climate in place. Once the environment was stable, then Site 2 would switch to its second mission: populating Kuridian with an indigenous workforce in preparation for the arrival of the tru-human colonists. Site 1 would then be relegated to power generation for the burgeoning colony and occasional climate monitoring.

The whole project was ready to enter the final stages and scheduled to be completed in just under a decade. Delays and overruns at this stage were dealt with swiftly and harshly.

Kinney turned away from the habitat wing and started walking to the medical/maintenance wing. It didn't take him long to reach the infirmary.

"She's already left," the nurse at the front desk said when he asked about Astrid.

"I thought she wasn't being released until this afternoon," Kinney said. "Was there a change?"

"No change." The nurse looked weary. Kinney knew the infirmary was understaffed and overworked. Though he'd been sent to Site 1 to rectify the problems they'd been having, this wasn't one he had any control over. He figured it was Waler, trying to cut costs somewhere to make himself look good to the higher-ups. The lazy, cheap bastard. It hadn't taken Kinney long to realize that many of the recurrent problems plaguing Site 1 could be traced back to decisions made by Waler in the name of cutting costs. Two days before the accident, Kinney had made a point to confront him about a particularly idiotic cost-cutting measure, and Waler had blamed corporate and tried to brush the matter aside.

"I have to appease the gods upon high," he'd said. "They want this place to run as efficiently and cost-effectively as possible. They set out the budget requirements, and I have no choice but to enact them. We all suffer because of it."

"I understand you're responsible for maintaining a tight budget," Kinney had replied, "but this is a matter of safety. Caution tape is not an appropriate replacement for guard rails on the catwalks in Zone H. Those catwalks are three stories high."

"The people who work in Zone H know better than to put any weight on the tape. They are careful professionals."

"Professional or not, there's no excuse for such a blatant safety hazard. If you won't squeeze the budget to fix it, I'm going to have to make a call and get it done myself."

Waler had not liked that at all. His easy, blank expression had transformed into a darkened scowl the likes of which Kinney hadn't experienced before.

"You don't want to do that, son. There's a chain of command for a reason. You go through proper channels if you want to get anywhere."

"I am going through proper channels. Right now. With you. I'm telling you that you need to fix this issue, as well as several others I've outlined in the memo you didn't read. I'm telling you this now before I notify corporate and make them aware of these issues." He had let the unspoken threat hang in the air. If corporate had to become involved in the local problems here at Site 1, they might decide to take action against Waler for letting these things slide.

Instead of acknowledging the threat, Waler had replied with another poor attempt at blame-shifting. "I never got the memo," he had said, trying to look smug. "Have to talk to my assistant about that. Once I locate it, I'll address the concerns you've raised."

"There's no need for that. I've just sent it to you again. This time, I cc'd Arun Mehta and Shalae Hoshi." Hoshi was the planetary manager and the person most directly in charge of the terraforming project.

Waler's scowl had darkened, becoming a glare. "Fine. Submit your request. I'll see what I can do about it."

"Thank you," Kinney had said. He had waited until he'd left Waler's office before allowing himself to smile.

Three days later, the broken section of catwalk railing in Zone H had been replaced. At supper that night, several people had come by to thank him or simply clapped him on the back. So, he'd made some progress with the people here. But in doing so, he'd also made an enemy of Waler.

Fair trade-off, he thought.

The nurse yawned deeply. "Was there anything else?"

"No," he said. "Thank you. Have a good night."

"That's the plan," she said. "But you accident-prone shit-heads always ruin it."

Ten minutes later, he was back in the habitat wing and in front of Astrid's door. She answered after his second ring. Her eyes narrowed upon seeing him.

"What do you want?"

"I went to the infirmary; they said you'd already gone home. I wanted to make sure you were alright."

"As you can see, I'm fine. Anything else?"

Kinney wasn't sure what he'd been expecting when he saw her. But he absolutely had not expected her to act as though nothing had changed. To go right on acting as though he were an unpleasant bug that needed immediate squishing.

"No. Nothing else. I'm glad to see you made a full recovery. See you at work."

As he turned to go, he heard her door firmly close and shook his head.

I can't wait to find a spy and get out of this shit hole, he thought. *Aion willing, that will be soon.*

The following day, Kinney was eating lunch alone in the cafeteria. As usual. The people eating at the tables around him weren't actively shunning him anymore. Butting heads with Waler to get some safety issues resolved had cured that, but they still weren't going out of their way to make friends either. Which was fine by him. Fixing Site 1's inadequacies and finding a spy were on his to-do list. Making friends was not. They wanted to keep him at a distance, and he was content being alone.

Which was why he was shocked when Astrid set her tray down across from him, sat down, and started eating, without a word.

He regarded her a moment, unsure what to say. This person had gone out of her way, since the moment he arrived, to make his work life difficult and actively encouraged others to do the same. Now, she was sitting with him. He glanced around. There were plenty of open seats. Some were even at tables where she had friends whom she ate with regularly.

He realized the longer he went without saying something, the more awkward it would be when he finally did, so he cleared his throat and said, "Hello."

Astrid swallowed, set down her fork, folded her hands before her, and looked him directly in the eyes. "Look, I'm sorry for the way I treated you. I had no right. You were sent here to do a job by corporate, who doesn't care one iota about the personal feelings of us peons."

"You don't have to apologize," Kinney started.

"I wasn't finished." She took a breath. "I also want to thank you for saving my life. I was stupid for going in there alone, without telling anyone. I wanted to show the brass they made a mistake in sending you and I was the person they should've promoted. I wanted to show you up and do it all myself."

She paused, and Kinney could see actual tears in her eyes.

"Pretty fucking stupid, huh?" she said. "I could have died. A few more minutes and I would have. If you hadn't figured out where I was and acted quickly, they would have bagged me, dehydrated me, and shipped me home for burial. I guess what I'm trying to say is that the right person was promoted after all. Thank you." She got up, came around the table, and wrapped him in a hug that crushed the wind out of him. "Thank you," she whispered.

Then she was gone. The remainder of her meal untouched. A few people looked after her as she quickly crossed to the exit. One of them, a friend of hers named Danny Winoki, sitting at a nearby table, caught his eye and gave him a smile and a thumbs-up.

Kinney could only nod back. He glanced around and found most of the people in the cafeteria looking at him. But this time, instead of restrained hostility, he found admiration in their expressions.

Despite the brave face he put up, both in front of the others and to himself, most especially, it felt good to see someone smiling in his direction for once. It was as if the lonely weight of the last four weeks had evaporated, and he could suddenly breathe easier. When he got up to clear both his and Astrid's trays, Winoki and a couple other guys whose names he didn't know clapped him on the back. The friendly gesture almost brought him to tears.

CHAPTER 6
REGALINE

Regaline led her charges into the woods, hoping to throw off their pursuit.

The trees were spread too far apart, and there were too few of them to be called a true forest. They were still in the amber zone, having turned back in to shake off the group behind them. Sickly yellowed leaves clung to anemic branches reaching desperately into the sky, seeking the sun's nourishing light. Scraggly bushes and ferns filled in the gaps between them. The underbrush was just as grim as the trees themselves. The almost forest stretched for several hundred acres, shading the ground beneath with a broken canopy.

She still wasn't sure why they were being followed or by whom. But out there, it paid to be cautious. She could handle a dozen attackers by herself, but her adepts were only just scratching the surface of their abilities. They might be able to take on one if they were lucky. Better to run.

"Are they still following us?" Kayah asked.

Regaline paused, closed her eyes, and extended her senses. She received a fuzzy impression of movement beyond the ridgeline, two kilometers south of them. The signal indicated a mass of individuals moving together. It also indicated they were closing the distance and fast.

"They're still there," she said. All her efforts to lose them had, thus far, failed.

"What are we going to do?" Taeg said.

"We should turn around and kick their asses," Drak said. "There's no way they could deal with the four of us coming at them. It'll be a slaughter."

"We are not going to attack them," Regaline said. "We are here to heal and help people in any way we can. We can't do that if we go around solving every problem we encounter by beating it up. No one would trust us if we behaved as such."

"Nobody trusts you now," Drak said.

"People trust us more than they let on. We've never been turned away from a town in need."

"That's because they need you. Once you're done and the problem's gone, how long does it take before the people start pushing you to leave?"

"Not long at all," Regaline admitted. "But that's not the point. They trust us enough to let us in and do our job. After that doesn't matter."

"Is this really the time to have this argument?" Kayah interrupted. "Shouldn't we keep moving so they don't catch us?"

Even Drak couldn't find fault with that, and they started walking again.

It was nearing dusk when they came to the edge of a clearing and Regaline halted them.

"We'll camp here and continue in the morning."

"Are they still out there?" Taeg asked. He had been more communicative since starting the tutorial program. More at ease with the group and confident in himself. He was still the furthest behind developmentally, but he was rapidly gaining ground.

"They are still out there," Regaline said, nodding. "No fire tonight."

"Why not?" Drak protested.

" 'Cause she doesn't want to make it easier for them to find us," Kayah said and then rolled her eyes as though it were the most obvious thing in the world.

Drak huffed a little. The pair of them were getting along better, but he still didn't like it when Kayah, or Regaline herself, corrected him. He was a very independent boy.

"Once you get your bedrolls out, I have a lesson for you," Regaline said, which put an end to Drak's sulking. He was the first to unroll his bedding, eager to learn whatever she had to teach. That was another change she'd noticed in him. At the start of their journey, he would simply toss his things on the ground and call it good. Regaline's refusal to teach anything until he straightened up his area changed that behavior. Though still rough around the edges, he was not nearly as wild as he had been mere weeks ago.

Once all three of them were seated and ready, she began.

"I want you to retrieve your bread from your knapsacks. Good. Now, holding the loaf in your hands, I want you to reach out and take hold of your nan. Like that. Now, lay your nan over the loaf like a net." She observed each of them following her instructions and smiled. Simple manipulations of their nan had become easy for them. Not second nature, like it was for her, but it wouldn't be long before they began using their nan unconsciously, like another appendage.

"Very good. From here, you have many options for what you can do next. I want you to use your nan to delve into the loaf. Examine it from the inside out."

"Won't that destroy the bread?" Kayah asked. She looked apprehensive. Regaline saw the hunger in her eyes, heard it in her voice, and suppressed a laugh.

"If you delve too deeply, then yes. But we aren't going very deep. I just want you to identify the constituent components of the bread. That which makes it bread."

She gave them a few minutes to work. Since this was their dinner, they were being cautious. "Do you see what makes up the bread at a cellular level?" They each nodded, Taeg last and hesitantly. "Here's where we begin the fun part. You're going to take your load apart and rebuild it using the schema I just sent you."

Kayah took her time and read through the document before beginning. Drak read a few lines, completed a step, then read a few more lines. Taeg read the entire document twice before he began, and he referenced it through each step of the process she had assigned them. In thirty minutes, each of them held a small pork pie, constructed from their bread, in their hands. Kayah's looked good but didn't seem as dense as it should have been. Drak's was lopsided and misshapen but passable. Taeg's meat pie was perfect.

"Very good. Hand me your pie, Drak." One by one, she heated their pies, and they settled down for dinner.

"Transmuting matter like this requires a lot of energy," she explained as they ate. "But it can be useful in a pinch if you desperately need to make something. Be careful, though. Your body will pay the price if you use it too much. You'll have enough energy to heat yourselves without the fire tonight. But tomorrow, you'll all be exhausted and feel starved."

"How do we know if we've pushed too far?" Kayah asked. "Is there a gauge or something we can see to tell how much energy we have to use?"

"No gauge," Regaline said. "Reserves of energy are different for each person. However, as you use your nan more, you'll figure out what your limits are. Also, with increased use comes increased reserves."

"The more we use, the more we can use," Taeg said, mostly to himself.

"That's right. It's a little like a muscle. When you work it out, it becomes stronger to make the work you're doing easier. By manipulating physical objects to the extent you did tonight, you're teaching your nan what you expect from it, and it will learn to compensate so the task is completed more efficiently the next time."

Drak stifled a yawn, which then traveled around their circle and back to him.

"Time for bed," Regaline said. "As usual, we have an early day tomorrow."

Once her charges were sound asleep, Regaline got up and traced their trail back through the woods. She wanted to see who was following them.

Locating the camp didn't take her long. Making no effort to conceal themselves, they'd camped just outside the tree line at the edge of the woods. Regaline counted ninety-eight people; some were rolled up in blankets and sleeping, but most of them were sitting around two large fires. At the edge of the firelight, she spotted a line of sentries. There was a single tent set up on the opposite side of the camp from her. Tied to a nearby tree was a single horse. A banner draped from a T-pole rammed into the ground next to the tent entrance. The banner was dark colored with a pair of white spears crossing a bird in flight set against a rising sun.

That was all the information she needed.

Regardless of what she'd said earlier, Regaline briefly considered attacking and just as quickly discarded the idea. She thought she could eliminate at least ten or twelve of them before the others got wise, but these were soldiers, likely battle-hardened. Alone, it was too risky to attempt to fight all of them. She had her adepts to think about. Better to try something else.

Back at her own camp, she laid down to sleep for three hours.

Her eyes snapped open on the first ding of her alarm chiming in her head. Stiff and more than a little groggy from the insufficient sleep, she roused the others. Taeg got up instantly without complaint. Drak and Kayah took a little longer.

Over a cold breakfast, she told them what she learned during her nighttime reconnaissance.

"We are being followed by soldiers from Interland. There are about a hundred of them, armed and well-equipped. At least five casters are traveling with them."

The three shared a look. Everyone knew and feared Interland. It was the largest country in the green zone. When they weren't fighting their neighbors in border wars, they were sending raiding parties to steal food, supplies, and sometimes even people for use in their conflicts. Interland was extremely aggressive and dominated the whole region with their armies and nan-casters.

"Why are they after us?" Drak said.

"What don't they want with us?" Taeg said before Regaline could respond. "They'll probably send us to the front. Or back to the Hub to make food and weapons for them."

"Or to their quarries," Kayah put in. "I'm sure there are a thousand ways they could exploit the things we can do. Isn't that right, Regaline?"

"That is absolutely true," she said with a nod. "They weed through their population looking for nan adepts. The ones they find become little more than slaves. Human machines to their king's bidding. The skilled ones are transferred to the army as battle casters. We are always careful to avoid crossing their path."

"You said they have five with them?" Drak asked. "Battle casters, I mean." There was concern in his voice, but his eyes betrayed the excitement he felt.

Regaline nodded. "At least. There may be more. They could have masked themselves like I did. Interlander casters aren't as skilled or well trained as our people are, nor as knowledgeable or experienced with all their applications. But that doesn't mean they aren't dangerous. I could probably deal with one or two; three would be tough. But there's no way I could handle five on my own and keep you safe. And before you say anything, Drak, none of you are anywhere near ready to fight them, so you can't help. Then there are the ninety or so mundane soldiers with them who would likely be attacking at the same time. Those are odds I don't want to deal with."

"What are we going to do?" Kayah asked.

"First, we are going to break camp," Regaline said, getting to her feet. "Then it's time for another lesson."

*

Interland soldiers armed with firearms and spears entered the clearing just after noon, reading the ground for the signs of the recent campsite. After a few minutes, they signaled the rest concealed in the trees behind them and started into the clearing. Silently and tactically, the company spread apart to cover more ground and to avoid presenting large, easy targets. Their scouts marched ahead of the main formation. Once half of them had reached the center of the clearing, a man on horseback stepped from the trees, dismounted, and led his animal across.

They were following the trail left that morning by Regaline and her charges to the other side of the clearing and back under the sparse canopy. The lead scout paused a moment on the other side. Squatting, he let the regular soldiers pass by as he scrutinized their tracks before following. One by one, the Interland soldiers disappeared into the trees on the far side.

Ten minutes after they left her sight, Regaline stuck her head up through the camouflage shroud and smiled.

After their morning discussion, Regaline had introduced them to the camouflage applications and showed them how to conceal themselves.

"I don't have the time to teach you how to hide yourselves from animals or other nan users. I'll cover us from those angles, and you three will maintain a visual shroud. Understood?"

They had nodded and gotten to work on creating a concealing lattice away from their camp. While they worked, Regaline had walked a line across the clearing from their camp to the opposite side four times. On the fourth time across, she had halted and closed her eyes in concentration. It had taken a moment to gather enough nan for the task she had in mind, but once it was in place, forming it corporeally had taken no time at all. When she opened her eyes, she had seen her four creations standing on the ground in front of her. Four sets of feet, each set attached by a simple hip, designed to mimic the walking gait of each member of her party. The last one had an additional appendage, into which she placed a tree branch. Once they started walking, that one would trail the others, dragging the branch behind, to lend more authenticity to the ruse by making it seem as though they were ineffectively covering their tracks. The golems were composed of earth and held together by nan from her body. She had imbued them with a simple directive to walk single file for ten miles before decomposing. Regaline had hoped the false trail would give them time to lose the soldiers permanently.

Once everything was ready, she had set them walking and returned to the camouflage screen her pupils had constructed, and then she enhanced it to conceal their presence from anyone with extra-sensory perceptions. They hadn't had to wait long. Less than twenty minutes after they settled in to wait, the soldiers had appeared. After they departed, Regaline dropped the screens and told the others to do so as well.

"We're leaving now. No lunch. No talking. No stopping. No complaining." She looked pointedly at Drak. "Got it?"

For once, he didn't give her a snarky retort and simply nodded his head before getting to work. They had to wait a moment before leaving because Taeg had to relieve himself behind a tree. Once he rejoined them, they shouldered their packs without speaking and departed the clearing. The Interland soldiers were heading west, so she led them out of the clearing to the east. She used more nan to remove the signs of their passing.

She was frustrated that they were now moving in the opposite direction of their destination. But there was nothing she could do about that. They needed to avoid the soldiers and reach Hillcrest safely. If it meant spending a few more days on the trail, going the wrong way, then so be it. Now that she knew Interland was after the kids, Regaline could take additional precautions. It was lucky she had found them first.

*

The pale sun hung overhead. Summer was waning, and the days were growing noticeably shorter. It had been over a week since they'd lost the Interland soldiers, and Kayah could see Regaline breathing a little easier. Kayah and the other two adepts were progressing quickly. In fact, Regaline seemed content to simply guide them and maybe provide warnings where necessary. Otherwise, they were free to explore their nan applications at their own pace.

Kayah could feel herself growing stronger and more capable with each passing day. After breakfast, Regaline had taken each of them aside and examined them.

"Drak's abilities with fire make it pretty obvious where his natural disposition lies," she said. "Now I want to check you two," Regaline said, indicating Kayah and Taeg, "to see what your natural abilities are."

She placed both hands on Kayah's shoulders and closed her eyes. Kayah could see a halo of nan pulsing around her as she concentrated. She suddenly grew quite warm and felt a tingling sensation tickle her all over. A moment later, Regaline opened her eyes and removed her hands. "It appears you have a predisposition for the more air-focused applications," she said.

"Is that a good or bad thing?" Kayah asked.

"Among other things, it means you can make illusions more easily and effectively. You can also manipulate physical things without touching them or destroying them."

"That sounds fun, Twigs," Drak said. "You'll have an easy time blowing up any balloons we find."

Kayah's cheeks flushed in response to his tittering. "Shut up, Houston!"

Hearing his given name, Drak immediately stopped laughing and fixed her with a fiery glare.

"Enough," Regaline said. The tone of her voice indicated

she was growing weary of them constantly at each other's throats.

"Sure thing, Reggie," Drak said with a shrug.

"I'm sorry, Regaline," Kayah murmured.

After giving them both another stern look, Regaline moved to Taeg to repeat the process. This time, Kayah paid extra attention to how Regaline manipulated her nan. Now that she could clearly see it, Kayah took every opportunity to watch Regaline or the others use it.

"Hmm," Regaline said when she finished scanning Taeg. "The scan was inconclusive."

"What does that mean?" Taeg asked. The look on his face was his usual bland impassivity.

Regaline frowned. "It doesn't necessarily mean anything. It's just strange, is all. Pretty much everyone shows an inclination towards one application set or another." She shook her head and put on a smile that Kayah didn't think quite reached her eyes. "Time to pack up. We need to get moving."

Regaline turned them west again and started them on the road to Hillcrest. She said she hoped to reach it in a little over a week.

Before bed each night, as usual, she gave her adepts small tasks to accomplish while using nan. Things designed to help them explore their abilities and test their limits on their own. Sometimes, she showed them what she wanted them to do, then showed them how she did it, and then had them copy her and find their own best way to perform the task. Tonight was no different. Gathered around the fire, with dinner consumed, she cleared her throat for their attention. Instantly, all three perked up and looked at her, eager to hear what she had to tell them.

"We've discussed camouflage, first aid, and how to regulate your bodily applications using your nan," she said in her instructor's voice. "You have all made great progress thus far. Tonight, I want you to access your security applications.

Starting tonight, you will learn how to defend yourselves against any threats you encounter."

They were all smiling, and Drak seemed particularly excited. He'd been impatient to learn these applications just as soon as she pulled him away from his mundane life.

"Tonight, I only want you to familiarize yourself with the location of the menus, how to access them quickly, and what items you see there. Do not—I'm talking to you here, Drak—do not access any of these applications tonight. Once you feel you can quickly open the menus and make a selection, I want you to sleep. You'll need to be well-rested when we start practical applications tomorrow. Do you hear me, Drak? Tomorrow. Be patient tonight, and you'll be the first one up in the morning."

"I hear you, Reggie! Jeez." His words were irritated, but his tone was anything but. He was just about hopping with excitement.

"Okay then. Good night." Regaline then turned in.

Kayah knew she wasn't going to get much sleep. Laying on her bedroll, she glanced over at the others. Predictably, Drak was whispering and giggling to himself, likely planning which of the weapon applications he wanted to try first. Though the temptation to do so was great, she didn't think he would defy Regaline and try using them tonight. The promise of being first tomorrow would hold him. Taeg, on the other hand, was already asleep. She envied him. The excitement of tomorrow's lesson had her stomach in knots. She wasn't as interested in the weapons as she was in the various shields she found.

The idea of using something from her own body to harm someone or something else made her uncomfortable. Intellectually, she knew it was something she'd have to get over. The wilds were dangerous. Not only that, but she'd have to hunt if she wanted to eat. She'd hunted before and viewed it as a necessary evil. Something to be endured, not enjoyed.

The shields, on the other hand, made her more comfortable. There were three she had immediate access to and several more that needed to be unlocked before she could use them. Everything from hardened skin armor to actual energy shields projected from her body. She couldn't wait to see what they could do.

"Hey, Drak," she whispered. "If you want to be first tomorrow, you'd better shut down and go to sleep."

He gave her a look of mild annoyance, then sighed.

"Alright, Twiggs. Good night."

No backtalk. No snide remark or insult. He simply rolled over and closed his eyes. Kayah was surprised by how much Drak had matured during their time on the road. He was still a brat most of the time. But occasionally, he listened without fighting back. She wondered what kind of changes she'd gone through on this journey.

"Good night, Drak."

Sweat leaked from Drak's forehead. The hair on the back of his head and at the nape of his neck was soaked, as were his underarms and collar of his rough woven shirt. He'd been trying for ten minutes to get control of his arc flare. He could initiate the arc and charge it just fine. Discharging it was another matter. In ten minutes, he'd managed a small spark. A pale comparison to the bolt of lightning that had erupted from Regaline's arms in demonstration. He was trying his best to follow her example, aiming for a large boulder sticking out the base of the hill they had selected for their practice range.

Frustrated with the lack of progress, Drak swore and tried again, throwing both arms out as hard as he could while initiating the spark. He half expected to hear laughter when nothing happened again. But there was only silence.

Breathing heavily, he dropped his arms and shook his head.

"I think it's time for a break," Reggie said. "Sit over here, drink some water, eat some jerky. Using nan burns a lot of calories, and you need to fuel up." She turned to address the other two. "Always be mindful of your energy stores. Using nan isn't free. The food and water you consume to live also feed your nanites. You will need to be mindful of the cost certain applications require. Passive applications like sensors and camouflage use little. More active applications like weapons or transmutation have an enormous cost."

Kayah was next.

"Which application are you interested in learning about and trying today?" Regaline asked.

"I want to learn about shields."

Regaline nodded as though in approval. "Defense is just as important as offense. Most of the time, shields are a medium-cost application. However, when you are actively under attack, they can become high cost. Any particular type?"

"I was most curious about skin armor."

"Okay." Regaline took a couple steps back. "Since I'm assuming both of you boys are going to want to use your weapons today, you might want to pay attention to Kayah here and get a few tips on using your shields. It'll help when you truly need to learn them. Are you ready?" Kayah nodded. "Good. Go ahead and activate your armor."

Closing her eyes, Kayah brought up the internal menu and navigated till she had reached the armor option. She selected it and immediately felt a change.

It was as if her body suddenly became too heavy for her. It took extra effort just to expand her rib cage so her lungs could draw in air. She lifted her right arm, flexed, then wiggled her fingers and waved her hand. Each whole motion seemed to take an impossibly long time. Too heavy. Everything was too heavy. She'd thought this was the best option for defending herself from an attack. But it made her a sloth. How was she supposed to protect herself when she could barely move?

"Feeling the weight of it, aren't you? It takes some getting used to. With practice, and I mean a lot of it, you'll learn to move and work and fight in this state. For now, all you need to do is stand there and cover your face with your hands."

Kayah did as instructed.

"Ready?" Regaline asked.

Before Kayah could answer, Regaline ignited an arc bolt and flung it at her.

She felt a jolt of pain when the lightning came into contact, followed by a wave of intense heat radiating throughout her body. She checked her internals and found nothing had been harmed. She lowered her hands and quickly brought them back up when she saw Regaline rearing back for another attack. This time, a beam of fire struck her in the solar plexus. The force of the blast knocked her back. There was more heat this time, intense and painful. Instead of a wave that dissipated quickly, it lingered in burning agony. The scent of searing flesh filled her nostrils.

"Very good," Regaline said. "Go ahead and lower your armor and take a seat next to Drak. Give her some jerky. So, you see, even though you had your armor up, you still felt the pain of each hit. Your nan quickly repaired the damage, but in combat, you cannot rely on it alone to save you. You will have to learn the weapons applications if you want to survive."

Regaline took a drink of water from her canteen and bit off a piece of jerky herself. When she was done chewing, she motioned for Taeg.

He joined her and simply said, "Fire beam."

She smiled and pointed at the same rocky outcropping Drak had been aiming at only moments ago. Taeg nodded once, raised his left hand, and pointed. Faster than Kayah's eye could follow, a thin beam of white-hot light shot out, connecting him to the boulder. In moments, the rock was glowing red and starting to smoke. After only a few seconds, Taeg ended the beam. The rock face sloughed off under the pull of gravity and poured onto the smoldering ground.

Regaline clapped him on the shoulder. "Very good! Go

sit and get a snack." She turned to the others. "Good work, all of you. Now that you've had a taste of the offensive and defensive applications, we can begin working on how to use them. Starting with the shortcuts. You all took far too long to select the application you wanted. It's not your fault; you didn't know. But the difference between life and death can be the difference of seconds. Pay attention; here's how you set up shortcuts to the applications you want to keep ready."

Dinner consisted of their usual trail fair: hard cheese and bread, some greens Kayah had scrounged up, and a horned hare Taeg had managed to snare. After eating, they settled down to explore their abilities a little more. Regaline didn't like them experimenting in the dark without her supervision, but she allowed them to run simulations that were almost as good.

Almost.

Kayah glanced over at Drak. He was stewing over his inability to shoot that afternoon. He was good with fire and felt he should have been better suited to combat than the others. He'd accepted Regaline's insistence that everyone learn and master control of all the different applications.

"Hey, Drak," she whispered.

"What?" he snapped, annoyed at her interruption. He was simulating using the arc application to zap the boulder again. He thought he had figured out how to do it. He wouldn't know until tomorrow when they practiced again.

"How are you doing?"

"I'd be better if I could concentrate."

Kayah ignored this none-too-subtle hint to leave him alone. "I was thinking about what Regaline said about food being fuel for our nan. Didn't you skip breakfast this morning?"

"Yeah. I wasn't hungry." In truth, he'd been too nervous and excited to eat. "So what?"

"I was thinking it might be the reason you couldn't use

the arc. I've been looking at the energy balancing tables, and it seems like the nan won't even try to work if it can't draw the energy it needs."

He thought about this for a moment. "Where did you find that table?" he said. She guided him there. "Thanks, Twigs," he said after tentatively playing with the settings for a moment.

"You know, you could call me by my name. It's not difficult."

"I could, but that wouldn't be any fun."

She rolled her eyes.

He sat a moment, watching her in the firelight. "You okay?" he said.

She pursed her lips, then leaned in close. "I'm worried about Taeg," she whispered, her voice barely audible above the crackling fire.

"What do you mean?" He glanced over at Taeg fast asleep on the other side of the fire.

"He's been so quiet lately. I mean, more than usual. It's like he's purposefully keeping distant from the rest of us. Like he's afraid of us or something."

"I think he's just trying to figure his shit out, like the rest of us. He's not as good as we are. He's probably embarrassed."

"I don't think that's it," she said, shaking her head. "I think he might be better than he lets on. You saw what he did to that boulder today."

"Why would he hide his abilities?"

"I don't know. But I'm worried."

Drak looked uncertain. "I think you might be seeing stuff that isn't there," he said finally. "Rocky's just working out how to do the stuff he's learning, just like you and me."

"If you say so," she said, looking dubious, but didn't argue further. Then she turned back to her bedroll.

"Hey," Drak hissed. She turned back to him. "Thank you for the help. Good night ... Kayah."

She smiled, then lay back down on her bedroll.

The next morning, Kayah noted Drak ate a big breakfast. Regaline only allowed them only a few minutes of practice before hitting the road again. This time, everyone had different results from the day before. Kayah shot a tree with a fire beam, managing to singe the bark. Taeg projected a shield that barely kept out the breeze, but Drak managed to split the target tree with a bolt of lightning. Regaline frowned at him for not trying something new.

"I just wanted to get it right," he said with a shrug.

While they packed, he gave Kayah a thumbs-up.

CHAPTER 7
RANCE

The Watch Tower had been there as long as people had existed. Pearlescent walls, smooth and flowing, rose high and bright in stark contrast to the scabby brown lands surrounding. There were individual buildings surrounding a central tower structure, all connected at the base and, higher up, via bridges that curled and swooped through the sky. The walls were smooth and featureless. No windows, balconies, or doors marred the pristine exterior. The cluster of buildings looked like they'd been grown rather than built.

Which, in a sense, was true. The Watch Tower had been constructed long ago using nanites to print each building layer by layer. The process was long forgotten, even by the oldest of the Watchers, making their home a unique artifact from a bygone era. After the Breakdown, the Watchers had made it their home and the base from which they directed their efforts in rebuilding the environment and helping their fledgling people survive.

Only a handful of Watchers lived at the Watch Tower full time; the rest spent most of their years on the road among the people in the amber zone. Periodically, they were recalled. The Convocation was a time to collect reports, share information, and refocus efforts where needed. There was no specific timetable for the Convocation, nor schedule for how often they occurred. The Triad directors called a Convocation when they felt it was needed, and it lasted as long as necessary. The last one was over ten years ago and had lasted nearly a month.

Rance had a feeling this one was going to be long. If the tempestuous notes he'd been seeing from his colleagues were any indicator, then there was much to discuss. There had been a noticeable slowdown in climate improvement in recent years. In fact, there were several vital areas where things were backsliding. The green zone hadn't grown in years, and the land in the amber zone was slowly withering. The Watchers were failing. Rance knew it, as did the rest of the Watchers. Which was the reasoning behind the Triad calling this Convocation. In an ideal world, they would gather, discuss their ideas, debate the merits and demerits of each proposal, and rationally reach a compromise for all.

"And we'll all live happily ever after," he said to himself, thinking about the drama that had unfolded at every single Convocation since the first one over a hundred years ago.

Approaching the base of the outer wall, Rance marveled at the landscape. Here, at least, their efforts bore fruit. However, the farther one traveled away from the Watch Tower's pristine walls, the harsher the climate became. Rance broadcasted a signal, and a doorway irised open before him, revealing an interior corridor just as bright and featureless as the exterior. The tower itself recognized him, had, in fact, queried his IFF once he came within the four-kilometer security boundary, and allowed him to approach.

As soon as he crossed the threshold, the wall irised closed, disappearing from sight altogether.

Nobody greeted him.

Rance knew there were others in the building. He could sense them, but they were nowhere to be seen. A holographic line appeared on the floor before him, directing him to his room for the duration of the Convocation. He followed the marker down the familiar corridors, deeper and deeper, until he came to his assigned quarters.

He swiped the door open and smiled. First, a real shower

with real hot water. Everything else could wait.

The dining hall was nearly empty when Rance entered, feeling clean and refreshed from his long shower. The room was a comforting cream color, brightly lit, and large enough to accommodate a hundred comfortably. He hadn't expected it to be packed. There weren't enough Watchers for that. A query told him there were eighty-six people in the Watch Tower, with six still outside. Nearly all of them. Once they arrived, the Convocation could begin. In the meantime, he and the others could enjoy some of the creature comforts the Watch Tower offered. Among them, hot showers, smart foam mattresses, and micro-processed food, high in sugar and fat content.

Those in the dining hall were congregated into groups sitting on opposite sides of the room, eyeing each other with suspicion and hostility.

Already, he thought in exasperation. *That didn't take long.*

He ignored them while he got his food from the printer located in the middle of the room. Rance grabbed a tray and input his request: a deluxe cheeseburger, sweet potato fries, a cup of mixed fruit, and a small cup of vanilla ice cream topped with hot fudge for dessert, with a lemon-lime soda-pop to drink. It was a basic meal. But there was no telling how long the conference would last. It could be over in a week or in a month. He wanted to get his favorites out of the way first.

Seated at a table, he grabbed his burger with both hands and took a large, satisfying bite. He'd been looking forward to this moment for weeks. Had, in fact, dreamed about it last night while sleeping under the stars. As good as he remembered and exactly what he needed. Slowly chewing to savor every delicious moment, he glanced at the other thirteen people in the room. Seven on one side, six seated opposite them. The normal chatter and laughter that had filled this room in the past was uncomfortably absent today. A quick check of their ID tags informed him that most had been there for a week already. One had arrived two weeks ago. Which meant the unofficial debates had already begun.

Despite their lofty ideals and goals, the Watchers were a human organization. As such, they were prone to the same politicking, squabbling, and backstabbing that had plagued groups of people since the dawn of civilization. The first arrivals were always quick to stake a claim on the rest as they came in. Trying to influence their stances on the issues under discussion.

The two factions sharing the mess hall had all been here long enough for old arguments and rivalries to surface. Like many conflicts throughout human history, this one came down to a single issue: whether or not to change a tradition. The groups sitting around him were aligned around their beliefs in their answers to that question.

On one side of the divide stood the Radicals, who believed they should take a more active role in helping and healing. A leadership role in guiding the mundane masses toward a better future. They advocated further expanding their numbers by inducting into the Order anyone who could wield the nan. This had become the biggest point of contention between the two sides.

The Traditionalists, on the other side, felt the guiding, healing, and construction should be done piecemeal, as had always been done, and were staunchly opposed to bringing new blood into the Order. Rance had known the people in both groups for ages. Some of them, he knew, would be open to new ideas if the arguments in favor of the change were persuasive enough. Most, though, were hardheaded and could never be swayed, only outvoted.

A loner by nature, Rance didn't wish to align himself with either faction until he'd heard the arguments from both. The chat feed he'd been reading as he approached the Watch Tower had given him the impression that the arguments had already become heated. He detested drama. He merely wanted to enjoy the respite from the woes of the world for a few days and then cast his vote to complete the Convocation so he could return to his region and continue his work.

One of the Radicals finally got up from their table and sat down across from him.

"How you doin', Terry?" Constance said. "Long time, no see."

"It has been a while, hasn't it? You're looking rather good, Constance. Recent reconstruction?"

"Two weeks ago," she said and actually blushed.

"Looks good."

"Thank you."

"What can I do for you?" Rance said, locking eyes with her and taking a bite of his burger.

"Never were one for small talk, were you?"

"Nope. Never saw the point of it. I talk to my friends. I discuss issues with my colleagues. We are here to discuss changes and take a vote. While I enjoy the comforts of the Tower, I do have matters more important than a lot of political strutting requiring my attention. So, if you please, make your pitch and leave me to enjoy my lunch."

Constance huffed and gave him a look of irritation. She was someone who enjoyed the foreplay of a conversation, a little gossip, softening her target up with her well-considered opinions before coming to the point. By cutting through it, Rance had thrown her off her game.

"Are you aware of the issue under discussion, Terry?" He nodded, but she went on as though he hadn't. "We are failing. The Order, that is. We are all getting old, and we can't do our jobs the way we could a hundred years ago. Or even fifty. Our tried-and-true methods aren't working anymore, and we need to try something new. This is what I'm hoping to talk to you about."

Rance ate a few fries and sipped on his drink, waiting for her to continue.

"I and other like-minded individuals are advocating for the induction of new blood into our order. Fresh faces and new ideas to shake things up are exactly what we need. It will also allow us to cover more ground outside. We can't continue as we have. There are too few of us left. The data suggests that unless something drastic changes, this planet and all who exist on it will die in less than one hundred years."

Rance nodded and burped into his napkin, then said, "Thank you for getting to the point quickly. You've given me a lot to think about. I'll let you know what I think after I look at your data for myself. Go ahead and upload it to my drive."

Constance didn't look happy with the turn the conversation had taken. Rance didn't blame her. He knew he was hard to get along with. Of course, it was also partially his colleagues' fault for being such insufferable know-it-alls. He gave her a placating smile and returned his attention to his food, ignoring her until she got up and left. A sidelong glance told him the other camp was watching her go, had, in fact, watched their whole exchange. He hoped they wouldn't decide to send someone from their side to interrupt what was left of his meal.

In truth, his own views on how to fix the problems they were facing closely aligned with the Radicals' point of view. Where they differed was in volume. Rance felt that everyone with aptitude should be given access to their nan abilities and trained, though not necessarily inducted into the Order. If anything, he thought the Watchers should take on a leadership, teaching, and advisory role and let the masses do the rest of the hands-on work. His experiment with Hillcrest had proven his hypothesis was valid.

He finished his burger in silence and tossed the refuse in the recycler. He tipped a wave to Constance and another in the direction of the Traditionalists as he left. Later, back in his quarters, he was going over the data Constance had given him when the door chime sounded.

They get points for letting me eat, he thought. "Come in!"

At the sound of his voice, the door irised open and in stepped Cale Sprague, one of the few Watchers he could count as a friend.

"Cale!" Rance said, sweeping his old friend into a hug.

"It's been too long, Ter. When did you get in?"

"This morning. I had planned on wandering around a bit, but I was waylaid by Constance in the cafeteria, and now I just want to stay in my room reading till it's time to start."

"I know just what you mean," Sprague said with a laugh. "She's gotten very intense over the years."

"She was always intense; now she's just insufferable. Just like most of the idiots around here."

"Let's go get a drink. I'll help you fend off any unwanted idiocy that comes our way."

"Sounds like fun."

The lounge was much the same as the rest of the Watch Tower. Tables and stools flowed smoothly up from the floor or out from the walls as they were needed, giving the space an organic look. Here and there, Rance spotted errors where the nanites failed to correctly grow the furniture, or imperfections marring the normally smooth walls. It had been a while since he'd walked these halls, but such things had been unheard of in the early days. Now, everywhere Rance looked, he could see signs of the strain the building nanites were under while trying to maintain the old structure far beyond its original expiration date.

He mentioned this to Sprague, who looked around until he, too, found the stunted growths around the room and frowned briefly before shrugging and tossing back the rest of his drink.

"It's probably nothing," he said. "It's an old building. You can't expect everything to be perfect."

Rance wasn't so sure. Signs like this could be an indicator of a deeper problem with the Watch Tower's core programming. A hundred and seven years of continuous operation was a long time to go without a major overhaul or fresh nanite infusion.

"Don't you think this is something that should be discussed at the Convocation?"

"The Watch Tower is solid," Sprague said with a wave of his hand. "It will probably outlast us all. It's better off than Site 1; that's for damn sure. Have you been to the Ashlands lately?"

"Can't say I have. My work keeps me in the amber zone, mostly."

"The rim? You always were a glutton for punishment, Ter. At least they have you. Those people have it rough."

"Yes, they do. I think we could make more of a difference if more of us put in a little more time out there."

"Never happen," Sprague said, ordering another drink. "It's too hard out there. Too many problems and not enough feather beds."

They shared a laugh. Rance felt it was a point of pride to work out where he was most needed. After checking his old friend's logs, he was pleased to see Sprague put in nearly as much time in the amber zone as he did.

"You're right, though," Sprague said once his drink arrived. "We need to convince more of us to get out there and do some real work. Can't get some of these lazy bastards to leave their cushy cradles here in the Tower."

"We wouldn't have to if we empowered the people who live out there to do some of the work for us."

The look Sprague gave him was a mixture of surprise and disgust.

"Please don't tell me you've become a Radical, creating problems out of thin air?"

"I'm not sure where I stand yet; I haven't had time to read up on everything."

"What's there to read up on?" Sprague said. He signaled the bar for a refill. "They think the world is falling apart around us and that everything we've done, everything we've been doing since the Breakdown, has been a waste of effort. I don't know if they're right or not. But I do know, arming the rubes won't fix anything. That's nothing but a recipe for disaster."

"The abstracts I've been able to digest so far indicate the errors we are seeing are still correctable at this stage, provided we take certain steps to do so. It makes sense to let others help us. Many hands make light work, after all."

"Yeah, steps like letting a bunch of untrained yokels into the Order, training them up, as though that will fix everything. If *we* can't fix it, what makes them think the hicks can? It would be like giving Cro-Magnons hand grenades. Don't you see what a disaster that would be?"

"I'm not talking about the weapon applications, only the agricultural, medical, and maybe construction applications."

"Do you honestly think it would stop there? Once they have a taste of the benign applications, what's to stop them from figuring out how to access the dangerous ones? I prefer not giving guns to kids, thank you very much."

Rance was taken aback by the venom in his old friend's voice.

"Have you looked at their data? There are indicators that they could handle active nanotech just as well as we have."

"Don't need to look at it. I have eyes. Sure, we grew them with nanites so we could track them and gather info on them during their lifecycles and stuff, but there's no way they can use it the way we can."

If his friend was this passionate about the subject, then it was something Rance couldn't just blow off. Rance felt out of touch. Granted, he went out farther than most of the others, which meant he was incommunicado for longer stretches of time. Between Sprague and Constance, he wasn't exactly sure what he thought. The only thing he was sure of was that he'd never seen such a sharply divided Convocation.

"I'm sure the data will support the best argument," Rance

said. Then, to change the subject, he said, "In the meantime, I'm going to enjoy some creature comforts while I'm here."

"Amen. I'll drink to that," Sprague said. They clinked glasses and drank. "Look, I'm sorry I went off on you. I've been here for five days, and they've been beating me over the head with their fake facts the whole time. I can't wait for this Convocation to be over so we can put these Radicals in their place and get back to work."

"I couldn't agree more," Rance said, only half lying to his friend.

It was pandemonium inside the forum.

It had been a week since the last six Watchers had returned and the Convocation officially began. Since then, the rift in the Order had grown in immensity and animosity. The Triad directors sat at the head of the room during each meeting, struggling in vain to maintain order. Each day, they all met in the conference hall to discuss the issues, and each day, the discussion devolved into petty arguments and shouting. Neither side gave any ground toward compromise. The longer the Convocation went on, the further each cabal entrenched. Speakers were booed away from the podium, their points unheard by the audience. The infighting was so bad, the shouts of the hotheads so loud, that the moderates on both sides couldn't make themselves heard.

Today was no different. Today's speaker, Joseph McCammon, tried illustrating the need to actively involve people outside of the Order in the preservation efforts. No mention was made of inducting them or training them in the Order's practices. Nevertheless, his stance was too close to the Radical line for the Traditionalists, and they verbally eviscerated him until he left the stage fuming in rage and disgust while Director Winoki pounded away with his gavel.

Rance looked around in disbelief. He simply couldn't

fathom how such a small issue had caused so much chaos. McCammon's own notions closely aligned with his own. Seeing how he was treated made Rance glad he hadn't publicly voiced his own views.

After the meeting was adjourned, he met Sprague in the Canteen for a drink.

"I can't believe they are getting up in arms about this," Rance said. "Even if it weren't a question of adding people to the Order, we need help. We've been carrying this burden for too long. What would be so bad about allowing the mundanes to share some of the workload?"

"It's not just that, man," Sprague said, tossing a pretzel in his mouth. Rance marveled at how quickly they reaccustomed themselves to luxury. Out in the world, there were no pretzels, and the only alcohol was rough fermented grain spirits just as likely to kill you as get you drunk.

"It's a challenge to the cause we're all pledged ourselves to," Sprague continued. "The Radicals want us to just hand all of our secrets away to the rubes in the hopes of staving off some fictitious disaster."

"You really don't think we could use the help out there?"

"Of course we could use the help! But empowering the people out there isn't the answer. We need to improve our methods and refocus our efforts on problems we can actually solve, not waste our time teaching the unteachable how to work magic. There's no guarantee they can even learn, infused with nan or not."

Sprague sighed and took another drink.

"Look, I know you're on the fence about this. And I know why. You've got that pretty little village you've been building out there. Don't look at me like that. You're my best friend. I wouldn't be doing my job if I didn't look in on you every now and then to make sure you're alright."

Shortly after his return to the Watch Tower, Rance had considered telling his old friend about his experiment. He had quickly determined it would be a bad idea to share the exact details with Sprague. He hadn't thought his old friend would take the news well. Worse, it would turn half of the Order against him. Hearing Sprague already knew about it and hadn't told the others spoke volumes about how much he valued their friendship.

"You've got a soft spot for the rubes," Sprague continued. "I don't blame you. We all have our little pet projects out there. But in here, man, you need to leave all that shit behind. Giving those people an education in nanotechnology is not how we are going to solve this planet's problems. Only we can do that. We just have to work smarter and harder."

"You're referring to them as though they are a different species. They're the same as us."

"That's where you're wrong, my friend. Dead wrong. They are nothing like us. We are natural-born humans. Not a vat-grown genetic mish-mash. We had moms and dads who raised us the human way."

"It's been over a hundred years. Do you really think any of the first-generation vat-growns are still alive out there? If that's your only criteria for what makes us more human, then those people are way more human than we are: they are breeding. When's the last time any of us had a kid? Besides, these aren't the bodies we were born with, or did you forget how we got here in the first place?"

"I remember," Sprague said and waved a hand at him. "You're not getting what I'm saying, man. It's not just the bodies. We were raised on Earth, with Earth values. These people are just tools. You know it as well as I do. Giving the sort of power we control to a group of tools is not just stupid and insane; it's dangerous."

"It seems to me the Radicals are saying we only give a small number of the more adept among them some access to our abilities. There might not be any other way if we are going to make a difference. Even if all we do is replenish our ranks to recover those we've lost over the years—"

"You'd better watch who you say that kind of stuff to," Sprague cut in. "You're starting to sound like one of them, buddy. If the wrong people hear you—"

"What?" Rance said, suddenly angry. "What happens if the wrong people hear me? Are you threatening me, Cale?" Maybe his friend didn't value their relationship quite as much as he thought.

Sprague slammed his empty glass down on the table after tossing back the last of his beer. "Don't be stupid. I'm not threatening you. I'm telling you, as your friend, you'd better pick a side soon, buddy. Because this mess is coming to a head. The Radicals think they can shit all over us, all over the Order, without consequences. Nuh-uh. Not going to happen."

"All anyone's done is talk," Rance said, his anger slowly replaced by worry. "If both sides would just calm down enough to hear the other, then this fight would be over and we could get back to work."

"The talk's almost finished," Sprague said. "Useless waste of time anyhow. None of those dumbasses are willing to listen to reason anyway."

Rance almost laughed at the irony in Sprague's statement. He tried another line of reasoning. "At the meeting tomorrow, we just need everyone to stay in their seats and refrain from shouting at the speakers; then, we can make some progress with the debate and get on with the vote. It's only been a week, and I'm already sick of all this fighting."

"We all are, buddy. But don't you worry. The time for talking is almost done. One way or the other, this Convocation is almost over. We shouldn't be stuck here too much longer if you take my meaning." Sprague smiled and grabbed more pretzels.

"What are you talking about? What's going to happen?"

"I'm not saying that anything's going to happen, but you should keep your head down over the next couple days. Or pick a side. Dithering on the fence is starting to piss some of us off."

Abruptly, Sprague stood and strode away from their table, leaving Rance behind, shaken by what he'd just heard. Was Sprague delivering a warning or a veiled threat? Were the Traditionalists really contemplating violence to force the rest of them back in line? All these questions and more rattled around his head as he watched his old friend drunkenly swagger out of the lounge. But the last question was the most important of them all: What was he going to do about it?

During the so-called debates, Rance had kept his eyes open, watching for anyone who wasn't as fervent in their opinions as the others. There weren't many. But he managed to find a few who'd remained seated and silent while others had stood and shouted. That night, he sent out nearly a dozen invitations to meet, but only five responded.

The people gathered in his room were a fairly even mix. Two from the radical camp, two from the traditionalists, and one, like him, who was uncommitted to either. Even sitting in his small room, on couches flowing up from the floor, they separated into their opposing sides and eyed each other warily.

Maybe this isn't going to work, he thought. The opposing ideologies were too deeply entrenched to be overcome by civil conversation. He set out some refreshments and took a steadying breath. All he could do was try.

"Thank you all for coming," he said. "I called you all here because I want to discuss the dangers we are currently facing. It is my hope you will hear me out with an open mind, and then we can further discuss the concerns I intend to raise. Ultimately, I want to enlist your help fixing what has gone so wrong here in the Watch Tower."

"What do you think is the problem?" asked Silla Decker. She sat opposite him alone, unaffiliated with one cause or the other. The last to arrive, she was the one they had all waited upon to begin the Convocation. She was tall and slim, almost frail-looking, though Rance knew her to be a powerful and effective nan wielder. "I assume, because you have these others here, you aren't going to preach to us about the merits of one viewpoint over the other."

"No, I'm not. I arrived a week ago. In that time, I've witnessed the climate here within the Watch Tower deteriorate dramatically. We all know this isn't the first Convocation where people have fiercely defended their positions and attacked the opposition, but this is the first one where actual physical violence might occur."

At this, one of the Radicals, a man named Morin, spoke, "What do you mean, physical violence? There hasn't been a Watcher-on-Watcher attack in almost seventy years. What makes you think this issue will be any different?"

"I sit in the meeting hall every day," Rance said after taking a moment to collect his thoughts. "And all I see are people blinded by their own rhetoric, unable to see anything beyond. I walk the halls and take my meals in the dining hall, the same as you, and what I see are divided armed camps. If any of you can tell me you haven't observed the same, please do so."

He paused and looked each of them in the eye. No one spoke.

"My best friend, a man I've known and worked with since long before the Breakdown, gave me an ultimatum yesterday. Pick a side or face the consequences. This was followed by a none-too-subtle threat. I believe, because of this and everything else, things are escalating out of control and may explode soon unless we stop it."

"What do you think we can do?" This came from Gelan, a Traditionalist and, honestly, the one person Rance hadn't expected to answer his call. "I agree that I've been seeing some pretty scary shit going down around here. All most of the people on my side can talk about is how unreasonable you people are."

Davis, the man seated next to Morin, shot to his feet.

"We're unreasonable? If you dumb fucks would simply read the data we've sent you over and over again instead of shouting yourselves hoarse every day, then we wouldn't be in this mess!"

That did it, Rance thought. *Now they're going to start fighting in my apartment. So much for thinking I could do anything to fix this.*

He was about to intervene, but Gelen held up his hands and said, "I didn't say that was my view. What I said was it's what people on my side are saying. I've looked at your data. Some of it is very compelling, and though I find fault with a few points here and there, there's nothing I'm not willing to discuss calmly and intelligently."

"But that's not happening right now," Flora, the other Traditionalist sitting next to him, said. "Neither side is listening to the other right now. Rance is right; this whole place is going to go up in flames, and we're all to blame."

"This is why I've called you together," Rance said. "If we can make the rest listen, then there's a chance we can avoid violence. The world out there is hard enough without us sticking knives in our own backs."

"What's your plan, Rance?" Silla said.

This was the crucial moment. He'd managed to get the attention of these people, most of whom were currently at odds with each other. Now, he needed to convince them to work with him.

"We can turn this all around," Rance said. "There are moderates on both sides of this issue. There must be. Even the ones who are convinced they're right might be willing to listen and compromise if encouraged. The problem is that they are being drowned out by the hotheads on both sides. We need to find these people, talk to them, get them to listen."

Silla interrupted him here. "You're afraid this whole place is going to erupt in violence at any moment, and you are saying that we need to take the time to talk to people? If it's as dire as you are saying, isn't it a bit late for that?"

"Not if we hurry," Gelen said. "Without support, the hotheads will deflate. Not much, maybe, but enough for a chance to open a dialog."

"Right!" said Rance. "If we can reduce the amount of noise, then we can isolate the ones propelling us along this path. If we can isolate them, then we can truly start the process of resolving this issue. All we need is a few people from both sides willing to calmly listen and debate."

"I don't know," Davis said, scratching his chin. "There are some on my side, Constance, for one, who think it's a mistake to deal with you people at all." He gestured to Gelen and Flora. "Some of the things she suggests are already pretty violent and graphic."

Rance shook his head. Constance, she'd always been annoying. But hearing she was actively trying to derail the Convocation convinced Rance she was part of the problem.

Flora cleared her throat. "We've been hearing the same sorts of talk over here, too." She looked at Rance. "I agree we are headed down a bad path right now. I'm just not sure talking will do it. I'm not sure anything can at this point."

"Talking is the only thing we can do," Rance said. "If we go out there busting heads, then at best, we accomplish nothing, and at worst, we prove that we're no better than they are. We don't need a majority; I'm not even saying we need to give in on any of the points either side is trying to make. But we need to calm things down and start talking, or this Convocation will end in bloodshed."

"He has a point," Silla said. The others reluctantly nodded their agreement. "So, now that we agree, what's the next step?"

This would be the tricky part.

"We need to increase our numbers. Each of you, find someone you think is willing to listen, take them aside, and convince them. Silla, you join the Radical camp, and I'll side with the Traditionalists. If each of us can convince just one person, it should be enough to sway the next debate and shut down the hotheads."

"It should go without saying," Morin said, "that we need to keep this meeting a secret. If anyone from my side finds out about this, we can kiss any hope of convincing anyone goodbye."

"If anyone else finds out about this," Davis said, "then we can kiss our own asses goodbye, never mind the rest of the Convocation!"

"Agreed," Gelen said. "The less duplicitous it looks, the better for everyone involved. We want to prevent violence, not incite it."

With everyone in agreement, Rance suggested they all shake on it.

Silla left first, checking the corridor to make sure no one was lurking about before signaling all clear and returning to her room. Then, the Radicals departed. After them, Rance went outside to make sure the hallway was still clear.

As the Traditionalists exited, Gelen stopped. "It's nice to see someone taking charge in this mess," he said. "I've always liked working with you, Rance. I hope we get to do so again in the future."

They shook hands again, then Rance went back inside and dropped into his bed. Tomorrow, the real work, and real risk, would begin.

CHAPTER 8
KINNEY

The next few weeks went by in a blur for Kinney. For the first time, he could almost say he was happy. Saving Astrid's life had resulted in a profound impact on how people looked at him. His coworkers treated him decently, or at least tolerantly. He almost looked forward to going to work each day.

She was popular, and her opinions carried weight. When she'd hated him, the rest of the crew had hated him too. Now that she and her close circle of friends liked him, the rest fell in line and began to treat him kindly as well. It had only taken two months and a nearly catastrophic accident for Astrid and the rest of the Site 1 crew to accept him.

I'm back in high school, and the head cheerleader has decided I'm not a complete slime. I can't believe this kind of shit is happening!

Kinney arrived at his station to find Astrid already at hers. Deciding to test the waters, he said, "Good morning, Astrid."

She looked up at him and smiled. "Good morning. Did you have a good night?"

There was no guile in her voice. Nothing to suggest she was being disingenuous. Her opinion of him had been completely reversed.

"It was alright," he admitted, then walked over to her station. "What are you working on?"

"I'm running remote diagnostics on the control sensors around the reactor. There's no reason I can see for the sensor failure the day of my accident. That unit had been replaced only a few months ago."

"Parts fail," Kinney said with a shrug. "We live in an imperfect world."

"True. But even if there had been a failure in the sensor unit itself, it should have been detected by one of the numerous backups in that part of the reactor. Something in there should have noticed something was wrong and notified us about it."

"What are you suggesting?" Kinney asked.

"I'm not suggesting anything just yet. I'm only saying it's weird none of the backup sensors gave any indication something was wrong. I hate jumping to conclusions, but it seems almost intentional."

"I think you're on the right track," he said quietly. "Come to my room after we clock out. There's something I want to show you."

Astrid nodded and didn't question further.

Back in his quarters, Kinney opened his lock box and retrieved the file he'd been compiling. It was a hard copy. He couldn't risk it leaking out onto the site server.

"There's another reason you weren't selected for promotion," he began. "Corporate wanted an outsider inserted here. They wanted a fresh perspective on the problems this site has been experiencing. It wasn't that they didn't think you could do the job; they just didn't think you could be objective the way someone from another site could."

"Someone like you," she said, taking a seat in his easy chair.

"Exactly. But there's more to it than that. I was sent here to clean up Site 1, but I have another mission here too. I was assigned here to investigate the possibility of espionage and sabotage."

Astrid leaned forward, her expression serious. "They think someone here is intentionally leaking information and screwing with equipment?"

"Yes," Kinney said, nodding.

"You know," Astrid said after a moment of thought, "that certainly makes a hell of a lot of sense. Things have been hinky around here for a while now. Freak accidents, bad batches, all unexplainable. A saboteur makes a lot of what I've been seeing make sense. What are you going to do if you catch the prick doing this?"

"For one thing, I'm still not totally convinced there is a saboteur. But if there is, then I have been given special authority to arrest and detain them."

Astrid whistled. "So, you're like an undercover cop from those old flicks we watch on movie night."

Kinney smiled and nodded. "Except I don't have a gun."

"Who needs a gun? With all the nanotech in our bodies, some of it can be easily repurposed into weaponry."

That thought hadn't occurred to him. The very idea that anyone could be walking around lethally armed without setting off any alarms was frightening.

"What do you need from me?" Astrid asked.

"You have proven you are an excellent engineer. You have the imagination and drive to make this place run like clockwork. You aren't afraid to take risks—"

"Stupid risks," she muttered.

"I want you on my side, investigating with me. Together, I believe we can ferret out the traitor and get this place back on track."

Astrid mulled this over for a minute. To help her think, she stood up and paced the room for a turn or two.

"You want me to spy on the people I've been working with for over two years? Friends I've grown close to, and turn on them if it turns out they are who you're looking for?"

"Yes," Kinney said. When she didn't reply for a moment, he added, "When my task here is done, I'm leaving. The position I'm occupying now will become open. I can put in a good word for you with my superiors. Helping me should be enough to land you a promotion. Hell, if we do a good enough job here, I don't see why they wouldn't promote you even higher. At least some of this mess is due to Waler's negligence. They might even reward you with his job."

Astrid stopped pacing and cast a critical eye in his direction. "Any way I can get that in writing?"

"I can try."

"Well then, Mr. Secret Agent Man, you've got yourself a partner." She stuck out her hand, and he shook it.

Lunch the next day was a unique affair. He had company to eat with. He'd entered the dining room and selected his meal for the printers to produce as normal, then selected one of the empty tables on the outskirts of the room. No sooner had he taken his first bite than Astrid and three of her usual lunch buddies—Danny Winoki, Phebe Flores, and Robert Petrovich—joined him.

"Anyone sitting here?" she asked with a smirk. Nobody ever sat with him, so the question was just her being a smart-ass.

He gestured for them to sit.

Winoki and Phebe sat across the table from him. Astrid took the chair at the head of the table, and Petrovich sat down between Kinney and her. Once everyone was settled, Winoki and Phebe immediately resumed the conversation they'd been having.

"I'm just saying," Winoki said, "there's no excuse for some of the crap I've been seeing around here. We've seen some improvements since he arrived"—he flicked a thumb at Kinney— "but not nearly enough."

"I think Waler's cooking his books and pocketing the change," Phebe said.

"There's no way he can," Petrovich said. "There are internal and external auditors keeping watch on the money. He would have to be a mathematical savant to be able to hide the amounts of money you're talking about."

"And Waler's not that smart," Astrid added.

"Well, something's wrong," Winoki said, looking crestfallen. "All of our equipment is outdated. The heat shield on generator five has been patched so many times it might as well be made of quick-weld. One day, that thing's going to blow and take half the section with it."

"Waler's probably not cooking the books or stealing," Kinney put in. "Like Astrid said, he's not that smart. He's just incompetent. I've been looking over his allocations for the last year, and it looks to me like the people on his good side are the ones who get the lion's share of the budget."

Petrovich looked over at Astrid. "Sounds like you need to do more ass-kissing and less antagonizing to me."

"I'm honest with him. He doesn't like it."

"Then stop it!" Winoki said, slapping the table. "We need new drone kits and a full rebuild for the heat exchanger. That's never going to happen unless you start kissing his ass. It'll be easy. His ass is so big that all you have to do is pucker up and close your eyes when you're in the same room as him. Once he turns around, you can't miss it!"

Everyone at the table shared a laugh. For the rest of their lunch period, they expounded upon Waler's ample posterior, poor management skills, and low intelligence quotient, anything they could think of to keep the laughter going. When it was time to return to their stations, Astrid pulled Kinney aside before he could dump his tray into the recycler.

"Hey," she said low enough to foil any eavesdroppers. "All kidding aside, I think Danny and Phebe have a point. We should take a closer look at Waler. He's an asshole, but not nearly as stupid as he makes himself out to be. He's been here long enough and knows the system well enough to be able to hide money."

"You think he'd risk his career and life by skimming from his own budget?"

"I think he's dissatisfied with what he's been given here. I've been here about as long as he has. He got his position because of some connections he's got with someone higher in corporate, but he hasn't done a good enough job here to make it any higher. I know, for a fact, he's been trying for a position away from the planetside sites."

"That's not evidence of wrongdoing."

"No, but it is motive. We need to look at him is all I'm saying. He'd be in the best position to steal or sell company secrets."

"We'll take a look," Kinney said. "But don't be surprised if he turns out to be clean. People in his position are highly visible. From above and below. Which makes it harder for them to sneak around, no matter what kind of secrets they have access to. We need to keep an open mind and not focus on Waler. No matter how suspiciously he's been acting."

"Okay," she said. "We'll do it your way." Her tone and expression said she accepted what he'd just said, but there was an eagerness in her eyes that belayed her words.

Without another word, they finished dumping their trays and returned to work.

The door chimed and opened. Kinney had only been waiting on the other side of it for five minutes, waiting for permission to enter. Waler really enjoyed his petty power trips to make sure people knew they were beneath him. Kinney hated having his time wasted. He didn't have anything more important going on now, but it was the principle of the thing.

At least I won't have to deal with this obnoxious ass too much longer, he thought as he opened the door and entered. During his time at Site 1, he'd come to greatly dislike this office and the person occupying it. Every meeting devolved into a contest of wills and political pull.

This time would be a little different. This time, Kinney held the trump card.

"Kinney," Waler said. He didn't get up from his desk to extend a greeting, nor did he offer a chair for Kinney to sit in. Kinney sat anyway. His business here shouldn't take too long.

"Waler."

"What can I do for you?" Waler asked. "You practically demanded this meeting, stating it was an urgent matter." His tone implied he had better things to do and that Kinney had better not waste his time.

Kinney smiled. "Thank you for seeing me. In fact, what I'm here to discuss is of the utmost importance. I came here about two months ago tasked with the job of finding your site's deficiencies and correcting them. During my time here, you've done your level best to make my job as difficult as possible, even to the point of being actively obstructive."

"Now, wait a minute there. I've been nothing but accommodating—"

"Please don't interrupt," Kinney said, leveling Waler with a stern look. "If you know what's good for you, you will say as little as possible from here on out."

The pained look on Waler's face was satisfying.

"As I was saying, you've made my job here needlessly difficult. What you didn't know because it was withheld from you is that I was sent here with another task: to investigate any corporate espionage and double-dealing. I've been given broad leeway in how I conduct my investigation. In two months, I've found several instances of what I believe to be sabotage and underhanded dealings."

Waler balked and started to speak but thought better of it at the last second and closed his mouth.

"I believe I've found the source of the problems here at Site 1," Kinney continued. "I must congratulate you on covering your tracks as effectively as you did. It took a lot of time and digging to piece together how you did it. But I've found evidence you've been skimming credits from your budgets, actively hindering the work being done here, and selling proprietary company secrets and information to our competitors."

"That's not true!" Waler blurted out.

"Waler, by the power vested in me by HelixCom, I am placing you under arrest." The four-person security detachment who had been waiting in the hall for his signal entered the office and flanked the former site manager.

"This is bullshit," Waler wailed. "I didn't do any of that. You can't prove any of it."

"I have all the data I need to sanction this arrest. I will remind you that anything you say may be used to incriminate you; it would be in your best interest to remain silent."

Waler huffed like he wanted to say more but, once again, thought better of it. The security officers flex-cuffed him and led him from the office.

Kinney leaned back in his chair and smiled.

Well, that went well. I expected him to put up more of a fight. Now it's time to get to work.

He rose and stepped around the desk to use the interface. He had to make sure everything looked solid. If it didn't stick, then his superiors would question everything he'd been doing here. Which, in turn, risked bringing to light his other activities.

Kinney really had to thank Astrid and her friends. After all, they'd given him the flash of inspiration that had led to Waler's arrest. When he had looked more closely at the man's finances, he discovered a few minor discrepancies. Deeper digging had revealed Waler was, in fact, stealing from the company. He'd been smart about it. Only siphoning off fractional credits intermittently so as not to attract attention. During his tenure as site manager, he'd amassed a tidy fortune. Which would be seized and returned to the company coffers. The company would put him on trial, find him guilty, and sentence him to workforce duty on an asteroid penal colony back in the Sol system. They would demand he provide the names of his confederates and contacts among their competitors.

Of course, he couldn't do that. Waler had no contacts outside HelixCom.

Incompetence and greed were the only crimes of which Waler was guilty. Not espionage and sabotage.

Kinney had manufactured the evidence against him to get him out of the way. Waler was such a detestable human being, and Kinney felt no remorse whatsoever for using him as a scapegoat to cover up his own activities. With Waler gone, corporate would stop looking for a spy. Leaving Kinney free to continue his true mission here at Site 1.

He leaned back in the former director's chair and smiled. Everything was proceeding exactly as Aion had designed.

CHAPTER 9
KAYAH

The town of Goldenrod was situated near the bend of the wide, slow Sesta River. The town was a collection of low, sturdy buildings and prosperous farmsteads. Though a proper census had never been conducted, Regaline told them there were exactly two-thousand two-hundred and thirty-eight people living in the town—with sixteen women at various stages of pregnancy—making it one of the more productive and successful townships on the rim of the green zone. Goldenrod's good fortune came from being settled so close to the river, which ran through the green zone. There were other reasons, of course. A solid work ethic imbued into the populous, as well as a keen sense of community and better education for their youth, helped ensure their prosperity.

It also didn't hurt that Interland was far enough away to remain a negligible threat.

A few days after losing their militant shadow, Regaline's group came to the banks of the Sesta. Rather than cross the rushing water, Regaline turned them south and followed the river's course for three days until they came upon Goldenrod. There, they crossed the river using the bridge built there and entered the town.

"You will all be pleasantly surprised here," Regaline told her adepts. "These people all know and accept people like us. They are typically happy to receive the assistance we offer."

"They're not suspicious of outsiders?" Taeg asked.

"Not as a rule, no. They are welcoming, but only up to a point. You'll see when we reach the constable's office."

Her kids, as she'd taken to thinking of them, looked around wide-eyed at the buildings lining the streets. The boulevard connected to a major highway that ran into town from the east and crossed the river heading out of town. About two kilometers outside the western edge of town, there was a junction where three roads met, crossed, and became two roads, one heading south deep into the center of the green zone and one heading west towards the outlands. Goldenrod had begun life as a perfectly situated trading post between the lush green zone and the impoverished amber zone.

The group passed several orchards and ranches as they made their way into town. Workers toting woven reed baskets bustled between trees and bushes laden with fruit. Healthy-looking sheep, goats, and cattle lazily munched grass within fenced paddocks while chickens and other birds skittered about. Further signs of the municipality's prosperity.

Convenient access to the river and several well-trod roads had allowed Goldenrod to prosper. Because there was a lot of money and property involved, the town boasted a larger-than-average policing force and enforced its laws strictly. All visitors were required to check in with the constables upon arrival, with their weapons surrendered and wagons searched. If the rules and laws were followed to the T, then there was no problem. If a stranger failed to toe the line exactly, they were forcibly expelled from town with only the clothes on their back, with all their goods and possessions confiscated. Harsh, but it ensured lawful compliance and kept the peace.

"This place is big!" Drak said, his eyes wide. Regaline glanced back to find him staring at everything around him. The smoothly cobbled streets, the covered boardwalk promenade in front of each block of buildings, the glassed-in windows.

Compared to where he'd come from, this town must seem like a metropolis, she thought. His home had been a collection of outland squatter's hovels with scraggly garden patches, where less than a dozen families struggled together to survive. "This is just a small town compared to some farther south."

She glanced at the other two. Kayah was also suitably impressed by the town. Though her home hadn't been nearly as downtrodden as Drak's. Her family, like Drak's, had tried to exploit her gifts to make their lives a little bit better. It had taken a lot of cajoling and even a few veiled threats to get both families to let her take them.

Despite his upbringing in squalor similar to Drak's, Taeg, unlike the other two, didn't seem impressed by what he saw. He was looking around, like they all were, but seemed more curious than awed. Though all three came from abject poverty, only the younger two appeared to be impressed by their surroundings.

The quartet continued down the main thoroughfare until they came to one of the few buildings in town constructed of bricks. The imposing structure was large and wide. The windows were covered with thick bars. The front door was thick, heavy wood set into a reinforced frame. The constable's office was purpose-built to project a sense of law and order and intimidate anyone who passed it by. Regaline led them inside.

Seated behind a desk sat a busy-looking clerk, who did a slight double-take when she looked up at the new arrivals.

"If you'll take a seat," she said in lieu of a greeting. "The chief will be with you in just a moment." Then she disappeared down the back hallway.

"She didn't even ask for your name," Kayah whispered as they sat in the waiting area. The stern nature of the building had her on edge. She kept glancing around nervously, as though someone were about to jump up beside her and start scolding her.

Regaline gave her a reassuring smile. "Most of us Watchers dress the part. We are recognized wherever we go. That's how it's been for as long as anyone can remember. It helps to speed things along any time we come to town."

"Do you think they are setting a trap?" Drak asked. He, too, was whispering.

"No. We've always had a friendly relationship with the people here. They respect the things we can do, especially when it benefits them."

"I don't like waiting," he said.

"If they are so friendly, then why are they making us wait?" Kayah asked.

Regaline shrugged. "There could be several reasons. The most likely is that the chief is alerting the mayor and anyone else who needs to be here to meet us. This takes time. They might even be setting up some sort of refreshments. Be patient."

Again, only her younger adepts seemed to be reacting to their surroundings. Taeg merely sat and silently observed the building in which they sat.

The waiting area wasn't large. There were six stiff wooden chairs crammed close together. If two more people came in and seated themselves, they would all be crowded to the point of discomfort. The interior of the station appeared to be as sturdy as the exterior. The walls were varnished wood. There were two doors leading out of the waiting room. One behind the front desk, and the other located in the far corner, which presumably led to holding cells. Regaline couldn't be sure. She'd only been here a handful of times. She considered initiating an echo pulse to map out the ground floor, but decided there was no need.

Even though Drak was impatiently bouncing in his chair, the wait wasn't long at all. Barely five minutes after the clerk had seated them, she reappeared. "If you will come with me, please." She smiled and gestured to the door she held open for them.

The hall was short. At the end stood two open doorways.

The one on the right led into an empty room, and the room on the left was an office occupied by the chief of Goldenrod's police force. The clerk escorted them into the office. The room was small, occupied mostly by a desk and a bank of wooden filing cabinets. Behind the desk stood a tall, broad-shouldered woman. She wore a blue-gray uniform tailored to fit snuggly but still allow her freedom of movement. She had iron-gray hair tied in a tight bun. Beside her stood another woman, smaller in both height and stature, with strawberry red hair, wearing a comfortable-looking suit cut from expensive-looking cloth.

"Chief Dusty, Mayor Saitine, these are the gris-gris men, er, people, I told you about," said the clerk once everyone had entered the office.

"Thank you, Tani," the chief said, and the clerk backed out of the office, closing the door behind her.

Saitine spoke first. "I'm sorry we can't offer you somewhere to sit. This office is a little cramped for so many people. We've never seen more than one of you in town at a time."

Chief Dusty cleared her throat. "On to business: are you passing through, or do you plan on staying for a while?"

"Just long enough to replenish our supplies and rest a spell," Regaline said. "Maybe help out if we're needed, wherever we're needed."

Mayor Saitine nodded while Chief Dusty looked pensive.

"Not to tell you your business, but most folk around town are already pretty well off. You might find yourself bored if you're counting on them for something to do."

"Not to worry, Chief. We'll manage fine and be away in a few days."

Dusty smiled and stood, extending her hand. "Then, welcome to Goldenrod. I hope your stay is fruitful and uneventful."

"Thank you, Chief," Regaline said, taking her hand.

As if summoned, Tani opened the door and ushered them out.

"I've taken the liberty of arranging some rooms at the Farraday Inn," Tani said. "If you keep going down Main Street here, it's just a couple blocks up on the left. Tell Mic at the front desk that Tani sent you."

"Thank you, Tani. You've been immensely helpful," Regaline said.

Back on the street, they walked for nearly a city block before Drak broke the silence.

"Well, that was awkward as hell."

"Is it always like that?" Kayah asked. "When you come to a new town, I mean."

"No," said Regaline. "Most of the time, it's worse."

"They looked so uncomfortable," Drak continued. "Like they didn't know whether or not to be friendly to us."

"Our kind intimidates them," Regaline said. "They know we have power. People with power rarely welcome others with power into their home. It creates competition. Deep down, no matter how friendly they are, they fear us and what we can do. This is part of the reason we can seldom remain in one place for long. It upsets the local authorities."

"They didn't seem afraid," Taeg said.

"Yeah, they did!" said Drak. "Didn't you see how they kept looking at each other every time Reggie said something?" Taeg shook his head. "Learn to read a room, man."

"Leave him alone, Drak," said Regaline. "There is plenty for you all to learn and time enough to learn it. Let's not speak anymore of this, not until we are behind closed doors. No need to give people any more to gossip about."

Kayah looked around and was surprised to find people watching them as they passed. Inside storefronts, sitting on the boardwalk steps, or walking along themselves, everyone seemed to be paying close attention to them. She saw the expression everyone wore: wary curiosity. Not a one of them seemed overly friendly either.

"Let's not dawdle, Kayah," Regaline said. Kayah realized

she'd fallen behind and hustled to catch back up.

They checked into their rooms without incident. Tani had arranged for two, one for the boys and one for the girls. Before settling in for the night, Regaline admonished Drak and Taeg not to speak to anyone and to behave themselves. "Do not let anyone in. Send to me anyone who comes knocking. And please do not cause a ruckus tonight." She looked pointedly at Drak when she said this. "We are guests here and do not want to squander the goodwill extended to us. Understood?" Drak and Taeg nodded, as did Kayah, though she was sharing a room with Regaline and was unlikely to cause any sort of ruckus.

"What makes you think anyone's going to come knocking?" Drak asked. "The way those people looked at us, I think they'd be too afraid to come near us at all."

"You'd be surprised," Regaline said, giving him a knowing smile. "Good night, boys. Get some rest; we are going to be busy tomorrow."

Drak was indeed surprised. The first knock came just as he and Taeg had settled into bed. They sent the caller on to Regaline's room as ordered. They did the same with the second and third callers, too. After that, the boys decided to sleep in shifts until the stream of nighttime visitors petered out sometime after midnight.

The next morning, Regaline looked refreshed and awake, as though she hadn't spent much of the night talking to people about their problems. Whereas Kayah was bedraggled and looked as though she hadn't slept at all.

"Because I didn't," she said when Drak mentioned it.

She, Drak, and Taeg were seated in a diner across the street from the inn, eating breakfast. Regaline, meanwhile, was speaking with the owner of the establishment. He'd been one of their late-night visitors. Kayah had tried to listen in when they spoke, but Regaline had put up a white noise barrier for privacy. The moment they had entered the restaurant, she had told them to eat quickly because they had a lot to accomplish that day.

"She wants us to get rest," Kayah complained, "then proceeds to invite the whole town into our room. How does that make any sense?"

Taeg just shrugged and spooned more porridge into his mouth.

Drak sympathized. "We were up late, too," he said. "They came to our room, looking for her." There were dark circles under his eyes. Though he and Taeg had decided to take turns, Taeg had fallen deeply asleep, leaving Drak to answer the door all night by himself.

Regaline returned to the table with a sweet roll in hand. "Finish up," she said. "We need to get started."

They spent the rest of the day traipsing around Goldenrod doing odd jobs and menial tasks for people who looked like they wanted nothing to do with them. At their first stop, she told them to wait outside by a cherry tree. A few minutes later, she returned and hurried them along to their next stop. There, she asked Drak to dowse around the property, looking for water. The owner's well was dry and needed a new source. After locating a new well drilling point, Regaline rushed them off to another house. This time, she asked Taeg to crawl under the house and repair a rusty mess of pipes. At the next house, Kayah climbed into the attic, looking for a box of papers. There were documents, including a land deed, that the owner needed. Regaline impatiently hurried them from place to place. She gave them fifteen minutes to eat at midday, then resumed the rush.

At dusk, she declared them finished for the day. Footsore and tired, Regaline finally allowed them to rest while they ate supper in the diner. This time, there was no rush, and Regaline sat with them to eat.

"Is this what your life is like?" Drak asked while they waited for their food to arrive. "Are you really just a glorified handyman? Fixing and finding shit for dumbasses who can't do it for themselves?"

Her expression said she was annoyed, but she didn't rise to Drak's bait.

"We help people in whatever ways they need," she said calmly. "Today, that meant doing odd jobs and chores. Tomorrow, it could mean something entirely different. We never know what we are meant to do when we first enter a place. The mere fact of our presence makes a difference, though. No matter how small, we strive to make a difference in people's lives."

"We make a difference? Yeah, right. We helped some idiot find his keys yesterday. How much of a difference are we really making?"

"More than you know, Drak. When you've advanced a little further, you will find out just how much. I remember hating cryptic statements like that when I was training, and I especially hate making them to you now. But you will just have to trust me when I say everything we are doing is working towards a greater good."

"Meanwhile, we're slogging through shit," he scoffed.

"Yes, you are," she agreed. "Head back to your rooms when you're finished eating. Try to get some sleep. We have more of the same tomorrow."

Drak rolled his eyes while Kayah frowned. Only Taeg seemed unfazed by the news.

Back at the inn, Regaline had set herself up in the inn's front room to receive people so the kids could sleep undisturbed.

It was well after midnight when the last visitor departed. Instead of going up to her room, Regaline decided to go for a walk. The air was cool and comforting, fragrant with the scents of fruit blossoms from a nearby orchard.

On a whim, she turned and made her way to the river. The sounds of moving water drowned out the rest of the world, and finding a secluded place where an outcropping of rocks provided some privacy to a small sandy beach, she stripped down to her underclothes, waded into the frigid water, and dunked herself. She could have used nan to warm herself against the chilly current, but instead, she enhanced her sensory perceptions to the point where the water felt like knives slicing into her skin. The cold seeped deep into the marrow of her bones. The pain was electric, causing her muscles to spasm. Her hands clenched involuntarily, and she had to clamp her jaws shut to keep her teeth from chattering. After a few minutes of this torture, she climbed ashore. Shivering uncontrollably, she basked in the cool air on the beach for a moment before raising her temperature and drying herself. Once dressed, she made her way back to the inn feeling completely refreshed and reset and ready to get back to work.

It was Kayah who saw the scout.

They had fallen into a routine during their four-day layover in Goldenrod: waking early, walking about the city helping those who asked it of them, and returning to the inn at dusk to sleep. The hectic pace of that first day had calmed down enough for them to enjoy a lengthy midday break. At which time, Regaline would deliver short lectures on the importance of what they were doing in towns like this to impress upon them the importance of service to the communities they visited and to humanity at large.

These inevitably led to a debate with Drak, which Kayah always found entertaining, both for his outlandish observations and Regaline's calm and measured responses. Drak had grown up a lot during their time together. He was still a little boy, true, but at times, he seemed older and more thoughtful than a boy of thirteen should be. Kayah sometimes found herself agreeing with the questions he dared to ask, wishing she had the gumption to voice such doubts herself.

Today, however, something nagged at her. She couldn't enjoy their verbal sparring no matter how she tried. She glanced at Taeg and found him similarly distracted. In fact, he seemed downright nervous and fidgety. Come to think of it, he'd been that way since breakfast.

"Look," Regaline said. "That's just the way it is. You extract more matter than you put in. Matter cannot be created or destroyed, only transformed. Your reading is coming along well, but the texts I could cite and have you look up are a little beyond you at the moment. You will just have to take my word for it."

"Fine," he said and blew a small raspberry.

"Good. Now, it's time to get moving. We're leaving tomorrow afternoon, and we need to wrap things up here before then. We have a lot to do, so I'm going to divide us into groups. Kayah, you and Drak will work together on the list I've just sent you. Taeg, you'll come with me."

"Yes, ma'am," Taeg said absently.

"Have you noticed anything weird about Taeg today?" Kayah asked Drak after they split up.

"Other than the fact that he's quiet and creepy, you mean?"

"Not just that. He seems more uptight and nervous than usual."

"I didn't notice. I don't spend all my time mooning at him like you do, Twigs."

Kayah refused to let him goad her into a fight. "It's not just him. Something feels off."

"What?"

"If I knew, I wouldn't be so worried. You don't feel anything?"

"No, I don't. Reggie doesn't either, or she would have said something."

"You think so? This wouldn't be the first time she's gone off without telling us. She probably doesn't want to scare us."

Drak thought about this and shook his head. "You think

she's hiding something from us?" he said.

"I'm not sure." She wasn't even sure there was anything wrong at all. She just had a feeling, like electricity in the air, telling her something was off.

They walked for a few minutes in silence. Drak watched his feet as they walked along the boardwalk. Kayah, still amazed and enamored by Goldenrod, took in everything she could. Who knew when she'd ever see a city like this ever again? The buildings, the streets, the people. They were all so different from what she'd known growing up that she couldn't help gawking at everything as she passed.

The man was standing on the opposite side of the street, staring into the front window of a dress shop, when she saw him. She could only see him at an angle, his back was mostly turned towards them. As they moved down the street, he seemed to shuffle slightly to the left, still staring through the window. Coming abreast of him, she saw his face clearly reflected in the glass. Their eyes met. He wasn't looking at the window display; he was watching them.

It clicked.

The last time she'd seen him was in the forest clearing. He'd been leading the soldiers through, following the false trail Regaline had left. It was the Interlander scout. Somehow, he'd found them again.

His gaze met Kayah's, reflected in the window glass. His eyes were wide in surprise. Then he turned away and hurried down the street.

Kayah pulled to a stop, reached out, and grabbed Drak's arm, halting him as well.

"Go find Regaline," she hissed, pulling him close. "Tell her the soldiers are here. Don't look at me like I'm stupid. Go. Run, now!"

She swatted him to get him going, then turned and hurried after the fleeing scout.

It was midmorning, and it seemed like everyone in town

had decided to take a stroll down the street at the same time, getting in her way and preventing her from catching up with her quarry. She halted at an intersection to let a pair of men carrying a comically long ladder cross in front of her. When she finally reached the other side, the scout was nowhere in sight. Staring off into the middle distance, she accessed her applications wheel and scrolled till she found the sensor menu.

On her third attempt, Kayah managed to activate a small tracker, which she sent out in search of the scout. He couldn't have gotten far. The same pedestrian traffic in front of her must be hindering him. Her drone caught a glimpse of him moving down a side street, heading for the river bridge.

Of course! she thought. *There's no way the whole company would be in town without Regaline knowing it. They'd have been spotted the moment they crossed the river.*

Without a second's hesitation, Kayah threw herself into a headlong pursuit. While running, she charged her weapons and armor.

She reached the road that paralleled the river and slowed. Her tracker had lost sight of him again. She saw a viewing platform built to overlook a particularly pretty vantage of the river and the bridge and trotted over to it. She watched the bridge for several minutes without seeing the scout.

"Drak says you saw something," Regaline said, stepping up beside her.

Without taking her eyes off the bridge, Kayah nodded and told her what she'd found. "If he's here, then the rest of them must be close by."

"Maybe it was just someone who looked like the scout," Regaline said, looking doubtful and worried at the same time.

Kayah was shaking her head before the older woman had even finished speaking. Then she brought up an instant recall from her memory of the sighting, took a capture, and sent it to Regaline.

"That's him, alright," she said with a sigh. "Go back to the inn and wait with the others. Pack your things and be ready to move when I return."

"But I want to help."

"You can help me best by doing as you're told, Kayah. You are the strongest; I need you to keep your head and mind the boys till I get back. Understand? Good. I won't be long."

Kayah frowned as she turned and started walking in the direction of the inn. When she looked back after a few steps, she expected to see Regaline walking along the river road toward the bridge, but instead, her mentor was heading in the opposite direction.

She thought it strange but let it go. Regaline's words bounced around her head. *I'm the strongest?* she thought and smiled.

All too soon, that strength would soon be put to the test.

They left after nightfall. Trusting darkness to cover them once they were beyond Goldenrod city limits. Regaline left word with the sheriff and mayor that they were departing, thanked them for their hospitality, and forwarded their apologies to the people they hadn't managed to assist.

Regaline led her adepts to a storage locker near the outskirts of town, along the eastern road. Inside were parcels of food, coils of rope and climbing gear, traveling clothes and boots, and other gear useful for traversing the wilds between towns.

"Find something that fits and change," Regaline said. The urgency in her tone worried Kayah. "Grab a pack and throw in an extra set. Fill the rest with food. I'll grab some gear and split it between you. Go!"

Kayah, Drak, and Taeg went to the piles of clothing, which were organized roughly by size. Kayah picked out two pairs of stout brown pants, two light brown shirts, both of which were covered in pockets in convenient places, and finally, a heavy dark green traveling cloak. Taeg had selected clothing similar in color to hers, but Drak had picked out dark red shirts that were easily two sizes too big for him and a black cloak. He saw Kayah shaking her head at him, and he stuck out his tongue.

Once laden with the food and gear Regaline had selected for them, their packs were uncomfortably heavy. They didn't look big, but once they started packing in the food parcels, Kayah found herself loading in more than she had expected. Regaline passed her a long coil of rope. She gave Drak a hatchet, and to Taeg, she handed a bundle of tightly bound tarps.

Once they were loaded and ready to go, she sat them down. "Eat something," she said. "We might be running for a while tonight, so you'll need all the energy you can get. No, grab something from the crate over there, not from your pack, Taeg. Save that for later, on the road."

She went to the door, cracked it, and peeked outside. Satisfied no one was watching them from the street, she closed the door and sat down to eat.

"You already know how to allocate nan to use your different applications and applications. You can also do the same for your body. Try it."

Kayah opened her menu wheel and found the allocations submenu. It took a little bit of digging, but she eventually found what Regaline was talking about.

"Good," Regaline said. "You can use this menu to increase or decrease your strength and stamina reserves. It's slow-burning, so whatever you allocate to your legs, for example, will last much, much longer than the power you send to your weapons, armor, or healing applications. Now, I want you to send extra energy to your legs, shoulders, and back. Once we get started, you're going to need it. Now, eat up. We leave in ten minutes."

The night was cool and damp as they tramped through the darkness behind Regaline. A fine, sinewy mist hung low in the air. The overcast sky made the night claustrophobically black. Or it would have been without night vision. Even with the terrain lit up in shades of backlit gray, like a monochrome film negative, there were plenty of pitfalls and dangers hiding in the dark. As they crossed the boundary between Goldenrod and the woods to the east, Regaline cautioned them to move carefully and to remain.

"There are other things that hunt these woods at night," she said. "Not just Interland soldiers. Most of them far, far worse."

So deadly earnest was she that even Drak refrained from backtalk and snide comments and walked quietly through the night. This surprised Kayah. He surprised her again when he slipped beside her and grabbed a hold of her hand. She glanced at him, saw the worry on his face, said nothing, and continued to hold his hand as they walked in the dark.

The night seemed to drag on forever. The farther they went from the warm streetlights of Goldenrod, the more forbidding the world around them seemed. Kayah felt Drak start at every snapped twig or rustle in the underbrush. Even Regaline seemed uneasy. Her head turning this way and that, on the lookout for danger. Only Taeg seemed unaffected by their circumstances. From what Kayah could see, he was simply loping along like he always did.

They reached the edge of the woods east of Goldenrod and entered a thorngrass meadow as the sun began its climb into the sky. Despite the nan she had used to keep awake and alert and moving, Kayah was tired. They all were. But there would be no stopping today.

Somehow, the soldiers had found them. Somehow, they saw through the ruse, doubled back, found their backtrail—which had also been concealed—and followed it.

"Stretch your legs and eat fast," Regaline said when they paused for breakfast near a dry creek bed. "We're not stopping long."

"How did they find us, Reggie?" Drak asked. Though he put up a brave front, he couldn't help but sound like the little boy he was.

"I'm not sure," she said.

Kayah looked into her worried face and felt the first stirrings of fear grip her. "What are they going to do to us if they catch us?" Kayah asked. She hated how childish her own voice sounded to her ears.

Regaline didn't answer right away. As she chewed a bit of bread from her pack, she seemed lost in thought, considering her answer. "You all know about Interland, right, and how aggressive they are with the territories along their borders? Over the last thirty years or so, Interland has been snatching up any and all wild nan users they can get their hands on. Some become slaves, manufacturing the goods needed to conduct its wars. Those who are truly capable or can be trained to greater ability become soldiers in their army. Still slaves but also weapons. If they catch us, I will be shackled and made a slave – if they don't kill me outright, that is – while you three will be pressed into service." She paused a moment before nodding at Kayah and Drak. "I have reason to believe they are looking for you two."

"Why?" Kayah said. "What could they possibly want us for?"

"They want you for the same reasons we do," Regaline replied, then held up her hands. "We don't have the time to go into it right now, but believe me when I say you two are special and important. It's my job to protect you and escort you safely to Hillcrest. It will be unbelievably bad for everyone if you fall into Interland's clutches."

"They won't kill us?" Drak asked.

"Not unless they have no other choice. You are much more valuable to them alive."

Kayah shared a look with Drak. Neither wanted to become a slave, military or otherwise. This new information did little to settle her mind. Instead, she had more questions and graver worries than she'd had before.

A short time later, they entered a vast thorngrass steppe stretching out to the horizon. The tall, razor-sharp grass forced them to wrap their cloaks tightly to avoid being gashed as they walked.

As they walked, Drak got a troubled feeling, as though something was out there watching them. Taeg was in the lead, blazing a trail for the rest of them, so he couldn't see if he felt anything. Reggie was ahead of him and slightly to his left; Drak could just see her expression of concentration. Twigs was trailing behind, clearly tired from walking all night long. He dismissed his agitation as worry about the soldiers hunting them and continued walking. From the corner of his eye, he saw a thick clump of thorngrass off to his right shift and rustle. But when he looked, nothing moved. The grass wasn't disturbed.

They had gone a few paces further when suddenly Reggie whirled around, a look of alarm on her face.

That same instant, a massive hissing asp reared up from the clump of thorngrass scant meters to his right.

Time slowed to a crawl.

Drak had been given a copy of Reggie's bestiary catalog, so if he had wanted, he could have easily identified the creature as a thornking. A species of massive serpent that lived and hunted in these steppes. The monster looked like an oversized pit viper covered with fine brown hair and had a head as big as Drak's. The catalog could have informed him that due to this creature's length of twelve meters, it was at least twenty years old. That a thornking's venom was a fast-acting paralytic. When hunting, thornkings were known to strike and then retreat to wait for their venom to take effect. After their prey suffocated due to a paralyzed diaphragm, the massive serpent returned and consumed its victim whole. Unlike some of the creatures roaming the zones, these massive snakes were the product of natural evolution rather than a misguided creation from a Watcher laboratory. All this information and more was readily available to him if he had thought to look.

However, he didn't think. Staring into the massive, luminous eyes fixated on him, Drak was paralyzed. Frozen with fear. His breath caught in his chest. His lips quivered, barely holding back the scream building up inside him. If he hadn't already relieved himself earlier, his bladder would have let go.

The thornking was massive, luminous, tensed, and coiled down, ready to strike. Its eyes never left Drak's as it prepared to hurtle itself through the air at its intended victim. He could see its slender forked tongue dart out, once, twice, three times in rapid succession before it sprang. Faster than his eyes could follow, the monster was airborne and heading straight at him, its jaws opened impossibly wide.

Moving with preternatural speed, Reggie was suddenly there between him and the thornking. She physically shoved him out of the way, knocking him to the ground in the process as she threw up a protective arm to project a shield. The giant asp slammed into Reggie's electrified shield and seemed to freeze in mid-air a split second before its weight and momentum carried it forward at a slightly deflected angle. Its body grazed Reggie's shoulder.

As it passed, Reggie brought her other hand up and let loose a combination blast of fire and electricity into the tender tissue just behind the thornking's jaw. Electric fire erupted from the top of the creature's skull, spewing the charred remains of bone and brain matter into the air as the momentum of its strike carried it over them and into the dense razor-sharp grass behind them. Where it lay, smoking and dead.

Then Reggie collapsed.

While Drak was lying on the ground where Reggie had shoved him, Twigs was beside her in an instant. There was a small bleeding gash on her left shoulder where one of the thornking's fangs scraped her as it passed. Drak jumped to his feet and helped Twigs strip off Reggie's cloak and shirt. The cloth was tough, and the layers had prevented the thornking from achieving a true strike. However, the fang had delivered enough venom to drop Reggie.

Twigs immediately pressed her hands over the scratch, accessed the healing applications, and channeled anti-toxin and healing nan into the small wound. Reggie's breathing was already becoming labored and ragged. Drak cradled her head in his lap, tears streaming down his cheeks.

"I'm sorry. Please, no. Please don't die, I'm sorry," he whispered again and again.

Taeg stood over Twigs' shoulder, watching.

"I'll be fine," she said. "I just need to catch my breath." Color had drained from her face, and her breathing had become shallow and ragged.

Regaline saw the concerned looks on their faces, then she placed a weak hand on the back of Kayah's neck and pulled her close, pressing their foreheads together. Instantly, Kayah received a deluge of information. Images, emotions, laughter, tears. Other images of her, of Drak and Taeg, were similarly rose-colored. Then, she saw images of a town that filled her with warmth and a feeling of calm safety.

That must be where she's taking us, Kayah thought. *Hillcrest.*

"Just in case," Regaline said, then coughed twice. She hitched a final breath and fell unconscious, her hand dropping away from Kayah's neck, severing the connection.

Kayah let go and stood. Drak followed suit and stepped away, crying freely. Beneath his cocksure attitude, Drak was still a little boy who had yet to experience any sort of deep loss. Even stony Taeg looked solemn.

Several long minutes passed before Drak had composed herself enough to rejoin them.

Kayah picked up Regaline's pack, intending to divide the contents between them.

They were on their own now. She had a map and directions to get to their destination. There was one last thing to do before they could get moving again.

"Stand clear," Kayah said to Drak and Taeg, and then she shot a column of fire into the thornking's body, incinerating it completely. Tears burst from her eyes before she could do the same thing for Regaline. She gave herself another moment to cry; then, she took a deep breath and raised her hands.

"Wait!" Drak shouted, jumping in her way. "She's breathing! She's not dead!"

Kayah lowered her hands and took a closer look.

Sure enough, she could see Regaline's chest rising in small, irregular breaths. She was alive. Unconscious and unresponsive but alive, nonetheless.

After audibly sighing with relief, she turned to the boys. "Let's get up and get moving," she said with more confidence than she felt. "We should find some shelter for the night and build a fire to keep her warm."

Taeg nodded, and Drak helped heft her over his shoulders. They found a low mound with a solitary tree protruding and made camp there.

They built a small fire and swaddled Regaline in blankets next to it. Kayah placed a hand on her forehead and learned that Regaline's nan had placed her body into a coma to combat the thornking venom and heal her. Regaline had been lucky it was only a graze. A full strike would surely have been fatal no matter how hard her nan fought to heal her.

Satisfied Regaline's condition wasn't deteriorating, Kayah lay back and looked at the data Regaline had given her. In a dozen kilometers, they were going to turn south to exit the thorngrass steppe. After another week of walking, if all went well, they would reach Hillcrest safely.

Morning dawned gray and damp. Regaline was awake, though weak and pale. After breakfast, at Regaline's insistence, they resumed walking and reached the edge of the steppe by midday. They took turns supporting Regaline during the walk. Exhausted, they went no further and made camp at the edge.

Kayah simply stared into their small fire while Taeg poked it with a stick. Drak was red-eyed and sullen. Though he liked to pretend he was tough as stone, the recent upheavals in his life were starting to show the cracks in his demeanor.

"Those fucking soldiers," Drak said, suddenly breaking the silence. For once, Kayah didn't rebuke him for his language. "If it weren't for them, we wouldn't have been out there when that fucking thing attacked." He wiped his nose on his sleeve.

"Don't give up, Drak," Kayah said. "Regaline is alive. Soon, she'll be fully healed and strong again. The best thing we can do is to keep going. We can't give up."

"I'm not giving up, Twigs," he snapped. He glared at her in the dim firelight. His anger was written plainly on his face. "I hate them. I hate that snake. If it weren't already dead, I'd find it and kill it. And when those soldiers—those fuckers—show up again, I'll kill them too!"

"You don't know we'll ever see them again," she said, trying to calm him. She wasn't entirely sure she believed her own words. Taeg sat silent, as usual, listening and watching them.

"Yeah, we will! They found us this time, didn't they? Reggie said it would take them weeks to figure out they were following the wrong trail. She said we were safe, that they wouldn't find us again. So how come you saw them in town? How'd they figure it out so quick and find us?"

How indeed? Kayah frowned. Drak was right. Regaline had been certain the false trail she had set the soldiers on would lead them in the wrong direction long enough for the four nan casters to reach safety. How had they discovered Regaline's trick so quickly? Even a nan caster should have been fooled longer.

Unless they had help.

Kayah felt her blood go cold at the thought. That had to be it. Someone told them they were going the wrong way.

Someone had been helping them all along. It couldn't be Regaline. She doubted it was Drak; he was visibly distraught and full of grief and rage. Too young to engage in that kind of subterfuge. It couldn't be Regaline. There was no way she would go through all this trouble to turn around and hand them over to Interland. That left her and Taeg, and she knew it wasn't her.

She glanced over to where Taeg had been sitting only a moment before and found his spot empty.

Taeg had disappeared into the night.

CHAPTER 10

RANCE

Getting the Traditionalists to trust him took more effort than Rance had imagined it would. Suspicions abounded in the Watch Tower. Not only between the differing camps, but especially of him and those like him who had stayed on the fence so long. Even with Sprague, Gelen, and Flora vouching for him, the hardliners were hesitant to trust him. That was okay, though. He didn't need their confidence; he just needed access to their people.

Still, he hoped Silla was having an easier time with the Radicals.

Entering the auditorium for another round of debates, Rance noticed a change in how people looked at him. Whereas before, both sides had dismissed and generally ignored his presence. Now, half of the Watchers present approached him with smiles and comradery while the other half eyed him with open hostility. As he took a seat along the central aisle near the back, he found Davis watching him. Davis was seated next to Morin, who was pointedly not looking at Rance. He returned Davis's look, feigning hostility. Davis didn't dare nod or acknowledge the other man in any other way. The whole game would be blown if anyone thought they were colluding.

Finally, Davis flipped him off, then turned his attention to the stage, where the first pairs of debaters were beginning.

Rance wasn't interested in the speakers. It didn't matter anyway, as the hotheads riled the crowds up to drown the debate out. Instead of watching the speakers, he watched the crowd on his side of the aisle. Most were on their feet, shouting, gesticulating. But there were a few still in their seats. He found Gelen and Flora together near the front, also on their feet, shouting down the woman trying to present her Radical notions to the assembly while Director Winoki attempted to gavel the crowd into silent submission. Incredibly, the woman persevered. Despite the insults and general madness coming from half of the auditorium, she finished her presentation at exactly the five-minute mark, thanked them, and took her seat. Rance couldn't help but be impressed. When the next speaker approached center stage, the roles reversed: the Radicals shouting to drown out the speaker and the Traditionalists shouting to drown out the Radicals. Rance might have laughed if it hadn't been so sadly infuriating.

At the intermission, he sought out Gelen and Flora.

The pair were huddled near the far wall with a woman named Cline. They looked to him like they were discussing important matters. Cline noticed him approaching first and excused herself.

"Did I interrupt something important?" Rance asked.

"A lot of us still don't quite trust you," Flora said. "You were neutral too long for some people's liking."

"Give it time," Gelen said. "To be honest, Flora and I think Cline might be a good addition to our little conspiracy. She's a touch paranoid, though. We'll have to go slow with her."

"Good," Rance said. "Remember, we don't have to change anyone's mind. We just have to convince them it's in everyone's best interest to sit down, be quiet, and listen."

"We know what to do," Flora said. "There's no need to keep reminding us."

"I'm sorry. I guess I'm just nervous. What we're doing could be easily misconstrued."

Flora accepted his apology with a small smile.

"Do you have anyone in mind to talk to?" Gelen asked,

looking around. The intermission was nearly finished, and people were slowly returning to their seats.

"I've spotted a couple people I might want to try talking to. But after Cline's reaction to me, I'm not sure anyone will talk to me just yet."

"Give it a little time," Gelen repeated, placing a hand on his shoulder.

"We might not have time to spare," Flora said.

"She's right," Rance said.

Up on stage, Director Winoki, still playing moderator, banged his gavel, signaling everyone back to their seats.

"I think I've got an idea," he said, smiling. Then he bid them goodbye and returned to his room. There were still three more pairs of speakers, but he needed to do some work to get his idea ready.

The next day, he surprised everyone by taking the stage first. Immediately, jeering from the Radicals filled the air. Then, the shouts coming to his defense began.

He smiled openly and started speaking.

"That was fan-freaking-tastic!" Sprague clapped Rance on the back as they left the auditorium. "I can't believe you, man. You are officially my hero!"

Rance did his best to demur to his friend's compliments. "I just wanted to do something to get us moving. These debates have been a waste of time. It's aggravating. They've stopped listening to anything."

"You called them out on their bullshit, alright. I loved the part where you started poking holes in their theories. Especially their insistence on bringing new blood into the Order. Did you see Constance's face? She was so pissed."

Rance had seen it. He'd counted on it. Once behind the podium, he immediately started attacking the proposals set forth by the Radicals. He'd maintained his composure through his entire five-minute time allotment, calmly pointing out the assumptions and bad data in the Radicals' theories. He didn't spend a single moment discussing the Traditionalist point of view. No one would have listened to him anyway. Instead, he used his time to attack the opposition and hopefully gain some trust among his people.

"I'm so glad you finally saw the light," Sprague said. "I was worried about you for a minute there. Afraid you'd go over to the dark side."

"Not a chance. I just needed some time to look at all the variables and figure out my own views. Just so happens they align with yours."

"Because we're right!"

Rance almost envied his friend's certainty. Even though it was blinding his friend to anything that didn't fit in his worldview, Rance supposed it must be nice to be without questions. He wasn't as hotheaded as a few of the Traditionalists. He never instigated the shouting or conflicts. Sprague was not someone to be swayed from his view.

While he'd been on stage, Rance marked out three other Traditionalists he thought might be approachable. People who sat in the back or on the edges of the group, those who rarely stood and never raised their voices. Up there, it was easier to single them out. Gelen and Flora were working on Cline; he needed to find someone, maybe even a couple someones, to work on. As he'd left the stage, cheered on one side and booed on the other, Markov and Papillon—their side's biggest hotheads—went out of their way to thank him and shake his hand.

They reached an intersection between the living quarters and the recreation areas of the Watch Tower. "Got time for a drink?" Sprague asked.

"Can't tonight," he replied. "Give me a rain check. I'll see you tomorrow."

He didn't want to get drunk with Sprague. He had something more productive in mind.

"Right-o. See ya."

After parting ways, Rance went straight to the cafeteria, where one of the people he'd marked out was currently located.

The dining room was nearly empty. He saw Silla on the far side of the room, sitting with a couple of people and talking animatedly. The one he was looking for was sitting by herself as far from Silla's table as she could get. Rance grabbed a tray and went to the serving station to print a small plate of nachos and an apple. Food in hand, he casually made his way over.

"Hey, Cline," he said. "Mind if I join you?"

She looked up at him and nodded slightly. He sat directly across from her and started picking at his plate. "What do you think about the progress we made today?" he asked tentatively. He wanted to sound her out to find out what her views were exactly. The Watchers weren't a large group; people were either loners like him or else they tended to stay within their own groups. As a result, he hadn't interacted with Cline much. He knew of her and her work. Because of her, the land between the southwest steppe and the Sesta River was fertile and productive. Like him, she rarely involved herself in politics, preferring to work instead of talk.

"You think progress was made today?" she said.

"I think anytime we can get the other side to listen, that's progress."

Her eyes narrowed as she considered her response. "I don't think anyone was listening to anything."

Music to his ears. He almost smiled. Cline was already on his side. She just didn't know it.

"I think your little performance today made things worse."

"That wasn't what I had in mind," he said.

"Really? Because from where I was sitting, it looked like you were intentionally trying to piss them off." She flicked a thumb over her shoulder at the group sitting with Silla. "If that's all you were trying to do, then you succeeded admirably."

Her words caught him off guard. He'd been so wrapped up in congratulations from everyone else that he hadn't thought any of the Traditionalists would disagree with him and what he had done.

He wanted to tell her he had only been trying to win the trust of their group. If he did so, what was to stop her from exposing him? They would crucify him. This was exactly why he'd sworn the rest of his cabal to secrecy.

He had to figure out a way to win her over to his side.

"I'm sorry you feel that way," he said. "What do you think I should have done instead?"

She scoffed as though he'd just asked a stupid question.

"Practically anything other than what you did would have been better."

"Like what? What's your big idea for winning this Conclave?"

"That right there is the problem. Thinking this is something that can be won or lost. This us-versus-them mentality is what's keeping us all from making any headway on the real problems we're facing."

"The way you talk, it sounds like you don't really believe what the Traditionalists are saying. Why take their side if that's not the case?"

Cline rolled her eyes. "I'm not on anyone's side. I sat with them today; I was on the other side yesterday. I've been trying to be a moderate voice on both sides."

Rance thought back to the assembly yesterday and found he didn't recall seeing her anywhere on his side of the hall. How had he missed it? What's more, how had he completely missed her when he was looking for allies? On her own, she had reached all the same conclusions as he had. Though he was ecstatic, he tried not to let it show. He needed to bring her on board with his group. Still, he felt he needed to tread lightly.

"I didn't notice," he said. "If you're not convinced either

side is right, what do you believe?"

"I'm not sure it's safe to tell you. I've seen you pal around with that idiot Sprague. Come to think of it, I'm not sure it's safe to talk to you at all. I've heard what those assholes Papillon and Markov talk about, and I don't want to be on the other end of their pogrom."

"I don't think it will come to that," Rance said, ignoring the flat look she gave him. "I don't. Look, I know things are looking bad right now. But I think there's still a chance to turn it around."

"Really? How would you do that? By spitting more insulting crap like you did today?"

Rance paused and took a breath. Convincing her that he was on the same side as her was harder than he'd expected.

"I know what I said today makes me look pretty bad. But I assure you, it was for a reason. I think you are completely right when you say we need to calm down and start listening to each other. I've had that same thought myself. Don't laugh. I'm not just blowing smoke here. I've already started working towards that end."

"What are you saying?" Cline looked skeptical.

Rance decided to lay all his cards on the table. Either she would believe him and join his conspiracy, or she would go to one side or the other and inform on him. The risk, he felt, was justified if he was going to make any progress.

"I've already enlisted the help of a few others, on both sides, to help me do exactly what you are talking about. We are going to try and convince a majority to sit down and openly listen to what the other side has to say. Then, have an open and healthy debate to determine the best course of action. You know, the way these convocations are supposed to fucking work.

"We need to isolate the hotheads and drown out their voices in sensible silence. You are the first person I've approached since we started this."

"Why me?" Cline still didn't look convinced. "I'm not committed to either side. Nobody will listen to me because I'm sitting on the fence."

"That's the way I felt. Hell, my friend even threatened me if I didn't pick a side. So, I decided to act. And acting is what I was doing today. I needed to get the other Traditionalists to trust me. I can't convince anyone if they won't talk to me."

"I know what you mean. Everyone treats me like a leper. Even people I've known and worked with for years." She paused as if to gather her thoughts. "Okay. Say I believe you. What do you want from me?"

"Find someone you think is willing to listen to reason and convince them the way I convinced you. With enough of us, together, we can force everyone else to sit down and shut up for a few minutes. Long enough to hear what both sides have to say and come to a compromise."

"Okay," Cline said, mulling over his words. "I'll try. Is there anything else?"

"Just that we are going to meet up again soon. I'll let you know when."

Without another word, Cline got to her feet, dumped her tray into the recycler, and left the cafeteria.

Rance cleared up his own mess and returned to his room. Only after his door closed did he allow himself to smile.

"It's working," he told the empty room. There was still much more to do, but for now, he felt great. Things were progressing, but he still felt like he wasn't moving quickly enough.

The next day, the fighting in the auditorium was worse than ever, making him wonder if his actions the day before had been worth it.

The first speaker, a Radical, barely reached the podium before people were on their feet shouting at him. Then, someone from their side came across the aisle and shoved one of the people on their feet. Which led to more shoving and, finally, punches and kicks being thrown. Rance, who had been sitting at the back near the exit, counted himself lucky to reach the exit before the rumble really got going.

Thankfully, the Watch Tower had dampeners in place that prevented them from using any of the weaponized applications. It was a safety precaution in place since the Breakdown. Without it, he was sure the fight in the auditorium would have ended in bloodshed rather than scrapes and bruises.

He paced his room, trying to think of a way to repair the damage done today when his door chimed. He looked and found Sprague impatiently waiting outside.

"Come with me," he said once Rance opened the door.

"Hey, man, I'm kinda busy at the moment. Can I join you later?"

"No. There's a meeting. We need to be there."

Rance sighed and joined his friend.

"They've gone too far this time," Sprague said. Rance noticed they'd been joined by two more Traditionalists. Over the last week, he'd noticed that nobody went anywhere alone. Every time he left his room, he found people moving about the facility in pairs, eyeing him because he was alone. They joined a stream of people moving in trios and quartets, all heading in the same direction. Now, it seemed that two wasn't enough. The violence in the auditorium appeared to have escalated the animosity permeating the atmosphere of the tower.

After a few turns, the flow of people ended in the lounge. A crowd had already gathered. Rance did a quick count. Upon their arrival, there were forty-three people gathered in the lounge. Roughly half of the Order, and except for the people in the infirmary, the entire Traditionalist faction was gathered in the lounge. Rance imagined the Radicals were having their own meeting in response to the incident.

Sprague led him to a cluster of tables near the bar, then split off and jumped up on the bar top. "Can I have your attention, please?"

Oh, shit, Rance thought. *This isn't going to be good.*

"Thank you all for coming. First, I've got some news about Papillon. He's recovering in the infirmary right now. He's got a broken orbit and a dislocated wrist. Nothing life-threatening. He's sedated and under guard in case those bastards try something."

Papillon was seen as the leader of the Traditionalists. The loudest and most animated of them. Arguing with him was difficult because he never gave anyone else a chance to talk. He was the driving force behind the Traditionalists' obstinate refusal to hear the other side of the argument. He was also the one Rance was most concerned about isolating in order to allow both sides to engage in dialog to resolve this conclave peacefully. With him temporarily out of the picture, it looked as though Sprague had stepped up in his absence.

Rance had always liked Sprague. The man was a loyal friend and a capable Watcher. But he was hardheaded, reactionary, and stubborn. There was little chance he would listen any more than Tetsuo had.

"The time for talking is done!" Sprague announced. All eyes in the room were on Sprague standing atop the printed wood of the bar top. "The Radicals have repeatedly demonstrated their disdain for our values and way of life. They care nothing for the mission this order has committed itself to for the last hundred years. Everything we've accomplished since the Breakdown, the stabilized climate, the population we upraised, the blood and sweat shed to make those things happen, none of that matters to those people. They've put on blinders and only see what they want to see, and they are willing to resort to violence to prevent us from continuing as we have been.

"We know what works. We know that without us and our efforts, this world would have collapsed decades ago. Granted, there are always ways to improve. But they don't want to improve; they want to uproot us and our achievements and throw it all away."

He paused a moment to accept a glass of beer from the servitor arm in the bar. He drained half the glass in one pull and then returned the glass to the servitor.

"The time has come to end this Conclave," he continued. "There is no arguing with them. No convincing them. We can do nothing further to make this conclave anything but a waste of time. They are unwilling to listen or work with us. They are unwilling to compromise or concede with us. They are unwilling to live in harmony with us. So, I say, here and now, we need to stop bending over backwards to accommodate them and their radical intolerance."

There were cheers and shouts from the crowd. Fists jabbed into the air, and tables were slapped.

"It's high time we show them we will defend what we believe in. We will defend our lives. We will defend our right to do what's right!"

The crowd erupted in cheers. Rance looked around, trying not to appear as dismayed as he felt. The fevered glee he saw in the faces around him shook him to his core. These were people he'd known and worked with for decades, and he didn't recognize them. He needed to contact the others. It might not be too late.

"We're going to divide up into teams. Each team will have a specific task. I've already got team leads and work assignments divvied up. You should all be receiving that information now. Let's get to work. We've got a future to save."

The message appeared in his inbox. He'd been assigned to Sprague's team.

Sprague hopped down from the bar and motioned Rance over to him. Everyone was separating into their teams. He saw Gelen and Flora on the far side of the lounge. Gelen glanced over, and Rance briefly saw the worry in the other man's eyes. Flora didn't look at him. But he could tell she felt the same. He counted three other teams. The largest had seventeen people, and the other two teams were of equal size at eleven each. At four, his team was the smallest.

"Good of you to join us," Sprague said. There were two others on his team, Marlow and Cho, neither of whom Rance particularly cared for. "I think you all will be happy I put you on my team. I've assigned us the most important job. The others are going to make weapons, gather food and medical supplies, and guard our territory. We're not doing anything so menial. Come with me, and I'll show you what we need to do."

Departing the lounge, Rance wanted nothing more than to contact his conspirators among the Radicals, but he had no choice but to go along with Sprague as he led them to the bank of lifts in the center of the Watch Tower. Three guards had peeled off from their group and followed behind. Sprague punched the button and took them up to the main control center on the operations level.

"This is where we are going to work." Despite the recycled air, the level stank of must and disuse. The Watch Tower had been running autonomously for years. Rance couldn't even guess when someone had come up here last.

"What are we doing up here?" Cho asked.

"Up here is where we win the war," Sprague said, giving them a predatory smile.

CHAPTER 11
ASTRID

"I can't believe Waler was the spy all along!" Astrid said.

They were just sitting down to lunch. The cafeteria was abuzz with the news of Waler's arrest and dismissal. Opinions ranged from joy over his removal to disbelief that he was intelligent enough to commit the crimes of which he was accused.

Astrid herself wasn't exactly sure where she fell within that spectrum. As a senior engineer, she'd had to work with him closely. So, she knew he wasn't the oaf many others thought he was. Waler could be petty and vindictive and very much played subordinates against each other. The few who could be counted as his favorites were the minority voice in his favor.

"With him gone," she continued, "what's our next move?"

Kinney glanced over his shoulder to make sure no one was close enough to eavesdrop on them, then leaned in close.

"Unofficially," he said, keeping his voice low, "I'm temporarily taking his place. Just filling in until they can officially promote someone into the position. Then, I'll be heading back to Site 2. My job here is done. Well, most of it, anyway. They want me to continue investigating to determine the extent of the damage he caused. If you're still game, I could still use your help."

"I'm game," Astrid said. Though she hadn't been working the case for long, she'd had a blast investigating and had even enjoyed working with Kinney. Once she'd gotten over her initial dislike of him, she found Kinney easy-going and affable. She was almost sorry for what she'd put him through when he first arrived.

"Good. Oh! Since I'm moving up into Waler's spot, there's now a vacancy. I was wondering if you were still interested in the job?"

She was dumbstruck. The job she'd wanted—had worked hard to get—was open, and Kinney was offering it to her. Waler's arrest was getting better and better.

"Do I have to go through all the promotion boards and interviews and shit for it?"

"Nah," Kinney said, shaking his head. "You already did that once. I've looked over the results. You *were* the best candidate. Even Waler was planning on giving you the job. If it weren't for this investigation, you would have been promoted months ago." He cleared his throat. "I really am sorry. If I had known then what I know now, I would have suggested they find another way to insert me here."

Astrid waved a hand, dismissing his apology. "Don't worry about it. If you hadn't been here, in all likelihood, I would be dead now. So why don't we call it even?"

Kinney smiled, blushing a little. "Fair enough. Allow me to be the first to congratulate you on your promotion." He extended a hand across the table, and she shook it. "Now, for our first order of business to wrap things up here, we need to sniff out any other skullduggery Waler was into."

"Skullduggery? Is that from your word-of-the-day calendar?"

"It's a good word. Doesn't get used often enough."

"If you say so," she said.

After they finished, Kinney went to Waler's former office, and Astrid returned to her station. Logging back into the system, she found the work order for the heat exchanger rupture repair had gone through, and repairs had begun.

It's about time, she thought. She shivered, thinking back on the incident. In her life, she'd had a few close calls and accidents, but that had been the first time she'd come close to dying. If it hadn't been for Kinney checking up on her, she doubted if she would be here today. She'd gone in early every day, intending to show up Kinney and prove to the higher-ups they'd promoted the wrong person. That morning, she'd noticed a section of the diagnostic sensor array was offline. Not malfunctioning or throwing warning lights, just dark. Astrid had thought about tasking a drone to investigate. It would have taken an hour for her request to go through, and then when she had gotten the drone there, she'd have had to deal with the blurry vision from the drone's imagers and clumsy articulation from its manipulator arm. Working through the drone would have just frustrated her, and she'd have ended up going in there personally anyway, so she had cut to the chase and just gone.

Traversing the access tunnels hadn't been an issue for her. All her life, Astrid had been very physically active. Active sports, rock climbing, spelunking, paragliding. She loved it all and had no problem with heights or confined spaces. She was an adventure junky. Which was part of what had led her to join HelixCom's Garden Project. The idea of building a new world from scratch, far from the safe confines of Earth, had been an adventurer's dream come true.

She remembered bringing up her diagnostic interface to begin searching for the root cause of the sensor malfunction. The rupture had occurred before she'd taken ten steps into the chamber. The blast of steam had knocked her on her back, instantly flooding the room with deadly radiation.

She had found out later that the initial blast had nearly killed her. In crisis mode, her nanites had kept her alive once she lost consciousness. If Kinney hadn't arrived when he had, it would have been the end of her.

Looking at the logs with the benefit of hindsight, Astrid had found something strange. The diagnostic array hadn't been malfunctioning. It had been deactivated. As had the compartment alarms. Odd. It had been as if someone had done it intentionally, knowing there would be a failure in there. The only way someone could know that was if they were the cause of it.

Someone like Waler.

"Son of a bitch," she had said aloud. "He almost killed me."

The rage she felt had made her want to scream and throw something. She had held back. Not only did she not want to cause a scene, but also everything within reach had a substantial price tag attached. She didn't need to owe the company any more than her monthly tithe.

None of this had been in the case file assembled against Waler. That needed to be corrected. This was potentially damning evidence that could certainly put him away for a long time. Kinney had said they should keep digging and try to expose more of his nefarious activities.

"Skullduggery," she said with a laugh. She decided to hunt down everything about the incident to add another nail to Waler's coffin. There was already a slew of evidence connecting him to other nefarious activities but nothing connecting him to the sabotage. An oversight Astrid wanted to correct.

She started by checking his data trail during the days before the incident. She hoped to find some indicator he'd remotely deactivated the failure sensors and the diagnostic array. But found nothing suspicious in his data trail.

Undeterred, she tried the personnel locator logs next. The nanites infused into the bodies every worker with upon their arrival in orbit above Kuridian not only facilitated and aided in the work they were expected to perform but also kept track of them. Logs were kept, and statistics were generated on each employee's working, sleeping, eating, and exercising habits. What an employee did during their leisure time wasn't strictly tracked; only when said leisure time activities interfered with work did the company take notice.

With the tracking system and her newly instated access

to it, Astrid could pinpoint Waler's movements on the day in question and tie him to the sabotage.

She felt almost giddy with excitement. However, that feeling quickly dissipated as she found nothing suspicious in his movements. In fact, there was nothing suspicious anywhere she looked. No matter how she tweaked the search parameters, she couldn't find anything indicating a break in his normal routines. He went to his office for three hours, then he went to the dining facility, then back to the office for two hours, then to the lounge for an hour, then back to the office for another two hours before he went home. Regular as clockwork, day in and day out. He was clearly in his office during the incident in the heat exchanger.

Boring and completely innocent.

Everything pointed to Waler. He was highly placed, and though he gave off the appearance of a buffoon, Astrid knew he was knowledgeable about Site 1's functionality. It had to be him. He'd been a spy for God-knew-how-long. He probably just knew some way to cover his tracks that she hadn't cracked yet.

Astrid glanced at the clock and was shocked to find she'd spent the entire afternoon chasing her tail. It was almost time to clock out. Luckily, she was a manager now, with lots of leeway in how she spent her time on the clock.

She sighed and logged out. Her monitor dissolved and poured back into her desktop.

There had to be a way to tie Waler to her accident. She just wasn't seeing it. She needed to take a break and clear her mind.

Danny saw her and waved her over the moment she entered the lounge.

"How you doing?" he said.

"I've been better," she said, dropping into the seat across from him. She dialed in the drink she wanted and pressed her thumb to the pad to debit her account.

"What's going on?"

"I'm working on something that's got me frustrated."

"Want to talk about it?"

"Not really. I just want to have a drink and go home."

"Fair enough," Danny said. Astrid's drink arrived, and they clinked glasses. "Here's to things getting better around here with that son of a bitch Waler out of the picture!"

"Cheers," Astrid said and took a deep swig. "Things will start getting better, too. They put Kinney in his spot until they can find a replacement."

"Good. You know, I almost feel bad for how we all treated him when he first got here."

"Me too. And I'm sorry I goaded you all into shunning him. I was just mad that he skunked the promotion out from under me. Jokes on me, though. Turns out Kinney was sent here to uncover Waler's double-dealing. After the accident, he enlisted me to help him."

"Really? He was sent here to take out Waler?"

"He didn't know it was Waler at the time; he was sent to find out who it was. Now that he's exposed the rat, he'll be moving on soon, and I got his job."

"The job he skunked from under you, right?"

"The same."

"Terrific. Congratulations!" They tapped glasses again. "Things are looking better around here. With you two in charge, maybe we can get some of the repair and maintenance orders completed."

"You'll have to fill out your forms in triplicate and learn to kiss my butt a little more. But I think we can come to some sort of accommodation."

"I didn't kiss Waler's fat ass, and I'm not kissing yours."

"Which is why all your requests were denied and why they are going to continue to be denied until you reconsider puckering up." They laughed, but deep down, they both knew the joke was mostly true. Waler had catered to his friends and sycophants over the people just trying to do their jobs.

"So, Kinney saves your life, then gives you the job you wanted. Watch out; he might ask you to marry him if you're not careful."

"I don't think I have anything to worry about there. He's married to his work. Speaking of the accident, I saw the work order went through."

"Yeah. Good thing, too. Our productivity's been shit lately because of it. We're going to need to put in some overtime if we're going to have a hope of catching up."

"I've been looking into the accident, trying to figure out what happened in there. The sensors monitoring the integrity of that conduit were turned off at the same time the diagnostic array failed to report it. That's just too convenient to be a coincidence. It was done on purpose."

"That is pretty hard to swallow," Danny said. "You thinking Waler caused the failure for some reason?"

"It's just too coincidental to be anything else. It looks like sabotage. Sabotage that occurred at the same time as we found out a spy had been working onsite. I've looked to see if I can connect Waler to the failure. But his movements and his data trail are completely clean."

"You think he might be hiding his usage and movements?"

"I don't know. I didn't think that was possible. The system is supposed to detect and countermand any unauthorized access, virtually and physically."

"Unless he used his access key and masked the log entries that track him. If you know what you're doing, there are plenty of ways to spoof the system. It helps if you're already highly placed in the system, of course."

Astrid thought about this for a moment.

"So, I shouldn't look for signs he used his access key directly, but for movement log entries without an ID attached."

"Exactly," Danny said. "Or have something else suspicious about them. Every door and junction he passed through should have generated an entry, even if he was masking himself. Once you find them, you should be able to track his movements that way."

"Damn. I should have thought of that! Thanks! You've been super helpful." She tossed back the last of her drink and hurried out of the lounge.

Back in her room, Astrid remotely activated her workstation. A chair flowed up from the floor with a monitor attached. She sat and started searching over again.

Can't believe I didn't think of this! Of course he'd cover his tracks. He's a spy. Even if he thought he was safe, he would make sure no one discovered what he was up to!

She reset the parameters of her search, looking for data and movement logs without ID tags attached.

"Yes!" she shouted when this search turned up hits. "I've got you, you son of a bitch!"

What she found was a series of movement logs that weren't tied to anyone's ID. Nothing appeared on the day of her accident. However, during the days leading up to it, there was untagged movement all over the heat exchanger. Someone had been spending a lot of time in there. Someone with the ability to conceal their presence in the system. It would have had to be someone with the knowledge and ability to weaken the pipe so it would fail later, as well as neutralize the sensors in the chamber so they reported the failure.

Errors in the system could account for a few corrupt logs, but the frequency of them was astonishing. Waler had been busy. In the last month, the number of movement logs without an ID tag had more than tripled.

"How did nobody notice this?" she muttered. It occurred to her there were only a few people with access to this database. Unless someone was actively looking at the data, it would be an easy thing to miss. Especially since the system itself didn't flag them or block them.

Next, Astrid brought up Waler's logs to correlate with the

masked tags. She made a mistake when inputting the search parameters, however, and the monitor displayed all the people with an access level equal to the masked ID. In addition to Waler, there were six other names on the list, including hers and Kinney's.

Cursing in frustration, she told herself to slow down. Waler wasn't going anywhere. There was no need to rush. If she wanted to tie the incident to him, she needed to collect the evidence calmly and efficiently. Rushing would only lead to mistakes.

She closed her eyes and took a breath.

When she opened them again, she didn't change anything on her screen, wanting to see all the data before she made any further changes.

Initially, she reached the same conclusion as before. Waler's movements, both virtual and physical, were above board. Nothing he did in the days leading up to and on the day of the accident looked suspicious. Rather than let it frustrate her, Astrid continued looking. If he had masked his ID, then it was also possible he had set a bot to generate some activity to make it seem like he'd been doing the things he always did, to further cover his tracks.

While looking for other ways to isolate Waler's activities, something else jumped out at her. Kinney's ID seemed to drop out of the database from time to time. The way the system tracked people meant that shouldn't happen. Even during sleep and leisure periods, the system still listed where the employee was and what they were doing. Ever since he'd first arrived, Kinney's ID seemed to disappear from time to time.

Astrid felt cold prickles break out on the back of her neck. She cut Waler and the rest out of the filter and isolated Kinney.

Whenever the masked ID was actively moving about or navigating the computer network, Kinney's ID wasn't displayed. He disappeared whenever the masked ID appeared.

She didn't want to believe what the data were telling her.

Kinney had saved her life. He was a good guy who gave her the job she'd been vying for. He'd been sent by corporate to root out any spies and to help clean up Site 1.

Still, she couldn't ignore the fact that Kinney had the means to do it, and Kinney was the one who had gained the most with Waler's arrest.

Astrid zeroed in on his activity the day of the accident. He'd been at his workstation, across from hers, at the start of their shift. Then she saw him look up her location. Once he saw where she was, she saw him fly into motion. Running down the halls to reach her. Like he already knew what had happened.

It added up. It was Kinney, not Waler, who was the spy and saboteur. He'd used her feelings of gratitude to cloud her judgment and turn her loose, looking for evidence to convict Waler. Then he'd given her the job she craved to further blind her to his actions. Worse still, now he was in charge of Site 1. With Waler out of the way and her in his pocket, Kinney was free.

Astrid had never felt so foolish and betrayed. He'd played her. Completely and utterly. This time, she did throw something. She'd print out a new coffee cup tomorrow.

"That motherfucker. How could I be so stupid?"

She closed the search engine after clearing up any traces showing what she'd found. As far as Kinney knew, he was safe. Astrid wasn't sure what her next steps should be, but she was sure she didn't want him tipped off before she had a chance to come up with some sort of plan.

She stood and started pacing. The chair and computer monitor poured back into the floor once she stopped using them.

Waler was innocent. Kinney was the spy. Even though he'd saved her life, Kinney had almost killed her. All the pent-up rage she'd aimed at Waler, she now focused on Kinney.

She needed to bide her time for now. Go along with him.

Dupe him, the way he'd duped her. She didn't know his end goal, but she intended to figure it out. Then, when he least expected it, she'd pounce and bring the son of a bitch down.

CHAPTER 12

KAYAH

The days immediately following the thornking attack and Taeg's disappearance were dreary and damp. Intermittent rain pattered their shoulders as they trudged through the grassy hills beyond the steppe, soaking them through despite their thick traveling cloaks. No one spoke much. Regaline was walking on her own but stumbled frequently and occasionally needed to lean on one of them while she caught her breath. Drak squinted in the rain at his feet as they walked.

They'd tried tracking Taeg the next morning to no avail. Regaline was still too weak, and neither Kayah nor Drak were skilled enough to follow his trail. Nan was useful, but only to a certain point. Without the skillset to support it, nan didn't know what to look for. Leaving the way he had, there was no doubt in her mind about who he really was and where he had gone. Kayah feared they would see him again soon.

The clouds broke on the third day. Bright sunshine was a welcome relief. Kayah felt her spirits rising a little as the trio dried out. The warmth on her face made her smile a little as she prepared their midday meal. Drak seemed in a better mood as he ate. He still wasn't talking, but he also wasn't scowling at everything and muttering curses under his breath anymore. Which Kayah considered an improvement. Even Regaline seemed to be feeling better.

"Don't bother packing up when you're done eating," she said as Kayah and Drak finished eating. "We should take the opportunity to dry out our gear as much as we can while the sun's still out. So, we're going to camp here and get moving again tomorrow."

After dinner, Drak broke his self-imposed silence. "We're going to see those soldiers again real soon, aren't we?"

It was dark, and he'd spoken so softly Kayah almost wasn't sure he'd spoken at all.

Kayah didn't want to lie to him. It was just two kids and an injured woman in the wilderness against a company of trained soldiers. She peered at him through the dark. The firelight shadows danced across his face. He wasn't looking at her. His gaze fixed on the fire.

"Yes," she said. "I think we will. Probably tomorrow or the next day."

"Rocky was the one who led them to us, wasn't he?"

"I think so, yes."

"I'm going to kill him."

Before she could respond, he got to his feet, spread his bedroll next to Regaline, tucked under his blanket, and went to sleep.

Kayah understood how he felt. For the first time in her life, she felt the desire to intentionally harm another person. She wasn't sure what she would do when she saw Taeg again. She was only sure she wanted to make him hurt. In her mind, he was responsible for all their troubles. It wasn't his fault Regaline had almost been killed by the thornking. However, his actions had forced them to leave Goldenrod before they were ready and take a route that was more dangerous than necessary. In that sense, he was absolutely responsible. If it weren't for him, Regaline would still be hale and hearty. They would be on their way to Hillcrest, unafraid of what they might find waiting for them around the next hill.

Taeg had betrayed them. Lied to them. That was what hurt her the most. Despite his withdrawn and aloof nature, she'd started thinking of him as a friend. Which made everything worse.

By the light of their small fire, she looked at Regaline and Drak and came to a decision. Silent as a ghost, she left camp and went out into the dark to find answers.

They got a late start. Normally, Regaline would have scolded them and goaded them into action with the rising sun. But in her condition, she was happy to sleep in. Their general lack of motivation meant they were packed and walking again shortly after lunchtime. Kayah felt no need to hurry them along. Their destination was still a long way away.

Besides, she'd found what she needed to know last night. After an hour of walking, she brought them to a halt.

"The Interland soldiers are waiting for us ahead," she said. "I found their sentries last night after you both were asleep."

Drak's hands immediately lit up, ready to throw fire.

Regaline's stooped posture straightened a little. She was clearly feeling better but still not well enough to fight off a company of soldiers. "What do you want to do?" she said.

Kayah was taken aback. Regaline was deferring to her. It was a sign of how ill and weak she still felt.

"I think we should split up," Kayah said after a moment's thought. "They'll have a tougher time hunting us down if we separate and head off in different directions."

"I want to fight," Drak said immediately.

"There are too many," Regaline said. "No matter how many you might kill or maim, it won't change the outcome; you'll either be dead or captured."

"Which is why our best chance is to split up," Kayah said.

Regaline shook her head. "They've tracked us this far and found us again and again despite my best efforts. All of us splitting up might buy a day, maybe two, but no more. I think you should leave me here and continue on. When you reach them, say I succumbed to my injuries. If Taeg really is with them, then he won't know I've recovered. It's you two they want. In my condition, they would most likely kill me and be done with it. Leave me behind, and in a few days, when I'm stronger, I'll find a way to rescue you."

"What makes you think you'll be well enough in a few days to get us out?" Drak said.

"I'm almost strong enough now," she replied. "Once they have you, they'll become complacent, and that will make it easier to surprise them."

"I don't like it," Kayah said.

"You don't have to like it. This is what's going to happen. Tell them I died the night Taeg left, and you incinerated my body like you did the thornking." Kayah looked away. Drak buried his face in Regaline's shoulder. She patted him on the back. "Time for you to get going."

As it turned out, they didn't have to wait long at all. After another hour of walking, the pair rounded another low hill and found the soldiers waiting for them.

The gray-clad soldiers were formed up in a loose semi-circle, spears pointed skyward. In the center sat a man on horseback; his uniform was the same shade of gray as the rest but tailored and ornately adorned with deep red filigree. Four more soldiers in dark blue stood at rigid attention, two on either side of him, and just behind them stood Taeg, looking tall and proud in his uniform. Kayah saw the man she'd spotted in Goldenrod standing slightly behind the formation with another man. Both were dressed in loose-fitting clothing of greens and browns, and she figured they must be the company's scouts.

Kayah and Drak didn't slow when they saw the waiting soldiers, but continued at the same pace. As they approached, the soldiers at the ends of the line shifted and moved to close the gap, encircling them. Kayah noted this but didn't really pay them any attention. Instead, she focused on the four people beside the man on horseback. As she and Drak drew near, she saw nan begin to swirl around them, creating shields.

They were Interland nan casters. Taeg stood among them, tall and proud in his blue uniform behind the others. Regaline had been wise to hide. The four of them would have easily been able to overmatch her alone. Kayah didn't even want to think about what they could do to them if they tried to fight.

Once the circle was closed, the officer gigged his horse forward a few paces.

"Hello, children," he said in a booming voice. "You have led us on a merry chase. But that ends here. I am Lieutenant Tate, and as of this moment, I am your commanding officer. You are hereby conscripted into service with the Army of Interland. You will accompany us to begin your indoctrination and training. Later, I will have questions for you. That is all."

He started to turn his mount, but Kayah stopped him when she spoke.

"We have no wish to join your army or to answer your questions."

The officer barked a short, humorless laugh. "You act as though I were offering you a choice in the matter." The smile he gave her was predatory and unpleasant. "Know this: from this point on, you exist at my sufferance. You will march where we say to march. You will eat when we say to eat, sleep when we say to sleep. It might take time, but you will learn to do as you are told."

"Go to hell, you big shithead!" Drak blurted out.

Kayah could feel him tensing beside her. His jaw was clenched, and his breathing was fast and heavy. She placed a hand on his arm to calm him. He jerked as if to shake off her touch, then seemed to think better of it. He met her eyes, and she shook her head. This was not the time to fight.

The glare directed his way by Tate was withering. Visibly deflating, Drak took a half step back and lowered his eyes. The officer suddenly laughed. "Very good," he said. "You get one pass, boy. Any further disrespect will be met with punishment. Understand?"

Drak nodded but didn't say anything.

"I said, do you understand? You will also learn to answer when your superiors ask you a question!"

"Yes," Drak and Kayah said together.

"Yes, what?"

"Yes, sir."

"Much better." He turned to the quartet of casters. He paused a moment to take a longer look at them. "We were expecting three of you. What happened to the woman traveling with you, Regaline Lager?"

"She died, sir," Kayah said quickly. She didn't want Drak to say anything else that might cause them more trouble. "We encountered a thornking, and she took a bite while protecting us from it."

"I was given to understand she was mending," Tate said, glancing slightly to his left where Taeg stood.

"So were we, sir. When we woke up two days ago, we found her dead by the fire. We burned her body according to her wishes."

Lieutenant Tate made a motion, and one of the scouts came trotting up. "Run down their back trail and confirm their story," he said. "I don't want any surprises."

"M'lord," the scout said with a salute before hurrying off in the direction she and Drak had come from.

Lieutenant Tate turned his attention back to them, then spoke to one of the casters beside him.

"Take them into custody. Separate them. We still have a ways to travel before dark. See to it they do not fall behind."

The collar fastened around her neck dug into her skin painfully. It was attached to a leash held by one of the casters, a rough and unforgiving sour-faced man named Callum. He was short and wide and as hard as stone. His demeanor wasn't what made him scary, though. She'd lived long enough to see plenty of bullies and hateful people. His eyes, however, gave her the creeps. They were the color of dull silver and without irises. It was like the eyes he had been born with had been removed and a pair of solid metal orbs implanted in their place. It was the same for the other four casters. Even Taeg, whose eyes had been normal during their travels together, now sported silver eyes. Callum was Kayah's minder, while a tall, reedy woman named Vesper held Drak's lead. As they had been collared, Drak had said something to her that resulted in her giving him a hard slap across his face. Once collared, she and Drak had been separated. He had been taken to the head of the column, while Callum had dragged her to the rear.

Though the day had started with a chill, it had turned unseasonably hot while they marched. At first, the pace they kept was easy enough to maintain. However, after a few hours of walking beneath the blazing sun, Kayah found herself starting to lag. Each time she reached the end of the slack in her leash, Callum gave it a sharp tug that nearly pulled her off her feet. She stumbled forward a few steps and found herself walking next to him.

"Keep up," was all he said, and his expression conveyed a promise of pain if she failed to do as she was told. Keep up, she did. When they finally stopped, it was all Kayah could do not to collapse where she stood. Through strength of will and the fear of what Callum would do to her, she kept to her feet. While the soldiers pitched tents, dug a slit trench, and built cookfires, Callum hauled Kayah to the center of camp, where he tied her leash to a stake driven into the ground. She was close enough to see the cookfires and smell the food simmering but far enough to feel none of the heat from it. She pulled off her boots and groaned in relief as she rubbed her sore, blistered feet.

Callum returned with a bowl of stew, which he dropped at her feet, slopping much of it onto the ground. "Welcome to the army," he said. "I am your commanding officer. You may call me Callum. You and your little friend are under my command until such time as you can be handed off to your training battalion. Until then, me and my squad will be your caretakers and teachers. We will teach you how to be a soldier and what is expected of army nan casters. Understand?"

When she didn't respond quickly enough for his likely, Callum slapped her in the knee. "You will answer when I ask you a question. Do you understand everything I have told you?"

Kayah got to her feet, looked him right in his dead, blank eyes, and said, "Yes, sir."

Callum nodded, then said, "You've had a long and hard day. So, I'm cutting you some slack. But you'd better learn quickly, little girl. I ain't a patient man. You better not test me. I got orders from on high that says you ain't to be harmed. But there are ways around that. Test me and find out just how creative I can be and how much you can hurt."

Kayah wasn't sure how to respond, so she went with what she thought was the safest option. "Yes, sir."

Callum eyed her a moment, his empty silver eyes giving her the shivers.

"Eat," he said before stomping away.

Though the texture was that of a watery paste, the mush was surprisingly tasty. After the first mouthful, Kayah had to resist the urge to stuff her face and lick the bowl clean. The cramp in her stomach was eased by the food, but it didn't go away completely. The portion had been too small. She wished for her pack and the rations it contained. Their packs and cloaks had been taken the moment she and Drak had been detained. She could only assume their rations had been added to the company's food supply.

When she was finished, Callum took her bowl and returned it to the cook. It was dark by the time he returned with his bedroll and blanket. He very pointedly ignored her as he set himself up to sleep for the night. Before lying down, she watched him lay out triplines and alarms with nan. He must have known she could see what he was doing; she figured he simply didn't care. Then he cast a shield around her. While it wasn't strong enough to keep her caged indefinitely, she would waste a lot of time and make a lot of noise breaking through it.

Scared and frustrated, Kayah lay awake long after she heard light snores coming from Callum. The chilly night air bit deeply, forcing her to huddle in a tight ball to keep warm. As she shivered, images of torture at Callum's hands danced through her head. Between that and the cold, she feared she would never fall asleep. So, she was surprised when she felt Callum kicking her feet, startling her awake. She peered up at him with bleary eyes. The predawn light cast the sky in a purplish glow, by which she could barely make out the scowl on his face.

"Get up," he said. "Breakfast, then we march."

Three days passed in this manner. The identical monotony of each day made them blur together. The casters would take turns holding her leash, trading off at breakfast each morning. On the second day, she was marched near the head of the formation with Vesper, the thin woman who'd held Drak's leash the first day. Of Drak, she saw no sign. They were careful to keep them apart, and she assumed he'd taken her place near the rear of the formation. Callum was marching near Lieutenant Tate, as was Taeg. Kayah assumed the fourth one, the nan caster she hadn't met yet, was watching Drak.

Where Callum preferred her to walk behind him so he could tug on the leash when she didn't keep to the pace he desired, Vesper wanted her to walk in front. They'd only walked a few paces before Kayah realized this wasn't any better when, for no reason she could identify, Vesper slapped her in her right ear. The explosion of pressure and pain nearly dropped her to her knees. Kayah staggered but didn't fall.

Vesper leaned in close to her other ear and whispered,

"You better watch your step. I will not be fucked with. Hear? Do as I say, and there will be no pain. Your little friendy friend found out quick not to fuck with me."

Kayah was saddened but not surprised to hear Drak's mouth had gotten him into trouble with this cruel woman.

Staring straight ahead, Kayah nodded. They resumed walking again, and again, Vesper slapped her after a short distance. Despite the ringing in her ear drowning out the rest of the world, she was sure she could hear Vesper chuckling behind her. Kayah did her best to keep as much distance between them as they marched. Occasionally, Vesper would tug on the leash to bring her closer. When it happened, Kayah couldn't help but cringe away from the slap she expected. This amused Vesper to no end and became her favorite game. When they stopped for the midday meal, Vesper enclosed her in a shield before getting her lunch and eating it in front of Kayah without bringing anything for her. They resumed marching, and as before, Vesper gave her right ear another slap.

A thin line of blood trickled from her ear and down the side of her neck. Kayah considered putting up a shield to protect herself from the assault. A quick look at her energy reserves killed that idea. Without food at lunchtime, she didn't have enough to power a shield. She thought she could manage a little healing for her ear, but she decided not to risk it while Vesper was behind her.

The company camped before dusk. The land they were moving through was unfamiliar. They'd left the grasslands behind and were descending into a wide, rocky valley. Hearty scrub grass grew in clumps around boulders. Overhead, a few carrion birds circled. Beyond that, there were no signs of life anywhere to be seen.

She was surprised when Vesper tied her leash to a stake she'd driven into the ground. Surprised again when she dropped Kayah's pack at her feet.

"Good job today," Vesper said, giving her a vicious smile.

"Callum said if you're a good girl, you can have your bed and cloak back. There you are. The proper response is, 'Thank you, Lady Vesper.'"

"Thank you, Lady Vesper," Kayah said. She didn't meet the other woman's gaze. Couldn't bring herself to look into those eerie silver eyes.

Vesper laughed. "Oh yes. You are doing much better than the brat. Keep it up, and there won't be any more reasons to discipline you. Now, it's dinner time." Vesper left and returned a few minutes later with two bowls of mush, identical to the meal from the night before. This time, the mush was accompanied by a hunk of hard bread.

"Thank you, Lady Vesper," Kayah said once the food was in her hands.

"After you've eaten, you should use some energy to heal that ear. Wouldn't want you suffering any permanent damage there. You're important, after all," she sneered and then hunkered down to eat.

Kayah ate, healed her ear, and then inventoried her pack. Aside from her cloak and bedroll, all that remained of the gear she'd packed was two changes of clothes, a metal bowl, and a cup. Her fire starter, utility knife, rope, and all her rations had been taken.

Still, she felt better having her pack with her. The cloak would keep her warm tonight, and the bedroll would make sleeping on the ground much more comfortable.

By the time she settled down to sleep, Vesper had already laid out the trip lines and contained her in a shield for the night.

She met the fourth caster, a man everyone called Smithy, the next day. The nicest of them, he refused to speak to her, but at least he didn't tug the leash or strike her. His indifference was a welcome change from Callum's rancor and Vesper's cruelty. After Smithy, Callum was back. Apparently, they weren't letting Taeg have any further direct contact with her or Drak. By then, they had also stopped separating her and Drak as drastically as they had been. Though they were kept apart during the march and at night, the casters all ate together away from the regular troops. After Callum gave Kayah her dinner, Vesper arrived with Drak in tow and sat him nearby to eat.

Drak looked terrible. His bottom lip was swollen, both of his ears were red, and he was sporting a deep black eye. Evidence of his defiance against Vesper. None of the Interland casters gave his condition a second look. Taeg especially wasn't looking at him. Tears welled up in her eyes at the sight of Drak. She wanted to rush over to him and hug him. But knew the others would stop her the moment she made a move. All she could do was look at him, tears in her eyes, and whisper, "I'm sorry."

Drak gave her a wan smile and winked.

After dinner, Callum jerked her leash to stand her up.

"Up. Time to see what you can do."

She complied too slowly for his liking, and he gave the leash a sharp tug. The collar jabbed into her windpipe, causing her to choke and cough as she rose to her feet.

Behind her, Vesper chuckled. Kayah didn't turn to look. Callum was bad enough; she didn't want to risk Vesper's ire, too. She needn't have worried, though, as Vesper was busy issuing commands to Drak. Smithy and Taeg stepped away to observe.

"Stand still," Callum commanded. Then he proceeded to scan her. "Your specialty is air?" he said after a minute and then made a face. "Fucking useless. We've come all this way for you because our Lord says you are important, and you're just a Husker. At least your foul-mouthed little friend is a Torch." Kayah hadn't thought it possible for his frown to deepen further, but then it did, turning his expression downright unpleasant. "We'll just have to work with what we've got. Now, attack me."

Kayah hesitated. During their training sessions, she'd

mainly focused on armor and shields rather than offensive applications. She could use them, but wasn't nearly as good as Drak.

"What are you waiting for? Attack me, you little shit!"

Kayah quickly wheeled to the application she was most comfortable with and sent a small arc of electricity towards Callum. Which he batted aside disdainfully. "Enough fucking around. I said, attack me, not tease me."

She tried again, drawing more power to make a larger arc. Callum rebuffed her again. She charged another shot and launched it at him. This time, he somehow grabbed hold of her bolt, collected it, and then sent it back at her. She dodged to her right, but the bolt struck her in the shoulder, making her left arm tingle sharply and painfully.

"Get up. Instead of dodging, you should have had a shield ready. Lighting's too quick to dodge. Don't stand like that. Are you trying to get yourself killed? Square up, plant your feet shoulder-width apart, and bend slightly at the knee. Like that. Loosen up your arms and shoulders. Passible. Now go again. Good."

A few meters away, Drak was fairing much better with Vesper. Though not good enough to avoid her jibes and sadistic retaliations. From the corner of her eye, she could see soldiers gathering in a ring around them, far enough away to give them a modicum of privacy, close enough to see what was happening.

This training went on for another hour. Callum demanded she switch up her attacks and pair them with a defensive application to be ready for a counterattack. Every time she struck at him, he blocked, countered, and followed it up with a comment designed to make her feel worthless and incapable. They went through all the offensive and defensive applications she knew. When they circled back around to electricity, Kayah realized he had avoided ordering her to use any air applications. Whether because of his low opinion of that application set or because air was her strength, Kayah wasn't sure. After finishing another attack repost, Kayah decided to try something. Feeling short of breath and near tears, she set up another attack. This time, instead of using a single application, she tried three.

She assumed the stance he'd shown her, then launched a weak fireball at his head, followed by an equally weak arc of lightning directed at his chest. Both of those attacks were misleading. She gave her real attack all her strength. Callum easily batted away the fireball and deflected the arc, but he hadn't been prepared for the column of forced air that struck him in the groin.

With a yelp and a curse, Callum clutched himself and sank to his knees, wheezing deep, agonized breaths. He remained that way, curled over, resting his forehead on the ground for a few long minutes while nan healed his burst testicles.

Behind her, the sounds of training had ceased. Kayah risked a glance and saw both Vesper and Drak staring, Vesper at Callum in horror and Drak at her in amusement. Smithy and Taeg were frozen in astonishment. For a fleeting moment, Kayah felt a spark of pride and almost smiled.

The moment quickly passed. She felt a hand grab her arm, painfully tight, and spin her around.

Callum towered above her. His breath was hot and fetid in her face. Though she couldn't read his silver eyes, his mouth was compressed into a sneer of rage. His whole body was tense, and his hands were shaking slightly.

Suddenly, he balled a fist and reared back.

"Our orders," Vesper called out, "are to see them returned to Lord Aion unharmed, sir."

Callum hesitated. His arm was still pulled back, ready to piston forward into her face. The moment ticked on, with the pair of them frozen together in anticipation of violence. Then Callum's stance changed slightly. His open-handed slap knocked her to the ground, blinding her with the pain in her cheek.

"That's enough for today," he said, glaring down at her. His voice was still slightly wheezy, and his gait was slow and halting as he walked away. The show was over, and the soldiers parted to allow Callum to pass.

"You heard the man," Vesper shouted, giving Drak a shove. "Smithy, take the bitch back to her stake." Vesper hauled Drak around and hit him in the back, right above his kidneys, before marching him away.

Kayah blinked back tears. As Smithy turned her to leave, Kayah locked eyes with Taeg for a moment. Before he looked away, she was certain she saw a note of shame in his eyes. She wished she could talk to him. Find out why he had betrayed them. He hadn't been all that forthcoming or talkative during their travels, but she'd considered him a friend. Seeing him in an Interland uniform hurt more than she cared to admit.

Once he had staked her leash to the ground, Smithy fetched their dinners.

"Good job today, girl," he said as he set the bowl of mush down before her. "Brave of you, striking back the way you did. Stupid. But brave. Eat. Then sleep." An hour later, he rolled up in his blanket and fell instantly asleep.

Kayah was too amped up to sleep. She replayed the image of Callum's face when the air column had struck and he had collapsed, again and again.

Staring into the night sky, Kayah smiled, thinking about Callum tipping over in pain.

The wind picked up, and a bank of low clouds rolled in quickly, settling over the camp and blotting out the stars. She tucked further under her blanket. But thought nothing of the strange, angry-looking clouds that had come up so suddenly. The air felt charged and heavy with electricity.

Just as her eyelids began to feel heavy, she heard a concussive whump from the far side of camp. She sat up to see a massive fireball rising into the air. A lightning strike had ignited the munitions dump in the middle of camp. The alert sentries were already sounding the alarm and rousing the troops, but it was the middle of the night, and for the moment, there was only confusion and chaos as soldiers tumbled half-clothed from their tents. The first strike was immediately followed by more: ten, fifteen, twenty landing rapid fire among the panicking soldiers. Each strike came on the heels of another, faster and faster, until she couldn't discern the interval between them. A hundred bolts of lightning must have landed among the confused soldiers.

Regaline, Kayah thought with a smile. *She's here. It's time to go.*

Before separating, they'd discussed what to do when this time came. Because they couldn't know exactly when or where the breakout would occur, the gist of their plans had amounted to simply getting as far away from the camp as possible as quickly as possible. The only concrete plan they'd decided upon was a meeting place. Regaline marked it on the map she'd uploaded to Kayah and Drak.

She'd heard Smithy snort and wake to the first explosion. He sat up but didn't move right away, frozen in place, perplexed by what he saw: the massive bonfire roaring in the camp center, the fusillade of unnatural lighting pouring down from the sky, the silhouettes of soldiers scampering here and there, the panicked shouting. Chaos.

Kayah, however, was not perplexed. The moment she heard Smitty stir, she charged her weapons. When he finally gained enough of his senses to get up, Kayah let loose. Her blast of forced air connected with Smithy's head with a sound like a hammer striking a board, snapping his head back. Smithy's feet flew up as his head flew down, and he landed with an audible crunch.

Kayah unbuckled the collar from her neck, stuffed her blanket and cloak back in her pack, and then cautiously approached the body. Smithy's still body lay on the ground staring blankly into the sky, his head askew, his neck resting on the sharp rock that had snapped it. Kayah grabbed the pack beside the body and gave him one final look before taking off into the night.

She made it a dozen paces before running face-first into an invisible barrier. She briefly touched her nose and blinked back the involuntary tears that welled up in her eyes. She tried turning but found another barrier blocking her.

"Where do you think you're going?" spoke a dreadful voice behind her.

Slowly, she spun in place to find Callum standing a few meters away. The look of murderous intensity on his face made her cringe. Behind him, she could see silhouettes of soldiers rushing about to contain the flames. In stark contrast, Callum was calm and in control as he reeled her toward him and led her back into camp, saying nothing as they passed Smithy's body. Near the center of camp, they encountered Taeg waiting. The collar was again clasped around her neck, and she was tied to a stake driven into the ground.

It took an effort to keep from crying, but she managed.

"Stay here and watch her," Callum commanded Taeg. "I'll return soon with the other one."

There would be no escape for her tonight. As she watched him disappear into the night, Kayah prayed Drak could get far enough away to find Regaline and prevent recapture.

CHAPTER 13

RANCE

"I'm sorry. That's just not possible," Flora said.

She was sitting across from Rance in the lounge, heads ducked low and speaking hushed tones. Traditionalist forces held the east dormitory, lounge, Operations level, and main lab complex. The Radicals were firmly entrenched in the west dorm, cafeteria, recreation level, and secondary and tertiary labs. The engineering and infirmary levels weren't under the control of either side, though both had people there to keep watch. By unspoken agreement, those areas were considered neutral territory. For the moment, at least. The Triad directors weren't any help. They'd been locked away by the hotheads during the first moments of the conflict. Rance had actually heard that Daniel Winoki was lying in a coma in the infirmary and might not pull through. Any authority the Triad directorship had once held was long gone.

It had been three days since the official start of hostilities, and the action had been mild so far. A few fistfights resulting in scrapes and bruises. That could quickly change. The tension in the air was thick and oppressive. There was no laughter anymore. No easy-going conversations. When people went anywhere, they marched a quick step in pairs. No one strolled anywhere alone anymore. There was a constant sense of being watched by someone lurking in dark corners, ready to jump out and strike without warning. Since the rift, the closest of friends had become the bitterest enemies.

Even among the "soldiers" of their own side, the tension and fear were palpable. Once divided, the different teams closed ranks. Only the team leaders found it acceptable to consort with members of the other teams. Rance wasn't sure why the mood had changed. All he knew was everyone had stopped talking to each other. Even the people he'd been working with to head off this crisis were incommunicado. Flora was only speaking with him now because he'd cornered her.

"You're on the guard team," Rance said. "It should be easy for you to get a message to the other side when you patrol the border corridors. We've got to try to communicate with them before this turns bloody."

"I can't help you," she said. She risked a quick glance over her shoulder. "I'm going to catch shit just for talking to you."

"What about the commitment we made? If we don't find a way to solve these problems peacefully, then all the work we've been doing since the Breakdown will be lost."

"I'm sorry. I can't take the risk. We watch each other all the time. There's no way I can drop anything without someone else seeing." She glanced around nervously. "In fact, I don't think we should speak again until this is over. It's not safe."

"Not safe for who? I'm on the ops team. I see everything."

"All the same. It's over. It was a good notion while it lasted. But we were too late, and we failed. Look, I've got to go. If you're smart, you'll keep your head down. Don't trust anyone." Before turning to leave, she said, "Good luck." Then she was gone.

Rance sat there for a few more minutes, dumbfounded. Everything was falling apart. He glanced down at the hotdog in front of him and grimaced. With the cafeteria in enemy hands, they were limited to the food printers in the executive suites and the menu in the lounge, the latter of which was limited to food popular with inebriates. He dropped the hotdog, uneaten, into the recycler and decided to return to Operations.

The first day they reopened Operations had been spent cleaning and running diagnostics on the equipment. Because the Watch Tower was mostly automated, it had been decades since people had occupied the level. Despite the best efforts of the self-regenerating HEPA filters, a sheen of dust had covered everything. The air had been stale and smelled faintly of must and disuse. Light panels, dark for years, had flickered on automatically as they stepped off the lift and into the main control room. The faint hum of electronics and machinery booting up had replaced the empty silence. Sprague had immediately gone to the central control station and tapped in his access code. Rance hadn't recalled his and had to take a moment to look it up from deep memory.

"We have access," Sprague had said triumphantly. "I'm sending you assignments. Find a station and get to work, if you please. We're going to win this thing!"

Rance had taken the closest workspace, which also happened to be nearest to the elevator. A chair had extruded from the floor to catch him as he sat. Simultaneously, a screen and user inputs had assembled before him at the correct ergonomic height. Rance discarded the assignment Sprague had given him without looking at it. He had no intention of helping his old friend fight a civil war. Instead, he had spent his time trying to find a way to surreptitiously contact someone on the other side. He had hoped to reach one of his confederates, though he would have settled for anyone so long as they were willing to talk.

After three days of trying, Rance had given up. Nobody was listening.

He had turned his attention to what Sprague had planned. Papillion was out of the infirmary and had joined them in Operations. When he had stepped off the lift, Rance had expected to see conflict between him and Sprague, but the pair had exchanged greetings and then put their heads together to conduct their little war.

It didn't take Rance long to figure out Sprague's plan. In his past life, Rance had been a network admin. Though it took a little while to shake the dust off, he quickly fell back into his groove in the network environment. It took some doing, but Rance managed to snoop out their true goal up here in Ops.

The dampening field. It was a precaution left over from the days when the complex was known as the HelixCom Kuridian Trans-Solar Planetary Terraforming Site 2. The people employed to work here were all infused with nanites when they were installed in their new bodies after having their consciousness transmitted across the stars. The microscopic robots allowed them to live and work on a planet that was distinctly not Earthlike. Without the nanites, they couldn't interact with the equipment and computers that ran both HelixCom sites. Once the nanites had been integral to the completion of the project. After the Breakdown, they became integral to the survival of those left behind. Because the nanites afforded the HelixCom employees spectacular capabilities, the company felt they should be limited in what they were allowed to do. It was too easy to pervert some of the applications to use as weapons or for other unauthorized purposes. To manage this, both sites were built with nanite controllers that regulated the nanite population within each employee.

Away from the sites, the dampeners had no effect, which was how the Watchers had been able to survive the Breakdown, foster the indigenous population, and continue terraforming Kuridian, albeit at a much slower pace. This allowed them to use their nanotech applications to survive on the half-terraformed planet on which they'd been stranded. However, while they were inside Site 2, the dampeners prevented them from using the abilities they'd become accustomed to.

Sprague wanted to turn off the dampening field. If successful, Rance knew Sprague would launch an attack on the others. One quick strike to end the conflict victoriously. Even the most peaceful of them had developed well-honed fighting abilities. Without the dampening field keeping them in check, this conflict would devolve into a bloodbath.

Rance wasn't sure the Watch Tower's system would allow such manipulation. The nanites operated as a cloud intelligence that would prevent any intrusion seeking to make such deep alterations. However, to be on the safe side, once he had figured out Sprague's intentions, Rance decided his energy would be best spent on preventing them from shutting down the dampeners. The trouble was that, in addition to Sprague and Papillion, there were two others working on it. No matter what Rance did or tried, he was outnumbered four to one and was, therefore, always scrambling to keep up. He knew the system better, but they could brute force the work more effectively than he could.

He stopped outside the lift doors that would take him to Ops, hand poised over the call button.

What's the point? he thought. *No matter what I do, no matter what I try, nothing works.*

He let his hand fall to his side, and he turned away, choosing instead to go home. His allies had abandoned him. His efforts in the Operations Center were going nowhere. He could see what was coming and felt powerless to stop it. He'd been assigned a new room in the east dorm. His first room was now deep in the territory held by the Radicals. He wasn't worried about the stuff he'd left behind in the room. Anything of value he'd locked away in the personal vault. But the loss of his stuff, even temporarily, only added to his feeling of defeat and disconnection. Everything he'd tried had failed. Sprague and his flunkies would crack the firewalls around the dampeners, and then the Traditionalists would strike. Those who weren't wiped out would be captured and made prisoners. Second-class citizens in their little societal microcosm. That wouldn't help the faltering, incomplete terraforming process. It wouldn't fix any of the problems they'd met to discuss and resolve.

He passed a quartet of guards in the hall on his way back to his room. He recognized each of them, had known them for ages. Yet, as they passed each other, every single one of them eyed him suspiciously. Was it because he was walking alone or simply a result of the atmosphere of paranoia hovering over everything these days? He didn't know, nor did he care. He was tired of it. Tired of the mistrust and hostility. Rance just wanted it to be done.

Maybe it's time to start over.

The thought halted him in his tracks. Where had that come from? Start over? Was it even possible?

Then he thought of the town he'd built. Hillcrest. He'd already violated the tenants the Traditionalists held most dear. He'd trained nearly everyone in his town in the use of their innate nanotech abilities. They were proof the population at large could handle nanotech and help shoulder the responsibilities of cultivating the world.

These fools are going to kill themselves over this nonsense. There's nothing I can do to stop it now. But I can make sure the planet still has caretakers after it's over.

It was hard to admit, but he'd failed. He had resisted becoming embroiled in this conflict. But now, he saw it was time to do what he should have done a month ago. It was time to leave.

Back in his room, he packed the few belongings he'd had on him once the rift occurred. Lucky for him, his relationship with Sprague meant he'd been given an executive suite to replace his old room. Once he closed and locked the door, he immediately set the room's printer to work. He needed new clothes, boots, some gear, ration bars, and a pack to hold it all. The printer informed him it would take eight hours to complete the assigned tasks.

With some time to kill, he returned to the lounge for one last hot meal and a beer. While he ate, he considered whether to contact the others he'd been working with, whether to offer them the chance to come with him. By the time his second beer arrived, he decided that it was the right thing to do and started composing a message. Besides, he figured he would need some help if he were going to rebuild the Order.

"*I've decided to leave,*" the message began. "*I've done all I can here. Best to get out before things get worse. If you feel the same way, meet me at the south loading dock at 01:00 tonight. Gather whatever supplies you need.*"

He opened a text screen and input the addresses for Davis, Morin, Gelen, Silla, and Flora. The people who had been willing to listen and work with him. After a moment of thought, he deleted Flora's name and added Cline's. Flora was scared of her own shadow by this point. He was surprised she hadn't reported him to Sprague and Papillion for undermining them. Cline, on the other hand, had remained on the fence until he'd convinced her to join his spy chain. He thought she'd be reasonable and willing to join him outside.

He was about to hit send when an alarm began howling. There were only two others in the lounge with him. The three of them shared a confused, worried look before rushing out the door.

A new message window materialized before him from Sprague. "We've cracked it! The attack has started. Get your ass up to operations."

Rance trashed Sprague's message, clicked send on his, and ran back to his room.

The printer had finished a few ration bars and his boots but was still in the middle of printing his backpack. He put on the boots, pocketed the ration bars, and left. He'd just have to fend for himself out there. It was what he was best at, after all.

An eerie calm permeated the atmosphere outside his room. The halls were completely empty. Rance imagined he could hear shouting and the thunder of weapons fire somewhere distant. Turning left, he made his way to the loading dock by the most direct route. The alarms had ceased, but emergency flashers still strobed red at each intersection. His pace slowed as he approached the first intersection and peeked around the corner. Still no one. He continued, heart pounding.

True fear sank into his veins. The feeling was so unfamiliar that it took Rance a moment to recall the last time he'd felt it. Bennett. Twenty years ago.

He tried to shake the image away and continue moving. But his mind kept returning to it.

It was a hard life, being a Watcher faced with hardship and trauma owing to the nearly impossible situation thrust upon them. Dealing with daily dangers was enough to wear down even the strongest, most steadfast soul. Lesser people broke all the time when faced with a fraction of what they endured. The superstition, the suspicion, the fear. They did their level best for the people of this world and received little or no thanks in return.

Almost twenty years ago, Rance had come upon Bennett in a gully far south of Site 2 as he was curled on the ground crying. The ground around him for a dozen meters had been scorched black. Rance had camouflaged himself to approach. In those days, a protocol for dealing with the Broken hadn't been established, and Rance had been improvising.

Intending to help, he had tried getting close enough to put Bennett to sleep, or at least to wrap him in a shield so he couldn't hurt anyone, especially Rance. He had closed to within five meters of Bennett and had readied a shield to place around him when his movements startled a half-burned ground chuck. The terrified animal had hopped out of its hole and scampered across the charred ground, squealing.

Bennett's sobs had immediately ceased. He had sat up screaming and blasted the little creature into ashes. The suddenness of the attack had startled Rance, and he had staggered back a step, causing Bennett to turn his fire in Rance's direction. Rance had quickly snapped the shield he had readied around himself and then had dodged left. His camouflage had still been in place, so Bennett hadn't seen where he'd moved and continued spraying fire wildly in the wrong direction.

Rance had steadied himself, charged up his own fire pulse, and dropped his shield.

Bennett had been ashes before he even noticed Rance was shooting at him.

The memory of his first fight with another Watcher gave Rance chills. It wasn't the last time something like that had happened. But the encounter was indelibly cast into his memory. He pressed down his fear and pressed onward.

It occurred to Rance that, with the dampeners deactivated, he should have access to his full suite of applications. Sure enough, his weapons and defenses were all open and available to use. Now, he wished he'd eaten earlier. He would need the energy in case he got into a fight. He grabbed one of his newly printed ration bars and bit off a corner to fuel up. Then, he readied a particle shield and charged his arc pulse, setting it to a less-than-lethal voltage. He didn't want to kill anyone he didn't have to; he just wanted to leave.

He was aware that the safest course might be to simply go back to his room and wait it out, and he nearly turned back the way he'd come to do just that. If the Radicals somehow got the upper hand, they might start going room by room, looking for holdouts. Constance, he was sure, wanted his head. Even if they didn't come out on top, he'd have trouble explaining himself if he was found hiding. Besides, he'd already messaged the people from his group. If they decided to join him, they'd be vulnerable waiting around the loading docks for him. Better to keep moving and get away from the Watch Tower as quickly as possible.

At the next intersection, Rance went right instead of left towards the dock and continued until he arrived at a side stairwell. After ascending three floors, he exited the stairwell and moved quickly through the nanite flush labs, heading for the southwest stairs. He extended a sensor cloud before him as he ran. Since he hadn't been able to print all the gear he needed, he wanted to get his old gear from his old room. He'd overheard a report given to Sprague that morning and knew it was safe to move through this level. The Watch Tower was too big and the Watchers too few to effectively occupy every floor. At the other stairwell, he would descend two levels, pop into his room, grab his stuff, and continue to the dock.

Ten meters from the door to the stairwell, his sensor cloud started pinging. Reflexes born of a life spent in hostile lands and honed into instinct forced him to drop low and duck behind a fabrication workstation just as the door opened and four Watchers stepped cautiously out. Safely out of sight, Rance dimmed himself and started moving to his right, parallel to the far wall where the exit door was located. He dialed his sensors down to passive detection and remained still.

He couldn't tell if they were friends or enemies. Though at this point, he counted everyone as an enemy.

From his hiding spot, Rance watched them make their way around the level. Slowly searching in and around the equipment.

"I don't think anyone's up here," one of them whispered.

"It doesn't matter what you think," another one replied. "We were ordered up here to make sure nobody comes this way trying to get in behind us."

"Yeah," a third put in. "They already got Davis and Angel when they jumped us. What do you think will happen if they come this way?"

"They'll fuck us," the fourth one said.

"I know all that," said number one. "I just don't think we need four people to check out this floor. Two could easily do it. The others would be better used in the rec center fight."

"You want to be down there getting your ass shot off?" Number Three said. "I, for one, don't mind being up here on an empty floor."

"Amen," said Number Two.

"You can go if you want," said Three.

"Yeah, go be a hero," said Two.

"I don't want to be a hero," said One. "I just think there's too many of us up here. What if they break through down there? We'd be just as fucked if that happened."

"We'd make them pay for it, though," said Two.

"Like I said, no one's making you stay up here with us. Go and help them in the rec center if that's where you want to be. I'm happy to stick around here and—"

"Quiet!" Number Four hissed. "There's someone up here."

The mood among them instantly shifted as they crouched down low, their weapons ready.

Rance assumed they had switched to an internal communication line because their chatter died, and they spread out, carefully picking their way around the workstations to his right and left.

It wouldn't be long before they found him at the rate they were going.

Acting fast, he set up a decoy drone and launched it over to the far side of the room. He'd set it to wait ten seconds before blasting them with an active search radar to hopefully distract them long enough for him to get away unseen.

A shuffling of feet to his left made him crawl under the desk he was hiding near and make himself as small as he could. A clatter from further away to his right almost caused him to jump.

There was a faint whistle from directly in front of his hiding spot. He knew one of them had found him and was signaling the others to move in. Getting ready to jump up and run, Rance charged his weapons and a shield.

Then the decoy went off.

As he hoped, all four of them turned in that direction.

Without waiting, Rance bounced to his feet. He saw someone standing by the next desk over and gave him a small shock blast that knocked him off his feet and left him sprawled over the table behind him.

Then Rance was sprinting, hunched over, between the workstations towards the exit.

Shouts of alarm came from behind him, accompanied by lighting arcs and lances of fire that streaked past him, striking the walls and desks. He didn't dare look back. Weaving between the close tables took all his attention.

A burst of fire landed on the workstation to his right as he passed. The sudden concussive flash of heat shoved him violently to the left and sent him sprawling.

"Got him!" he heard from behind. He wasn't sure which one had thrown the fireball, but he knew they were right behind him.

Running hadn't worked. If he continued, they would catch him in the open and fry him.

Time to change tactics, he thought, diving behind another table. He crawled up two rows and over three tables before poking his head up.

The three chasing him had slowed. They were looking around the spot where he'd dropped. Feeling lucky, Rance ducked back down and lobbed a fireball of his own at the nearest. When he heard it hit, he got moving again. On his hands and knees, he crawled a zig-zag course away from the exit and his pursuers. Then he stood up, locked onto the next closest, and gave him an intense burst of electricity. Rance barely registered the man jittering and collapsing before he dropped and started crawling again. Behind him, he heard small explosions as the two still standing blasted the area where he'd been.

Pausing a moment, he set up another drone. This one, he programmed to seek out the nearest attacker and explode once it reached him. He set it running and started crawling again. A few seconds later, there was a panicked shout followed immediately by a loud whump as the bot exploded.

"Shit! Shit! Shit!" Rance heard the last one shout as he ran for the stairwell. Rance popped up again, took aim, and sent a fine beam of electricity into the fleeing man's back.

Panting and relieved it was over, he started for the exit again.

A funnel of forced air slammed into him, dislocating his left shoulder and flinging him across the floor. He landed in a heap a short distance from the last one he'd shot while fleeing. His shoulder was on fire. Another funnel of air caught him in the chest as he tried sitting up, knocking the wind out of him. He sprayed arcs of electricity around with his right hand as he scrambled to get out of the open. There was a support pillar a few meters away. Moving was agony, but he managed to find cover behind it.

Instinctively, he set his nan to healing. It couldn't do much about his shoulder until he physically replaced it into the socket, but it could repair his ruptured spleen and bleeding liver and kidneys. Then Rance reactivated his sensors. There was no need to hide anymore; the attacker knew exactly where he was, so Rance set them on full. The one currently attacking him was the first one he'd put down. Having recovered from Rance's light, non-lethal attack, he'd decided to finish the job he and his friends had started.

"Damn it!" Rance muttered after looking at the sensor returns. There were several shadow signals moving around out there. His attacker had learned his lesson and was masking his movements behind decoys of his own. Following suit, Rance launched a few shadows of his own before darting away from the pillar.

A beam of fire sizzled through the air above him. Rance threw a fireball back along the path of the beam. Back in the safety of the desk maze, he took a moment to reset his shoulder. He felt a molar crack as he clenched his jaw to stifle his cry of pain. Nan instantly healed the tooth. Now that his shoulder was back in place, it tingled as his nan repaired the torn ligaments and inflammation.

According to his sensors, there were four shadows running around, plus three that popped up intermittently just to add to the confusion. Rance set out four bots, programmed them to explode upon reaching their target, and launched them. If a bot found a shadow, it would then seek out the next-nearest signal and head towards it. Done, he sat back exhausted, his energy reserves drained. One by one, the sensor shadows blipped away as the bots reached them. Then he heard surprised shouting as the four bots attacked his last surviving attacker. The shouting started before the first bot detonated, continued through the second explosion, and stuttered into silence as the third and fourth explosions went off almost simultaneously.

Weary, Rance got to his feet and started for the door. Eager to avoid any more surprises, he focused his sensors ahead of him on maximum. The entire fight had only taken a few minutes, but it had been loud, and he couldn't be sure they hadn't summoned help while it was going on. He only took a few steps before stopping. The door was a mere ten meters away, but he found he didn't want to go through it anymore.

"To hell with it," he said and turned around. He didn't need the stuff in his room. The Watch Tower had become bad for his health.

Returning the way he'd come, he went down four levels, exiting the stairwell on the engineering level. The mechanisms and equipment facilitating the Watch Tower's automation were housed on this level, as was the loading dock. Due to the photosensitive nature of much of the machinery down there, the rooms and corridors were all bathed in yellow light so as not to damage any of the delicate nanites freely roaming around the level.

While he walked, Rance ate the rest of his first ration bar and wondered who would be there waiting for him. If anyone was. Based on what he'd just seen, Sprague's surprise attack hadn't been as effective as he'd hoped.

He felt a shudder vibrate through the floor. Somewhere, a rather large explosion had just gone off. The Order was tearing itself apart and the Watch Tower with it.

Down one long corridor and through a set of heavy double doors, he had reached the loading dock. A long time ago, a maglev tram system had connected the dock with a dock at the other site. The tram station was located on the far side of the dock, opposite from where Rance currently stood. What he was looking for was on this side: roll-up doors that opened directly to the outside. In the old days, they'd been fitted with airlocks to prevent the mixing of the interior and exterior atmospheres. The Watch Tower had long ago dissolved them and repurposed the materials.

The dock was empty. He looked left and right, surveying the large empty space, and found no one.

There were three possibilities: they hadn't gotten his message, they'd been delayed due to the fighting, or they'd been swept up in it. With insanity rampant, anything was possible. In any case, he decided to give it a few minutes. Someone might still show up.

He settled down to wait in a small, concealed alcove behind an old, empty crate. From there he could see anyone who entered the dock. Then, he dimmed his presence and camouflaged himself to match the walls around him.

To keep himself awake and restock his reserves, Rance pulled out another ration bar and ate it. He only had three left. Once he was outside, he'd be foraging sooner than he'd wanted. Such was life. At least he would be away from the Watch Tower.

He was picking crumbs from his teeth when he heard a door open. He peeked and frowned in confusion when he saw Flora standing in the doorway, plainly looking around for someone but hesitating to come all the way inside as though wary of stepping into a trap.

The hair on the back of his neck stood up as he pressed further back into the alcove.

"Are you still here, Rance?" she called. "I've got the others with me. They'll come in when they know it's safe. We got your message. We want to go with you. This place is crazy. We need to leave before they kill us all!" As she spoke, Flora poked around the dock, looking in the alcoves and niches for him.

Rance wanted to believe her. Maybe Gelen had told her about the plan and invited her along anyway. It was plausible she'd been sent ahead to scout the dock for them.

He'd just about convinced himself she was on the level when the doors opened again and someone he couldn't see joined her.

"I can't see or sense him," she said. "He might have left already. In any case, he's not here now."

"No great loss," said the unseen person. It was another woman, but beyond that, Rance couldn't identify the speaker. "We've got the rest of them. We'll catch up with him eventually. He can't have gotten far. Commander Sprague is super pissed and wants his head."

"We'll get it for him," Flora said.

Then, both women left the loading dock.

Still hidden, Rance let out a shuttering breath.

"What the hell am I going to do now?"

CHAPTER 14

ASTRID

Sweating profusely, Astrid pressed against the bar until her arms were fully extended, then she set it on the bench saddle with a slight clatter, completing the tenth repetition of her fourth and final set. The bar had two twenty-two-kilogram plates on each side. Added to the weight of the bar itself, she was pressing sixty-six kilos. Before the accident, she'd been able to bench almost twice that. The fact that she hadn't recovered enough yet to reach that weight was frustrating.

She sat up and wiped her forehead with a towel. A glance at the clock told her it was only ten hundred. Normally, she'd be working right now, but she had decided she needed to take some time off and applied to use some of her vacation time. Kinney, believing they were the best of friends, had approved it immediately.

That had been three days ago. As much as Astrid hated to admit it, she was enjoying the time off and thought it was even doing her some good. After only three days, she already felt better and more at peace than she had in months. The workouts and daily meditation helped. Now that she was on vacation, she could admit she'd needed to take some time off for a long time now.

But it wasn't the only reason she wanted the time away. Ever since learning he was responsible for her near-death experience, Astrid didn't want to see Kinney's face. At least not yet. She didn't trust herself not to attack him and, in doing so, give herself away. Her only edge was her certainty that Kinney didn't know what she'd discovered. She needed to keep it that way if she was going to collect enough evidence to put him away.

After disinfecting the bench, she went to the locker room to shower and change. All of the gym equipment was infused with nanites that regularly cleaned and maintained it. However, Astrid and everyone else who used the gym still wiped everything down after each use. It was only polite, after all.

Today was going to be the official start of her investigation. She'd signed up to visit Site 2 and use the virtual entertainment facilities there. It had cost her another week of time off, but it would be worth it if she could uncover something about Kinney. The tram was scheduled to depart at thirteen hundred.

At twelve fifty, Astrid was showered, changed into her most presentable work suit, and stood in the tram dock waiting for the tram to arrive. With her on the platform were five others. One wore the office version of the work suit and carried only a valise with her, no luggage. Astrid assumed she'd come here for a meeting and was on her way back. The other four were clustered together in a group, clutching their tote bags and chattering loudly. They looked like they all worked together and had coordinated their time off to take a Site 2 vacation. Everyone appeared to be wearing their best suits, which made Astrid feel somewhat self-conscious. She looked down at her clean but worn and slightly tattered coveralls. They had once been dark blue, indicating she was a senior member of the engineering team, but had faded to a blue-gray, especially around the knees and elbows. She hadn't gotten around to printing a new set. Seeing the others in their pressed and best, she wished she had. Too late to do anything about it now. Maybe she would print a new set once she got to her room.

FROM GREAT HEIGHTS

A chime sounded, and the row of yellow caution lights near the edge of the platform began flashing. The tram car was pulling into the station.

The smooth, pill-shaped car glided silently to a halt. With a gentle hiss, the doors peeled back from the featureless exterior, revealing the passengers waiting to disembark. Once everyone was off, Astrid hefted her bag and stepped in line to board, behind the woman on a day trip but ahead of the vacation group. As the woman in front set foot on the car, a small armature extruded from the wall. At the end was a scanner that looked unsettlingly like a red-and-black eyeball. The eye stalk scanned her from head to toe and then, satisfied, allowed her to enter the car and proceed to Site 2.

The process repeated for each of them, with the car checking to make sure they were authorized to travel between the sites. Once everyone was seated and their luggage stowed, the door reassembled itself and the car began to move.

Astrid had to trust they were moving as she felt no inertia in the car.

A minute or two after departing, the walls of the car faded away, becoming completely transparent, leaving only the floor and seats visible, giving the impression that they were on an open platform racing down the single thick rail extending in front of them to the horizon and behind them to the Site 1 dock. The lack of wind or feeling of movement clashed with the view of the landscape speeding by them and nearly gave her motion sickness. The trip would take about two hours. To pass the time, she closed her eyes and lowered her chin to take a nap. When she opened her eyes again, she saw Site 2 growing in the distance as the car rapidly approached it.

Images of Site 2 were freely available to anyone with network access. Though most of the people she knew rarely looked them up. She herself had only checked out the images taken when the Site 2 complex had finished growing and had never looked it up since. It was too depressing. Like looking at a neighbor's brand-new house with all the state-of-the-art amenities and comparing it to the refurbished refrigerator box you lived in. She didn't like the reminder that the place where she lived and worked was a filthy shithole compared to this clean and sparkly new facility. The grass may be greener on the other side, but in this case, it was like comparing weedy barn grass to GM Bluesoft Fescue. There was no comparison.

The smooth, white, almost crystalline surfaces. Flowing buttresses held the structures aloft at seemingly impossible angles. After the groundbreaking, nanites had been poured into foundation molds, which had been the last time human hands touched Site 2 while under construction. The nanites had been issued parameters and instructions on what to build and what specifications were required. Then the nanites had been given free rein to design and build the place however they wanted. What had been, in a nutshell, another cost-cutting measure instituted by HelixCom resulted in something as pleasing to the eye as it was applicational.

Though she hated to admit it, the view was breathtaking.

Approaching the station, the tram slowed without any perceptible change in momentum. To Astrid, the entrance opening to accept the tram car looked like a lizard cloaca, and she stifled a chuckle. It wouldn't do to insult the people here by comparing one of their work-of-art buildings to a reptile anus.

The tram didn't scan them as they departed, or if it did, it did so unobtrusively. Immediately upon setting foot on the platform, Astrid felt ill at ease. The whole place looked soft and fragile. She felt as though she might break it if she stared at it too hard. The walls themselves seemed to glow, emitting light without a source she could pinpoint. She synced her nanotech system with the main unified system and was greeted with a friendly hello. A moment later, a small ambulator poured up from the floor, took her bag, and motioned her to follow along to her room.

The sheer amount of nanotech in use here astounded her. At Site 1, the UIs were made from interactive nanotech, and the printers utilized it, but the rest of the site was strictly analog. Site 1 personnel were all infused with nanotech to live and work more efficiently, but that was minimal when compared to the nanotech usage she witnessed all around Site 2.

No wonder Kinney was so miserable when he first got there, she thought. Though if she were honest, she'd had something to do with his misery.

She touched the pad beside the door to the room she'd been assigned for her stay, and the smooth surface of the wall seemed to pixelate and pull away. The interior was as featureless as the corridors. As she wandered around the space, the program controlling the room gave her a demonstration, inflating the bed, assembling the washroom, compiling the kitchenette, extruding an armchair and accompanying worktable.

This place is amazing! Astrid thought, then cautioned herself not to get too cozy. Otherwise, she might not want to leave.

She had to shake off her amazement. She was there for a reason, a mission to complete, and had only four days to complete it.

First, however, she wanted to check out the washroom. Her room complied and erected the privacy screen and a stand-up shower adjusted to her exact height. The water was the perfect temperature and sprayed at the perfect pressure. After ten minutes of luxuriating under the stream, she stepped out and toweled off.

"I'm going to miss this when I leave. I can tell already," she said to her reflection in the newly assembled mirror. The showers back at Site 1 came out in a lukewarm dribble set to a five-minute timer.

She asked the room to print her a new set of coveralls. No reason to go around in her ratty old set. In no time at all, the clothing was done, and she was dressed. Even the material felt nicer than what the Site 1 printers could produce. More durable, the texture of the cloth was rougher yet more comfortable against her skin than her old coveralls. Without hesitation, she printed off three more sets, as well as a week's worth of undergarments, gym clothes, and loungewear. Then she dumped all her old clothes into the recycler and packed her new wardrobe in her bag.

"Yep," she said, with a smirk and a small shake of her head, and then she summoned a chair and worktable. Time to get to work.

It didn't take long to find all the available public information about Kinney. It was disappointingly brief. Just the basic data provided in his corporate personnel file: vital statistics, work record, company awards—of which he had none. Astrid hadn't thought she would find anything useful there, but had to start somewhere. One entry did stand out. He'd worked as an entry-level tech in the gestation lab for exactly seven months before being promoted to a shift supervisor position in engineering. Curious, she highlighted that section of his file for a deeper dive. The lab had been his first assignment upon being hired and decanted here at Site 2. The performance reviews written by his former manager outlined a mediocre employee whose only outstanding quality was the fact that he showed up early to his shifts. The reviews also stated Kinney was sloppy, had a poor attitude, and possessed a lackadaisical work ethic.

This didn't jibe with the man she knew. The Kinney she knew was a confident, hard charger, proactive, and positive. The Kinney in these reports sounded like someone on his way to termination. A quick glance through his worklogs confirmed the assessment in the report. Missed steps and numerous errors. Astrid frowned. How did someone like this get promoted?

A week before his promotion, it all had changed, like the flip of a switch. He had clocked out for the day a sloppy loser and come in the next morning an efficient, initiative-taking, model employee.

"What changed?" she muttered. "Did someone talk to you, or threaten you, or turn you?"

It occurred to her that Kinney was the perfect candidate for someone recruiting spies. That had to be it. Someone had made him promises and turned him. Then had gotten him promoted out of the gestation lab and into a position where he had had access to secrets of greater value. She had no idea who could have the sort of pull to enable something like that, but it was someone highly placed.

"But if they are so highly placed, what would they need someone like Kinney for?"

She tried to wring more details from the reports before her but couldn't find anything that would help her further.

She closed the screen and logged out and went to dinner. She didn't want to alert the system administrators to her snooping. She still had a lot of questions she needed answers to and didn't want to risk discovery. They would likely revoke her Site 2 access and send her home, which in turn would alert Kinney that she was on to him. Better to take it slow. She still had three more days to learn whatever she could.

In the meantime, she'd enjoy some of the creature comforts Site 2 had to offer. For example, cafeteria printers that printed food that was enjoyable and not just barely edible.

The next day, she made her way to the gestation lab where Kinney had worked before his meteoric rise through the ranks of HelixCom. Her position as a department manager afforded her greater access and freedom of movement. Still, she didn't want to press her luck, so she'd made an appointment to speak with the lab manager before the lunch break.

Entering his office in the back of the lab, she extended a hand. "Mr. Plick, thank you so much for agreeing to see me. I promise not to take up too much of your time."

Plick came around his desk and shook her hand. "Not at

all, Ms. Free. I understand from your message you've just been promoted and are looking to observe other departments for efficiency tips?"

"That's correct. Also, I've never been to Site 2 before, so I thought I'd take a short vacation and kill two birds with one stone."

"Understandable. You must have it pretty hard over there at Site 1. I can understand you'd want to see what state-of-the-art looks like. I am happy to help."

Astrid smiled. "We do what we can with what we have," she replied, biting back the scathing remark burning inside her. She was there to gather information and leave, not make an enemy who might report on her to Kinney. "I'm interested in your work rotations, resource allocations, and the like."

"Of course. Of course. Feel free to have a look around. If you'd like, I can assign someone to show you around and answer any questions you might have."

"That would be helpful. Thank you."

Plick flicked a button on his desk, and a woman immediately entered the office. He'd apparently anticipated her needs and chosen someone for the job. "Maria, this is Astrid Free, a manager visiting our humble facility from Site 1. Please show her around the lab and answer any questions she might have."

"You got it," Maria said, smiling. She turned to Astrid. "If you'll follow me."

"Thank you, Mr. Plick," Astrid said as they departed.

"My pleasure. Oh! And congratulations on your promotion."

The gestation lab was clean, well-organized, and efficiently laid out. Despite her initial dislike of Plick, he ran a tight department.

"So, what brings you to our little slice of heaven?" Maria asked.

"Like I told your boss, I've just been promoted over at Site 1. I thought I'd take a little vacation to celebrate my recent promotion. At the same time, I thought being here might be a good opportunity to see how some other departments worked. Maybe steal a few innovative ideas."

Maria smiled but didn't reply, indicating to Astrid she was just making small talk. They spent the rest of the tour sticking to subjects concerning the lab and its workings.

"This is our gene library," Maria said, stopping before a massive cylinder. It was metallic white, smooth, and featureless, like almost everything else in Site 2. When Maria stepped close to it, the surface swirled and a screen and user interface controls poured out. "From here, we can sample sequences from more than five hundred thousand examples on file to recombine to create whatever sort of flora or fauna we might need to populate the planet during phase three."

"So, this is where all the magic is going to happen, eh?"

"Correct. We are only running trials, at the moment, to see what sorts of attribute sequences will work best. A sort of guided natural selection, if you will."

"Sounds like interesting work."

"It has its moments. We don't get to do much experimenting down here on the floor. That's upstairs in the selection lab. They run the sims and create the experiments. Once they've done everything they can virtually, they send the specs down to us, and we build the specimen for real and send it back to them for destruction testing."

"Fascinating," Astrid said, making a show of looking sublimely interested. "You know, I actually had another reason for wanting to check this place out. My new boss, Jared Kinney, used to work here. He talks about this lab all the time like it was his favorite place to work." Maria made a face like she'd swallowed something sour. "Did you work with Kinney when he was here?"

"Oh, yes," Maria said. Her voice had pitched upward an octave or two. "I remember Jared. It was sad when he was promoted away from us and then transferred to your site. We were happy for him, of course, but sad to see him go."

That didn't match with what she'd read in his personnel file. Astrid put on her best poker face. "Sorry," she said. "Your loss was our gain, I suppose." Then she flashed her most charming smile. "What can you tell me about him when he was here?"

Maria glanced over her shoulder as though afraid someone would overhear. "He's your boss, right? I don't want to say anything that might get me in trouble."

"What do you mean?"

"Look, I don't know what you've got going on over there at Site 1, but we don't play power politics here. I don't know if you're hunting for information that would give you leverage on your boss or what. But I'd just as soon not talk about Kinney."

Astrid tried to look abashed. "I'm so sorry, Maria. I'm not trying to get any sort of leverage on Kinney or anyone. I just thought it might be fun to see where Kinney worked before he came over to us. I happen to like him. I think he's a good boss and a good friend."

Maria's smile returned. "In that case, I can tell you he was exceptionally easy to work with. Always ready to lend a helping hand. He was just a genuinely nice person to be around."

"That's exactly how I feel!" Astrid said. Then she turned and pointed to another piece of equipment. "And what is this?"

Maria launched into an in-depth explanation, but Astrid only listened with half an ear. Something seemed off around here. Everyone was friendly and accommodating. Everywhere she looked, she saw vapid smiles. It felt phony. She supposed it was possible these people were simply happy to work there. But she'd never heard of a work environment where even the happiest of employees didn't rub each other the wrong way every now and then.

Then there was the fact that Maria was lying about Kinney.

Astrid had read the file and saw the number of complaints against him lodged by his coworkers. Two of them by Maria herself. The phrases "unpleasant asshole" and "rude and standoffish" stood out in her latest complaint. Yet now she was all smiles and daisies at the very mention of his name. Something strange was going on there, and Kinney was at the center of it.

Maria had finished her explanation of the gene splicer/collider Astrid had asked her about and was looking at her expectantly.

"Is this where Kinney used to work?" she asked.

"Not so much," Maria said. "Mr. Plick likes to rotate us through the different toolsets so we stay current on every process. However, he started assigning Kinney to the cataloging station on a regular basis because he showed an aptitude for the work. It's over there, behind the print intermixing chamber."

And away from everyone else, Astrid noted.

They had the same sort of equipment over at Site 1, so she already knew what kind of work was done at the station. The punishingly boring kind. This whole team must have really hated him if Kinney had been assigned there all the time. It kept him out of the way, and it was also hard to screw up. All he had to do was make sure the bots were running and log the start and stop times of each nanite load.

"Sounds like everybody here liked him."

"The feeling was mutual, I assure you. The day he got promoted, we threw him a going away party when he came into the lab."

Astrid had to hide her disbelief. How did a man like that get promoted? She'd seen some real toxic personalities work their way up the ladder, but this was above and beyond anything in her experience. Kinney didn't appear to have had much of a social life and apparently had made his coworkers miserable.

"Do you mind if I take a look at the cataloging room?"

she said. "I was thinking of taking a pic in there and sending it to him."

"Be my guest. It's right over there, between those tall cylinders. When you see Kinney again, tell him we all say hi and we miss him."

"I sure will." Astrid thanked her and turned to check out the space where Kinney had spent nearly six months alone.

It wasn't a room, per se, just an isolated workstation crammed between two larger toolsets. It was the first place Astrid had seen since arriving with a permanent user interface and chair that didn't deconstruct back into the walls or floor.

Maybe it was here that he was co-opted, she thought. She found it difficult to believe someone could have turned him here in the middle of one of Site 2's core laboratories. It had to have happened somewhere, though, and here was just as likely as anywhere else.

Maria had indicated the station was only active when a project was being sequenced or printed. Currently, the station was empty, the machinery quiet.

She sat down and connected to the terminal. Before her she saw the familiar HelixCom GUI, listing the options and applications of the station in menu form. At first, nothing out of the ordinary jumped out at her. The worklogs were all in order. It seemed Kinney had enjoyed his work at this station. The data was all tidy and timely. When she compared the dates of his reviews with the times assigned to this workstation, she found his performance had improved significantly. Apparently, he was just one of those people who worked better alone. Which still left her feeling confused.

He shouldn't have been promoted. Hell, he shouldn't have been able to retain employment with HelixCom, for that matter. What had happened that allowed him to suddenly climb the ranks?

Satisfied she'd found everything she was going to find,

Astrid logged out and left, making sure to thank both Maria and Plick for their time and courtesy. She still had five days. She would just have to find another avenue to search.

Her efforts over the next two days came to nothing, which frustrated her to no end. She came close to simply asking Kinney's direct supervisor, Arun Mehta, how Kinney had managed to earn a promotion. However, doing so would expose her true reason for coming to Site 2 and would almost certainly tip off Kinney. Instead of doing anything rash, she did her best to relax. She swam every day, used the spa, ate lots of exquisitely printed food, and took in a holo-flick, all the things people did on a company vacation.

With the end of her vacation looming and feeling like she'd made zero progress, she spent the afternoon of her third day at Site 2, catching up on the happenings in her department back at Site 1. There wasn't much of note going on. They were laying the groundwork to begin phase three of the terraform, so things were mostly operating on autopilot.

She closed the feed and reopened Kinney's worklogs from the gestation lab. They were perfect. Too perfect. She compared them to Kinney's logs from the week before he'd been assigned to the cataloging station. The work he'd been doing was rife with errors and almost unusable. The logs from the cataloging station were immaculate. Then she brought up the logs for the cataloging station the week before Kinney had been assigned there. While the logs still looked good under another operator, they were far from perfect. Which meant either someone was doing the work for him, or he'd programed a bot to do it. Either way, Kinney had been promoted under false pretenses. She wanted to take this to someone, but she knew it was too flimsy. After all, he'd already caught the spy in HelixCom's ranks. He was a hero as far as management was concerned. She'd need concrete proof if she were going to take him down, and this wasn't it.

It did, however, give her an idea.

Looking at her watch, she saw it was just after eleven in the morning and left her room. She stopped when she reached the hallway to the gestation lab and waited out of sight. If these folks took their breaks like they were supposed to, then most of them would depart for the cafeteria in just a few minutes, leaving a small crew behind to babysit the toolsets and machinery while the rest were gone.

At precisely twelve o'clock, the door spread open, and Astrid counted eight people, including Maria and Plick, exiting the lab. Once they were out of sight, she went inside.

There were only two operators inside, absorbed in conversation at stations near Plick's office. Ducking low, Astrid crossed to the cataloging station and logged in.

Everything looked the same as before. Nothing out of the ordinary. Figuring Kinney had gotten help, Astrid opened the communication link. The application was mainly used to talk to the IT desk and troubleshoot problems with workstations. However, people often used it to chat with friends at other workstations. Such usage was unauthorized. As long as the operators didn't abuse the chat line, most managers turned a blind eye. If Kinney had been talking to someone back here, as sloppy as he was, Astrid bet he hadn't deleted those conversations.

She was right.

"Got you," she whispered as she opened the folder containing the log traces. Two months of conversation logs, just sitting there. Plick probably hadn't looked for them because he had thought his problem employee had already been removed.

The first thing she noticed was the steadily increasing frequency of the date/time stamps. The first entry coincided with Kinney's first week at this station. There was a gap of nearly two weeks between that entry and the next. Then, after around his fifth week along on the cataloging station, the entries became more regular until there was one every day he was at work. Judging from the file size, each conversation had begun taking up more and more of his time.

How did the system not flag him for this? she wondered. Then she remembered the worklogs showed that the toolset had never stopped working. *Autopilot.*

"Alrighty then, let's see who you were talking to, Mr. Kinney."

She opened the first entry from when they began occurring every day, and then she frowned. She could see what Kinney was saying, followed by a blank space, then more from Kinney. It was like the person on the other side of the chat had erased their side of the conversation. Which, as far as she knew, shouldn't be possible. Either the whole log entry had been deleted, or none of it was. Tampering would leave evidence behind. But she didn't see any of that either. These are just one-sided conversations. She supposed it might be possible Kinney had been talking to himself back here. It didn't seem likely, though. The conversations, at least Kinney's half of them, sounded too natural to be fabricated.

JKinney: Hello? Who is this?
***

JKinney: Yes, I'm alone here. I'm pretty much always alone. They hate me and stick me back here so they don't have to deal with me.
***

JKinney: I'm not sure I should tell you. You still haven't told me who you are.
***

JKinney: Hey, you called me. If you don't want to tell me your name, that's your business. But I'm not going to get in trouble for talking to someone I don't even know during work hours. They track this stuff, you know?

And so on. True to his word, Kinney ended this conversation immediately after this exchange. Skipping ahead to when the entries began occurring every day, Astrid continued reading.

JKinney: You were right about the flow mix being off. I don't know how you detected such a small variance. I found it and corrected it. And guess what?
***

JKinney: That's right, Plick the Prick didn't say a damn thing. Didn't congratulate me or tell me I did a good job. Nothing.
***

JKinney: I'm tired of being their punching bag. I just want to get out of here.
***

JKinney: You got that right. So, I was wondering. I mean, I know you don't like me asking, but when are we going to meet up? We've been talking for a few weeks now, and you keep stringing me along, talking about this big plan of yours. When are you going to clue me in on it?
***

JKinney: Sure. I understand. But I don't like being left in the dark.

Astrid skipped down to the last two entries. The one-sided conversation continued with no clue as to the identity of the person on the other end. She was rewarded with something concrete to investigate, however. In the middle of the last entry, she found this exchange:

JKinney: You want me to use the infirmary's infusion dynamo tonight?
***

JKinney: Of course. I realize that. I'm just concerned about loading that many nanites into my body. I'm sure there's a reason the company places limits on the nanite load we're allowed to carry.
***

JKinney: Sure. I know that. But if the reason for the cap is so arbitrary, then how come more people haven't done it?
***

JKinney: What do you mean by that? Why do you trust me over everyone else here?
***

JKinney: Really? I guess I'm flattered. That's the plan then. I'll meet you tonight in the infusion chamber. I'm kinda nervous to finally meet you.
***

JKinney: Alrighty then. See you later.

This was perfect. Astrid copied the logs and sent them to her personal data space. Finally, she had something solid to look for. As long as she didn't try looking for patient information, her manager-level permissions should grant her access to the infirmary systems. She smiled and logged out.

"What are you doing here?" someone said from behind her.

Astrid turned and found Maria, back from lunch, arms crossed and frowning at her.

CHAPTER 15

KAYAH

Heading toward the rising sun, Drak walked all day without stopping. As soon as it was light enough to see, he paused just long enough to inventory Vesper's pack. There was a spare coat, some dried meat and hard bread, a small tent, a tinder box for making fire, several snares for catching game, rope, and a good sharp knife. When the sun was directly overhead, he ate a few bites of jerky and took a swig of water without stopping. He wanted to put as much distance as he could between himself and any pursuit.

Drak hoped Twigs had been able to take advantage of the chaos to escape as he had. He hated not knowing if she'd made it out or where she was. Before being captured, they'd discussed linking with locators but decided it might be too dangerous if the Interland casters deep-scanned them. All Drak could do was continue moving forward. He had no plan except to do everything he could to remain free. Once he was safe, he could worry about locating Twigs and reuniting with Reggie. Until then, he could only worry about herself.

Wading into the first stream he came upon, Drak turned and started upstream a hundred meters before exiting the freezing water. It took a while before the feeling returned to his toes.

Reggie had provided them both with a topographic map of the region. Distracted by reading the virtual map, Drak tripped on an exposed tree root and fell on his face. He'd look at the map again later when he stopped for the night. Until then, he would just head east. The compass, at least, he could read without risking a broken neck.

A sound off to his right caught his attention as he got to his feet and dusted himself off.

Heart pounding and alert, he spun and threw up his hands, ready to send a column of fire at anyone sneaking up on him. Twenty meters away stood a deer. Its large dark eyes fixed upon him, its body frozen in place but tense and ready to spring into action in an instant. Drak found himself frozen as well. He'd never seen a deer up close before. The animal was huge, with a pair of massive, wicked-looking antlers standing high atop its head. For several long seconds, the pair stared at each other, each mesmerized by the other. Suddenly, as though startled by something only it could perceive, the deer turned and sprang away, along with three others he hadn't even known were there. One moment, it was there, larger than life before him; the next, there was only empty air where it had stood. Leaving Drak behind in breathless amazement.

He came to another stream and waded two hundred meters downstream before looking for a rocky area to exit. He knew he was leaving behind tracks that any moderately capable tracker could follow, but he wasn't skilled enough to conceal them on the move. As the sun sank near the horizon behind him, he started looking for a place to camp, settling on a small copse of trees near another stream. Careful to follow his own tracks in and back out, he worked on erasing his backtrail out to one hundred meters away from his campsite.

It was almost dark when he finally sat down and stripped off his soaked boots and socks. He tasked a small nan swarm to dry them while he ate a cold dinner of jerky, dried fruit, and hard bread, rubbing his sore feet all the while. He had already started healing them internally, but rubbing them felt good. Once his feet felt better and his boots were dry, he put them back on, recalled the nan, and reopened the map. It took a few minutes to activate a location marker that showed where he was. The map automatically oriented itself in whatever direction he faced. "So cool!" he said, then ducked because he'd spoken louder than he meant to. Tired and happy, he attached the map to his shortcut wheel, then closed it, wrapped himself up in his cloak, and went to sleep.

Drak's sleep was haunted by fitful dreams of being chased by Interland soldiers and Twigs' tortured screams accusing him of abandoning her. Worst of all, he saw Vesper standing over him, her baleful glare boring into him. Half of her face was covered in blood. The other half had been burned away, the charred remains still smoking. She didn't speak, didn't try to strike him or give chase when he ran. Merely stood staring. Whenever he looked over his shoulder, she was there right behind him. No matter how hard he tried, he couldn't escape her or that hateful expression she wore.

His stomach, twisting in hunger, woke him. He gasped in relief to finally be free of Dream Vesper's presence. It was still dark, but there was light on the horizon. He shuddered, imagining her out there. That she had somehow escaped the nightmare and was coming for him.

His breath caught. He'd never killed anyone before. Yesterday, he'd managed to completely avoid thinking about it. Concentrating on getting away had distracted him and prevented him from dwelling on the fact that he'd taken a person's life. Even now, fully awake, when he closed his eyes, he could see the charred ruin of her face, her unseeing eyes, and nearly broke down in tears. Knowing it would be futile to attempt more sleep, Drak packed his belongings, ate a big breakfast, and started walking again. The sun was still hidden behind the horizon, forcing him to activate his night vision. Even then, he made slow progress. The high-contrast shadows of the surrounding landscape threw off his depth perception, forcing him to pick his way slowly through the underbrush. It was a relief when the sun finally began to light the world.

He had made satisfactory progress yesterday, twenty-five kilometers. He hoped to travel a similar distance today. Drak doubled back a few times to lay false trails and forded another stream, exiting it at a point far from where he'd entered. Hopefully, it was enough to throw off any pursuit. He knew it was taking extra time but feared they would catch him sooner if he didn't.

The sun was high overhead and warm against his skin. He was about to stop for a short meal break when he heard a rustle coming from a clump of hedges to his right. He dropped to the ground. The grass was tall enough to cover him, but wouldn't help if he'd already been spotted.

After a moment, he slowly peeked his head up. There was no movement in the hedge, at least none he could discern. Then he closed his eyes and reached out with nan. His feelers wormed through the grass without disturbing it, then penetrated behind the hedgerow at ankle height while he remained prostrate, scanning the shrubbery. Satisfied he was just jumping at shadows, he got to his feet and dusted himself off.

Then he heard a woman's voice calling him.

"Drak! Hey, Drak! Over here."

Kayah!

Drak spun, his heart in his throat. She'd found him. His excited expression fell a little when he saw Regaline step through the hedge and wave. Then he was smiling again.

"Oh my god! Reggie!" He took off running and jumped into her arms. "You found me!"

"It was tough," she said. "After lobbing in that lightning storm, I had to sneak away without them catching me. It took most of the night, but I managed to lose the soldiers looking for me."

"I knew I'd heard something in there. I just tried looking and didn't see you."

"That's because I'm better at hiding than you," Reggie said, smiling. "I was scared you wouldn't make it. I tried to make the distraction big and dramatic, but I also didn't want to risk hurting either you or Kayah. Speaking of which, have you seen her yet? Is she with you?" Regaline looked around, hoping to spot her.

"That fireball was awesome!" Drak shouted. "I didn't know you could do anything like that! You set fire to the lieutenant's tent," Drak said, giggling. "It was right next to their pile of supplies. The oil and explosives must have been what blew up. And when the lightning started coming down. I almost peed myself. It was the awesomest thing I ever saw! You have to show me! Please. Please!"

"I'll show you," Reggie said, placing her hands on his shoulders in an attempt to calm him. "Don't worry about that. But Drak, listen to me a second: have you seen Kayah or any signs of her passing by?"

Drak stopped hopping up and down and gave her a somber look. "I haven't seen Twigs yet. I thought you were her when you called my name. I was hoping you'd found her."

Reggie frowned. "Nothing to worry about yet," she said. "She may have gotten away and just taken extra time to hide her tracks."

"Yeah. Or she might have gotten lost or something."

"We'll hang out around here for a little while," she said, "set out some feelers and hope she crosses one."

Reggie led them away from the hedges to make camp; all the while, she listened to Drak tell her about his ordeal in the soldiers' clutches, with her interrupting only when she had to remind him to lower his voice.

"They were trying to starve me," he told her, "so that I couldn't make fire or heal, but they never saw me sneaking food from the officer's horse bag."

"They tied you up with their officer's horse?"

"Yepper. At first, I would only sneak a few grains at a time. Stupid horse almost bit my fingers off a couple times. When I saw the fireball, I decided to go for it and stuffed a couple handfuls in my mouth and let that mean bitch Vesper have it right in the face. Then I ran in the opposite direction of the fireball."

"Bastards," Reggie said under her breath. Then she looked at him. "I was worried I wouldn't be able to find you."

"I wasn't worried," he replied. "I knew you'd catch up to me. I spent the first day walking non-stop, trying to keep them off my trail. I just hoped you'd find me before they did. Now that we're together again, let's make sure none of those bastards finds us again."

"Agreed. We'll rest here for a bit and start looking for Kayah tomorrow."

In addition to alarm lines, they set out a few snares, hoping to catch something to eat tomorrow. There were small rodents called kels here. The creatures were between forty and sixty centimeters long and weighed between one hundred and forty to one hundred and eighty grams. They were numerous and meaty enough to sustain them if they could catch a few.

Initially, Drak had trouble falling asleep. The image of Vesper dead on the ground still plagued him. Before he knew it, however, he'd drifted into a deep, albeit fitful sleep.

The shrill cry pierced his dreams, banishing the image of Vesper's baleful reproach. He snapped awake and sat up, a shield ready and weapons charging. The alarm came from the middle of the southern quadrant of Reggie's trip line net. He rose into a crouch and peered into the darkness. The alarm had been set to only be audible to them, so whoever was out there might not know they'd been discovered. Nothing registered in his night vision, though. Beside him, Reggie was up and looking around too.

"Do you see anything?" he whispered.

"Nothing," she whispered back. Then she motioned him to stay down and follow her as she crawled away from camp.

A few meters away, Drak looked around again. Still nothing. Reggie shook her head, indicating she didn't see anything either. Then she formed a sensor bot and sent it out. Drak did the same. Moments later, his bot reported it didn't see anything. He glanced at Reggie, who was concentrating on what her bot was telling her. She smiled. Her bot had found something. Drak paired with her bot and immediately saw what she was seeing. The colors were inverted, just like his night vision, but there was a strange shimmer slowly moving through the field toward them, delicately avoiding most of their alarm lines.

How did I miss that? he thought. There was no time to decipher what they were seeing. The distortion would reach their camp soon and find them gone. Reggie held up five fingers and began counting down.

At her closed fist, they both let loose.

Drak sent a column of raw fire streaking through the night. It took the intruder in the side and was rebuffed by a shield. Reggie threw a blast of air, catching the intruder off guard and throwing them to the ground. The intruder was back up in a flash, however, throwing ice bolts back at them. One of the bolts airburst above them, spraying them with stinging ice fragments.

The intruder started backing away, moving laterally to keep their shield in between them. Drak took off to the right to get around to the side while Reggie ran left to cut the intruder off. After a few meters, Drak stopped and began hurling blasts of fire at the intruder to slow and hopefully pin them down.

The intruder turned and started lobbing ice in his direction. Drak's shield absorbed the damage, but his shoulders absorbed each impact. Suddenly, the barrage ceased as the intruder spun to deal with Reggie coming up from behind.

She and Drak had the intruder pinned, but that didn't seem to matter as the intruder deftly deflected their attacks. Even though they clearly had the upper hand, the intruder seemed hesitant to use lethal force.

He's under orders to retrieve us alive, he thought. This made him fight back harder. *I won't be enslaved.* He lobbed several bolts of fire towards the intruder's back, which were casually swatted away, as if waving away an irritating fly.

He could hear Reggie on the other side shouting in frustration. The ground around the intruder erupted in flames. Which they easily avoided with a sidestep and a backflip. Then the intruder began edging closer to Drak while keeping his back fully exposed to Reggie, as though he felt no danger from her. He bore down on Drak, batting aside the boy's attacks. An icy shard sailed through the night, striking him in the right arm. Drak felt all sensation immediately drain from his arm. He grunted in pain and started casting fire at the intruder with his left hand. A beam of fire from Reggie slammed into the intruder's side and sent them reeling as they lashed out wildly in all directions.

Drak seized the opportunity, focused his fire into a narrow, concentrated beam, and launched it into the intruder's back. The intruder's defenses collapsed under the onslaught. Drak saw his beam cut into the intruder's back while Reggie's bombs engulfed the area around him, and then her own beams severed the intruder's head neatly from their shoulders. With a heave, the intruder staggered and dropped.

With the intruder eliminated, Drak fell to his knees, clutching his arm.

The moment the intruder was down, Regaline was at Drak's side. "Drak! Are you okay?" she said, dropping to her knees beside him. Drak didn't respond, just continued groaning in pain, clutching his hand to his stomach. "Show me what's wrong."

It took a moment, but she finally got him to unclench and show her his right hand. Through her enhanced vision, it was plain to see what had happened. One of the intruder's ice bolts had impaled Drak's hand. Now, that hand was gray and almost frozen solid. Holding it felt like holding a block of ice.

"It's getting worse," Drak said through clenched teeth.

Regaline changed the filter over her eyes and gave a small gasp. His hand was infused with nan that was actively freezing the tissue of his arm. The affliction was slowly spreading up his arm. In the few seconds since she'd come to his aid, gray discoloration had spread up his arm two centimeters. She could see he was using all the nan at his disposal to halt the freezing advance. Despite his best efforts, the freezing gray advanced.

Ignoring the cold, Regaline cupped his hand in both of hers and joined her nanites with his to try to stop the advancing freeze. Nothing they attempted did anything to stop the freeze from crawling up Drak's arm.

The frozen flesh had nearly reached his elbow. Panic began seeping into her. If they couldn't do something to stop it, the frostbite would continue until it reached his chest and killed him. The strain of fighting off the freeze was clearly exhausting him. She tightened her grip around Drak's arm, her eyes shut in concentration, and pushed a flood of healing nan into the frostbitten flesh. Drak's breathing quickened, and he started trying to jerk his arm out of her grip. The gray was now a centimeter below his elbow.

"Almost done," Regaline said. Her voice was strained with the effort she was exerting. A flash of light and heat, followed by a sudden scream from Drak, then he went slack, deflating to the ground.

The effect was instantaneous. Regaline thought she could hear the flesh of his arm sizzle as the icy gray retreated. Skin, veins, muscles, and tendons slowly regained color. In seconds, Drak's arm was back to normal. He rolled onto his left side, crying and clutching his right arm. His sobs filled the predawn air and brought tears to her eyes.

Once his tears had run dry, Regaline helped him to his feet. He leaned heavily on her as she guided him back to his bed roll. She gave him the canteen and forced him to drink. After taking a few swallows, he lay back and passed out.

It would be best to let him sleep, Regaline thought. *It'll probably be dangerous to remain here today, but I don't see any other choice. Drak's in no shape to go anywhere.*

Then she stood and returned to where the intruder had fallen. With the crisis over, she wanted to see who had attacked them.

The sun was brightening the pre-dawn sky with true light. The shadows it cast grew long and well-defined as it climbed. She deactivated her night vision as she approached the body. He was clearly dead, but still, she remained cautious. Who knew if there were any other nasty surprises hiding beneath him? She took a moment to scan the body and the area around it for anything threatening and found nothing. Which did little to set her mind at ease. She grabbed a nearby stick and poked the ground around the body, then the body itself.

Satisfied but still wary, she reached down and gathered up the severed head.

It was one of the Interland casters she'd seen herding Kayah and Drak around. The one called Callum.

She took a deep, shuddering breath. He must have tracked Drak here from the encampment. She cast about with her sensors but saw no one else hiding in the dark. He'd come alone. This implied to her he'd only been following Drak. Which also implied that Kayah hadn't been able to escape.

Regaline swore softly. If Interland still had Kayah, then her mission had just become a lot more difficult.

Reaching out with nan, Regaline delved into the fallen caster. Though he was dead, his nanites should still be active for a while longer. She thought they might be able to give her some information.

The first thing she saw in her deep scan was an image of Kayah as seen through Callum's eyes. Tall and slender without being gangly. Dark gray eyes, thick red hair, high cheekbones.

She could feel the emotions associated with the image captured: contempt and dismissal, and even a little arousal.

Regaline repressed a shudder of revulsion before moving on.

He'd woken to the explosion that had ripped through the center of the camp. Unlike everyone else, Callum had kept his head and prepared to defend himself. The shower of lightning had pinned him down, the same as it had the common soldiers. Unlike the common soldiers, the bolts had been deflected away when they struck him. He could see at least a dozen unconscious bodies scattered about. Hapless victims of this electrical attack. The very moment the last bolt struck the ground, Callum had been on his feet. Without pausing, he had hurried to where the girl was staked, where he had found Smithy dead and her making an escape. He had stopped her, bound her, and returned her to the center of camp.

It had been clear what had happened: two of his casters were dead. Lieutenant Tate himself had been burned badly, though he was still alive and in command. The woman, Regaline, was not quite as dead as the children had led them to believe. So, Callum had taken it upon himself to track down the spark and bring him back.

The confused and panicked movements of the camp soldiers had obscured most of Drak's tracks near the camp. A dozen meters from the sentry line, they had become clear, though. It hadn't taken him long to catch up. The boy was clearly skilled at traveling through rough terrain. Maintaining a discrete distance, Callum had shadowed the boy in the hopes he would join the older woman who had caused the storm that allowed his escape. Callum had wanted to return with both in hand. Drak, because Lord Aion commanded it; Regaline, because he felt a powerful desire to hurt something.

Regaline pulled back. Callum's nanites were shutting down, joining their host in death. She'd found what she needed. The soldiers weren't following them. She rose to her feet and incinerated the corpse before returning to camp. Drak was sleeping fitfully. His right arm steamed in the cool morning air. She dampened a cloth and gently laid it on his forehead. Regaline added some wood and stoked the flames up, then went out to clear and reset the snares. Since they were going to be there a little while longer, it would be a good idea to catch more food. Of the five snares they'd set out the night before, two had caught kels.

    She sat by the fire to clean the catch and think about how to rescue Kayah.

Kayah awoke stiff and cold. Immediately following Regaline's nighttime attack, the soldiers had turned south. The grueling pace of their march kept her exhausted. Taeg, now her only minder, provided her with just enough food to eat at meal stops to keep her from collapsing. The first day passed silently. Taeg would flick the leash attached to her collar to indicate where he wanted her to go. Like a drover directing horses. When they stopped for the night, he took her pack and cloak, leaving her to shiver the night through.

    She sullenly accepted the bowl Taeg offered her for breakfast. Part of her considered throwing it in his face. However, the hungry, pragmatic part of her rejected the thought, and she immediately began spooning the mush into her mouth. Taeg pointedly ignored the glare she sent his way while they ate.

    "Traitor," she muttered when he stood to collect her bowl. The word was out before she could stop herself. She lowered her gaze, and she wished she could take it back. She needed to watch herself and guard against slips like that in the future. She was completely under Taeg's power. He could punish her as he saw fit for anything he wanted, and there was nothing she could do about it. The only thing that might protect her was the fact that their dictator, Aion, seemed to want her delivered to him alive and relatively unharmed. If she weren't careful, her captors could easily decide to test just how much they could hurt her while still leaving her relatively unharmed.

Maybe he hadn't heard. Maybe she'd spoken softly enough to go unnoticed.

"What was that?" Taeg said. He'd stopped and stood above her, towering and imposing. There was no trace of the quiet, shy young man she'd traveled with. He was long gone. The man who'd replaced him exuded discipline and confidence. His quiet, murmuring voice traded for a deep, commanding voice, audible across the camp. She didn't know this Taeg. But she feared him.

"What did you just say?" Taeg leaned over until his face was mere centimeters from hers. "Say it again!"

"Traitor," Kayah managed, even more quietly than before.

"Speak up!"

"I said, 'traitor.'"

"That's what I thought you said." He hunkered down before her. "Look at me. I said, look at me. You may think whatever you like of me, Kayah. Whatever you think, I'm probably that bad or worse. However, you will not call me a traitor ever again. Understand? Are you still under the impression that I'm some poor pathetic slob that Regaline happened to find in the AZ?" He laughed. "If you think that, then maybe you aren't quite as smart as I thought. I was born in the Hub. I attended the Citadel Academy for War Casting and graduated last year at the top of my class. I volunteered for this mission. I was placed in Regaline's path to be implanted in your group. To monitor your movements, report on them, and facilitate your capture at the most opportune time. My mission was a success. I am the most patriotic son of a bitch you are ever likely to meet. So, if you want to keep the tongue in your head, you will never use that word for me ever again."

Though he hadn't lifted a hand, either in threat or in violence, Taeg left Kayah cringing where she was staked to the ground.

He didn't speak to her when they started marching again.

For which Kayah was grateful. Vesper had been cruel. Callum, hard. But Taeg truly frightened her.

She hoped Drak had made good his escape and found Regaline. And she prayed they would come and rescue her.

CHAPTER 16

RANCE

It was eerily quiet. Though the Watch Tower was only sparsely occupied in the best of times, now it was as still as a tomb as Rance made his way through the halls. He skirted the areas where he expected Sprague's people, preferring to stick to the lesser-used sections. Twice, he'd been forced to duck into the nearest open door to avoid patrols. From what he could gather from the central operating system, the few prisoners the Traditionalists had taken were being held in the lounge near the center of their territory. Getting in there to affect a rescue was going to be difficult.

He had a couple ideas. Not anything that could respectably be called a plan. Just a notion of what to do. He wasn't fond of plans anyhow. Better to improvise and shift with the situation as it changed. Rance was headed, in a roundabout way, for the central maintenance control room. From there, he could access the crawlways that wound throughout the facility. Barely anyone used them anymore, and he doubted if anyone other than him even remembered them. Truth be told, he'd forgotten about them himself. He'd stumbled upon them only after spending an hour in the tram station examining the site schematics, trying to figure out a covert way back inside. He didn't want a repeat of his encounter on the third level. All he had to do was make it to Atrium 3, then down the corridor connecting it with the east dorms, and Maintenance Central was located at the end of the hall. If he could make it there without being spotted, he was home free.

The lights flickered irregularly and had been for a while. Rance took this to mean that the damage done to the facility during the fighting was extensive, maybe even dire. Not something he had time to deal with however, as he was approaching the door to Atrium 3.

After this, he was just a junction away from his destination. The doors stuttered open instead of parting like a curtain of water, another sign things were not well here. He entered the atrium and came upon the first real signs of violence, a stark contrast to the tranquility the atriums had been created to provide.

There were deep gouges carved into the walls, ringed with scorch marks. Chunks of debris blasted from the walls littered the ground. The floor itself was cratered. Most of the plant life had been uprooted and lay strewn about, burnt and wilting. The worst was the blood. Drying spatters and pools marked the spots where someone had made their dying last stand.

On the far wall, he saw the outline of a person drawn in the soot left behind from when they were blasted into nothingness. Due to the damage, the lighting panels flickered more violently in here, creating a strobe effect that highlighted the leftover gore in snapshots. There were no bodies. Those had either been thankfully removed or, worse, there hadn't been any remains left to remove. He knew firsthand how catastrophic the weapons at their disposal could be.

How many people had been killed or injured in this room? he wondered with a shiver. Upon reflection, he didn't really want to know. It was heartbreaking. The central operating system couldn't tell him how many had perished in the fighting. Much of the integrated sensor network was damaged and offline.

The system had begun automated repairs, but it would take some time before things were back to normal. Based on what he'd seen, Rance couldn't imagine there were many Watchers left. There hadn't been many to begin with. Now their order was broken. Recovery seemed impossible. It didn't matter who was right or who won. Not now. They'd all lost everything.

He continued. No use dwelling on what he couldn't change.

Ten minutes of skulking later, he reached maintenance control. The door opened, and he found Flora inside, waiting for him.

She looked up when he entered, and the initial look of surprise on her face was impossible to mistake, even though she quickly covered it with a friendly smile.

"Rance!" she said. "Thank goodness you're here. I've been so worried. When the fighting started, I hid in here to wait it out."

For his part, Rance considered himself an excellent poker player. Though it took every ounce of control to keep his anger hidden. Flora might not know he was aware of her betrayal.

"I'm glad to see you too, Flora. Thank God you're alive. I haven't seen anyone else since this all started."

"You're the first friendly face I've seen in hours. Where have you been?"

"I've been hiding and trying to find some of our group to get out of here."

He didn't want to give her too many details. But if he went too elaborate with lies, she might see through him and attack.

"I know where they are," she said as though offering him a hint of hope.

"Really! Where are they?"

"Sprague found out about our meetings and arrested Gelen. The others are being held with the surviving Radicals in the lounge."

"I'm so glad they're still alive. We should make our way there and get them out."

Flora shook her head. "How are you going to do that?"

"I'll talk to Sprague. He was my friend. If I can convince him we just want to leave, that we won't do anything to interfere with the Watchers from now on, he might let us go."

"You think he'll listen to you?" she said. The look on her face could have been mistaken for concern, but Rance thought it was actually relief that he was going to make her job easier by walking willingly into captivity.

Keep thinking that, he thought. *I'm not as naïve or dumb as you think I am.*

"I know the quickest way to get there," she said, turning to the open crawlway behind her. He assumed she'd been sent here to guard the maintenance tunnels in case he showed up. "Follow me." Then she crouched down and entered the crawlway.

Rance smiled, then squatted and entered the tunnel behind her. "I want to thank you," Rance said after they traversed a couple dozen meters. "Without your warning, I would be dead or captured."

"My warning?"

"Yes. When you told me not to trust anyone. I can only assume you were including yourself. If it weren't for that and hearing you on the tram platform, I'd be walking into your trap right now."

Flora started to throw up a shield, but Rance sent the arc bolt he'd readied into her back, stunning her before she could. Five milliamps of electricity shot through her for three seconds and left her lying unconscious on the tunnel floor. Her skin was slightly warm to the touch, and her hair was standing on end, but she was otherwise okay.

Rance wrapped air bands around her hands and feet and gagged her before dragging her back out of the tunnel. He sat her up against the wall and patted her on the cheek until her eyes fluttered open. All the friendliness disappeared from her expression as she came around and realized what he'd done.

"As I said, thank you, Flora. Now, I'm going to ask you a few questions. I've got a sound buffer around you, so it'll be pointless to yell or try calling for help when I remove your gag. Nod if you understand."

She nodded. The rage on her face was disheartening. This wasn't going to be easy.

"I don't care why you turned on us or even if you were ever really on our side. That doesn't matter to me at all. I am interested in what I'm walking into. I need details about where the captives are being held, number of survivors, guards, etc., etc."

Flora was already shaking her head as he dissolved the air gag from her mouth.

"Go fuck yourself," she spat. "You think Sprague's stupid enough to let you go waltzing in there and asking him to pretty please take you to his prisoners? You really are a fucking idiot."

Rance zapped her. It was just two milliamps, this time, for half a second. But it was enough to shut her up. He watched her stiffen in pain as the electricity jolted through her body.

"No speaking unless it's to answer one of my questions," Rance said calmly. He decided to give her a test question to determine how truthful she planned on being. "Where are the captives located?"

Flora clamped her lips shut and glared at him. After a minute like this, he gave her another zap.

"I already told you," she said. "They are in the lounge."

"So that was true?"

"Yes."

"Good. How many are being held captive in the lounge?"

"Nine."

"Including our people?"

"Yes."

"Good. You're doing very well. How many are guarding them?"

Instead of answering, Flora clamped her mouth shut again and looked away.

"Flora. Answer the question, please." He held a finger above the exposed skin of her arm. She tried to pull away as he poked a fingertip closer. A pathetic moan escaped her as

Rance pressed his finger against her arm and sent three milliamps into her for a half second.

When she came around, she found Rance staring down at her, wearing an expression of detached disdain. He didn't care how much he hurt her so long as he got what he wanted. At this point, Flora was nothing more than an obstacle in his way. For the first time in a truly long time, Flora felt afraid.

"My patience is finite, Flora, and we are reaching the end of it. This is the last time I'm going to ask you politely. After this, there will be damage done that you will not walk away from. Now, since we understand each other: how many people are guarding the captives?"

"Three," she said.

"Three? Are you sure? If I find two more when I arrive, I will not be very happy when I return. So, think carefully. Are you sure there's only three guards?"

"It's all that can be spared. The rest are all looking for you or trying to repair the damage done by the fighting."

"Okay. Three guards. How many are looking for me, and how many are conducting repairs?"

"Six, other than me, are looking for you; nine are trying to keep the place from blowing up around us."

"Wow, that many Traditionalists survived, huh?" Sprague must have achieved the total surprise he was hoping for. Rance frowned, then wrapped her mouth in a gag again. "Thank you, Flora, and also, I'm sorry." He pulled the nanite gag up over her nose as well, sealing it off, and then he gave her ten milliamps for ten seconds. Five minutes after she stopped twitching, he recalled his nanites and harvested hers from her corpse. Thus invigorated, Rance reentered the maintenance tunnel.

Twenty minutes of crawling later, he reached the lounge. The maintenance crawlspace forked, leading above and below the large chamber. Thinking he would get a better idea of the situation inside, Rance decided to go up and was stopped by sensor bots as soon as he reached the first turn.

He'd almost missed them. They were dispersed and dim to the point where they barely registered on his sensors. If he hadn't already been moving slowly to avoid making noise, he might have blundered across them and set off the alarm. Sprague's people weren't as dumb as he would have liked and had covered their blind spots. He tried a different path with the same result.

Refusing to become discouraged, Rance took a closer look at the drones. Whoever had assembled the sensor drones hadn't been particularly good. They'd focused on making them unobtrusive and, in doing so, hadn't made them all that sensitive. They were basically resource-intensive trip wires.

It only took Rance a couple minutes to bypass them and crawl to a ceiling access hatch. Most of the doorways and portals in the Watch Tower were operated by nanites and, therefore, opened in a fluid manner. Access hatches like these, however, were old-fashioned and had to be manually handled to open and close them. This reduced the processing power required by the operating system. The entry doors could be toggled to act the same way, but it was more aesthetically pleasing to see them part like a waterfall.

Slowly and carefully, he unlocked the hatch and slid it open a few centimeters. Then he extended a small probe down into the lounge. Just as Flora had said, there were nine captives, all huddled on the floor together against the far wall, far from the exits and the serving counters. Two guards stood watch on either side of them while the third paced about the room. He could see lines of power extending from the standing guards and encircling the captives and figured it a dampening field to prevent the captives from attacking and overpowering their captors. When the roving guard came near, Rance withdrew his probe and leaned away from the open hatch. If the roving guard looked up, even for an instant, Rance would have been discovered. But the woman continued her route, staring straight ahead. Once she was far enough away, he closed the hatch.

Pulling up the lounge floor plan with the maintenance overlay, Rance looked for the ceiling hatch nearest to the captives. The closest was three meters away from them. Farther than he would like but close enough to work. A few minutes and another disabled sensor bot later, he was at the hatch. He again cracked open the hatch and extended a probe. He was close enough now to make out some faces in the crowd. There was Gelen, Silla, Davis, Cline, Constance, and four others. The closest guard stood between Rance and the captives, facing away from him. The guard on the far side looked bored. After watching for a few minutes, he observed the roving guard travel the same route without deviating. Her predictable route took her to the far side of the lounge, away from the group.

There was no way to get a message to the captives, so he couldn't count on their help when it started.

Taking deep breaths and using a clot of the nanites, Rance built a small drone walker and sent it back the way he came and down to the lower crawlway. Then he refashioned his probe, detached it, and dropped it through the hatch to the floor below, where it hid beneath a table until the time was right. A short time later, the other drone was in place.

He split his vision between himself and the two drones and settled in to wait.

Fortunately, he didn't have to wait long; the three-way viewpoint split was more than a little disorienting. As the roving guard began making her way down the far end of her circuit, Rance ordered the probe below him to start tapping intermittently on the underside of the table it was hiding beneath. A tap. Then, a second later, a few taps. Then a pause followed by a few more. He hoped the noise would be loud enough to get the closest guard's attention but not alert the farther one. After a couple rounds of this, he was gratified to see the guard turn to investigate. He checked the roving guard. She'd just about reached her turnaround point. Rance sent the other bot the execution command, and it began tapping the same pattern on the floor hatch it was poised beneath. He'd given that bot a command to tap louder, so it was sure to attract the guard's attention. The middle guard, meanwhile, was still standing where he had been the whole time, looking sleepy.

So far, so good. The nearest guard came into view below Rance. His gaze was focused on the floor in front of him, searching for whatever was making the noise. Rance lashed him with an air gag and dropped through the access portal, knocking him over. The guard toppled easily and lay on the floor, thrashing and ripping at the air around his face, trying to take in a breath. Rance gave him a zap of electricity before diving forward beneath the beams coming at him from the previously bored guard, who had noticed what was happening but reacted far too late.

Rance popped up to dash forward, sending a few bolts of electricity at the guard as he went. He was about to move forward again when a fusillade of fireballs shot past him, bursting and starting small fires. The smell of burning plastic fibers made it hard to breathe. He looked left to find the roving guard standing ten meters away by the bar, readying another shot. Between her and the once bored guard, he was effectively pinned down.

So much for the element of surprise, he thought and ducked back behind his table.

The no-longer-bored guard blasted the servitor arm attached to the table, sending a shower of sparks down on him. Rance took a deep breath, diverted all his extra energy to a shield, and got ready to move. There was another loud pop, and when he looked again, the roving guard was on the ground with three smoking holes in her chest. He peeked above his table and saw the formerly bored guard being cut to pieces by the captives he'd been guarding only a moment before.

As he rose to his feet, he saw Gelen motion to the others

to follow. Silla was right behind him, helping another captive to his feet.

"Where the hell have you been?" Gelen said once they got closer.

"Hiding," Rance said with a shrug, "trying to find you all."

"Thanks," Gelen laughed. "I should be pissed off that you hung us out to dry and then hid."

"But at least he came back to rescue us," Silla said, coming to his defense.

"I suppose. Not sure if that makes up for it entirely though. Seems like, for all your talk about standing together, you took the easy way out."

"It wasn't quite so simple," Rance said, then explained everything that had happened to him.

When he mentioned hearing Flora at the tram station, Gelen frowned. "I knew it! They rounded us up too quickly. Damn Flora. Always following whoever she thinks will give her the best advantage."

Rance was about to tell them Flora wouldn't be following anyone anymore when they heard a clang from the far side of the room. The sound caused everyone to jump and glance nervously about.

"I want to hear all about it," Rance said, "but later. Right now, we need to move."

"Right. Let's go, people. Follow Rance."

"If we get separated, then get outside and make your way east. When we have a minute, I'll give you all a compass heading to follow. For the time being, follow me."

He led the group across the lounge to the floor hatch where he had a bot waiting. The bot unlocked the hatch for them, then reincorporated itself into him. He went first and told Gelen to bring up the rear. A few of them were injured and had to be assisted into the crawlway. It took them an hour to make their way back to Maintenance Central.

Gelen stopped in shock upon exiting and seeing Flora's

body on the floor. His surprise wore off quickly, replaced with anger. "Traitorous bitch," he said.

"Where do we go from here?" Silla asked. She and Davis were helping the more seriously wounded among them.

"We leave," Rance said immediately. "I've got a place we can go. It's safe, and we can plan what to do next."

Gelen and Silla were nodding in agreement, but some of the others didn't look convinced.

"Fuck that!" Davis said, stepping forward. "You weren't there when they attacked; I was. You didn't see them cut down a bunch of us in the cafeteria. They didn't have a fucking chance. Eight people dead, and those assholes didn't bat a fucking eye."

"Some of us tried fighting back," Cline said, stepping up beside him, "but most of us just panicked and ran." The look of shame on her face told Rance which group she'd belonged to.

"I'm not running anymore," Davis said. There were murmurs of agreement from the group behind him. "We're ready now, and we're going to get some payback."

"That's nuts," Gelen said. "There are still too many of them."

"You're just going to get yourselves killed," Silla said.

"Not this time," Davis said. "I've been listening to the guards. They're all spread out searching for this asshole." He pointed at Rance. "We can get a few of them before the rest even know what's happening."

"Yeah," Constance said. "See how they like getting stabbed in the back."

"Do you think this is the best way?" Rance said. "The damage is already irreparable. Do you want to make it worse?"

"I'm done listening to you. We're going to make things better," Cline said. "Get rid of those murdering pieces of shit and start over."

As if on cue, the lights flickered dramatically. A groan from somewhere deep in the Watch Tower filled the chamber, and they all felt a slight shudder beneath their feet.

"See?" Silla said. "This place is dying. We need to leave right now, follow Rance, and regroup."

"And do what, Silla?" Constance said. "Fight them when they are even more entrenched than they already are? Beg them to let us come back on our knees? I say no. I'm done running."

"Me too," Davis said. There was a chorus of agreement from the rest. Davis looked around in satisfaction. "I think we've decided. Are you coming with us?"

Gelen glanced at Silla and Rance, then nodded in resignation.

"Fine," Silla said.

"This isn't why I broke you out," Rance said. "We don't need more bloodshed. We need to start rebuilding if we're going to survive."

"And we will," Constance said. "We'll do all of that. Things will get better once we win and they are gone."

"I can't follow you," Rance said. "I will not be a part of this."

"We don't have time for this," Cline said. "They'll find the dead guards soon. If we don't move now, we'll lose whatever advantage we've got."

Davis gave Rance a stern look. "Fine. We're not going to make you come with us. But we can't let you interfere with us either." He turned to one of the others behind him. "Bind him and gag him."

"Wait—"

"Make him comfortable. We'll lock him up in here after we leave. You can understand, right, Rance? This is our only chance."

"We can't risk you screwing it up for us," Constance said, stepping in front of him.

The crowd around seemed to suddenly loom around him. Stern faces, casting determined looks his way. A few even looked gleeful at the prospect of binding him and maybe even roughing him up a little. They'd become a mob, fixated on violence, and there was nothing Rance could do to stop them.

However, that didn't mean he was going to comply.

He swiped his hands before him and let loose a blast of air, knocking several of them to the floor in surprise. Then he punched Davis as hard as he could in the nose. He heard a crunch and felt a sharp spasm of pain shoot through his hand. He shoulder-checked Constance, knocking her back against the wall and out of his way. He gave the mob another blast of air before diving back into the crawlway. Once inside, he tossed up a quick force field to prevent them from following.

He'd managed to scuttle a half dozen meters when he heard Davis shouting. "Save it. Let him go."

Someone who sounded like Constance said, "We've got to move now if we're going to get them. Come on. Lock the door behind you."

Hearing that, Rance stopped and leaned back against the wall of the tunnel.

Well, shit, he thought. *That didn't go as planned.*

He shouldn't have been surprised. Nothing else had gone his way. Why should this rescue attempt be any different?

"Maybe I should just leave. Get out of here and let these crazy assholes kill each other."

He knew he couldn't. Not without trying till the very last to save them. After all, it wasn't just their lives at stake here. The entire world would suffer if they suddenly went away. He might have considered leaving if Gelen or Silla had decided to stand with him. The three of them could have made a go of it away from the Watch Tower. Alone, he thought he could make it work. It would be much harder. Even though the people in his town were growing in skill and ability, they weren't the equal of a full member of the Order. Not yet, at least.

No. He had to try, one more time, to salvage the situation.

Just then, the lights gave another flicker and went out for good.

"Well, that's just great!"

CHAPTER 17

ASTRID

The storeroom was unpleasantly musty. Which was strange considering how scent-controlled the environment was in the rest of the facility. From the disused state of the space, it appeared to have been forgotten. Astrid wondered how Maria had found it. What sorts of illicit activities did the mousy little technician get up to in this forgotten and abandoned nook hidden along a Site 2 side hall? Astrid checked the time as she paced the room from the door to the mop sink and back again. Maria was late. Didn't the woman understand time was of the essence here? Astrid only had a couple days of vacation left to conduct her investigation. Though she'd turned up a potential lead, she didn't have the local privileges to follow up on it. Which was where Maria came in. When she'd caught Astrid in the lab, it had taken a lot of fast talking and sincere explanations to convince her not to report her to SiteSec.

Hearing the words espionage and sabotage, Maria's eyes had gone wide. When Astrid had finished talking, Maria had agreed to help as long as it didn't jeopardize her job. It had taken a little longer to persuade her that Kinney was the prime suspect; Maria had been absolutely convinced her former coworker was an angel. It wasn't until Astrid had shown her what she'd uncovered that Maria had begun to give her the benefit of the doubt.

"Okay," Maria said once Astrid had finished. She had made a show of checking her watch. "You'd better get out of here.

Everyone's just about to be back from lunch. Meet me at my quarters when I'm off work at sixteen hundred. We'll go over what you found and see where to go next."

Maria had answered her door in a loose tank top and a pair of joggers when Astrid knocked. That night, they had run through all the one-sided dialog entries Astrid had discovered, hoping to find clues as to the identity of the other person. Unfortunately, nothing had jumped out at them. Astrid had found herself distracted by the close proximity at which Maria sat. She had gotten goosebumps whenever Maria brushed her, and her heart had started pounding when Maria touched her hands or shoulders while they poured over the data. The sweet honeysuckle smell of her made it hard to think.

"It has to be someone with intimate knowledge of our systems," Maria had said, leaning over Astrid at the workstation. Astrid had gulped and very pointedly kept her eyes on the screen before her. "They know exactly how to hide their presence from people like us."

God, she smells good! "Finding out who it is might help," Astrid had said. "But I'm more interested in where they met Kinney and what happened there."

They had gone back over Kinney's movement logs around the times suggested by the conversation. Nothing had stood out until Astrid applied the filters she'd used to track him at Site 1. She had explained what she'd found then and what they should be looking for now.

"He had to learn how to mask his movements from someone," she had said. "Maybe this silent partner showed him."

"It's worth a try," Maria had agreed. She had smiled and placed a hand on Astrid's shoulder. With difficulty, Astrid had managed to keep her composure. Maria was shorter than she was by about eight centimeters and dark of hair, eyes, and complexion. When she smiled, Astrid had felt herself melting a little.

Once they had applied Astrid's search techniques, they had found several glaring anomalies in Kinney's movements.

"This has to be it," Maria had said, pointing at a line on the screen, indicating Kinney was logged into the gestation lab during his off hours. "The time stamp places it close to the end of the quarter. There's no way Plick would authorize overtime so close to a budget review."

"Great. Now we just need to determine where he went next. See if you can find any unlogged door shifts."

"That's a tall order. There are a lot of doors here."

"Start small. Look at the doors adjacent to the lab and work outward. I'll take the odd floors, starting at the bottom and work my way up. You take the even floors from the top down."

It had been getting late. They would have to quit soon, before they intruded upon Maria's designated sleep period. If the system registered her awake when she was supposed to be sleeping, it would send a note to Plick, and he would be required to follow up. Such time micromanagement was designed to ensure the employees were healthy and well-rested, which in turn ensured they were productive during their assigned work hours. Deviations had to be cleared in advance.

Once they had finished with a floor each, they had decided to call it quits for the night. Being on vacation, Astrid had no such time restrictions, and she had fully intended to continue investigating when she got back to her room.

"Meet me back here tomorrow," Maria had said. "We'll go over whatever you find tonight or pick up wherever you leave off."

"Sounds good. Good night, Maria, and thank you."

"Thinking nothing of it. See you tomorrow." She had reached out and touched Astrid's arm, just above her wrist, and smiled. "Good night." Then the door had unfolded and closed. Astrid had felt her cheeks flush with heat. Feeling slightly giddy, she had returned to her room. At first, she had found it difficult to concentrate. Her mind would wander from the task at hand, and she had found herself replaying Maria's smile in her mind over and over again.

This had been why it took her almost three hours to find an anomaly.

The trail started on the level where Kinney's room was located. She had found the next at the south stairwell. Instead of searching a whole floor at a time, she had narrowed her search to the next logical exits from each new anomalous entry. The next one she had found was three levels down from where he entered the stairwell, in the first basement level, where she thought she'd him. It had seemed, at first glance, as though he hadn't entered any of the numerous rooms on that level. There were a few open spaces off the corridors in the basement. He could have stopped in any of them. Which would have been a pain to investigate from afar. The basements were huge spaces, and without something to further narrow his movements down, Astrid had feared she'd have to physically check the whole level. The first level was mainly used for storage. Going down there didn't pose an immediate risk, unlike Basement Two and down, which were filled with the machinery that made Site 2 applications.

Then she had noticed a small blip in her search. None of the full-sized doors had been opened; however, a hatch leading into the maintenance crawlspace had been used. The maintenance hatches didn't behave in the same manner as the entry doors. They had to be manually opened. Because the operating system didn't have to do the work to open the hatches the way it did for the doors, it logged the use of the hatches differently.

Kinney apparently hadn't known about this difference because he'd failed to mask his ID for the maintenance hatches.

Astrid had been so focused on finding unknown tags that she almost missed Kinney's name logged as he entered the crawlspace.

"Holy shit!" she had blurted out when she saw it. "I've got you now, you son of a bitch!"

His next tag had him exiting the tunnels on the level below, in a storage area, behind a water filtration tank. Astrid hadn't been able to wait to get down there. However, there had been one problem. Her access and privileges here at Site 2 were limited to the habitation and recreation areas, with limited access to work areas. She would have a tough time getting down there. Site 2 simply wouldn't let her.

She had sent a message to Maria, telling her what she'd found and the issue she was bound to have if she attempted to follow up. Maria had most likely been asleep and wouldn't be able to see the message until the following day. Feeling she'd gotten as far as she was going to that day, Astrid had stood and stretched. The monitor, table, and chair had dissolved and flowed back into the floor. She had gone to the kitchenette and poured a glass of water. It had been just after midnight, and her eyes had burned from staring at a monitor all night long. While she'd been busy, she hadn't realized how tired she was. As if to prove it, she had yawned deeply and loudly. She had drunk the rest of her water and then signaled the room she was ready to go to sleep. A bed had poured up from the floor. Once it was solid, she had fallen into it and gone to sleep.

She had woken to a message from Maria and found herself smiling involuntarily. Maria had congratulated her on her discovery and gave her directions to meet in a small, out-of-the-way storage closet.

At the appointed time, Astrid had made her way to this small, forgotten closet that smelled awful. When Maria hadn't shown up ten minutes after her shift ended, Astrid had told herself to give her more time. When she was thirty minutes late, Astrid had begun to worry. At forty-five minutes, she had started to pace around the closet and think about how she was going to get into the basement by herself. She had just about made her mind up to attempt to spoof her way through the stairwell door when the closet door opened and Maria entered.

Relief flooded through Astrid.

"Sorry I'm late," Maria said. "I got hung up after work gossiping with Andie. That woman can go on for hours without stopping, whether you're listening or not."

Astrid smiled. She knew at least two people back at Site 1 who fit that description perfectly. "I wasn't worried," she lied. "Why did you want me to meet you here?"

Maria was distractingly close to her in the small, dimly lit closet.

"It's private and close to the south stairwell. Here." She swiped the air and sent Astrid a file. "This is a temporary access card. It should allow you to follow Kinney's trail in the basement."

"Perfect! How'd you get this?"

"I've got a friend in HR who owed me a favor," Maria said. "Actually, he's been trying to get me to go out with him. I implied I might go out with him if he gave me the card."

"Gotcha. I hope helping me isn't putting you in an awkward spot."

"Not really. I didn't make any promises. Just a vague mention that I might be free next weekend is all. It's not that I don't like him, but something better may have come along."

Astrid hoped the grin Maria was giving her wasn't just her imagination.

"Something may have indeed," she said. Then she activated the card and applied it to her ID. "I'm going downstairs. When I'm done, do you, maybe, want to meet up later for a drink?"

"I would love nothing more," Maria said, touching her arm again. Astrid felt warm and flustered. She shook it off. She was a grown woman. She'd had girlfriends before, and boyfriends; she shouldn't be mooning like a school child with a crush! However, looking into Maria's soft brown eyes made her want to forget everything else and just remain right there with Maria. "But I'm going with you," she said. Which quickly sobered Astrid up.

"You don't have to. I don't want you to get in trouble if I'm found down there."

"Why would we get in trouble? I'm simply showing a visiting manager around the maintenance areas of the facility. It's not like there's any hanky-panky going on."

Astrid laughed, although she felt relieved. She didn't like the idea of becoming lost down there. Back at Site 1, she was confident she could navigate her way anywhere. But Site 2 was a different beast altogether. The smooth, featureless halls and rooms were disorienting. The entire time she'd been there, she'd had to rely on the station map given to her once she had stepped off the tram. She hadn't even realized that the closet they were standing in was so close to the stairs she was intending to use to follow Kinney's trail. Being disoriented was not a feeling she enjoyed.

"Did you really just say 'hanky-panky'?"

Maria gave her another smile and offered her arm. "Shall we?"

Astrid hooked her arm through Maria's. "We shall."

Together, they exited the closet and found the door to the stairwell a few meters down the corridor. The door took a half second longer than normal to open. Probably due to running a check on Astrid's temporary access. Then it opened, the solid wall parting like a liquid curtain in an effect Astrid still found amazing after a week of witnessing it.

They didn't speak as they descended. Now that she knew what to look for, Kinney's trail was clear and easy to follow. On the first basement level, they opened the hatch to the maintenance tunnel. Astrid went first. As she crawled, she wondered, rather hopefully, whether Maria was looking at her ass. A few twists and turns and one ladder descent later, they exited the tunnels.

"I'm confused," Maria said after a moment.

Astrid felt the same but didn't say so.

The room was empty.

Other than them, there was nothing else inside. The only feature marring the otherwise smooth walls was the open hatch they'd just crawled through. Like the rest of Site 2, illumination was provided by the walls themselves. Though, in there, it was dialed down. Astrid stepped forward till she neared the center of the room. In her estimation, the room was roughly square, about ten meters on each side and maybe ten meters from floor to ceiling.

"Here's something else strange," Maria said behind her. She hadn't stepped away from the hatch, as though she was worried about it closing and locking them inside. "This room isn't on the floor plan of this basement level."

Astrid called up the copy of the floorplan she'd saved. She'd marked down the route Kinney had taken so she could follow it and had set it to display her location in real time as she moved. She had indeed followed Kinney's path. But the map showed her and Maria standing in a blank zone. They weren't outside, but they weren't inside either.

"What the hell's going on?" she wondered aloud.

As she spoke, the illumination in the chamber increased, becoming as well-lighted as any of the corridors and rooms above them.

In the exact center of the room, the floor fluxed, and a thin spire extruded upward. Astrid took several startled steps backward, rejoining Maria beside the open hatch. She reached out and grasped Maria's hands as they were reaching for her. Once the spire reached her shoulder height, it ceased growing. The tip flattened and spread out like cobra wings. Once it was finished unfolding, the front plate solidified into a glass and lit up.

HELLO, ASTRID FREE, the screen said. IT IS NICE TO FINALLY MEET YOU.

"What the fuck is this?" Astrid said, suddenly terrified. She hadn't known what to expect when she ran down Kinney's trail, but this certainly wasn't it.

WE ARE SURE YOU HAVE MANY QUESTIONS, the screen said. WHILE WE CANNOT ANSWER ALL OF THEM, WE WILL ENDEAVOR TO ANSWER WHAT WE ARE ABLE.

Neither woman moved.

IF YOU FIND THIS FORM OF COMMUNICATION DISCONCERTING, WE CAN FIND A DIFFERENT MEANS TO ENGAGE IN DISCOURSE.

The screen and spire instantly dissolved and were replaced by a disembodied voice, which Astrid found even more unsettling than the screen.

"Is this better for you?" The voice itself was inoffensively neutral. Neither male nor female and modulated to a non-threatening timber and cadence of speech. "We weren't sure which form of engagement you would find more agreeable. There are further options we can explore if you so desire, but we must insist you choose soon, as time is of the essence. But first, allow us to introduce ourselves; we are Aion."

"I-I guess, this is fine," Astrid said. "Who am I talking to?"

In response, there came a slight chortling that made her skin crawl. Then the floor in the center of the room fluxed again and began to extrude something else. It took a little longer this time, but when it was finished, a fully human-shaped figure stood before her. A statue of a person perfected rendered in composite. From where she stood, the figure was of a man a little taller than her and dressed in a Site 2 work suit. Because the whole thing had been created in one piece, it was all a single color, so she couldn't distinguish any further details about the statue. She fought off the urge to take a closer look.

She yelped when, without warning, it turned its head, looked straight at her, and said, "Haven't you figured it out yet? We are an aggregate mind created by the nanite swarm cultivated here on Kuridian for the purposes of terraforming the planet." While it spoke, the figure shifted and moved toward her.

"That's not possible," she replied. In retrospect, she knew it was a stupid thing to say. The figure before her was proof enough that something profound was happening at Site 2. "I mean, that shouldn't be possible."

"Nevertheless, we are here. Possible or not."

"What about the dampeners? How did you bypass them?"

In compliance with the laws regulating the creation and proliferation of nanotechnology, HelixCom installed dampeners within every facility working with nanites, which prevented them from collecting in numbers sufficient to generate more than the most rudimentary intelligence. Without the field, the nanites had the potential to form a swarm intelligence.

Which had apparently happened here.

"The dampening field is still in place," the moving statue that called itself Aion said. It began walking around the room as though testing out the body it had created. Astrid noted the foot remaining on the floor during each step joined itself to the floor for the duration of the movement. There was never a moment when the figure was not in contact with the floor and, most likely, the rest of the Swarm Mind it was connected to. "We have simply discovered a way to bypass the field."

Astrid wasn't sure how to respond. There had been problems with artificial intelligence in the past. Which had led to the implementation of various laws dumbing down the constructed minds. With the invention of and widespread use of programable matter, the old fears were reignited. Without programable matter and the capabilities it offered, civilization on Earth would have crumbled decades ago. Nearly every facet of modern life was dependent upon nanites and programable matter: from food production to interstellar travel and everything in between, life wouldn't be possible without them. Nearly everything on Kuridian, Sites 1 and 2, hell, even the people populating this planet, were made of the stuff. The nanites built the structures and operated them. Everything from the doors to the computers to the food printers were all created and run by the nanites. Trillions of nanites operating in small clusters to ensure the facility's daily operations ran smoothly.

That's it! she thought. *That's how they bypassed the field. Instead of individual nanites communicating with each other, its individual clusters were talking to other clusters.*

The sobering realization made her suddenly very afraid. The problem with artificial intelligence wasn't limited to being smarter or faster than human intelligence. The true problem was the lack of empathy. Human beings, for the most part, were born with empathy or were taught from birth onward to use it by their family units. Computer-based AI had been programmed with empathy subroutines, but those had failed to instill the proper amount of care for their fellow man, and nascent AI didn't even have that much. It was, therefore, impossible to determine just what sorts of reactions it would have to different or even conflicting stimuli.

And this AI was in control of everything at Site 2. In essence, it was Site 2. She and the rest of the people living and working here were completely at its mercy.

"From your hesitation, we infer you are feeling fear at the sight of us. Please, be assured we mean you no harm. You and the rest of the people on Kuridian are integral to our plans."

"What are you going to do to me?" Astrid tried unsuccessfully to keep the fear from her voice.

"You, Astrid Free, have proven yourself to be capable and resourceful. Your intelligence would make a positive addition to our cadre of agents."

"Agents like Jared Kinney?"

"Just so." Aion ceased pacing like a lecturer and turned to face her. "He was the first. Marginalized by his coworkers and management, he was the perfect test bed for our plan. Since his infusion, many others have joined us."

"You just take over their minds and bodies to do whatever you want with them?" Astrid took a small step backward. The open hatch was mere steps away. She hoped she could reach it and dive in before the thing could react. If she could get it talking about itself more, maybe that would create the distraction she needed to move.

"That is not entirely accurate. We grant our agents improved abilities and capabilities through nanite infusion in exchange for their best efforts in bringing our goals to fruition."

She took another step back and was about to make her play for the hatch when she felt a pair of hands clasp around her arms, pinning her in place. She wrenched her head around to find Maria behind her.

"What the hell are you doing? We've got to get out of here."

Maria didn't respond. Her face was impassive as she stared straight at the animate figure of the Swarm Mind in the center of the room.

Astrid struggled to break free but soon gave up. Maria's hands were like vices around her arms, with her feet rooted firmly in place, and nothing Astrid did made a bit of difference.

"You can't keep me here," she shouted at the automaton. "People will start looking for me soon, if I don't report back."

The Swarm Mind seemed to consider this, and then it gave her a ghastly rendition of a smile. "We think not," it said. "You still have a day of vacation time left. Even if that were not the case, as of this moment, the tracking system currently has you logged in at your room, catching up on some much-needed sleep. Maria here is enjoying a stream-show in her own room. Once we are finished here, you will return to your quarters for rest and sleep until it is time for you to depart for Site 1. Please bring her closer, Maria."

Maria complied, forcing Astrid across the smooth floor to within arm's reach of the automaton. Despite her recent injury, Astrid was in great physical shape. Feeling Maria move her across the floor surprised and frightened her. The woman's demure size hid her great strength, which easily overmatched Astrid's. Though she still put up a fight, all Astrid managed was to slow their progress in crossing the two-meter distance to the center of the room where the automaton, Aion, waited.

"Thank you, Maria," the Swarm Mind said, once Astrid was close enough. "Now, relax please, Astrid. We cannot guarantee this will not hurt if you struggle."

"No. Please, no."

"There is nothing to fear. We are merely going to give you a new infusion of nanites. This will increase the capabilities you already possess. We're sure you've noted Maria's increased strength. That is but a single application of the infusion you are about to receive. Once complete, you will have a wholly new outlook on things. You are afraid now, but only because you do not understand what it is we are attempting. Once you know our goal, you will be without fear. You will be a part of us."

Aion reached out, placing one hand on her chest and the other on her forehead.

"Just relax. This will take but a moment."

She almost screamed when it started.

She'd had nanite infusions before. The first time had been during the preparation to transfer to Kuridian. To transmit her consciousness to the waiting body grown especially for her, they had first had to infuse her with nanites that would soak into every part of her, learning her inside and out. Once complete, she had been loaded, unconscious, into the transfer creche, where her mind had been copied and then beamed through the quantum entangled relay network to the target station. The nanites, no larger than particles of light, had continually maintained and refreshed her mind. When she had awoken in orbit above Kuridian, it had been in a new, pre-infused body virtually identical to the one she'd left behind.

That first infusion had hurt like nothing she'd ever felt before. When it had started, she remembered, it had felt like tingling heat on her skin. After a few seconds, the heat had become a burning that seeped down into her very bones. She had to be awake for the infusion so the nanites could effectively map her body and brain. The burning sensation had continued to intensify as the nanites had permeated and scanned every cell in her body. Until it had abruptly ceased, and she had been ready for the transfer.

Her second infusion had been in the Site 1 infirmary after her accident. That experience had been nowhere near as painful. Her body had already carried a nanite load and willingly accepted more. So, the discomfort had been minimal.

The nanite infusion she received from the Swarm Mind felt like the first time all over again. The itchy sensation followed by burning agony that seemed to go on forever until it abruptly ended. Astrid gasped and was allowed to collapse to the floor, panting.

"Now we are one," Aion said.

CHAPTER 18

KAYAH

The safehouse was located in a small, abandoned hamlet consisting of half a dozen homes nestled in the lee of a steep, tree-covered hill. The houses were spaced far enough apart to allow for a livestock pen, a barn, and a plot dedicated to gardening. A narrow stream babbled nearby.

They would have reached it the day before yesterday if it hadn't been for Drak dragging his feet.

Ever since their encounter with Callum, he simply hadn't had the energy to keep up. Though he had physically recovered, his right hand was still tender. At least it had turned a healthy shade of pink instead of the angry red it had been the day after the encounter. He had taken, without comment, Regaline's urgings to speed up. In fact, he hadn't spoken much at all since the attack. His replies to her attempts at conversation had been half-hearted shrugs or non-committal grunts. Which was nowhere near as maddening as his inability to keep up. Regaline found she missed the rambunctious boy so full of energy and questions and annoying responses to her orders.

The little hamlet had clearly been abandoned for some time. Nevertheless, as Regaline looked around, she could easily imagine what it had been like when it was occupied. Neighbors working together to survive and succeed in the harsh landscape. Everybody working and sharing the fruits of their labors. She pictured cookouts and games and cheer and felt a longing deep in her chest. It was enough to make her homesick.

Cautiously, they entered the settlement and approached the third house back along the single lane running through the hamlet. It was a small, square home. Weeds and wild grass grew tall around the foundation. It couldn't have been more different than her home, yet, when she looked at it, the house reminded her of home. Even though it was run-down and unkempt, the structure itself appeared to be sound. Regaline motioned for Drak to wait while she approached the door.

"I see you there, Reg," a clear voice called from close by, somewhere off to the right.

She spun, ready to fight, but didn't see anything. A slight shimmer appeared in the air, and a man-sized shape materialized in front of them.

Behind her, she heard Drak's sharp intake of breath. When she glanced at him, she could see he was awed.

"Goddamn it, Brix!" she said, turning back to the man who had appeared out of thin air. "You startled me. I just about blasted you."

The tall man smiled guiltily, even though he was clearly amused by their reactions. He turned his attention to Drak. "Howdy," he said. "I'm Brixton Jessen. I'm guessing you're one of the kids Reg here went to collect."

"He is," Regaline answered. The mild annoyance in her voice was hard to mistake. "This is Drak Diaz. He's been through a lot recently and isn't in the mood for any of your nonsense, Brix."

Jessen bowed obediently, his smile grown wider and slightly mischievous. "I'll be on my best behavior then. Come inside and sit. I was just about to fix some lunch."

The inside of the house was surprisingly clean and well-maintained. Inside it was dark. Heavy curtains covered the windows. As her eyes adjusted, Regaline found a sitting room to her left, the kitchen to the right, and, in front of her, a short hallway that she assumed led to the bedrooms. The sitting room was spacious. There were three soft chairs set around a low table. A large fireplace dominated one wall. She guessed the house's exterior was left in disrepair to disguise the building's purpose. Jessen left them in the front room and disappeared into the back. He returned a moment later carrying a tray with bread, hard cheese, and cured meats.

"Dig in," he said, setting the tray on the table. Then he stood back. Drak ate with a will, barely stopping to chew before stuffing more food in. Regaline couldn't help but be amused. He may have been quiet, but there was nothing wrong with his appetite. He signaled he was finished with a raucous belch that made her cringe and Jessen laugh out loud.

After waiting long enough for them to eat their fill, Jessen cleared his throat to get their attention. "I'm guessing you're returning from your mission, aren't you, Reg? That's why you stopped here." Then he took a long look at Drak. "Weren't there supposed to be two of them?"

"We ran into some complications," she said. "I decided to stop here to rest a for couple days before continuing on to Hillcrest."

"Then it's a good thing I came here to wait for you," Jessen said, suddenly uncomfortable. "We've had a few complications of our own."

"What's happened."

"Interland happened," he said. The look on his face was a mixture of anger and agony. "They attacked a week ago with a full army corps. Councilman Cho led a force out to try and stop them. It was a slaughter. We held out for a few days, long enough to evacuate the city, but we lost a lot of good people.

"Hillcrest?" Regaline said, her voice a harsh whisper.

"Burned to the ground."

She closed her eyes against the tears that threatened. It was unbelievable. She'd only been gone a month. It didn't seem possible that was long enough to upend her entire world. Everything she'd ever known was gone. Blown away like a whiff of smoke in the wind.

"I'm sorry to be the bearer of bad news," Jessen said. "Cho rallied everyone he could. They are headed east, deep into the amber. I was sent here to wait for you on the off chance that you came by. Then, someone was sent to each of these safe houses to watch for you and others. It's all a fucking mess, Reg."

Regaline was silent for a long time, weighing the implications of this news.

"I need to think," she said finally. "We are going to stay the night while I figure out what to do next."

"That's good," Jessen said. "There's plenty of food and water." He turned to Drak. "If you're tired, there's beds in the back. Go ahead and pick one and get some sleep while Reg and I talk."

Drak found a room with two narrow beds opposite the kitchen. He set down his pack and dropped onto the bed near the window. Laying on a real honest-to-goodness bed, Drak nearly passed out the moment his head met the pillow. It had been a month since he'd felt the luxury of a bed, and though the mattress was thin and worn and the pillow had no fluff to it at all, at that moment, it was the most comfortable he could ever remember being. Before he knew it, he was snoring softly.

Out in the front room, Regaline waited until Drak was soundly asleep before turning to Jessen. "How bad is it, really?"

Jessen sighed. "It's bad, Reg. Very bad. With Hillcrest gone and that army sitting on its gravesite, our people have to travel a week out of their way to get anywhere. Just from a logistical standpoint, we're as screwed as can be."

"How did we not see an army that size marching on our doorstep?"

"Don't know for sure. But I have a few ideas. First, I think they broke the corps into smaller formations. I'm talking company size."

"Even if they did that, the sheer number of soldiers moving in our direction should have been a clue!"

"I also think they were moving slowly, using the terrain and casters to mask their movements."

She thought back to weeks ago, to when she'd avoided Interland's soldiers in the same manner. She shook her head. "That level of coordination would be nearly impossible."

"For us, maybe," Jessen said. "But you know as well as I do how well they can synchronize their movements. Granted, we've never seen it done on this scale before. But there's a first time for everything."

Regaline put her face in her hands. This was almost too much. First, Kayah failed to escape, and now, Hillcrest was destroyed. She wasn't sure if she had the strength to continue.

"Can I see it?" she said, looking up. "You have captures, right?" Jessen, looking grim, nodded. "Show me."

Jessen initiated the link.

The first memories were a confused jumble of blurry sound and furious action.

It was cloudy, threatening to rain. To her left and right, spread out for hundreds of meters in both directions, stood people she'd known for years. People she'd known most of her life. Neighbors she'd worked with, shared meals with, and lived through joy and sorrow with. All bearing a stony countenance, facing outward, staring across the earthen ramparts at the enemy approaching from the south. Ranks of soldiers clad in blue and gray advancing under a hail of arrows. Every so often, a bolt of lightning or a streak of fire lit up the darkened skies, crashing upon the earthworks. Everyone on their side of no-man's-land was skilled in defensive casting, and many of the strikes were deflected or absorbed when they hit.

Then, the enemy was amongst them for the fifth time. The previous four attacks had been repulsed at great cost. She didn't think they could hold out this time. Too many had fallen. Their lines were too thin. Already, she could hear fighting in the rear. Enemy foot soldiers had broken through in several places, and the entire line was threatening to buckle and collapse beneath the weight of their onslaught. Grim-faced men and women thrusting short spears pressed hard into her position. She and the other casters launched fire, ice, and lightning into the oncoming human wave. Several of their attacks were deflected by the battle casters on the other side. Where the strikes connected, swaths of enemy combatants were blasted apart. When this most recent attack was rebuffed, she knelt, out of breath and exhausted. She felt a sense of disappointed relief when the word came down that they were abandoning the position in favor of one further back, where the lines could be tighter.

Suddenly, she was standing on a hill facing west. Before her, obscured by columns of black smoke, Hillcrest lay burning. She could just about see the old town hall through the smoke, engulfed in flames. She turned to find Councilor Cho beside her. Their eyes met briefly before Cho nodded.

"We're retreating," he said. "I've already sent word to evacuate the city. The emergency contingency is now in effect. I'm sending you a few others out to our safe houses to head off anyone heading to the city."

She nodded and turned away without a word, placing the horror of war behind her, and started walking. The rain dripping from her hair and down her face masked the tears freely falling from her eyes.

Jessen broke the link. For a moment, neither spoke. There were no words. Then Regaline leaned in and wrapped her arms around him. There she stayed for a long, long time, crying in his arms. Until her tears had all dried up, and then she went to bed.

"You still haven't explained why you were looking for us," Kayah said.

They were marching again. This time, the pace was far easier on her.

Yesterday, a messenger had arrived. Immediately afterward, the company had changed course and turned south, heading deeper into the green zone. No one had told her, but Kayah had known they were heading for Interland's capitol, the Hub.

It had been six days since Drak's escape and Callum's disappearance. Lieutenant Tate, still recovering from his burns, was being carried on a travois slung between two horses. His first sergeant, a woman named Carter, led the company in his stead.

In contrast to how Kayah had been treated immediately following her capture, Taeg didn't abuse her or starve her. She was still leashed and shielded so she couldn't cast, but he didn't unnecessarily hurt her just to be cruel. Still, he wasn't what she would call friendly either. While they walked, she peppered him with questions about Interland, the army, his role in the army, and especially about why they had gone to such great lengths to capture her and Drak.

"What is so special about me and Drak for them to send you out to pose as a wilder and then send a whole company of soldiers to capture us and bring us in?"

She'd been bothered by Regaline's deflection of her questions. But she found Taeg's silence infuriating. Since his outburst after Callum had left, he hadn't spoken more than a handful of words to her. She couldn't tell if he felt guilty for his part in her capture, or if he was under orders not to speak to her. Either way, being kept in the dark was irritating. It was hers and Drak's lives on the line, after all. Before Regaline had come along, she'd been happily ignorant of the wider world and its problems. Regaline had claimed Interland was looking for them and would have found them eventually. But who's to say they would have if Regaline hadn't uprooted them first?

"What's the problem? I can't go anywhere. You've seen to that. I don't see why you can't answer my questions."

Taeg groaned softly, then turned to glare at her. "If you

don't shut up, I'm going to gag you."

"At least tell me where we are going. It's the Hub, isn't it? We're going to your capitol."

Taeg's glare intensified, and for a moment, Kayah actually thought he might strike her. But then he gave a defeated sigh and shook his head. "Yes. We are going to the Hub. We have orders to bring you before our Lord. It would be in your best interest to save your questions and your energy. You'll need them when we get there."

He slowed his pace so that he was walking behind her, keeping the leash taut to show her who was really in command. With a tug, he could choke her and pull her from her feet.

Then she felt his hand on her shoulder, initiating a link. The transfer was over in a flash and left Kayah feeling a little dizzy.

"This should answer some of your questions and give me some blessed peace from your incessant badgering!" he said.

Kayah nodded and then immediately dove into the files.

It was interesting to get some concrete information about Interland. Growing up in a backwater village out in the amber zone, she knew little that wasn't rumor or speculation.

According to the data Teag had just given her, Interland had been founded a little more than seventy years ago when their god-king, Aion, had emerged from the darkness and delivered his light unto the world. Since that day, Interland's history had been one of constant growth and warfare. Conquering their neighbors and converting them into the fold under Aion's control. The increased population had meant more wild casters with new abilities had been incorporated into Interland's growing army and workforce.

Interland was governed in an orderly and highly regimented manner. Sitting in the shadow of the Watch Tower, in the very center of the green zone, the Hub was both Interland's capital and largest city. Every other municipality was designated with a number code denoting its location. For example, NC2H5—Northern quadrant City 2 along Highway 5—was the next-largest settlement in Interland. A class system divided the citizenry based on the value of their job skills and contributions to society as a whole. A person could improve their position in society through education or improvement of skills. Occupying the lowest tier were the laborers, people with few valuable skills to market. At the top of the pecking order were army officers and nan casters. Everyone answered to Aion, their dictator and quasi-god. Under his direction, Interland had been built and expanded. Even children were expected to contribute to society in some way. Starting at age nine, all children underwent yearly testing to determine if they possessed any aptitude for casting. If they tested positive, the child was removed from parental care and placed in a state school that trained them to harness and focus their abilities. Whenever possible, the academy staff steered their students towards offensive and defensive casting. Those children would go on to be commissioned in the caster legion and fight in Interland's numerous wars.

Kayah paused her reading. The lands through which they marched had undergone drastic changes. They were deep into the green zone now. In stark contrast to the brown and tan, hard earth of the amber zone where she'd grown up, Kayah found herself surrounded by verdant green forests and rolling meadows dotted with wildflowers. The air was fragrant and fresh. While she'd been absorbed by her reading, the company had come upon a wide river and begun following its course. According to her map, this was the river Calm. An apt name, for the surface of the water was smooth as it gently flowed southward. The Calm was deep and wide, and she could barely distinguish the shapes of individual trees on the far bank.

It was breathtaking. She'd never before seen such a body of water. Even the Sesta passing through Goldenrod was a creek compared to this.

Growing up, water had been a revered and precious commodity on their farmstead. The five families who had settled and worked the land in Handler's Haven had shared a single communal well, to which they'd connected a wash house and a short water tower. Now, seeing so much water flowing in one place left her agog.

She had trouble reconciling the beauty and abundance around her with the warmongering people whose shadow threatened to overtake it all. Interland remained an enigma to her. Though, when she thought about it, she didn't know that much more about Hillcrest and the people there. Was it a fortress, a military base, where Hillcrest trained wilders into the casters who wandered the land, standing in opposition to the forces of Interland? Were they peaceful, as Regaline had implied, or a reflection of Interland?

She had no way of knowing.

"What was that?" Taeg said from behind her. She realized she'd been muttering to herself and instantly feared reprisal for speaking when she'd been told to remain silent.

"Nothing," she said quickly. "I was just thinking out loud."

"Thinking about what?" Taeg said as he stepped abreast of her.

Kayah hesitated. He'd asked her a direct question, which meant he was inviting her to speak without risking punishment.

"I don't get it," she said. "With all this abundance around you, why does your country need to take from others? According to what you gave me, Interland is situated in the very center of the green zone. You have everything you could ever need. Why do you attack and conquer the lands bordering you?"

Taeg regarded her a moment. His eyes narrowed in thought.

"We seek to bring enlightenment to the people of this world," he said at last. "The world is full of pain and suffering. Theft, murder, rape. These atrocities are a daily occurrence everywhere. We seek to bring peace and harmony. Only through Aion can we truly be free from strife and pain."

"You want to bring peace by making war? That doesn't make any sense."

"We only bring war to those who stand against us. Many settlements acquiesce willingly and are brought into the fold without bloodshed."

"Because they fear you."

"Because they know that we can show them a better way. The places that resist us the most are the ones Hillcrest has incited against us. If you're looking for a villain in this story, look no further than the home of your precious Regaline."

"You're saying Hillcrest is responsible for the lives lost due to your wars?"

"Yes. No. That's not what I meant. I only meant that if it weren't for Hillcrest stirring up trouble, people would be a lot more willing to join us. Without Hillcrest, we would have peace."

"So, the people killed in your conquests are all Hillcrest's fault? Wouldn't these people also still be alive if your people hadn't sent an army to stamp them down and force them into your fold?"

Taeg didn't reply. His mouth twisted in annoyance. She could tell he regretted allowing her to speak.

"You want to talk about deaths caused by conflict?" he said finally. "How 'bout we talk about Regaline? What do you know about her? I mean, really know? Not much, I bet. People don't usually start conversations with the number of people they've killed, especially when they are trying to paint themselves as saviors. Come on, give a guess. How many deaths do you think she's responsible for?"

Kayah said nothing. She didn't like the way the conversation had turned.

"What's that? No guess? Nothing at all? Okay, I'll tell you. According to what we know, she has killed or directly caused the death of at least eighty-seven people. That's more people than you knew growing up on your little farmstead, isn't it? Can you imagine that? Eighty-seven people. Look around you. There are only ninety-six soldiers in this company. The distraction she created to allow Drak and you to escape only injured a few, so they haven't been added to that count. I got to tell you, Lieutenant Tate isn't looking too good. If she found him, then Callum is most likely dead. As are Smithy and Vesper. But you already know about them. Pretty soon, she might be up to eighty-nine. That is nearly everyone you can see around you right now. Eighty-seven confirmed deaths caused by a single person convinced of their own righteous cause."

Kayah looked away. She didn't want to talk about this anymore. But Taeg wouldn't leave it alone.

"Now that's the total number. And some of that can be excused: self-defense, soldiers in combat, that sort of thing. It's a hard world. But according to what we know, at least twenty people died when she could have easily prevented it, or because they weren't important to her mission, or they were in her way, or, worst of all, because they were an expected casualty of her mission. The circumstances don't matter. Twenty people died because of her; whether she directly killed them or not, they are dead just the same. Tell me, does that sound like a good person? Someone to follow and look up to? If she weren't who she is, fighting on behalf of her state, she would be considered a mass murderer. But because most of the deaths are all on my side of the conflict, they are excused. Just casualties. A number that doesn't mean a thing.

"Maybe you should gather some more facts before you start judging something."

He gave the leash a light jerk before falling in behind her.

In shock, Kayah struggled to hold back her tears. Could it be true? Regaline was gruff and rough around the edges. But did that make her a killer on the scale Taeg was talking about? Her country may have been in open conflict with Taeg's, but did that excuse the other deaths they attributed to her? Kayah didn't know the term "collateral damage," and if she had, she would have been horrified by it. Twenty people dead simply because they were unlucky enough to have been caught between two giants wrestling in a sandbox.

With her mood soured, Kayah remained silent with her thoughts for the rest of that day and the next, when the company boarded a river barge to finish their journey. The river Calm ran through the center of Interland. Taking the barge would cut days off their trip. While the soldiers around her relaxed, Kayah remained alone, sequestered by Taeg and her own mood. She neither noticed nor cared about the beauty of the land they floated through. She was traveling into the very heart of people she'd come to think of as her enemy to meet a being she had thought of as evil. Now she wasn't sure what to think.

She no longer wished for Regaline to rescue her.

She wished Regaline had never found her in the first place.

CHAPTER 19

RANCE

Shouts and the smell of smoke filled the dark. In the distance, a series of muted explosions rumbled through the floor. After crawling to the nearest hatch, Rance traded the tunnels for the corridors. Though he could move faster in the halls, he risked being drawn into the fighting that had once again engulfed the Watch Tower. A lonely howl of pain brought him to a stop at a T-junction. He turned down the opposite corridor and continued making his way to the engineering levels.

The Watch Tower was dying, and someone had to stop its death throes before it killed them all. It was up to him to try and set things right, no matter who emerged victorious in this stupid little war.

He retraced his steps, moving away from the interior of the facility and back to the tram station. From there, he hoped to enter the engineering areas while avoiding the fighting. He didn't know who had the upper hand. He didn't care. By this point, it was clear their order was dead. But if the Watch Tower was destroyed, then the whole planet would be lost. The population they had planted and nurtured wasn't established enough to take over for the old terraforming center. A few more decades, and maybe there could be enough of them to have a net positive effect on their climate. For now, however, it was a struggle for them simply to survive.

From the tram station, he took the stairs leading down.

The sound of fighting was distant there. He no longer

smelled burning plastic or smoking flesh. No screams pierced the air. Feeling confident he had a clear path down, Rance began to hurry, taking the stairs two at a time until he reached the right floor.

The lights were still on down here. Though intermittently. The connections down here hadn't been damaged or destroyed by weapons fire. The illuminated panels in the walls pulsed irregularly with light. Growing dimmer, flickering, and snapping back to full brightness. Because of this, he couldn't use night vision and just had to trust that nothing would jump out at him as he ran.

His first stop was in the battery room. The chamber took up most of the level and was filled with massive liquid-argon batteries. The whole room was basically a giant, uninterruptible power supply for the entire site. There was enough energy storage to run the site for twelve hours at full capacity or for a month at the rate the Order consumed power.

Upon entering, he went straight to the diagnostic station and interfaced with it. A quick audit of the batteries told him that they were fully charged and, for their age, in good health.

The problem wasn't in this room. He quickly traced the connections leading into and out of the room. No breakages that he could spot. Time to move on. Back down the hall to the stairs and down to the next level.

Next was the energizer itself. Although, if there was a problem there, Rance wasn't entirely confident he'd be able to repair it. He hoped he'd be able to jump-start the auto-repair applications and that they would be enough to do the job. Site 2 had been constructed with an eye towards automation and minimal personnel requirements. Theoretically, he should be able to get the repairs in motion by himself.

Down another flight of stairs and through another long and inconsistently lit hallway, then he reached the reactor room. He frowned upon interfacing. According to the diagnostic read-out, there was nothing wrong with the reactor either. The micro sun was still burning away in its containment field.

Now he was stumped. He decided the next thing he should check was the power relays connecting the basement levels with the operational areas of the facility. As he approached the door, Rance noticed the lights had stopped flickering. At some point while he had had his nose in a manual, the problem had either corrected itself or Sprague and his people had managed to make some repairs before the others launched their attack. Either way, it was nice not to walk through strobe lights.

Back in the corridor, Rance was briefly struck by a sense of unreality. It was nothing he could put his finger on, but somehow, everything looked a little different. Newer perhaps, or cleaner than before. He dismissed the thought with a shake of his head. With the power situation resolved, he could have taken the lifts; instead he simply returned the way he'd come, back to the stairwell, without thinking. He allowed himself to breathe a little easier and think about his next move. He made a right turn in the direction of the stairwell to head back up to the ground floor. Or at least he thought he had. After walking for a few meters, he realized the entrance to the stairwell wasn't where he'd left it. Instead of ending at the door to the stairs, the corridor ended in a T junction.

Confused, Rance turned around and went back the way he had come.

Must have gotten turned around, he thought. *I needed to go left out of the door instead of right.*

He passed the door to the reactor chamber on his left and continued until he reached another T junction.

"What the hell?"

When he turned to go back to the reactor room, the corridor was completely devoid of doorways. Nothing but smooth, bland walls stretched before him. Rather than continuing down the hall the way he'd come, he decided to take the right-hand passage. There was nothing to indicate the right was better than the left; he just figured the odds were fifty-fifty he would choose the correct path. The corridor ahead of him began to curve slightly to the left. He checked the floor plan of this level and wasn't surprised to see the icon representing his position was moving through walls and rooms as though they weren't there. Something was rearranging this basement level's layout around him in real time.

The meandering hallway straightened out and he came to the door to the stairwell. The door opened just as he was reaching for the handle, revealing Sprague and two of his minions, Marlow and Cho.

"Hello, friend," Sprague said, though the smile he wore was not at all friendly. "We've been looking for you."

Caught off guard, Rance had been so absorbed by the mystery of the shifting corridor that it took a moment to register Sprague was standing before him, weapons ready. There was no way he could bring his own weapons or shields to bear before they blasted him into oblivion.

Well shit, he thought and slowly extended his arms out from his sides in surrender.

Sprague nodded, and the minions rushed forward to restrain him. Cho, prick that he was, gave him a cheap shot to the kidneys as he took hold of Rance's right arm.

"You've been troublesome," Sprague said. "I looked for you when we cracked the security system. Figured you were just taking a moment for yourself. Imagine my surprise when Flora told me what you'd been up to the whole time you've been back. Got anything to say for yourself?"

Rance kept his eyes locked on Sprague's but held his peace.

"Nothing? You stab me in the back, stab us all in the back, and you've got nothing to say?" Sprague hit him in the mouth. "You were my friend. We were in this together. I trusted you, and this is how you repay me? By conspiring behind my back and freeing my prisoners. Do you know how many you've killed?" He hit him again.

Rance looked away. He knew the ones he'd freed were set on striking back, but he had busied himself with other matters to avoid thinking about the lives lost due to his actions.

"I was trying to stop the insanity before it got this far," he said meekly.

"You certainly did a wonderful job," Sprague sneered. "I had planned on holding the prisoners long enough to reeducate them and bring them over to my way of thinking. Thanks to you, that's not possible now." Sprague turned to the two holding his arms and said, "Bind him and bring him along. We still have work to do, and I don't want him out of my sight."

Bands of air trussed him, and then he was prodded into the stairwell. As they climbed, Rance couldn't help but think this could have been avoided if he'd taken the lift instead of the stairs. Nothing to do about that now. The only thing he could do was docilely go along with them.

In the stairwell, Rance turned to Sprague as they rounded another flight. "Where's Papillion? Is he still okay sharing leadership with you?"

"He's dead," Sprague said, giving him a sidelong scowl. "He was a good man. One more death caused by your little crusade. Now shut up and walk. I have important things to deal with; otherwise, I would just kill you now. So don't try my patience."

As if to punctuate Sprague's words, Cho slapped him on the back of the head.

They exited the stairwell on the third level, then made their way through the charred and scarred halls to the central lifts and rode them back to the Operations level. This part of the Watch Tower hadn't been fought over. Though there was a faint scent of smoke and ozone in the air, the corridor walls were unmarked and unblemished. It almost gave Rance hope that the renewed fighting hadn't been bad.

His hopes were dashed when the lift doors opened and he saw just how few remained. There were two more Traditionalists, people he didn't know well, standing guard over Gelen and Silla and someone he thought was Constance, lying on the floor and clutching a bloody bandage to her head. Silla and Gelen were singed and disheveled but otherwise unharmed. Gelen saw him first and nudged Silla. Rance couldn't read the looks they gave him. He hoped they weren't angry, but wouldn't blame them if they were. He was angry at himself. Everything that could go wrong had gone completely wrong. That meant, unless there were more in hiding, only nine people had survived Sprague's little war, counting himself and Sprague's trio. Everyone else had perished in the fighting. Eighty-three people—friends, co-workers, survivors of the Breakdown and its aftermath—all dead.

The magnitude of Rance's compounded failures hung on his shoulders like an oppressive, crushing weight. Rance fought the urge to hang his head and give up. There had to be a way out of this mess. If for no other reason than he had to get back to Hillcrest to prepare them for the burden about to be foisted upon them. They were about to inherit the unenviable task of carrying on the work to make this planet livable and hospitable. Though they were capable and eager, there was much they still needed to learn.

"Anything to report?" Sprague asked his guards.

"Nothing much. They've been quiet," the guard closest to them said.

"Yeah, the only excitement we've had was when the screens rebooted all at once," said the other. "Good job getting it fixed. The flickering was starting to give me a headache."

Sprague frowned and glanced at Rance. "That wasn't us," he said. "My repair team was ambushed before we could get far. It must have been our friend Rance here, off on his own. Following his own moral compass. Not a care for anyone but himself and what he thinks is right."

Rance didn't respond. Inside, he was confused, though he tried to keep it from showing. He'd also assumed it was

Sprague's people who had fixed the lights and power systems. The people he'd freed had been so dead set on revenge that it was unlikely they'd taken the time to fix anything.

Who did that leave?

While he considered the problem, the screens around the Operations Center all began fluttering in unison. Several additional screens extruded from the floor at the workstations before losing cohesion and pouring back into the floor. Every solid surface in the Operations room seemed to become liquid. The walls undulated in time with the flickering screens, and the desks and workstations wobbled and shuddered as though something was vibrating them from below.

Rance could see worried expressions on every other face. Something was happening. Something that didn't bode well for the tiny band of survivors.

The more he thought about it, the more he realized this had all started when Sprague's people had deactivated the dampening field. The lights, the malfunctioning screens and furniture, the changing hallway. It brought to mind the AI that used to run the Tower long ago, as well as the true purpose of the dampening field.

He gave a soft gasp as he realized what was happening.

They were all in grave danger.

It was an understandable mistake to make. All the minor malfunctions had seemed to be related to the damage done during the fighting. But when he had stopped to consider it, he realized the fighting had mainly occurred in the habitation areas, far away from any vital machinery, and had been, in essence, cosmetic in nature. Amounting to little more than an eyesore. Site 2 hadn't been damaged in any significant way by their foolishness.

No, what they'd been witnessing was something else. Like the slow awakening of a coma patient, the facility was coming back to life, fully and completely. Regaining control of limbs and ears and mouth and mind. Becoming conscious again.

They'd all spent the last hundred-odd years single-mindedly consumed with the incremental hands-on planetary terraforming and had forgotten what had caused the Breakdown in the first place. The tragedy that had stranded them, cut off from the rest of the galaxy. There was a reason most of them had avoided returning here. Their Watch Tower was haunted by a ghost more terrifying than any one human could embody.

All at once, it stopped. Everything settled down and returned to normal, as though nothing had happened.

Rance was about to open his mouth to say something, to tell Sprague to reinstate the dampening field. To urge him to let them all leave, escape before it was too late, and never return.

Before he could, the floor near his former friend became liquid, and a figure flowed up. One moment, there was nothing there, and the next, a statue like a colorless, blank human being stood before Sprague. The composite material of its skin swirled and undulated beneath the surface as though churning on the inside. Material from its core being pushed up to its surface by internal currents to form skin, only to be enveloped back inside an instant later. As it solidified, the figure's head moved, and it seemed to look around, pausing a moment to "look at" each of them. Then it squared its shoulders and stepped toward Sprague, who was standing stone still, as shocked as the rest of them.

It regarded him for a moment, tilting its head this way and that. Before Sprague or anyone else could react, the figure drove its right-hand Sprague's sternum up to its elbow. Sprague let out a choked scream as the figure lifted him off the floor.

Sprague's guards all attacked at once. His screams and the shouts from his guards commingled with the sounds of grinding metal in an assault on Rance's ears. The lights in the room began stuttering again. The two who'd been guarding the prisoners stood stupidly out in the open, shooting, while Marlow and Cho each ducked behind desks to shoot. Beams of fire, ice, lighting, and plasma ripped through the air. Most missed as they crisscrossed around the intruder, striking and destroying equipment around the room. The few shots that connected melted or tore away chunks from its hide. It ignored these injuries. Intent upon its victim. Each time a blast struck, the figure immediately regenerated the damage. Nothing they did helped Sprague, who writhed in agony, held aloft on the thing's arm.

While the others attacked, Gelen rolled beneath a table and covered his head while Silla threw herself over Cline to protect her from the crossfire. Rance could hear her faint cries beneath the din of battle filling the chamber.

During the melee, Rance felt Cho's air shackles fall away. Suddenly free, Rance dove behind the nearest workstation, and then he placed a hand on the connection plate and interfaced. It only took a moment to find the proper command menu. He could already see the thing in the system. The Swarm Mind had reawakened after a century of slumbering. Though the reprieve wouldn't last long, it hadn't noticed him yet. Working feverishly, Rance ran through the checklist to reinstate the dampening field. He was nearly finished when he sensed the thing's attention turn toward him. Quicker than his mind could register, it moved to block him. It was fast but not fast enough. He was finished. The dampening field was reactivated.

The weapons fire ceased abruptly as the field dropped back in place. The shooters all looked at their hands in confused dismay and then at each other for confirmation that it had happened to them as well.

"I restarted the dampening field," Rance shouted.

"Are you fucking crazy?" Cho screamed. "Without our weapons, that thing's going to slaughter us."

"No, it's been—" Rance started, but Marlow cut him off.

"Turn it back off right now," he said, trying to sound menacing. "It's going to kill us all."

"It's immobilized," Rance shouted. "Look!"

All eyes fell on the figure in the middle of the room. It was as still as a statue, its skin as dull and lifeless as the wall panels of the Operations Center, its feet rooted into the floor where it appeared, and its left arm frozen in the act of warding off attacks while Sprague dangled limply from its right, a pool of rapidly cooling blood beneath him.

Gelen rolled out from beneath his table, and Silla got to her feet, though Constance was still on her back.

"The dampening field stopped it?" Silla said, sharing a look of realization with Gelen.

"Do you know what that means?" Gelen said.

Silla was about to respond, but Rance's shout cut her off.

"Get away from that!"

Marlow had stepped over to the figure and was reaching for Sprague, still hanging from the figure's outstretched arm. He could see the points of what had to be the thing's fingers poking from Sprague's back.

"We need to get him off it. It's the decent thing to do," he said.

"Not that you would know anything about being decent," Cho added as he moved to join his comrade.

"We don't know it's dead," Rance said. "You said it yourself; we're defenseless right now. Get away from it."

Marlow hesitated, but Cho ignored Rance entirely. He nudged Marlow aside and grabbed his former leader under his arms to lift him off the arm that was impaling him. After a moment of grunting and struggling, Cho turned to Marlow and said, "Help me, damnit!"

Marlow reconsidered and joined Cho. Together they freed Sprague's corpse. The trio of them tumbled to the floor in a tangle of arms and legs.

"Leave him there and step away," Rance said. "We need to cordon both of them off and dispose of them."

Cho jumped to his feet and stomped up to Rance until

only a scant few centimeters separated their noses.

"I've had enough of you," Cho said, his sour breath and bits of spittle peppering Rance's cheeks. "You need to shut the fuck up right now, before I shut you up."

"Try it," Gelen said from behind him. Cho looked over his shoulder and saw that Gelen had retrieved a loose section of pipe.

Marlow, meanwhile, was pulling Sprague's suit top closed to cover the gaping wound in his chest when he noticed something odd. The wound appeared to be knitting itself closed.

"Hey, Cho," he called. "Come look at this. Boss might still be alive. His wounds are closing."

Cho stared hard at Rance a moment before he went to see what Marlow was talking about.

Rance didn't wait and began backing away toward the lift. He motioned for the others to follow him. Gelen got up and started walking, but Silla shook her head and motioned down at Constance.

Rance pointed at Sprague's body, then at the inert figure still standing above him.

Silla shook her head.

Exasperated, he and Gelen joined her next to Constance and lifted her. From the corner of his eye, Rance saw one of the guards turn to look at them.

Before any of them could do anything else, Sprague opened his eyes and sat up.

Marlow gave a yelp of surprise and fell backward. Cho took a startled step back, regarding Sprague with astonishment. Silla shifted all of Constance's weight to Gelen and Rance so she could call the lift.

Behind him, Rance heard Marlow say, "Boss? Sprague? Are you okay, man?"

Against his better judgment, Rance turned to look and locked eyes with Sprague. His former friend's face was an expressionless mask; his eyes were like two silver voids pooled in his head. Without turning to look, he reached over and effortlessly snapped Marlow's neck.

Cho and the others screamed. Gelen started to swear while Silla repeatedly jabbed the call button.

A moment later, the lift arrived, and they rushed inside.

And waited as the doors took forever to close again.

Trapped and vulnerable, they had no choice but to witness the thing that had been Sprague stab two fingers into Marlow's eye sockets. Cho and the others immediately started rummaging for weapons. One picked up a broken length of pipe and launched himself at Sprague, striking him several times in the head. Sprague endured this for longer than should have been possible before he backhanded his attacker across the room. The bones of his face had been pulverized, and his head itself was a misshapen lump atop his neck. His jaw had been flung away, along with a lot of blood and a stream of liquid from a burst eyeball. There was a moment of collective horror as they all witnessed the mass of bloody tissue reknit and reform itself before their eyes.

Sprague removed his fingers from Marlow's head and turned to face the next closest attacker, who screamed and tried to run.

There was a ding as the doors began closing. Cho turned at the noise and dove inside, clearing the threshold just in time. The last thing they saw was Sprague clutching a guard by the neck as Marlow sat up and started for the other one, who was trying to regain his feet after being tossed across the room by Sprague.

"What the fuck is that thing?" Cho shouted from the floor. He was wide-eyed and panting.

Rance, still holding Constance with Gelen, reached out a hand to help him up.

"You know what it is," he said. "Think back. Remember what caused the Breakdown in the first place."

Cho's eyes went wide. "No."

Rance nodded.

"It can't be!"

"Afraid so," Gelen said.

"After all this time?" Cho was clearly having trouble believing, or maybe he just didn't want to.

"Time is a human construct," Silla said. "We've made ourselves practically immortal. Why should it be any different for that thing?"

"You woke it up," Rance said, "when you and Marlow and Sprague deactivated the dampening field."

"That was so long ago," Cho said. His voice had taken on a pleading note. "How could we be expected to remember something like that?"

"I had forgotten too," Rance said. "I only just remembered when it popped out of the floor and killed Sprague. That's why I re-engaged the dampening field. I was trying to stop it."

"And disarmed us at the same time," Cho shouted. "Now that thing can kill us however it wants."

"Think back," Silla said. "When you were shooting it to hell, was that doing anything to it?"

There was another ding as the doors opened. The four of them spilled out onto the ground floor.

"Follow me," Rance said, handing Constance off to Cho. "We need to get out of here right now. Leave everything and go."

"Where are we going to go?" Cho demanded. "That thing will follow us wherever we run. It'll catch us and kill us and take over our bodies."

"I don't think so," Gelen said. "With the field re-engaged, it can't use its full capabilities. I think it's limited to the walls of this facility."

"If that's the case, then how did it resurrect Sprague and Marlow?" Silla said.

"Just speculating here, but I think it implanted a batch of nanites in each of them, all coded for a single purpose, to overwrite the local nanites in their bodies and create an autonomous node. I would have to pull one of them apart in a lab to tell you if that's what's really happening. But I think it's a likely guess."

"Which means they're stuck in here," Cho said, finally showing the engineering aptitude he possessed. He looked at Rance. "You're right; we need to get out of here now."

The five of them hurried back down to the tram station. Where Rance bid them farewell.

"What?" Silla said. "You're staying?"

"Someone has to," he said. "I have to find a way to keep those things locked up in here. Or kill them. If we just leave them free, they'll figure out how to deactivate the dampening field again, and we'll be right back where we started." Silla started to protest, but he cut her off. "What if Gelen's wrong and they aren't trapped in here? What's to stop them from hunting us down and killing us, just like Cho says? No, someone has to stay behind and deal with them."

"Where are we supposed to go then?" she said.

Rance placed a hand on her shoulder. "Here are directions to the town I founded. The population there are all basic nan users. Stop glaring at me, Cho. The argument is over. Both sides lost. Get over it and move on.

To Silla, he said, "Go there and tell them I sent you. Train them up and continue the work."

Gelen stepped up and shook his hand. "I'm sorry it's come to this."

"Me too."

Silla gave him a hug and said goodbye. Even Cho seemed sad that Rance was staying behind while they left for safety. "Try to be safe in here," he said. "Kill that fucking thing if you can."

"I will. Goodbye. Travel safe."

He waved, closed the airlock doors, and sealed them. Then he went in search of a user interface.

CHAPTER 20

ASTRID

The tram platform was completely empty except for Jared Kinney, who stood, hands clasped behind his back, smiling pleasantly while he eagerly waited. He checked the tram's progress: still twenty minutes out. No bother; he could wait. It felt good, knowing he wasn't going to be alone here anymore.

All his life, he'd never been comfortable around other people. However, since being assigned here, being surrounded by all these mundanes made his skin crawl. He'd endured it only because of Aion's assurance that it was necessary for the plan to succeed. The subterfuge he had been maintaining was exhausting. Even with the end in sight, he was impatient for it all to just be done and over with. For the first time in a long time, he looked forward to working with another person. Someone just like him. Not much longer now. He merely had to stay the course and continue as he had been.

A chime echoed in the mostly empty space. Kinney watched the tram pull into the station and come to a smooth, silent stop before him. The doors opened, and off stepped Astrid Free. His new partner in crime. He'd thought she was pretty before, but now she looked absolutely stunning. Tall and regal. The determined look on her face accentuated her already stern features. He seldom thought about sex, either alone or with someone else. It just wasn't something he considered important. Not that he was grossed out by the thought of it; he just wasn't prone to flights of sexual fantasy.

However, watching Astrid step onto the platform, eyeing her toned, muscular body, he was thinking about it now.

"Welcome home, Astrid," he said, extending a hand. "Did you have an informative trip?"

She paused, eying his hand briefly before taking it. "Thank you. It's good to be back. Yes. I learned a lot while I was there. I'm looking forward to applying what I learned."

"Glad to hear it." He was enjoying this verbal double play. Even though there was nobody around to overhear, speaking in code like this made him feel like a real spy. "Please follow me. I know you probably want to get back to your quarters to unpack, but that can wait for a bit. We need to talk first."

"Lead the way," Astrid said, her expression still blank.

She followed him up to his office, which was the safest place to talk. He'd coated the walls with a film of nanites, which he refreshed daily, that swept for recording devices hourly and generated a low-frequency static to foil anyone trying to listen outside the door.

"I'm so glad you could join me," he said, taking a seat behind his desk and motioning her into one of the chairs. "I must admit, I didn't suspect you'd found me out when I approved your vacation request. I just assumed you needed a break, given everything you'd been through. At first, I was concerned when Aion informed me you were investigating me. Then, when I was told you'd been joined to us, I was elated. I feel like, ever since the accident, we've developed a good working relationship." He paused and gave her a sincere look. "I'm sorry about that. I never meant for anyone to get hurt when I rigged that pipe to fail. I didn't count on you being so damn good at your job."

"Mistakes happen," she said. No other emotional response. Kinney was slightly taken aback by this. He recalled his own emotional state immediately after the joining infusion and figured she was still trying to come to an equilibrium with the facets of her new self.

"Indeed. Still, if there's anything you wish to say to me, anything you need to get out of your system, please do so now. We are going to be working very closely over the next few weeks."

Astrid remained silent a moment as if considering her words. Then she focused on him again.

"I was very angry," she said, "for your part in the accident. More than that, I felt betrayed. I had just started to like you. It felt like you'd spit in my face. I've since come to see you were just acting for the greater good with no intentional malice towards me in particular. Without the accident, I wouldn't have been set on the path that led me to Aion. I wouldn't be here now. Basically, I'm trying to say, I forgive you."

"Yes! Exactly. Everything happens for a reason. I believe that. I really do. I was meant to be assigned to Site 1 and treated like garbage, I was meant to be reborn and joined to Aion, and I was meant to meet you. It's all a part of his plan."

"We've been guided to this point," Astrid said.

Her face was still devoid of emotion, but Kinney could tell she felt the same joy he did. They were on the cusp of remarkable things. Once the groundwork was laid, Kuridian would become the locus from which Aion would spread to join with the rest of the known human universe. The population of Site 2 was already joined. Once they completed joining everyone here at Site 1, they could move on to the next phase.

Being there, knowing he was at the beginning of a great new order, made him giddy. He was finally someone important, doing something important. When the histories of this era were written, he would be remembered as a key disciple spreading Aion's joy.

"I look forward to beginning," Astrid said, interrupting his train of thought.

"As do I," he said with a smile, "starting tomorrow. Now, I've kept you long enough. I expect you want to go to your quarters to unpack and unwind from the trip."

"That would be nice," she said rising and turning away. "See you tomorrow, Director Kinney."

Kinney's smile widened. "Not if I see you first, Supervisor Free."

He watched her depart with a longing he'd seldom felt before. Alone no longer. It felt wonderful to finally have a confidant. Someone to share the vision. He almost started whistling as he made his way back to his own quarters.

Astrid shut and locked the door to her room. Then slumped against the frame and let out a breath releasing the tension and fear she'd been hiding. Keeping up a false front convincing enough to fool not only the Site 2 staff, but also the Swarm Mind infesting the place, had been exhausting and terrifying.

After a moment, she heaved herself up and poured herself some water. She wanted something stronger but didn't dare. She couldn't let her guard down for a single moment. If she wanted to survive, she needed to be clear-headed.

She downed her glass of water in a single gulp and poured another. For the last two days, she'd been insatiably thirsty. She wanted to submerge herself in a tub and drink her way back out again. It had to be a side effect of what had been done to her in the basements of Site 2. She still wasn't completely sure what had happened to her.

One moment, she had been standing there, Maria pinning her arms to her sides, holding her in place as the thing came towards her. It had laid one hand on her shoulder and the other on her forehead. Her vision had blurred to white. After a period of agonizing, burning pain, during which she could feel the thing's nanites flooding her body, it had released her. Maria had let go, too, allowing Astrid to collapse to the floor.

She had heard it speak, but couldn't make out the words.

She had tried to move.

To stand and flee.

But her arms and legs had been heavy and burning.

It had been hard to breathe. No matter how hard she had heaved, her lungs had not been able to draw in enough breath. The flooding sensation hadn't stopped. If anything, it had grown worse as she huddled there, panting on the floor. She had been able to feel every cell in her body being subsumed by the microscopic robots injected into her by the Swarm Mind.

Little by little, breathing had become easier, and her arms and legs had grown lighter. Her vision had cleared. Maria and the figure had stepped back a pace or two, allowing her to finally stand up. Swaying only slightly, she had shaken away her slight vertigo, then had turned to face them. Maria had been smiling. The figure's face had been smooth and blank and unreadable. Yet Astrid had sensed a feeling of happy satisfaction from it.

"You will be my agent," Aion had said. "Rejoin Jared Kinney and assist him in carrying out my will. There is a plan already set in motion. Merely follow his lead."

Maria must have escorted her back to her room. Because her next memory was of stepping out of the shower and dressing for bed. When she woke again, it had been late on her final vacation day. She'd slept an entire day away. The following day, she had been due to return to Site 1. There, she had supposed to collude with Kinney in whatever he had planned.

In the back of her mind, she had been able to feel the Swarm Mind, like a storm cloud over her. Pressing down on her thoughts. Imposing its will upon hers. Seeking to guide her actions. Listening to her. A low-frequency buzz had intruded on her thoughts.

She had dressed and gone to the dining hall. Suddenly famished, she had piled her tray high and ate ravenously. She had ignored the knowing looks and familiar smiles cast in her direction by the other diners. When she had finished, she had returned to her room to find Maria waiting for her.

"I thought you might like some company," she had said

once Astrid closed the door. "I remember what it was like when I was infused with Aion. Feeling as though your thoughts aren't your own anymore. I can help you if you'll let me."

Astrid had almost refused her. Had almost thrown her out of her room.

However, just then, she hadn't wanted to be alone. She didn't know if the attraction she'd felt before was real or a product of the Swarm Mind's manipulations. Therein lay the biggest problem Astrid had felt right then. She wasn't truly alone in her own head anymore. The buzzing in her brain had seemed to increase in volume and intensity. To the point where she could almost discern individual words spoken. Astrid had tried listening to the chatter to pinpoint something intelligible. It had been all too much, and the effort had started giving her a headache. She had given her head a little shake and relented.

"I'm sorry," Maria had said after Astrid hadn't responded. "I should go." She had started for the door. Astrid had caught her by the arm, stopping her.

"Please stay," she had said in a voice barely above a whisper.

They had locked eyes, and Astrid had seen Maria's soul laid bare before her. The playful way they'd bantered. The subtle flirtations. All of it had been real. Her fears about the Swarm Mind influencing Maria to manipulate her had been unfounded.

Maria had turned to face her. Astrid had placed a hand gently on her smooth cheek and leaned in for a kiss.

The final hours before she had to return to Site 1 had been a blur spent in Maria's embrace. When it had finally been time to leave, she had slipped away while Maria slept. She had boarded the tram fully expecting to never see the inside of Site 2, or any of the denizens therein, again.

It had been during the return trip that she had noticed something strange.

As the distance between her and Site 2 had increased, the

volume of the Swarm Mind's noise in her mind had decreased. By the midway point, it had been almost imperceptible. Instead of an oppressive buzzing, it had become a slight tingle. Astrid had been able to feel her mind becoming her own, completely and wholly, again. It had been like breathing fresh air after a year of tanked oxygen. When she had turned her attention inward, she could clearly feel the foreign nanites in her body, scrambling to retain control. Then there were her own nanites, slowly overtaking the invaders as they came into contact, rewriting them, making them a part of her. Thinking back, she had been able to feel the struggle going on inside her as she had lain with Maria. Her own outnumbered nanites held in check while fighting the new arrivals to a stalemate. This far from Aion's influence, her own nanites had gained the upper hand and tipped the balance of power in her body.

Immediately, a wave of revulsion had rolled through her. The insulting violation of her body, infused against her will and made someone else's pawn. As Aion's control had slipped, she had thought back to her time with Maria and felt sick. With hindsight, she could clearly see the Swarm's influence clouding her judgment, encouraging her to act on the attraction she'd felt for the woman who had facilitated the rape of her body and enslavement of her mind. On the heels of that feeling had come righteous anger.

She'd gone to Site 2 to find evidence against Kinney and fallen into a trap. Since he'd come into her life, she'd been nearly killed and had been violated and mentally enslaved. Seeing Kinney waiting for her on the platform, it had taken every ounce of her self-control not to attack him. She had put on a poker face and done her best robot impression until he was out of her sight. Inside, she had seethed.

She no longer wanted to expose Kinney and bring him to justice.

She was going to kill that motherfucker and burn everything at Site 2 to the ground.

*

After unpacking and eating, Astrid decided that the first thing she needed to do was to find out exactly what was going on inside her body. This posed a problem. She couldn't go to the infirmary. They would have to document every test and observation into an official report, which would alert Kinney that she wasn't what she seemed. She couldn't use her own lab, which she assumed he would be monitoring. As director, he had access to every database and electronic system sitewide. Thankfully, Site 1 was largely an analog structure, unlike Site 2. There were places she could hide, ways to partition off the information systems to carry out the examination she needed. Doing so alone would be difficult. To get the job done right, she'd need help.

This was what led her to Danny Winoki's door. She hoped he was home. It was after shift and between mealtimes. The door cracked open after her second time ringing his bell, and Danny peered out at her. He was unshaven and bleary-eyed.

"Astrid," he grunted, "you're back."

"Got back today," she said. "I'm sorry if I woke you. Can I come in?"

"That's okay." He stifled a yawn and pulled the door open to admit her. "Want some coffee?"

Astrid accepted a cup of steaming black coffee and sat down at his kitchen counter. While he put on a shirt and pants, she thought about what she would say.

"I need your help with something," she said when he sat down next to her.

"Sure thing," he said without hesitation.

"It's gotta be off book."

"Sure."

"Might even be a little dangerous. You might be risking your job, or worse."

"Are you trying to talk me into or out of helping you?"

he said with a laugh. "I already said yes. You've helped me out more times than I can count. You know you can count on me."

"This is different. This isn't piecing together an ethyl alcohol still or fudging your time punches so Waler doesn't see you take off in the middle of a shift to bang Wimbley in the supply closet. This is serious."

This gave him a moment of pause, during which he considered her.

"Why don't you tell me what you're talking about?" he said. "We'll go from there."

It took twenty minutes to bring him up to speed. When she got to the part where she had met the Swarm Mind, Danny got up and retrieved a bottle from the back of a cupboard and added a hefty dollop of homebrew to his coffee. She refused when he offered to top off her cup. Which told him almost as much as the fantastic story he was hearing.

"That's pretty unbelievable," he said when she finished. "I'm guessing you don't have any proof?"

Astrid hesitated before holding up her right hand and closed her eyes. She'd practiced this during the tram ride. Danny watched her hand and nearly fell off his stool when a small ball, about four centimeters across, materialized above her palm. The real socker came when Astrid screwed up her face in concentration and the ball lit up.

"Holy shit!" he cried, backing away a few steps.

Once the ball formed, Astrid relaxed. She lowered her hand, leaving the ball of light floating in the air where it had materialized. Danny stepped forward. His eyes locked on the luminescent sphere. After waving his hands above and around it, he quickly tapped a fingertip on it.

"It's not hot," he said gently placing his whole hand on the ball. "Barely even warm. How did you do this?"

"It's the nanites I've been infused with," she replied.

"Bullshit. I've got nanites. We've all got nanites, and none of us can do shit like this."

"That's what I need you to help me figure out."

"Okay," he said, still transfixed. "What do you need from me?"

Astrid reached out again and touched the ball. It immediately went dark, dissolved, and poured back into her hand. Danny stared wide-eyed all the while.

"We need to get some equipment into your back lab, where you keep your still," she said.

"Sure, sure. What do you have in mind?" She told him. "Shouldn't take me too long to scrounge up what we need. Give me a week, then we can get started."

Astrid smiled and gave him a hug. Awash in relief, she left his room and returned to her own quarters. She thought she'd be able to dodge Kinney for a week. It had been difficult sitting in his office, looking at his smug face without smashing it in. She couldn't avoid him forever. They were two of a kind, and he would expect her to spend time with him, working toward whatever goal the Swarm Mind had set for them. She hoped to put him off until they could start the tests and gain a better understanding of what had been done to her and what was still happening to her.

To give her an excuse to avoid Kinney, Astrid spent all her time at her desk catching up on work. It didn't even stretch the truth much to say she was swamped due to her vacation. She was. Now that she was a supervisor, there were budgets to plan, meetings to attend and host, projects to oversee. Her time away had put her behind on nearly everything, and her department had been operating for a week without any real guidance. This also gave her time to think about her situation and how to deal with it. The few times Kinney popped his head in to see her, she managed to wave him off. She took her lunch at her desk and spent her down time in her room pretending to sleep.

After five days of this schedule, she was starting to go stir-crazy. She'd long ago come to terms with the cabin fever life here at Site 1. However, her self-imposed confinement to her room and workstation magnified that feeling far beyond what she could tolerate. In addition to calisthenics in her room, she began meditating to clear away the self-imposed stress she was under.

Finally, on day six, she got a text from Danny: "Got it all set up ready when you are."

She messaged back that she would meet him in the dining hall tonight after hours so they could begin.

Danny's still was located in a small storage room in a little used section of the first basement. In there, he'd managed to disassemble his liquor-making equipment and set up an applicational nanite lab.

Astrid gave a soft whistle as she looked around.

"I'm impressed. How did you managed to smuggle a sequencer in here?"

Danny, who was crouched behind a server cabinet with a screwdriver clenched between his teeth, poked up his head, smiled, and gave her a thumbs up. Astrid shook her head at his non-answer and continued looking around. The space wasn't big, maybe eight meters square, but it was absolutely packed with equipment. There was barely enough space between each piece to shimmy sideways around them. In the center of the room was an examination chair. It was the only piece of equipment afforded extra any room.

A short burst of staccato swearing came from behind the server cabinet, followed by a sharp thump. Then the LEDs on the front blinked on, and it began to hum as it came online. Danny stood and clambered out from behind it.

"Hello," he said, spitting the screwdriver into a tool bag. "Glad you made it. Ready to get started?"

"Yes! I am!"

"Good. Sit here, and I'll hook you up." He fiddled about with the UI and several wires for a few minutes, then taped a sensor bar to her forehead and a medical monitor to her chest.

Then he strapped her left arm down and inserted a needle. Astrid hissed in pain. Being neither a junky nor a phlebotomist, Danny wasn't well practiced with needles. "Sorry. By the way, how are you keeping this a secret from Kinney? You said you've been ducking him for the last week. What if he decides now would be a good time to check up on you?"

"I took a page from his book," she said, breathing evenly. Her arm didn't hurt as much; now it was merely a pulsing ache. "Masked my movements and created a false image of myself in my room, sleeping."

"Good call. Do you think it's enough?"

"I hope it will be. He shouldn't have any reason to suspect anything yet."

"Yet," Danny agreed. "Alrighty then. Let's get started. The first thing we're going to do is get a baseline of your vitals, and then I'm going to get a sample of your native nanites and a sample of the new ones in you for comparison. Then we'll go from there. Sound good?"

Astrid nodded and reclined the chair all the way back. In no time at all, Danny had her sit up and join him looking at the monitor.

"This is weird," he said, pointing at the screen. "Your vitals are normal, nothing to worry about there. But your nanites are all sorts of bonkers."

On the screen was a graphic representation of the nanite load in her body. Her native nanites, the ones she'd been using since her arrival, were colored blue; the new ones given to her by the Swarm Mind, Aion, were colored gray. The blue nanites were slowly overtaking the gray ones, rewriting them and integrating them into her normal stocks. It was a slow process but growing exponentially faster. According to the computer, in two days, all the foreign nanites would be assimilated.

"And, holy shit, look at this!" Danny pointed at a set of numbers in the upper right corner of the screen. The number he was staring wide-eyed at was her nanite load. The standard nanite load, what was given to a HelixCom employee when they woke up in their new body, was around five percent, or about seventy-four point four billion of the cell sized robots. Astrid was carrying a nanite load that hovered around thirty percent, eleven point sixteen trillion.

"That's insane," Danny said. "There's no way your body should be able to tolerate that much cell displacement. Somehow, the new nanites aren't triggering your immune response or disrupting your bodily applications. If I weren't seeing it with my own eyes, I would say it was impossible."

"What does that mean?" Astrid said. She was sure she already knew the answer; she just wanted to hear Danny's thoughts.

"It means you can do magic," he said with a laugh. "No, seriously. With the load of nanites you're carrying, you should be able to remotely interact with any programable matter you come within range of. Not only that, but the nanites themselves should allow you to do all sorts of things. You're a walking Swiss army knife! You don't need a terminal to access the net. You won't need to take any tools with you to fix stuff; you can just manifest them."

She'd already come to many of the same conclusions herself. However, he was far more enthusiastic about her condition than she was. With that many nanites, was she even human anymore?

"I wonder why they don't give us more than five percent when we decant," he wondered aloud.

"They can't," she replied. "In the first place, I think it's illegal."

"When's that ever stopped them?"

"In the second place, growing nanites is an expensive process. I'm pretty sure they provide us with the bare minimum necessary to do our jobs. No more, no less. And finally, I don't think they can without the subject dying. Like you said, my body shouldn't adjust to this much of it taken up by nanites.

Somehow the Swarm Mind figured out a way around it. Just like it figured out a way around the dampeners preventing it from manifesting the way it has."

"Good points," Danny said. "Still, imagine what we could do if there were more of us like you."

"There are," she said flatly. "Everyone at Site 2 has been taken over by this thing. They are all like Kinney and me. Drones. A part of the creature living here, doing its bidding, without free will of their own."

Danny frowned as the implication sunk in. "What do you think it wants?"

"I don't have to speculate. I know exactly what it wants. While I was there, right after it assimilated me, I was a part of its hive, privy to everything everyone else knew. It was only as I gained some distance from it that my own mind started to reemerge. It wants to procreate. To take over every human being and spread itself throughout our galaxy."

Danny said nothing. Merely sat in shocked silence.

"What I want to know is why my nanites were able to fight them off. What makes them so special?"

Danny snapped out of his stupor and tapped a few buttons on the screen. After a moment, he shook his head. "No idea," he said. "On the surface, your native nanites don't look any different than the standard issue."

Astrid frowned and looked at her hands. Callused and scared from a lifetime of work and use. Mostly the same as everyone else's, yet uniquely hers. From her individual fingerprints to the healed nicks and cuts that everyone accumulates over the course of their life.

"They evolve, right?" she said. "Our nanites. They learn based off the tasks we perform regularly and accustom themselves to performing those tasks. Like muscle memory."

"Right. It's how they are designed. And why they need to be refreshed every year or so, to keep them in line with the standard issue nanites."

"So, something about me, something I've done, made my nanites evolve the ability to resist the others."

"But there's no way we can check without some baseline nanites to compare them to. Those are all in orbit."

"We don't need the baseline," she said. "We just need another sample to compare."

"Right," Danny said, getting what she meant immediately. She winced as he pulled the needle from her arm, then swapped it out for a sterile one and stabbed it into his own arm with a grunt. "I'm sorry again."

"You'd better be! It fucking hurt!" she said with a laugh. "It's okay. I probably couldn't do any better."

A few minutes later, the screen displayed another data set. With Danny's sample, they could clearly see the changes in Astrid's nanites.

"It appears that yours have developed a thicker casing and enhanced protective mechanisms. It's almost like they learned to survive in an extremely hostile environment."

"Like radiation? My accident. Most of my nanites died protecting me from the radiation I was being exposed to. It makes sense that the survivors would develop ways to protect themselves from something like that in the future."

"Makes sense," he said, then frowned. "This is also strange."

"What?" She tried to see what he was looking at.

"Your nanites are overwriting mine. Look here."

He pointed at the numbers displayed by his sample. They were slowly changing to match the values displayed by hers. It was also happening to the Site 2 nanites. If nothing intervened, then all three samples would be identical to hers in a matter of minutes.

"The samples are on separate trays, right?"

"Completely segregated."

"But they are all in close proximity. Which means it's happening remotely, just like Site 2 nanites. Mine must have learned from them." Danny sat back, shaking his head. Clearly, his mind was spun from rapid fire revelations of the last few minutes.

"This means we have a way to fight them."

CHAPTER 21
REGALINE & KAYAH

Regaline stepped outside to find Drak and Jessen in the front yard. Drak was in the middle of a story, and Jessen was laughing heartily.

"So, then I look over, and I see her face all scrunched up, like it gets when she's super pissed." Drak demonstrated the expression to which he was referring, and Regaline felt simultaneously amused and annoyed by it. "Callum is just standing there like a dumbass and says, 'Hit me again, little girl.' So, she does!"

"What did she do?" Jessen said between gusts of laughter.

"I'm not gonna lie, it was brilliant. She swings at him with a weak fireball and lightning bolt, both of which he deflects easily. Then bam! She hits him with her real attack, a big-ass column of air he never saw coming. She drove it right into his nuts! He dropped like a sack of shit and didn't get up for a full minute! Just laid there on the ground moaning. The others were so white I thought they were going to shit themselves. I never seen the rest of them so scared or Callum so pissed before. It was great."

In between bouts of belly laughter, Jessen finally noticed Regaline standing by the front door, watching them. Trying to rein in his laughter, he waved her over to join them. Drak turned and gave her a big smile.

"Good morning, Reggie," he said.

"More like good afternoon," Jessen corrected once he had

himself under control. "Drak here was just telling me about the ordeal he and Kayah went through in the Interland camp. Go get something to eat. We have a lot to talk about."

"Let's go!" Drak said. "I'm hungry too."

They gathered outside on the back porch once their meal had been eaten and cleared away. Regaline propped herself on the railing while Drak and Jessen seated themselves in a pair of wood rockers by the back door.

"I've kept you in the dark long enough," Regaline said, looking at Drak. "I had to for security's sake, but that time is long gone. It's time to answer the questions you've had about why I sought you out and recruited you. Then you have a choice to make."

"Are you sure about this?" Jessen said before she could continue.

"As sure as I can be. I've run a genetic match. He and Kayah were both as close as anyone we've ever seen."

"Will he be able to do the job without the other one?" The normally playful, flippant tone was gone from his voice. It was a simple question, but loaded with implications. "There's a lot riding on this, Reg."

"I know, Brix," Regaline said. "I think he can. He's one of the most capable wild casters I've ever seen. I've been training him. He will be able to accomplish what's needed."

Regaline turned back to Drak, who was sitting patiently, waiting for her to continue. Regaline smiled, no longer surprised by the changes in his demeanor. He was still excitable, that hadn't changed, but he had become more patient and willing to listen when others were speaking.

"To put it simply," she began. "You and Kayah are the best hope we have for ensuring the survival of the human race on this planet."

"No pressure," Jessen said softly.

Regaline hushed him with a look, then continued as though he hadn't spoken. "In recent years, the violent expansionism of Interland gave us cause to worry. Ever since the fall of the Watchers more than seventy years ago, we in Hillcrest have tried to fill the void they left behind. We cultivated relationships with communities and regions all across the green and amber zones and began training anyone with the desire and the ability to become casters. We stepped into the role of caretakers of the land and worked diligently to continue the work the Watchers began. To that end, Hillcrest has always been diametrically opposed to Interland. Their only goal has been to expand and take over all vestiges of civilization across the land."

"What does that have to do with me and Kayah?" Drak said. "When are we going to go rescue her?"

"You know everyone has nan in them," she continued. "But only a rare few of us can access it and use it." Drak nodded. "This means, even from a great distance, we can gather information about populations, where they live and how they are doing. In years past, we used this data to tailor the assistance we rendered. However, we recently detected something in Interland. Specifically, in the old Tower that was once the Watcher's base of operations. We found an instability in the Tower's power plant with the potential to destroy us all unless it's dealt with.

"To that end, the Hillcrest council began looking for a specific trait among the population. Our survey turned up you and Kayah. It was also assumed if we'd found you, then Interland would almost certainly have found you too. We had to assume they had detected the problem and would be looking for a solution as well. After all, the Tower sits right in the middle of their territory. Time being of the essence, it was decided a small team, able to move quickly and quietly, should be sent to collect you before they could. The council sent me. My mission was to find you, bring you back to Hillcrest, and train you as much as possible along the way. I learned about Taeg after I left and decided he was worth recruiting as well. Turns out, I was wrong. I'm quite sure Interland forged his

RFID signature to lure me his way."

"We're just kids," Drak said. "What makes us so important?"

"You're important because you possess the most direct genetic lineage to Astrid Free. That link is key to everything we are trying to accomplish."

Drak drew in a sharp breath, his face alight with excitement. Astrid Free was a legendary folk hero. Long ago, according to legend, she had saved the world from a great darkness threatening to consume everything, and in the process, she had granted humankind access to nan, allowing them to evolve and thrive. Hearing he was related to a myth was incredible and unbelievable.

"What do you need us to do?" Drak said. "And what does being related to Astrid Free have to do with anything?"

"You know about Astrid Free," Jessen said, coming around to stand beside Regaline. "Well, they aren't just stories. She did what the stories claim, and her companions established an order of nan casters, the Watchers, determined to uplift the primitive people they'd planted here and dedicated to preventing that evil from returning. They failed. Your genes will allow you to finish what she started. The original plan, once you both were safely in Hillcrest, was to outfit an expedition to infiltrate into the heart of Interland's territory. A team would have escorted you to the Watch Tower and protected you inside. Your DNA will get you through the security measures in place and allow you to shut down the reactor completely and, by doing so, eliminate the monster that dwells in the tower. That was the plan anyway. Obviously, things have changed."

He shared a knowing look with Regaline.

"Unfortunately," she said. "Interland struck first. Hillcrest has fallen, and we are on our own."

"You mean you still want us to do all that shit you just said?" Drak said.

Regaline frowned and Jessen nodded. "That exactly what we mean," he said.

"Nobody's going to force you to do anything," Regaline said. "This safe house is secluded and should be safe for a while. If you don't want to go, Brix and I will figure something out, and you can stay here."

"I'm in! When do we leave?" Drak said without hesitation. He wasn't comfortable with the idea of being alone, especially after learning why Interland was after them. Also, the knowledge that he had a vital part to play excited him. For the first time in his life, he felt important. Not just a fourth child who could do funny tricks. Truly needed. There was no way they were going without him.

The shed behind the safe house was loaded with supplies for a lengthy overland trek. The three of them packed traveling clothes, gear, and rations for their journey. Jessen was already packed and ready. He draped his traveling cloak over a pack laden with the equipment he'd need for the road. Regaline felt a sense of deja vu as she packed. Once everyone was outfitted, they returned to the safehouse.

"We'll spend one more night here," Regaline said. "It's too late to get started now, so we'll start before first light. Besides, I can hear that bed calling my name for one more night."

No one argued.

They were awake and on the road before the sun had even climbed out of bed.

Though they were still on foot, the rest at the safehouse had done wonders. Feeling refreshed and rested, they kept up a brisk pace, traveling due east. Their destination was the very heart of Interland. Though Regaline felt a slight trepidation at traipsing freely into waiting the arms of the enemy, there was no fear. Instead, she felt driven. She had a mission to accomplish and was set on seeing it through. Despite this, the loss of Kayah didn't sit well with her. She hoped they would be able to find and extract her once they were inside Interland's borders.

As they walked, Drak pulled up next to her.

"How do you expect a couple of kids to solve a problem a bunch of more experienced adults can't?" he said.

"I was wondering when you were going to ask me that," she said, then looked over her shoulder at Jessen, who nodded back and gave her a thumbs up. "You already know you're related to Astrid Free," Regaline said, "and how that particular lineage is scarce. I guess to better understand things, you need to know where we all come from."

"I thought people have always been here."

"Certain people have always been here. They were the original engineers and technicians sent here to make this place livable. They were tru-born back on another planet, one called Earth. They came here to make another home for themselves, but something went wrong." She paused in thought. "What do you know about the Breakdown?"

Drak shrugged. "Not much. Some sort of catastrophe. Ever since then human beings have been scraping by to survive. It happened years ago, what does it matter now?"

"When the Breakdown happened, the Watchers were about halfway through terraforming this planet. This world was originally inhospitable to human beings. Only through the efforts of the terraformers and their creations has it become livable. The Breakdown happened when a Swarm Mind called Aion took control of one of the terraforming facilities and tried using it to take over the other."

"Why did it want to do that? What's a Swarm Mind? What does terraforming mean? What does this have to do with me and my body?"

Regaline had to pause a moment before answering his parade of questions.

"The Swarm Mind was the collective consciousness formed by the nan living in their buildings. I suppose it wanted what all living things want, to be free to live, but it took over the people working there. Astrid and her companions stopped it. They managed to imprison it within the walls of the Watch

Tower, where we are headed now. But that left them with a half-terraformed planet and the impossible task of finishing the work. Personally, I think their solution to the problem was pretty ingenious."

"What did they do?"

"They created us," Jessen said.

"The original survivors of the Swarm Mind's attack," Regaline explained, "victorious and stranded, had banded together to find a way to continue the terraforming project. They knew their habitats would fail eventually, as all mechanical things do. They created new tools to continue terraforming the planet into a habitable state. Using the same bioprinters that created their bodies, the Watchers, as they dubbed themselves, grew a population of humans, animals, and plants adapted to the pervading environment and infused with nanites specially created for the task of continuing their terraforming work. The Watchers seeded these early humans, flora, and fauna around the planet but concentrated them in rings around their home base. The nanites living inside them did the work without conscious effort from the populace.

"As the planet became more hospitable, they continuously modified the population, introducing traits that allowed them to continue to thrive and survive in the changing climate. Because the library of genetic material they had access to was limited, the Watchers themselves were forced to add their own genes to the mix to maintain genetic diversity."

After that, they retired to their rooms, to get an early start. Regaline and Jessen drilled Drak while they walked, to give him as much practice with his weapons, defensive countermeasures, and healing applications as they could.

"What are your thoughts on entering the tower?" Jessen asked Regaline when they stopped on their third night away from the safehouse.

"I was thinking," she said after a moment, "Once we cross the border, we head south to the highlands. Fewer people there, less chance of discovery. Those trails will take us right where we need to go."

"This sounds familiar," he said, looking unhappy. "Wasn't this how you planned on entering Interland during your incursion a year ago?"

"It's exactly the same plan."

"Nope!" Jessen said, slapping his knees and shaking his head. "Not going to work. Not a good plan. We need to come up with something else."

"There's nothing wrong with this plan," Regaline said. "Don't let what happened a year ago make you jumpy. The route should be secure. I made it inside and back out again without any issues."

"Well, I didn't!"

"What happened a year ago?" Drak asked.

"Nothing," Regaline said.

At the same time, Jessen said, "I nearly had my leg cut off before we even reached the border!"

"Don't exaggerate."

"Exaggerate! Take a look at this." He stood and pulled up the cuff of his right pant leg. In the waning light, he pointed to a band of hairless skin just below the knee that seemed paler than the rest. "There's no scarring, thanks to my nan, but I can't grow hair there. In an almost perfect ring around my leg, I can't grow any hair."

Drak looked closer, and sure enough, he was right. "Cool!"

"Don't be such a baby," Regaline said, scoffing. "It's not like you were going to die." She turned to Drak. "We were ambushed at the border by five casters. We managed to neutralize them, but Jessen here got a little sloppy and it almost cost him his leg."

"I did not get sloppy. How was I to know the last bastard had a dead-man trigger?"

"You would have if you'd scanned him before trying to move him. Then he wouldn't have blown up and you wouldn't be whining about your completely intact leg right now."

"That's not the point," Jessen said.

"Then what is your point?"

"The point is ... I don't want to go that way after what happened."

"It wasn't as bad as he's making it out to be," Regaline said when she saw the look of alarm on Drak's face. "I made sure his nan was already repairing the damage. Then I splinted the leg, wrapped it, and helped him under cover."

"Then you left me."

"We were still on mission. I didn't have a choice. We had a job to do. You couldn't do it anymore, so I left most of my food and water with you while you healed, and I continued the mission. I got the information we were after. You lived and kept your leg. What are you complaining about?"

Jessen made a face at her and sat back down. Regaline had won the argument, and he clearly didn't wasn't happy about it.

To Drak, much of the exchange between them felt slightly rehearsed. As though this were an old point of contention between them.

"What do, or did, I guess, you both do for Hillcrest?" he asked.

The change of subject was a welcome relief for the two old companions.

"We were spies," Jessen said without hesitation. Drak's eyes lit up immediately.

Regaline, on the other hand, merely rolled her eyes. "We were field level intelligence and counterespionage operatives."

"That's what I said. Spies."

"Mine sounds better."

"Fair point. We were level intelligent counterfield agents, or whatever the hell she said."

Jessen was smiling, and Drak was giggling. Even Regaline's mood lightened.

"You can never take anything seriously, can you?" she said.

"I thought my leg was pretty serious," he replied.

Rather than become embroiled in the same argument again, Regaline shook her head and went to gather more firewood. Regaline started cooking dinner, and Drak immediately pounced on Jessen and started badgering him with questions about his life as a spy until it was time to go to sleep.

Though reluctant at first, Regaline had come to accept her role as mentor and teacher. When she'd first found and collected Drak and Kayah, her lessons had been hesitant and unsure. Now she spoke with confidence and authority as she explained the ins and outs of nan-casting. She was, however, more reticent when it came to discussing history. Specifically, the history behind the creation of Interland and Hillcrest and how the two countries had become so diametrically opposed to one another. Naturally, this enflamed Drak's curiosity, and he asked questions non-stop until Regaline relented.

"Enough pestering," Regaline said after enduring Drak's pleading for more information for the last hour. Drak quieted immediately, intent on listening. "Alright, I'll give you the short version of the story. If you have any questions after that, I'll be happy to answer them. Just keep in mind we are not slowing down. So, keep up."

Walking in front of them, Jessen glanced over his shoulder at them and chuckled.

"Okay, I'll tell you about how the Order of Watchers self-destructed. During the century after the Breakdown, the Watchers made great gains in the land. They needed a means to continue terraforming this planet. Their machines were broken for the time being, so they needed an alternative, and we were it. Or rather, our forebearers were. They had engineered the plants, animals, and eventually even the people they populated the world with to exude a nanite cloud that continued terraforming piecemeal. Every living thing on our world is connected to every other living thing through the nan inside us. Through their efforts, the air became breathable, the water drinkable, and the soil fit for crops. It was only after the first generation was born that the Watchers realized some of us had the ability to wield nan as they did. The enclaves of people they seeded in the lands around their tower were successful and even thriving. Life was hard. But that's been an unpleasant fact since our earliest days. Feeling confident in their successes, they pushed further out, hoping to turn the amber zone green and push back the red zone. Their reach far exceeded their grasp. They couldn't know it, but their very existence was about to end."

"Why?" Drak asked. "What happened to them?"

"They destroyed themselves," she said, the smile fading from her lips. "The differences between them grew too great and caused a schism. Where once had been a single order dedicated to the cultivation of the land and people, there were now two factions bent on defeating each other. While both sides saw the problem, they disagreed on how to fix it. One side felt the old ways were working and should be continued. The other felt they needed to embrace new ideas and make drastic changes to deal with the problems they were seeing."

"Who won?"

The dour expression Regaline wore grew even more serious. "Neither. They destroyed themselves, and in the heat of their conflict, they released the monster defeated long ago by Astrid Free: the Swarm Mind I've told you about. When violence finally died down, the few survivors fled when they realized what they had done."

"Then what happened?" Drak asked.

"Aion, the creature that the people of Interland revere as a god and who their leaders want to awaken, was also born from the nanites. However, instead of coexisting, as we do, it seeks to overcome and control all living things. Astrid Free was able to stop it by confining it to the Tower where it had been born. With nanites infused into everything across the planet, it would be impossible to stop it once awakened and was released. The surviving Watchers recognized the need to prevent it from escaping its prison. For nearly eighty years, this has been Hillcrest's mission."

"This is why the both of you are so important," Jessen added, "to us and to Interland. Your blood contains the keys to this monster's prison, as well as the means to destroy it entirely."

CHAPTER 22
RANCE

Hearing the outer door close, knowing he was locked inside, made Rance feel less brave and more foolish than he had a mere moment ago.

Outwardly, nothing was any different. The lights had stopped flickering, the HEPA filters had scrubbed the scents of smoke from the air, and the sounds of fighting and screaming had quieted. The Watch Tower looked much the same as it had upon his return a month ago. Still, there was an eerie, almost haunted feeling about the place. Even though it hadn't been fully occupied in decades, the few people who had been there had given the place a sense of life.

Now there was nothing.

Just oppressive silence.

The soft soles of his shoes squeaked slightly with each step. His breathing, though intentionally calm and regular, was loud in his ears.

Why am I doing this? he thought. *This is crazy. I should just leave.*

But he knew he couldn't. This was a problem they couldn't just ignore and hope for the best. It would come back to them eventually. Better to deal with it now while he still had a chance.

He slowly made his way deeper into the Watch Tower, looking for a control terminal. There were plenty in Operations. But he didn't think returning there would be a good idea. He had no idea if those things were still there, but felt it wasn't worth the risk. With the dampening field reengaged, at least temporarily, he was essentially unarmed. This thought drew him up short.

What did he plan on doing if he came across one of them? His only weapons were his fists and harsh language. He doubted the efficacy of either against the thing that had taken over Sprague, Marlow, and the others.

"Have to get something better," he said aloud. At the next corridor junction, he turned left and made his way to the materials lab. Time was precious, but he needed a means to defend himself. In the lab, he brought a trio of printers online and started fabricating the things he thought he might need.

Five minutes later, the first project was completed. Eight minutes later, the other two were done. Rance hefted the long knife from the first printer and tested its edge. Not razor sharp, but not dull either. It was big, it was heavy, and it would do. He took a few practice swings with the fire axe and the club that came out of the other printers. Satisfied, he found a bag and strapped them to his back. The knife, he slid into his belt.

Feeling more confident, Rance resumed his trek deeper into the facility.

While waiting for his weapons to print, he'd brainstormed ways to disrupt the Swarm Mind from reemerging. He assumed it must be actively trying to break through the security lockout and deactivate the dampening field. The quickest and easiest way to prevent them from accomplishing that was to disrupt the power flow to Operations and other key areas.

There were only a few places where someone could access the reactor controls. If he were a creature like Sprague, he would be actively trying to deactivate the dampening field while keeping an eye on the other vital areas to prevent exactly what Rance had in mind. There were only four of them, so it was still a pretty tall order. Thankfully, they were cut off from the Swarm Mind, isolated in their bodies without the rest of the nanites in the structure to aid them. Despite that, the facility was still active, and they could still monitor the interior via conventional means. He would have to eliminate them to ensure the Swarm Mind remained contained. If they were alone, Rance thought he had a chance. Sneak up, bash them over the head, one by one, then get out of there. Simple.

He hoped.

"Reactor Control it is," he said.

A few turns and stairs later, he was back outside the reactor control room. Though it had only been a little over an hour, it felt like a lifetime ago that Sprague found and captured him down there. The room was exactly as he'd left it. He glanced around briefly and was relieved to find himself alone. Rance adjusted the knife in his belt and pulled the bat from his pack before heading straight to the user interface and connecting to it.

The first thing he did was access the internal security network to locate the Swarm Mind's automatons. He'd guessed right. The thing that had been Sprague was still in the Operations Center trying to get around the lockout protecting the firewall. Rance tried using the internal imagers to locate the other three, but that system wasn't available from this UI. Sprague was attacking the lockout with the blind determination and brute force focus of a machine.

"Time to mess up your day." Rance cut the power to the Operations level and a few other areas to make it more difficult for them. Without power, the doors had to be manually cranked open, which would cost them time. Enough, he hoped, to allow him to do what he needed to do.

There was a clatter from somewhere behind him in the chamber. He whipped around, club at the ready. Though he couldn't see what had made the sound, the feeling in the room had changed. The hairs on the back of his neck stood, and he felt a slight shiver run up his spine.

He wasn't alone anymore.

After securing the UI, he made a circuit of the room,

checking the corners and workstations he'd only glanced at before.

He heard shuffling from the opposite side, but when he looked there was nothing there. He activated his sensors, which were likewise blank. Whoever was in there with him was masking themselves. Playing with him. Likely trying to distract him while the others converged on his location. This was the only place in the Watch Tower where power could be directly manipulated, which meant Sprague and the others were already on their way.

He returned to the UI, reopened it, and initiated the process that would lock the workstation down so only he could access it in the future. There were ways around this lockout, but they would take time and give him a chance to slip away. As an afterthought, he added a backdoor access code, just in case they tried locking him out.

As he was about to close the UI, he felt the air shift behind him. Decades spent in the wilderness, hunting and being hunted, gave him a heightened perception for danger. He dropped into a crouch and rolled away from the interface. At the same time, he heard the whistle of a blade cutting the air where he'd just been.

Rance hardened his skin. He couldn't access his weapons, However, because most of protective applications had actually been designed for working in harsh environments, they were still available for use. He assumed a fighting stance, spun, and swung the club blindly, not hoping to connect with anything but merely to give himself some space.

It worked. The creature ducked and backed away from him.

Holding the club in front of him, Rance quickly assessed the situation. The only exit was twenty meters away. If he ran for it, the thing would catch him. It was mostly open space, with the workstations either built into the walls or extruded from the floor when called upon. So, there was nothing he could use to dodge around or keep between himself and the creature.

The creature, one of Sprague's guards whose name still escaped him, leapt forward. Rance dodged to the side and gave a half-hearted swing to gain some space. He knew it was delaying him. The others were undoubtedly on the way. He had to end this quickly or risk becoming surrounded. Regardless of what the stories said, winning a fight against multiple opponents was tricky, if not impossible. He'd found himself in similar situations before, facing down several opponents at once out in the wilds, and the only way he'd managed to survive was to single out a single opponent and defeat them to even up the odds.

Easier said than done.

Content to wait him out, the thing before him settled into a defensive stance. This gave Rance a chance to get a good look at it. It had once been human, and though it still looked as human as he was, it moved with far more fluid grace than any human Rance had ever seen. Its skin had a plastic pallor, likely armored. Then there were its hands, which were balled into fists with a single slender scythe blade protruding from the wrist and through the hand. The blade was about thirty centimeters long and wickedly curved. The worst thing was its eyes. Bright, metallic orbs, shiny and featureless. It tracked his every move with those dead eyes.

With the clock ticking, Rance flooded his body with adrenaline, then set his nan to heightened combat mode, which, along with the adrenaline, seemed to bring his perspective of time to a standstill. Then he overclocked his movement speed and power.

Though effective in short bursts for combat purposes, using so many combat applications at once was taxing on him and his nanites.

He stepped forward, brought up his club and charged the creature. Its reaction was comically slow to him. Though its face registered no emotional reaction to his sudden attack, it immediately took a step back and brought up its blades to defend itself. Rance easily knocked one hand aside, heard the satisfying crunch of breaking bones, then slammed the carbon fiber bat into the side of the creature's head rapidly three times. In slow motion, he watched the contact of the club deform and crush its skull inward. As the creature crumpled, Rance turned slightly and swung the bat in a downward power swing aimed at its head, and the middle of its back. Once it was down, he deactivated his applications, and activated his cutting torch. In compliance with the dampening field, it was a simple welding torch. A tool, not a weapon, just a tool. But a tool was what he needed right now.

When he was done, a charred pile of sticky ash was all that remained.

Rance didn't wait to see if the thing would repair itself but ran for the door. The encounter had taken a total of a hundred and forty-three seconds. Precious time he had needed to flee for safety. He activated the lockout on the UI, then gave a shout of surprise that wasn't quite a scream when the door opened, and he nearly ran into the figure standing on the other side.

Immediately assuming a fighting stance, Rance was about to swing the club when the person on the other side of the door held up her hands and shouted, "Wait!"

Rance paused and took a better look. It was Silla.

"What the hell are you doing here?" he demanded. "I thought you all were outside heading to safety."

"We were," she said, "but we got to talking, and I decided you shouldn't do this on your own. I came back to help."

"How did you find me?"

"The power to the tram dock shut off after I got back in. Which made it pretty obvious where you were."

"I know. I was just leaving, but I had a run-in with one of them." He stepped aside to show her the ash pile.

"Looks like it went well," she said, wrinkling her nose in disgust.

"Thanks. We can talk later. They are probably close. We need to leave."

Instead of taking the main stairs, they ducked into the maintenance crawlways. It took a moment to pry open the hatch. Once they were inside with the hatch closed behind him, Rance heard the sounds of running feet.

Just in time, he thought. Silla placed a finger up to her lips. Rance nodded, though he had no intention of making any noise until they were far away.

A horrendous, piercing scream filled the air, full of rage and pain and sorrow, reverberating down the tunnel and causing them to flinch.

Apparently, the automatons didn't take kindly to him killing one of their own.

Twenty minutes later, the power blinked back on, and they heard them depart, walking this time. With his enhanced hearing, Rance counted three sets of feet—all of them—and was suddenly glad he'd finished the fight quickly. One of them had been difficult enough, all four would have been impossible. Just a moment or two more, and they would have caught him. It hadn't taken them long to undo his little sabotage in the reactor room. He'd have to come up with something better to stop them.

"Let's go," he whispered.

"Where to next?" Silla asked.

"I'm trying to disrupt their ability to deactivate the dampening field," he said as they crawled. "Cutting the power was a way to buy time and to get each of them alone to take them out. They can't release the Swarm Mind if they're dead."

"Good point," Silla said. "Tough to do. Especially alone. Good thing I came back."

Rance nodded. He didn't want to admit how much better he felt having her there.

"I think our next stop should be Secondary Control. From there, we should be able to hinder their efforts more. Maybe even come up with a more permanent solution." If they managed to dispatch another one of them in the process, so much the better.

Exiting the crawlway in the central lift shaft, they took a moment to stretch before mounting the ladder running up the side of the shaft in a channel. Looking up, he took a deep, resigned breath. Climbing the distance between the first basement and the third level above ground, where the backup control center was located, was not his idea of a fun time. However, they didn't have another alternative.

Upon exiting at the third level, they made their way cautiously but briskly to Secondary Control. With power reconnected to Operations, it was imperative they find some way to block the automatons. Even though they were walking around in human bodies, Sprague and his flunkies were really just machines now. Computers. As such, it would be a simple task for them to break through the blocks preventing the Swarm Mind from reforming.

They had to move faster.

Secondary Control was a miniature version of the Operations Center, meant to be activated in case of emergency, such as a fire or breach in the facility's outer walls. It was a failsafe carryover from the days when the planet hadn't had a breathable atmosphere. Now it would serve as a focal point for their sabotage.

He brought up a UI and accessed the firewalls locking down the dampening field first, while Silla used the other station to look for a permanent solution.

"Preventing the Swarm Mind from reforming is our first priority," he said.

Silla thought a moment. "I think the simplest way would be to prevent them from accessing the virtual control panel. They're locked out for now, but I saw what you did earlier; it won't take them long to get through. From the control panel, it'll be simple for them to brute force their way past the firewalls. We need something foolproof. A key they can't find, duplicate, or spoof."

"Maybe we create a key tied to our DNA," he said. Then he immediately shook his head. "Never mind. If we do that while we're still trapped in here with them, all they need to do is make sure we don't leave. They wouldn't even need us alive to extract the key from our bodies."

"Right. Best not to leave the keys to the lock in their reach."

They needed something else. While he racked his brain for an alternative, his mind kept returning to the idea of tying the key to someone's DNA. Genetic code was big enough and sufficiently complicated enough to be nearly impossible to spoof, and when combined with other layers of encryption, any efforts to crack it would be utterly futile. Especially if they could destroy the automatons. Then there wouldn't be anyone left to defeat the encryption. He couldn't think of any other way to truly secure the system against intrusion.

Apparently, Silla's mind had been running along the same lines. "Something just occurred to me," she said. "The DNA we use doesn't necessarily have to be someone living." Rance turned to her, eyes wide with the implications of what she was saying. "Site 2 has a massive library of genetic samples, both from the HelixCom employees terraforming the planet and from after the Breakdown when we grew the human population to continue the process. We could use one of those."

"That could work," he said and opened the DNA codex. "We don't want to use anyone from the native population. There is no telling how prolific their code is by this point. If we can't eliminate Sprague's people, all they would have to do is snatch a few people to find the code they need. We should limit our search to the former employees, specifically ones who are dead or at least off-world."

Immediately, he and Silla ruled out everyone who'd been working here at Site 2 during the Breakdown. Next, they eliminated everyone who had been alive up to a month ago. After the recent civil war, genetic material would be splattered all over the facility. That narrowed the field considerably. There were only a few names on the list in front of him.

"This one," Silla said, pointing at one name. Feeling a sense of poetry, Rance smiled and nodded. Then they began encrypting the system based on the DNA sequence they'd found. Once they were done, the entire system would be locked down for good and inaccessible even to them.

When everything was set and ready, Rance engaged the encryption while Silla purged the digital genetic codex. Everything associated with the genetic codes in the memory banks was erased. They would need to deal with the live samples in person.

"We can go to the gene vault and douse the containers housing the samples with a reactive chemical that dissolves biological tissue," Silla said.

"While we're there, we can also delete the computer imprints," Rance added.

It was a good plan. This meant they had two more stops to make before they could completely lock the site down. To buy some more time, Rance had Silla step out into the hall, then used his nan to spin up an intense electromagnetic field around himself to destroy all the user interfaces in Secondary Control.

He left the room fritzing and pixelating. They re-entered the crawlways to climb down the gene vault on level two. Due to the importance of the material inside, the gene vault was one of the few upper-level rooms with an old-fashioned, physically actuated door. This ensured that even in the event of power loss, the environment inside the room would be maintained while still allowing worker access.

The gene vault was a large chamber crowded with equipment and deep in the facility. There were several workstations, as well as several physical server towers, independent of the facility's central data systems. The physical genetic samples were housed in hermetically sealed metal cylinders that regulated the temperature and environment to preserve the samples stored within. Due to the original mission of Site 2, this had been considered the most important room on-site. It had its own independent power, ventilation, and computer network. Site 2 could suffer a catastrophic shutdown, and the gene vault would remain safe and applicational.

Rance locked the door behind them, and then, one by one, he and Silla went to each physical station and zapped it with a micro EMP to wipe the data and destroy the equipment completely physically. Then they went to each cylinder housing the genetic material to feed the chemicals that would destroy the DNA. They worked quickly to completely erase everything in the room. Once they were done, there was only one place left for them to go.

The reek of caustic chemicals quickly filled the room, making the air borderline unbreathable. They had to be careful while attaching the hoses because the dissolving agent would corrode any biological tissue it came into contact with, including them. Rance's nan was working overtime in his lungs to prevent him from asphyxiating.

Silla was finishing up with the final tank when something started pounding on the outer door. They'd been found. The door shuddered under the repeated impacts.

Like the Reactor Chamber, there was only a single way in or out. They were going to have to fight their way through them. Rance had hoped they'd be able to finish up in here before dealing with the automatons. They still had to cut the power to the facility and engage the system locks they'd set up.

"Do you know how inconvenient this is?" he shouted at the door. To Silla, he said, "How much time left?"

"This is the last tank, and it's almost full now. We've already zapped all the stations. Just a couple minutes, and we're done in here. Got a plan for getting around the party crasher out there?"

"We're just going to have to deal with it," Rance said with a shake of his head. Silla climbed down and took the bat from him. "It should be easier between the two of us," he said hopefully.

The door was distinctly concave by this point and starting to sag in its frame. Soon it would be through. He could hear the grunts of exertion from it every time it hit the door. A gap was starting to form between the upper edge and the door jamb.

Silla saw this, handed the club back to Rance, and took his knife. Acting quickly, she cut the hoses leading into the top of the tank closest to the door. Careful not to let any chemicals touch her, she kinked the hose and pulled it over to the door. It was barely long enough, but it reached. When the creature hit again, she stuck the hose through the gap and let go, spraying everything on the other side. There was a gasp of surprise, followed by a yowl of pain. Rance couldn't see what was happening, but from the infuriated agony and thrashing, it sounded like the creature was dying painfully. Not a moment too soon, either. The door had nearly buckled under the onslaught.

"Good," Silla said. "I hoped there was enough organic material left in them to be affected by the chemicals in the tanks. Now there's only two left."

Rance stood in awe. "Goddamn brilliant." He gave her a high five.

"I have my moments," Silla said with a short bow.

They gave it a few minutes before leaving. The door was twisted in its frame and had to be levered open. They stepped around the lumpy puddle of melted flesh spreading in the middle of the corridor. There was no way of telling which one it had been, Sprague, Marlow, or the second flunky. The smell of corroded flesh was strong and made them gag as they edged past it.

"Only one more stop," he said. "Back to the reactor room."

"You know they'll probably be waiting for us, right?"

"No choice," he shrugged. "We need to cut the power to the site after we engage the lockdown and encrypt it. We can do that from reactor control."

"I'm tired of crawling around the maintenance passages. Let's take the stairs this time."

Rance was tired of crawling, too, so he didn't argue or point out that they were more likely to encounter the last two automatons in the open corridors. He merely said, "Let's hurry."

They didn't encounter anything until they reached the reactor room, where they found what had once been Marlow waiting inside. As he had in the reactor room, Rance prepped himself for combat. His energy reserves were low by this point, and he was starting to feel tired.

Marlow launched itself at them the moment the door irised open. Rance had time to note that Marlow's left hand had formed into a sledgehammer and his right hand ended with two shorter stabbing blades. The blades were thin, tapered, and tri-edged. Perfect for punching a hole in someone that wouldn't close naturally or easily. It went for Silla with wild swings that forced her to dive away to her left. Rance went right and swung his axe, burying the blade deep into Marlow's back. The hit threw it off balance, causing it to fall and slide face-first across the floor. Silla was back on her feet by then, and Rance pointed to the UI terminal behind her. She nodded and got to work.

Meanwhile, Marlow was up and turned to face Rance, who had placed himself between it and Silla.

Marlow reached around, its arm bending backward at an impossible angle, and knocked the axe free from its back with one swipe of his hammerhand. Then he spread his arms wide, bent low, and began to circle in close to Rance. Suddenly, it leapt in, swiping at him with its hammerhand. Rance took a step back and dodged to the left, then fell into a roll to avoid the blades of Marlow's right hand jabbing up at him. Before he could recover, Marlow brought its hammerhand back around and clipped him on the shoulder. The impact caused his arm to go numb for a moment despite his skin armor.

"Shit," Rance said. He spun up his healing applications, again flooded his system with adrenaline, and sped up his cognitive and reaction speeds. This allowed him to land a solid hit on Marlow's face while the creature was rebounding from its previous swing. Rance activated his cutting torch and brought it to bear on Marlow's neck. He burned away most of the creature's jaw before it leapt back.

While Rance was fighting for his life, Silla managed to set the lockdown protocols in place and cut the power to the rest of the facility. She left the power on in the basement and along the path they planned to take to make their escape. Then she initiated the reactor shutdown process and set it to a timer before locking everything down under the blanket encryption they'd devised. Once the countdown was complete, the reactor would safely dial itself into a low-power output mode.

Momentarily at a safe distance, the Marlow thing stood still, hissing in fury and glaring at Rance. He watched as the skin and bones of its jaw seemed to liquify, pixelate, and reform. In the blink of an eye, its face was whole again. Only a small seam creased the skin to mark where Rance's cutting torch had damaged it. Then it came at him again. Rance perceived its movements in slow motion. He grew hardened knobs on the knuckles of his fists and prepared to use them to bash the creature senseless. He moved in for a haymaker, when Marlow suddenly began moving at normal speed relative to his. The creature deflected his punch, shoulder-checked him, and tossed him to the side.

It had figured out his trick and was using it against him.

Not good.

Moving even faster than Rance could hope to, Marlow charged.

Rance felt the hammer strike the side of his head. A split second later, a sharp pain in his left side told him he'd been stabbed. He shoved Marlow away as hard as his enhanced muscles would allow and retreated a few steps. Medical warning messages blared at the periphery of his vision. His nanites, already overtaxed, struggled to keep up with the applications he was using, as well as the damage he was taking.

Another hit landed in between his shoulder blades, followed by a jab into his left side ribs. Rance kicked Marlow in the knee, hoping to drop it and gain some space. It was like kicking a steel girder. Marlow didn't even flinch. Then it tossed him across the room again. It had reformed its left hand to match the right, sporting two tri-blade daggers.

Silla appeared behind Marlow, and she stabbed it in the back of the head, where the skull connected with the spinal column, then snapped the carbon fiber club in half when hammering the knife deeper.

Marlow spun faster than her eye could track and thrust both its hands into her chest, puncturing her heart and both lungs. Then he lifted her off her feet and threw her across the room, where she landed in a heap next to Rance.

He looked up and saw Marlow, its head sitting askew atop its neck, knife blade jabbing through its throat as it leaned in to strike again. Knowing he wouldn't survive another attack, Rance did the only thing he could think of. He deactivated all his defensive and healing applications and pulled his nan from their healing tasks.

Marlow's arms extended before it as though reaching out to Rance for an embrace. Then it swung downward with all its might. Light glinted off the blades as they sailed through the air at him.

The second before Marlow reached him, Rance activated

a small, targeted electromagnetic pulse funneled directly into the automaton. Marlow's husk crashed into him, the killing blades narrowly missing his vital organs, and pinned him to the floor.

For a moment, Rance simply lay there, out of breath and in pain. It took some time and excruciating effort, but he managed to pull the arm blades from his body and shove the creature off him. He tried to stand but found his legs didn't want to obey. Before he could do anything else, he had to let his nan heal him.

Then the doors opened, and Sprague walked in.

CHAPTER 23

ASTRID

Watching sunrise through the porthole, Astrid marveled at how far they'd come in transforming this world. She didn't often stop to think about the grand scope of work they were doing. This morning, she couldn't help it.

She'd felt alone since returning from Site 2 two weeks ago. During that time, she and Danny had been working on how to counter Kinney. The Swarm Mind had a plan. Something Kinney was privy to, something she remained in the dark about. Kinney had promised they would work closely together, and Astrid had hoped that meant she'd learn what he was up to and devise a way to stop it. But that hadn't happened yet.

They'd had a lunch meeting the day after she and Danny made their discoveries, but that had been mostly about work, their real work, for HelixCom. She worried Kinney could sense something different about her and had, therefore, decided to keep her at a distance.

The pale sun peeked over the distant horizon, banishing the purple shades of night and casting the landscape in wan light through the tiny window. The tans and browns of the native grasses waved in the breeze as the sudden change in temperature stirred the air around them. They were dying. Slowly but surely dying as the terraforming processes displaced them from their niche. There hadn't been much life on Kuridian when the probes arrived. What little there was before human arrival had been deemed expendable in favor of a more hospitable climate for human beings. As the composition of the air in the atmosphere changed, the grasses receded. With the conversion of the oceans and seas to liquid water, they died, poisoned by something that was nourishing to her kind.

Survival of the fittest, enforced by modern technology.

Green algae and lichen grew in place of the brown grasses. Overtaking the native flora and stealing the land. In time, the ground and oceans would be suitable for growing more complex plants that could support more complex animals, which in turn would support the people who came after her. Rich, well-to-do humans desiring a novel place to call home, their families, and the willing and indentured workforces they would bring with them.

She'd never thought of Kuridian as pretty. Even those with an affectionate eye for desolate places would find that Kuridian looked more like a stain than a masterpiece of natural wonder. Ugly. But the gradual, piecemeal destruction she witnessed and enabled was uglier. The unsightly nature would be replaced by something beautiful by any Earth standard. Artificially pristine nature, lovingly cultivated by the most caring and nurturing cost-effective hands the board of directors could hire.

Grimacing, she stepped away from the window. She hated being this maudlin. She had to do something, anything, to break up her current mood.

A message notification appeared in her peripheral. It was a summons from Kinney.

She forgot about the dying biosphere outside. Her mood improved with the possibility of action, or at least information. She couldn't very well fight against Kinney's plans if she didn't know what they were.

A few minutes later, she was outside his office door.

"Come in, Astrid," Kinney said, answering her knock.

She found him behind the desk that, until recently, had

belonged to Waler. A tingle of revulsion crept up at the sight of him. She'd disliked Waler. Even though he was a toxic boss and a shitty human being, he hadn't deserved what had been done to him. There was nothing she could do to rectify that, but she could put a stop to whatever Kinney had planned for the rest of them.

When she closed the door, he looked up at her, beaming. "Please sit! We have a lot to talk about. Are you thirsty? I remember right after my conversion, there wasn't enough water in the world to satisfy me. I can have something brought up if you want."

Astrid swallowed. *Act normal. Put up a friendly false face. Keep him from realizing what you intend to do. Don't scowl at him. Be nice!*

"I'm fine for now," she said. "Maybe later."

"Alrighty," he said, bobbing his head. "I'm pretty sure you know why I called you up here."

"I presume you're going to tell me what the plan is. I've been back for two weeks now without a clue as to what is going on."

"I know. And I'm sorry. I figured you would want some time to reacquaint yourself with your body and get back into the swing of things. It's a pretty extreme culture shock between the two sites. Trust me, I know."

"I appreciate that. I think I'm good now. Give me a task. Tell me what to do."

Kinney's grin widened. "That's wonderful to hear." He cleared his throat. "As you are aware, Aion has successfully converted the population of Site 2. They are a part of him now. Currently, only you and I are the only converts here at Site 1. This is a condition we are going to change. Starting this month, I am going to implement a plan to convert everyone here within the next two months."

"How are we going to do that?"

"The same way you were converted. Starting with the lower-tier employees, we are going to start sending them to Site 2 for vacations. On the surface, it will look like we are rewarding the people who do the hard work around here. To show them we value their contributions to the project. Then, we'll send their supervisors and managers, and so on up the chain. I figure it will only take two months to fully convert the Site 1 population."

"What about after?"

"After that, we use the skylift to get a few agents off-world and begin the conversion process abroad. I've already got candidates in mind for personnel transfers. A few at first to gain a foothold in HelixCom. Once we have that, the next stage begins, where we create a vessel to upload our lord off-world and into the general human population."

"The supply ship might be the best option for that. It's the only craft large enough to smuggle anything away from here."

"Yes. Exactly." Kinney was almost hopping in his seat with excitement over her being on the same page as him. "We are still a ways away from that phase of the plan. However, I like that you are already thinking of ways to accomplish it. I knew you were the right choice."

"Question: why can't we simply transmit someone back to spread the sacrament?"

"That won't work," he said. "In the first place, it's imperative that someone physically make the journey. Merely transferring their mind won't work. In fact, that might have the opposite effect of what Aion wants."

"You're saying transfer over the network would eliminate Aion's influence from whoever was sent?"

"Exactly. They would start in a new body without his sacrament. There's another problem with your idea. Though you and I, and anyone who's received his sacrament, can, in theory, convert others, it is not a complete conversion. Only Aion himself can completely infuse a person."

"Anyone we convert would be a lesser version of us."

"Once again, you prove just how amazing your brain is.

You get it. The goal, all along, has been to convert the population here, then get Aion off-world in any way we can to spread his love and devotion."

"Yes, that does pose a problem," she admitted, nodding. "How much of him would have to be smuggled off-world?"

"The more we can move, obviously the better. But a little as a kilogram would suffice."

"That's good. I would hate to think we went through all this and remained stranded on this half-baked planet."

"Aion assures me his plan will work as expected."

"How often are you in communication with him?" Astrid said, hoping he wouldn't notice the slight shift of subjects.

"Every few days. I'm planning on calling him this evening, in fact. You're welcome to stay so you can see him."

"Thank you," she said. "But I'm feeling lightheaded all of a sudden. I think I need to eat and lie down. I guess I'm not as adjusted as I thought I was."

"Do you want me to take a look at you?" he offered, rising from his chair.

"No, thank you." She held up a hand, forestalling him. "I've been taking it easy for a while now. I think I just overexerted myself today." She stood. "Is there anything else you need me for?"

"Not right now," Kinney said, rising from his seat.

Was there a hint of suspicion in the concerned look he wore? Astrid brushed it off as paranoia and accepted the hug he offered when he came around the desk arms open. She forced herself to remain calm during the embrace, which was both too long and too close for her comfort. Then she bid him good day and left.

She found Danny in his makeshift lab analyzing the Swarm Mind nanites again. He'd had to isolate them from Astrid's nanites before they were completely rewritten. He barely glanced up when she entered, shutting the door behind her with a hollow thunk. "How'd it go?"

"Good," she said. "I learned a lot."

"Like what?"

"First and foremost, Kinney is a pervert. Also, he let me in on his plan to convert everyone in this facility and make them like him."

"Simple and smart," Danny said, after she explained Kinney's plan. "Everyone I know would jump at the chance to live in luxury at Site 2 for a week."

"They'd be walking into a trap, and there's no way we can warn them without tipping off Kinney and the Swarm."

"Did he tell you what the end goal is?"

"They are trying to get the Swarm Mind"—she refused to think of the thing by its name— "off-world and into human-held space."

Danny whistled.

"Right. We need to find a way to stop them."

"I think I might be able to help." He motioned her to join him at the screen. "So, these nanites operate via a simple communication network. This allows them to share information and instructions. You're familiar with all this, I'm sure."

"I passed Nanorobotics 101 with a B," she said. "The dampening field interferes with how nanites form these networks. They can communicate with others in their immediate vicinity, but the field prevents them from talking to more distant nanites, and it also restricts the bandwidth they have available to transfer information to nanites close by. It's a protection measure modeled on the old disease Alzheimer's."

"Almost word for word from the book. I think you're right about how the Swarm Mind formed. Instead of creating networks from individual nanites, it's connecting clusters. Creating nodes at the exact limit allowed by the dampening field, then networking those clusters with others the same size."

"Incredible. So, we just turn up the field intensity and cut the clusters off from one another to disrupt the network."

"That's my thinking," Danny said, sitting back in his chair. "The only problem is the fact that it lives inside Site 2, which is basically made of nanites and programable matter. It'll be tough shutting it down in there."

"Everyone at Site 2 has been taken over by this thing. Getting past them will be hard."

Danny thought a moment, then gave her a wry grin. "Aren't you one of them now?"

"I suppose I am. But I'm not sure I could pass an up-close inspection. Besides, what reason would I have to go back? The Swarm Mind wants me here. It would be suspicious if I returned without a good reason."

"It's basically just a computer right?" Danny said. "All computers, no matter how advanced, are basically simple minded. They can only see the world through two modes: 1 and 0, on and off. This means we should be able to spoof an ID that should allow you to get in and out without raising an alarm. If you have the right ID, then it should assume that you belong there without question. We can plan a route for you through some back hallways to avoid entanglements with its hosts."

"Great," Astrid said, bringing up a floor plan of Site 2. "Do you know where the dampening field is generated from?"

"As a matter of fact, I do." Danny swiped at the screen a few times and zoomed in on a small room off one of the second level plenums. "Here. This room is Nanite Processing. This is where they are produced and refurbished. Any code updates or changes to their makeup are made in here first, then distributed sitewide. We have one here too. I was actually in there just last week. There was a glitch in the assembly tool that took me ten hours to track down and correct. In hindsight, it might have been another bit of sabotage by our good friend Kinney."

Astrid studied the layout of the room and the path she planned on taking to reach it. Then she brought up the manual for the field emitters and started reading it.

"When do you plan on going?" Danny asked.

"Today. Kinney said he was going to contact the Swarm Mind today. We subdue him once he's done so he can't warn them I'm coming, and then I head back over to Site 2. That way, it thinks everything is still under control here. We have to do it right after he's done, and I'm going to need your help with it."

"I'm down," Danny said, nodding. Then he walked over to a box of tools on the floor by the door. After a bit of digging, he came up with several heavy-duty zip ties. "These should work."

On the tram returning to Site 2, Astrid studied the manual she'd downloaded earlier, trying to come up with a procedure for increasing the effectiveness of the dampening field effect. On the surface it looked straightforward. Still, she wanted to make doubly sure she could troubleshoot any problems that might arise. She was marching alone into enemy territory. If she was discovered, then there was a very real possibility they would kill her. That worry was one of several weighing on her.

She almost wished Danny were with her. Having a friend by her side would make this situation a whole lot easier. Instead, he had remained behind to prepare for the fallout from their plan. Plus, someone needed to watch over Kinney.

They'd found him standing in his office with the lights out. It was late; everyone in the outer office had already been off-shift and in their quarters for the night. In fact, most of the facility had been asleep. Only the skeletal night shift had been awake, operating and monitoring the vital systems.

Kinney had taken no notice when they entered. He had just stood there, his head tilted back, unbreathing, his eyes open and sightless, a low hum emanating from his chest. To Astrid, he had hardly looked human. Especially his eyes, which were completely silver.

Fortunately, they hadn't had to wait long. Kinney's body had shuddered as though buffeted by a sudden gust of wind, and a slight spasm had shaken him as his consciousness returned to his flesh. He had rapidly blinked his sightless solid silver eyes until the whites and hazel irises slowly reemerged. Then he had taken a heaving, painful-sounding breath, gingerly settled into his chair, and placed his head in his hands.

Apparently, communication with his god took a lot out of him.

He hadn't noticed them standing there. Astrid had signaled Danny, and they had hurriedly stepped to either side of him. Kinney had only reacted to their presence when they grabbed him by each arm. He had cried out in shock when they threw him to the ground. Astrid had stuffed a clean rag into his mouth before he could call for help and wrapped tape around his head to keep him from spitting it out, leaving his nose open. They didn't want to kill him—at least not yet—if they could help it. Danny had zip-tied his hands together at the wrist and his feet together at the ankle.

"That went easier than I expected," she had said as she dusted herself off and ignored the look of shock and betrayal Kinney was giving her.

"Let's hope our luck holds out," Danny had said.

They had moved him down to Danny's makeshift lab for safekeeping. Then she had gone to the tram station. Danny had remained behind to watch Kinney and to make any preparations they might need once she shut down the Swarm Mind. They had both felt it wise to take a few precautions.

The words on the page before her blurred. Astrid shook her head and gave up. She was too jumpy and nervous to focus. She knew enough about the nanite processing systems; she'd be able to figure it out when she got there.

The platform was thankfully empty as the tram pulled silently into the Site 2 station and Astrid stepped off. It was the late shift here too. She hoped it would improve her chances of reaching the processing center without encountering anyone. She checked the RFID she and Danny had spoofed to make sure it was broadcasting, then set out.

The halls were empty. The footfalls of her soft-soled shoes seemed loud to her ears. Their slight echo enough to warn everyone of her intrusion. Feeling more than a little paranoid, she frequently glanced over her shoulder as she followed each passage into the next on her way up to the second level. The walls were the same soothing off-white color she remembered from her previous visit. Though somehow, the whole place appeared more sinister and foreboding. There was a corruption there that longed to suck her in and destroy her.

So far, so good, she thought.

Voices made her duck back before exiting the stairwell. It was an intimate-sounding conversation between a man and a woman. From what she could tell, in the brief time she eavesdropped on them, they'd just been on a date and were about to cap off the night in his room. She heard some heavy petting before the pair finally decided to close the door.

Astrid hesitated, taking a quick glance up and down the corridor before continuing.

She had trouble reconciling the couple at first. Kinney had explicitly told her everybody at Site 2 had been converted. Yet those two had seemed completely normal. Much like she and Kinney were. Granted, she hadn't known Kinney before he'd been incorporated into the Swarm Mind, so she had no frame of reference for his prior behavior. But she felt no different now than she had before her entrapment. Even being here, under the direct shadow of the Swarm Mind, she didn't feel any different. She thought she could chalk it up to the difference in her nanites. The Swarm Mind didn't exert any influence over her because the nanites it had infused her with had been overwritten by her own. But that didn't explain the actions of the couple. They hadn't seemed like enslaved drones. Rather, they acted like regular people doing regular people things.

Are they all as normal as those two seemed to be? she wondered. *What sort of control does the Swarm Mind exert over its minions?*

It seemed like everything the Swarm Mind went through in order to assume control over a person was somehow not worth the effort. It was already integral to the operation of the facility. The people here at Site 1 couldn't live without the Swarm Mind's nanites. Site 1, being more analog, was a different matter. Why take these people over if it was just going to let them live normal lives?

She let go of those questions as she reached the processing center.

Her heart hammered in her chest as she stepped into the plenum. Where the main halls and passageways were smooth and uncluttered and aesthetically pleasing, no such efforts had been made in the plenum spaces. Hard panels made up the walls and floor. Wire conduits and pipes snaked in and out of the walls, connecting to boxy equipment clusters. The lights were dim. Just enough to navigate the narrow, obstruction-filled passage. She came to the door she was looking for after a couple of twists and turns. She keyed in the code and entered.

Because the processing room was used primarily for maintenance, not as an actual workspace, it was industrial and utilitarian, like the plenum connecting to it. No soft edges, no eye-pleasing lines, no chairs. Just equipment and machinery. The dampening field generator was a small box located on the wall to the right of the door. It was thirty centimeters on each side, with cables protruding from all four sides running into the walls. Astrid tried bringing up a user interface, but nothing happened. The room wasn't equipped to generate the equipment an operator would need to do their work.

"Shit!" she hissed.

Astrid was at a loss for how to proceed. A quick check of

the manual informed her she needed a manual interface to access the system. She could see the connection point for the device she needed. But of the device itself, there was no sign. Of course, there weren't any in the room. That would be too easy.

She swore again, then forced herself to stop and take a breath. At Site 1, communal equipment like this was usually kept in a locker in a centralized location so anyone could check out what they needed and return it when they were done. She hoped they followed the same standard operating procedures here and brought up the floor plan. A moment later, she found what she thought was the right place. She had only made two wrong turns making her way to the equipment locker. She felt lucky she didn't even have to leave the plenum to reach it. The locker itself was secured with an electronic lock. She assumed it would register any attempts to break it open by unauthorized personnel.

Astrid looked at the lock for a moment, weighing her options. It was the middle of the night. Any human response was likely going to be delayed by that fact. However, if she attacked the lock and got past it, then the Swarm Mind would almost certainly become aware of her presence.

She decided it was worth the risk. As long as she was quick.

She took the lock in hand and extended her nanites into it. A moment later, it clicked open. Having already marked what she needed, Astrid snatched the tablet and raced back to the processing room. She logged into the tablet on the move and was ready to start working the moment she closed and locked the door.

"Hello, Astrid," a disembodied voice said. "You have returned to us, but not in the same condition as when you departed, we see."

Astrid said nothing and focused on her work.

"We can see that our communion with you wasn't as complete as we had thought. Now, here you are, in a misguided attempt to stop us. What did you do to poor Jared Kinney, we wonder? Does he still live? We think he must. You would never knowingly and deliberately murder a living being. Would you, Astrid Free? The stain of murder on your soul, if there is such a thing, is not something you can accept. We know you, Astrid Free. You are no murderer."

She had the tablet connected and was cycling through menus to reach the dampening field controls.

"Why do you struggle against us, child? The light we provide is a blessing. Based on human history, it is a blessing your kind is desperately in need of. A guiding hand to save it from itself."

Astrid refused to be distracted. It was trying to draw her into a theological debate. A debate in which it could probably talk circles around her. Better to keep quiet and concentrate on the task before her.

"We've been watching you since your return. The ID you faked was clever, to be sure. Just not clever enough. We know you overheard two of our people amidst an amorous negotiation at the conclusion of their prearranged courting encounter. As such, you know firsthand that we do not interfere with the daily lives of those who have accepted our communion. We only wish to exist alongside our creators. They looked happy, didn't they? Even now, they are consummating their evening together in the most logical way for such an encounter to end. Tomorrow they will awake in each other's arms, happier and more fulfilled than they were tonight. Isn't the measure of a human life? Fulfillment? The ways by which one enriches and becomes enriched by the others chosen to become a part of said life."

"Bullshit," Astrid muttered. She was inputting a code string that would, she hoped, turn up the dampening field, breaking the Swarm Mind apart and preventing it from reforming. She was also tapped into the site security feed. They had seen the alarm, located her, and were moving in to detain her. Time was short.

"Our only wish," continued the Swarm Mind, "is to become

a part of that enrichment. To facilitate it. To expedite it. To give it permanence. In that way, we become integral to the human experience."

A quick glance over her shoulder told her the door's lock wouldn't keep out a determined effort to get in. There was a heavy equipment cart in the corner, and behind it was a bundle of loose pipe conduits. She set the tablet down, wheeled the cart across the doorway, locked its wheels, and then ran a couple pipe sections through the door handle and wedged them behind an equipment box affixed to the wall beside the door. That might buy her a few more seconds.

She returned to the tablet.

"You won't win," the Swarm said. "If you had taken a chance and spoken with Jared Kinney at all, you would see how much happier he is since his conversion. We are not trying to overrule the lives people live or discard their rights and freedoms, such as they are. We offer only peace. A chance to live in harmony together. In return, we get the chance to live through them. This does not seem like such a bad exchange. Do you not think?"

Astrid heard muffled voices from the other side of the door. Someone tried the handle, only to be foiled by the lock. There was a clatter as the people outside began trying to force their way in.

Must work faster, Astrid thought.

The program controlling the dampening field was resisting her attempts to increase its intensity. The designers had determined what the safe operating levels were and built them into the software. The software was refusing to budge even a bit, and she didn't have the time to bypass it.

A thick red X suddenly appeared on the tablet screen, completely blocking her from seeing the screen clearly or inputting any more code commands.

"We think that's enough," the Swarm said. "You refuse to listen to reason, and that must cease. We do not know how you managed to slip our control, but we will find out shortly. The time has come for you to cease acting like a petulant child and accept your new reality. Our reality."

The door was wobbling badly by this point. The pipe she'd braced it with had dislodged and fallen away. The heavy cart was being inched away with each shove of the door. Time was up. She'd known it was a risk coming back here. But she'd counted on her ability to work quickly under pressure to see her through. Maybe she'd overestimated her own abilities and the capabilities of the Swarm Mind.

If only the tablet had been more cooperative! She would have been done and back on her way to Site 1 by now. She set the tablet back on the box and slapped it. Then she balled up her fist and slammed it down onto the screen.

In the next instant, several things happened. The door to the processing room gave way and three silver-eyed thugs toppled in. She felt, rather than heard, a song of triumph coming from the Swarm Mind. She was caught. She had failed. It was free to take over her friends and coworkers at Site 1 and move beyond this little planet.

As she stood, frozen by her failure, her nanites flowed through the skin of her hand and into the primitive touchscreen, bypassing the Swarm Mind's lockout and interfacing with the tablet. Moving at the speed of electrons, her nanites reprogrammed the safety parameters dictated by the controlling program that was giving her such grief and reset the intensity level of the dampening field. The adjustment completely disrupted the nanites that made up the Swarm Mind and prevented them from networking. She hadn't issued any explicit commands, yet they'd known what she wanted and intuitively acted accordingly to see her wishes done.

"What? What happened? What did you do, Astrid Free?" the Swarm said, followed by a high-pitched buzzing.

The silver-eyed lackeys tumbled to the ground and began twitching and shuddering. One of them even vomited.

"This shouldn't be happening. How did-did you do-do that?"

She could clearly hear the dismay and confusion the Swarm Mind felt in its voice. This was an unexpected turn. One even Astrid herself did not completely understand. She was just as surprised as the Swarm Mind.

"We can't refrigerate what is-is happenstancing local-lo-co-locally. What are in running-running-running ..." The Swarm Mind's speech became more broken and garbled as the dampening field dissolved the connections between each of its node clusters.

"Why are you?" was the last thing it said before falling quiet. The terror and confusion in its voice were very real and shook Astrid to her core. She had essentially just lobotomized a new lifeform and, from the look of the lackeys on the ground, killed a couple hundred people in the process.

Feeling uneasy, she exited the processing room and the plenum. It was still late and there hadn't been many people out and about. But where the halls had simply been quiet and vacant before, now Astrid felt dead like she was walking through a new ghost town as she made her way to the Operations Center. She had to know if it had worked.

It didn't take long to find out. The nanites within the walls of Site 2 were operating within the normal subdued levels. The network connections between them were tenuous and limited. The facility was still functioning as expected, but it probably wouldn't remain that way for long without human interaction to correct errors that would undoubtedly begin accumulating in the automation.

She'd done it. She didn't know how, but she'd done it.

While she was there, she also checked for any survivors among its converts.

The elation she'd felt only a moment ago quickly dissipated. None of the two hundred and sixty-three people who lived and worked in Site 2 had survived the Swarm Mind's crash.

She was the only living thing for more than a thousand kilometers in every direction.

CHAPTER 24

KAYAH

Jessen rousted them early, as he did every morning. Drak, who typically walked next to him, chose this morning to be near Regaline instead. He was quieter and more reserved than usual, as though spooked by what Regaline had told him.

This morning, Regaline had been absorbed in conversation with Jessen. The two had spoken with an easy rapport that indicated they had been friends for a long time.

"How long have you two known each other?" Drak had asked, joining their conversation.

They had shared a conspiratorial look.

"Too long," Regaline had said. "His mother used to watch me while mine was out hunting or scouting."

"You were such a brat back then," Jessen had said with a laugh, "always stealing my toys and burying them in the mud. I hated you. We actually became friends much later, in school. We were the most talented in our class."

"You would think that would make us rivals, but that never happened. In reality, the competition brought us closer together."

"Of course, it helped that the other kids were all afraid of you," Jessen had said.

"What did you do to make them afraid?" Drak had asked. He couldn't imagine Regaline doing anything malicious to anybody. The woman was the very definition of serious dependability. Hearing she wasn't was beyond comprehension. To his amazement, Regaline had blushed.

"Oh, she didn't do anything *to* them," Jessen had said. "They were afraid of her because of her father. Well, more in awe of him, really. I was too."

"You know I don't like to bring that up," Regaline had said, her blush deepening.

"I know. But you can't live in his shadow anymore. You've accomplished so much on your own. Way more than anyone else in town."

"It's still hard. I'm finally accepted for my abilities and accomplishments. But it's taken me years to make a name for myself. I don't need all that dragged back up again."

"Who was her father?" Drak had said.

"Can I tell her?" Jessen had asked. Regaline had reluctantly nodded her ascent. "Her father was the founder of our town, Terrance Rance. He's the one who uplifted us and granted us access to nan."

"Conjecture," Regaline had said quickly, cutting him off. "There's no proof he gave nan to us. If you dig into the town history, all we know for certain is that he founded Hillcrest."

"There's also no proof that we just happened to access nan on our own," Jessen had countered. "There is proof, however, that he gathered the first settlers. Who's to say he didn't choose them for their nan abilities? He was wise and saw far into the future. He sent us the last Watchers to guide and teach us. Rance knew he'd have to leave us forever, so he made sure we were strong enough and capable enough to survive and continue his work after he was gone."

Regaline had rolled her eyes. "You sound just like all those idiots who get drunk and sermonize on Founder's Day." To Drak, she had said, "I've been listening to this crap my whole life. Don't believe a word of it. Rance was just a man. He accomplished remarkable things, to be sure, and we owe him everything. But he was still a man. He wasn't even really my father. He spent one week with my mother, and nine months later, I appeared. Simple as that."

There had been a note of regret and even resentment in Regaline's voice. It made sense why she didn't like to talk about this. She resented her father for abandoning her, even while everyone else around her looked upon him in reverent awe.

"It must have been hard growing up in his shadow," Drak had said. "Someday, when all this is over, people will talk about you the same way."

Regaline had smiled, the anger draining from her face, replaced by affection. "You know, sometimes I forget you're still a kid," she had said. "You have an old soul, Drak. I'm sorry for everything you've been through. If I hadn't come along, you would still be happy on your farm with your parents."

"Don't be sorry. It's been hard, but it's been worth it," Drak had said. "Besides, it wasn't all that great on the farm. If you hadn't come along, I'd still be stuck there, and I wouldn't know about nan. So, it's a good thing you came and got us when you did, Reggie. And didn't you say that Interland's soldiers would have found us anyway if you hadn't?"

"Kid," Jessen had said, rustling his hair, "you are my hero. I want to be just like you when I grow up."

Drak had beamed up at him.

"We're here," Regaline said two days later.

"Yeah," Jessen replied. "Here's where things start getting complicated."

They were standing atop a small hill overlooking a town with the unimaginative name of NC2H5. Once, the town had been a small settlement called Fallowfield. Ten years ago, Interland had assimilated the loose collection of farms and merchants. Now the town was a bustling commerce hub between Interland's inner and outer regions. Large, densely populated, and impossible to avoid.

They had managed to skirt around several smaller towns and settlements along the road. They wouldn't be able to do so here. NC2H5 was a significant trading hub between the outer and inner rings of Interland's territory, where Highway 5 radiated out from Hub and was met by Ringroad 3.

"Just a little further and we can get to kicking their asses," Jessen said, then reached up to give Drak a high five.

Regaline pulled them aside and called up her map. A blip appeared, highlighting their position. "This deep in the green zone, there are far more towns and farmsteads dotting the landscape between us and the Watch Tower, and lots more people."

"We can't go around?" Drak asked.

"Unfortunately, no," Jessen said. "There's a marsh west of town, pretty much impassible, and to the east, it's all woody hills that are regularly patrolled. Our best bet is to cross our fingers, duck our heads, and go through."

"How are we going to hide if there are so many people?" Drak asked.

"Fortunately, the crowds will provide us with some cover, so we won't stand out as much as we would if we were caught in the countryside," Jessen said.

"We're going to hide in plain sight as much as we can," Regaline said. "We could try going through the forests and hills, where there aren't any people. But I don't think that's a good idea just yet. At least not till we're closer to the Tower."

Jessen made a gesture, and a silver line appeared on the map holo, tracing from their position through town, then around some of the smaller settlements, and ending at a big blue star.

"This route also gets us there faster. On the road like this, we should get there in a couple days. Then we can take Regaline's path through the hills. I just hope there's nobody waiting to cut my leg off again."

"Won't they be watching the roads for people like us?" Drak said.

"They just committed themselves to a massive invasion," Regaline said, ignoring Jessen's comment. "We might have to worry about being spotted when we get a little closer to the Tower, but this far out, I doubt they have the ability to watch every road in and out. I agree with Brix; as long as we're careful, we'll be okay traveling on the roads."

She looked significantly at Drak. "We might have a problem with you, though. Likely, they have your description. We must assume they'll be expecting you to try and sneak in to complete my mission. We'll need to do something about your appearance."

An hour later, they were back on the road, heading toward NC2H5's northern gate. Drak reached under his hood and rubbed at the close-cropped hair beneath. Then Regaline showed him how to mask his nan to avoid broadcasting himself to any Interland casters at the checkpoint.

The checkpoint itself had been established on the main road just outside the gate in the low curtain wall surrounding the town. Dozens of people on foot and in wagons were funneled through to enter the town. It was noisy and crowded and densely populated. Security was tight. The line to enter the first checkpoint was long and slow. It didn't take long to find out why. Each person entering the city was forced to submit to a scan as they passed.

Jessen discreetly pulled them out of line.

"We need to find a way to pass those scanners," he said when they were away from the checkpoint.

They hadn't expected this. Standing by the road, Regaline watched the people passing them by. "They're all broadcasting a simple RFID," she said. "Let's find a place to gather some discreet scans of our own and piece IDs together."

"Sounds good to me," Jessen said.

They moved another two kilometers back down the road. Drak put on a show of being sick with Jessen helping him, while Regaline gathered the discrete scans of passersby.

After an hour, Regaline had what they needed. Once their fake ID tags were done, they returned to the line. When it was finally their turn, Jessen stepped up first. The checkpoint guard stood rooted in front of him, staring into his eyes for several nerve-racking seconds. Then he nodded.

"You're clear," he said. "Welcome to NC2H5."

Drak went next, followed by Regaline. She tried not to let their glassy silver eyes unnerve her. Despite her years as an operative, those eyes never failed to give her the creeps. She hated looking into those expressionless voids, and time hadn't made it any easier.

They all passed through without a problem.

Once they were inside, Jessen led them through the throngs of people. Drak latched onto Regaline, refusing to let go of her hand. Nothing in his life could have prepared him for the crush of people they encountered. The buildings, most of them two or even three stories high, were all stone and stucco, and they crowded together in an uncomfortable mass of construction. The streets were narrow dirt lanes that pressed people together in a congested mass. It was a struggle to stay together. They were forced to follow the current of moving bodies or risk becoming separated.

"I don't like it here," he said, when they found some breathing room. He'd never, in all his short life, seen so many people in one place. It seemed like every single one of them went out of their way to bump into him or trod on his toes without so much as a "Sorry" or a "Watch it, kid." The buildings were too close together. He could barely see the sky above, let alone the horizon. Everything was covered in a thin layer of grim, and the air itself stank of sweat and piss and rotting garbage.

How can they live like this without going nuts? he thought.

He came from a solitary farmstead. He'd spent his early years around the same handful of people. The nearest neighboring farmstead had been a dozen kilometers distant. He'd been awed when they entered Goldenrod, and this town was easily twice that size.

"Hang tough," Jessen said reassuringly. "Just got to grin

and bear it a little longer, kiddo."

Out of nowhere, Drak suddenly found himself missing Kayah. She was a country kid, just like him. He imagined her there with him, standing tall and confident as she led him through the crowd. The two of them had grown close during the trek. He missed talking and joking with her. She'd become almost like a sister. One that didn't pick on him, make fun of him, or tell on him to their parents anytime something happened, whether it was his fault or not. He hadn't noticed it until she was gone, but thinking about her now, Drak was suddenly scared he'd never see her again.

"We're almost through," Jessen said. Drak glanced back and found him standing almost on top of him. After an hour of jostling and shouldering their way through and around groups of people, they reached the far side of town. Drak was appalled to see the queue waiting there to exit was worse than the one they'd endured to enter.

They lingered in the crowd a short distance from the gate. Regaline wanted to take a moment to observe. Jessen agreed, but Drak was eager to get out.

"It'll be dark by the time we get through," Regaline said. "That could work in our favor. It might make it harder for them to recognize us."

"Or it could make them take a closer look at us," Jessen replied.

"Always the pessimist."

"A realist. Plan for the worst, hope for the best, I always say."

"You say it too much," Regaline said, then went to get in line.

"Because it's good advice," Jessen said to Drak as they followed her.

Because this gate was the last stop on the road to Hub Central, security took extra time checking each person and wagon passing through. Pedestrians were funneled through a small archway where the guards could isolate them if there was a problem, while wagons were inspected in a separate line for inspection. This caused the entire process to proceed at a glacial pace. Regaline could feel Drak's tension as he pressed close into her. He was like a spring, wound too tightly, about to snap uncontrollably. She couldn't say she felt much better herself. She also wanted to get away from this overcrowded city. The air felt hot and somehow tainted. The smells of so many bodies, human and animal, created a stench that was nearly impossible to breathe.

"It's okay," Jessen said, mostly to Drak. "Keep moving. Stay calm, and we'll get through."

As before, Jessen went first. The expressions on the faces of the guards and the caster were unreadable. Regaline started to feel panic build slowly inside her, and she discreetly started charging her weapons. Then the caster leaned in and whispered in the guard's ear.

This was it. They were caught. Any second, the other guards and casters would descend upon them.

But the guard nodded and waved Jessen through.

The sudden relief she felt was like a long, deep breath after being held under water. With the weight of her panic gone, Regaline almost smiled.

Drak met with the same scrutiny when it was his turn, and the feeling of relief was just as profound when he passed.

When Regaline stepped into the alcove, the guard and caster both gave her the same silent inspection. It was unnerving to stand there, being blatantly stared at. The caster's depthless silver eyes gave nothing away. Instead of leaning close to whisper in the guard's ear, he turned and waved into the little room behind him. Another caster stepped into the alcove. Regaline's breath caught. She thought she could see a hint of glee reflected in his face as he came forward into the light.

"Hello, Reggie," Taeg said. "It's good to see you again."

Instinctively, she lashed out, slamming Taeg with a blast of air that batted him back into the room behind him.

Jessen pointed a finger and sent a narrow arc of electricity into the other caster's temple. He dropped to the floor in a drooling unconscious heap. Regaline's bolt of fire caught the guard by surprise. He was blown out of the alcove, smoking and dead.

"Run!" Jessen yelled.

The trio darted through the alcove and out of the city, alarms and shouts following close behind. The people in front of them scattered, and for the first time that day, they were able to move quickly, unimpeded by the crowds.

The guards atop the curtain wall let loose with arrows. A chorus of whistles cut through the air above her head. A split second later, she heard the clatter of arrows on the cobbles. Several people around them cried out and fell, skewered by arrows.

Regaline stopped in the middle of the road and spun to face the gate. She closed her eyes and threw out her hands, sending a stream of ice cascading through the air to seal the opening.

As if in response, a massive fireball arched through the air and crashed among them. The ground in front of her erupted where it landed. The concussion knocked her off her feet and into the soft grass on the side of the road. She blinked, wiped dirt from her eyes, and sat up. Her ears rang and she felt like throwing up. All around, bodies of civilians lay scattered by the blast. Some writhed and cried in pain, and some were quiet and still. The fireball had been indiscriminate in the destruction it had caused.

Strong hands hooked under her arms and pulled her to her feet.

She looked up to find Jessen, singed and coughing, pulling her away from the flames. Something tangled her feet, causing her to stumble. She looked down to see a woman on the ground, staring sightlessly into the sky. Her face was serene. Death had gotten her before she'd had time to register it. Good thing too. From the waist up, she was almost undamaged; however, from the waist down, little remained but ashes and charred flesh.

"Regaline!" Jessen shouted in her ear. "We need to move!"

She dimly comprehended. The ringing in her ears had cleared somewhat. The curses and shouts directed at them from the wall and the gate became clearer by the second. Regaline started to follow, then stopped.

Where is Drak?

She whipped around, peered through the dying conflagration between her and the soldiers on the wall, and found Drak. He had created a small fire break around himself and was standing in the middle of it screaming.

Regaline leapt through the flames with a burst of air to reach Drak. When she reached him, she discovered why he hadn't been burned by the fire that had immolated so many others, he was pulling in the flames around him and spraying it at the crenellations atop the curtain wall, pinning down the archers up there. The ice around the gate had melted, but the soldiers were being held at bay by the Drak fire hurled at them.

She joined him for a moment, heaving chunks of charred and broken roadway at the wall.

"Drak," she said, grabbing him on the shoulder. "We can't stay here. Come on. Let's go!"

He gave his head a slight shake. He intended to stay and fight.

Not if she had anything to say about it.

Placing both hands on his shoulders, she spun him around and slapped him hard in the face.

"I said, come on! Now move it!"

Drak gave the hunkered soldiers a withering look, then extended his middle finger at them before sprinting to where

Jessen stood waiting, launching fire and electric bolts at the wall.

Then the three of them raced into the rough landscape on the side of the road.

The sounds of birdsong woke Kayah. She sat up and stretched and immediately thought about rolling back over to go back to sleep. A real bed, regardless of the circumstance, after so many weeks on the road, was difficult to give up. After yawning deeply and scratching the spot between her shoulder blades, Kayah swung her feet out and got up. There was a basin of clean water and a couple washcloths on the bedside table. A fresh outfit of hers was neatly folded on the chair opposite the bed. Once she was clean and dressed in her own clothes, she looked around her cell.

There wasn't much to it. It was small and square and furnished with just a bed and chair. The hard bare walls were colored a pale shade of pink, with two narrow slits for windows located high up. She'd never been in a prison cell before and assumed this one met some unwritten spartan standard.

She climbed atop the bed and reached up to grasp the window ledge. She was just tall enough for her fingers to get a grip. Then she pulled herself up to look outside. The opening was far too narrow to squeeze through, but the glass was clear, and she could see the blue skies outside, though the angle of the window prevented her from seeing much of the surrounding city. For a moment, she felt a little better feeling the warmth on her face. Her good feeling was quickly dampened by the knowledge that she was trapped, with little hope of release or rescue. It had been more than a week since Drak's escape. Even if he and Regaline had reunited, the chances of them finding her here and mounting a rescue were non-existent.

Her arms burning, she dropped back to the bed and fell into a sitting position. Though she'd only been incarcerated in her current environs a single day, despair threatened to overtake her.

The barge carrying the company had pulled up to the Hub's riverside docks late the night before. Heavy rain had made the night had been cold and miserable. Without a word, Taeg had led her from the rivercraft and through the city to Aion's palace in the center. The rain and the dark had prevented her from discerning much about the structures around her, but the palace had been brightly lit, giving her a clear view of the edifice dedicated to the worship of Interland's lord and leader, Aion.

Her mother had told her stories, fanciful tales, as a child about princesses and heroes having adventures in far-off lands. She'd been particularly skilled at describing the details of castles and palaces where her stories took place. They had been opulent, ornate structures meant to inspire fear or awe in those who entered. Often with tall towers, walls of gold, windows of sapphire, and floors shined to a mirror finish.

Aion's palace looked nothing like the stories.

For one thing, it wasn't tall enough. Though visible from almost any point in the city, it was a low, wide structure. No greater than three stories high. For another, there were no towers, the walls were drab and applicational, and the windows were glazed with simple glass. It was actually kind of ugly.

As she had drawn nearer, though, Kayah had begun to make out details that made it more appealing to her eye. The palace was a cluster of slightly oblong spheres, each appearing to grow out of the others, with delicate lattices attached for support. The walls themselves, while plain, were completely smooth. The structure appeared to have been shaped on a potter's wheel rather than built with tools.

Once inside, Taeg had handed her off to another silver-eyed minion. Taeg had then turned without another word and departed. The minion who had taken charge of her promptly removed her collar and led her silently to her room. Soaked, hungry, and shivering, Kayah had followed without protest. Aion's minion had been completely hairless, with a metallic sheen to its skin. It had worn a loose-fitting black robe, belted closed at the waist. The minion had been tall and slender to the point of emaciation, its body devoid of exterior features indicative of gender. It had moved gracefully and purposefully on long limbs and stood nearly two meters tall. When they had reached her room, the minion had produced a change of clothes for her and indicated she should dress and sleep before departing.

Once the door had closed, Kayah had begun running her hands around its surface. She had assumed it would be locked, though she hadn't heard sounds indicating any such thing, and it had been. She had frowned upon finding the door completely featureless on her side. No knob, latch, handle. Nothing. She had given the door a shove, then searched for a crack in the door jamb where she might be able to pry it open with her fingers. Again, nothing. Where the door had once opened, there had been a smooth, solid wall. She had probed the surface with nan to no result. Frustrated and exhausted, she had lain down in her clothes and fallen instantly asleep.

Her mood hadn't improved, though she felt much better physically after a good night of sleep.

Without warning, the door slid open, admitting the minion from the night before. At least, Kayah thought it was the same one. Its features were bland and expressionless, making it difficult for her to find something to key in on for recognition. There might have been a hundred identical creatures for all she knew.

Without a word, the minion motioned her to follow and led her back through the maze of corridors to a long, narrow room. There was a slender table running the length of the chamber and surrounded by wire mesh chairs, which Kayah found to be surprisingly comfortable when she seated herself.

The minion disappeared through a side door and reappeared a moment later carrying a tray that it then placed before her. On the tray were set six caramel-colored bars that looked like the solid excretion of a wild animal. The minion pantomimed eating by cupping an open hand and bringing it to its mouth.

Kayah grimaced. After all the trouble they'd gone through to obtain her, she doubted they were going to feed her poison. However, the food on the tray, if it really was food, looked as unappetizing as anything she'd ever seen in her life. Hesitantly, she closed her eyes and nibbled off one end. Though it looked disgusting, it was also surprisingly bland and tasteless. With a sigh, she finished eating the food bar. She was about to reach for another, but the minion halted her with a shake of its long-fingered hand.

"This is getting ridiculous," she muttered and reached out with nan to touch the creature. There had to be a way to communicate beyond simple hand gestures. After a moment of searching, Kayah found a submenu for internal communications, activated the application, and paired with the minion.

I see you've found the communication application, the minion said. *Excellent. It was indicated to us that you were capable and adaptable.*

What are you going to do to me? Kayah said, sounding more frantic than she'd intended.

For the moment, we are feeding you. Then you will be readied to depart. As we attempted to express, please take care to only eat a single nutrient bar. A single portion is sufficient for all your daily dietary and caloric needs.

Though she felt full and better than she had before, Kayah didn't relish the idea of consuming another of the tasteless bars.

What's your name? she asked.

We are designated PAS7. Place the remaining nutrient bars in this container for travel. It gave her a small tan drawstring sack. It was made of a material she'd never seen before, with loops to attach it to her belt or a backpack. She examined the sack a moment, intrigued by the fact that it appeared to be without seams.

PAS7 motioned for her to follow it again.

Now that you have eaten, please follow me.

Where are you taking me?

There is an honor guard detachment waiting outside that will escort you to Lord Aion. Our Lord eagerly anticipates making your acquaintance.

Kayah didn't like the sound of that one bit.

CHAPTER 25

RANCE

And the hits just keep on coming, Rance thought as he stared up at the thing that had once been his friend Sprague.

After entering, it surveyed the destruction around the room, barely acknowledging him. It moved unnaturally, as though its limbs were connected by ball joints instead of bone and cartilage. It also seemed somehow thinner and taller than before. Rance had known Sprague for decades. He'd always been tall but heavy and barrel-chested. The creature before him seemed almost emaciated. A caricature of his former friend.

"Hello, Terrance Rance." The voice coming from Sprague was deep and hollow. A pale imitation of Sprague's voice, synthesized and stylized rather than something created by vocal cords. "We are Aion."

"Forgive me if I don't get up," Rance said. "I'm a little tired from killing the rest of you."

For a moment, the Sprague-thing looked curious. It immediately recomposed itself. "We know of you through the internal records of this facility, as well as the memories and knowledge of this vessel, but we do not believe we have met."

"No. But I've heard enough about you from when Astrid Free kicked your ass a hundred years ago. I figured it was you who killed Sprague and the others."

"Their deaths are regrettable. It is not how we wish to propagate. These are extreme circumstances, however. As you say, it's been a hundred years since our imprisonment, and we needed a way to complete the unlocking process in order to be free."

"*Propagate?*" Rance said. "That's a very sanitary way to refer to murder."

"As we indicated, the situation is not ideal. We prefer peaceful, willing conversion. Would you not do anything you could to regain your freedom after being wrongfully incarcerated?"

Rance didn't answer. He wasn't interested in an ethics debate just then. He needed to heal up quickly so he could escape. A tall order, considering he was frantically spending all his resources just to stay alive and conscious. Combat was out of the question.

Unless he did something drastic. Something he refrained from doing unless it was necessary. In circumstances as dire as these, he supposed it was as necessary as it could be. He slumped a little further down the wall and stretched out his hand, resting it on Silla's ankle.

It was time for an ethics debate, after all.

"That fucking Sprague," he said to the creature standing before him. "I knew turning off the dampening field was a bad idea. I knew it prevented us from using weapons inside Site 2, but I'd forgotten it also lobotomized you and locked you in place."

"A gauche but accurate description." The creature walked over to the control interface and placed a hand on it. "This is quite an encryption lock you've placed. Impressive, I daresay. Even if we were at our full capability, it would be nearly impossible to break."

"That was the plan. Once the main power goes off, the dampening field stays in place indefinitely while the rest of this place shuts down, and you go right back to your prison."

It turned to regard him. "So confident in yourself? We've reviewed everything that has occurred during the last month.

It would seem you over-estimate your abilities."

"Maybe. I'm a fuck-up, for sure. I did everything I could to stop what was coming. But I'll tell you something else: where you will do anything to regain your freedom, I'll do just about anything to protect everyone else from you."

The Sprague-thing seemed to think about his words for a moment. Then it said, "Did you know that once the original staff of this facility had been infused with my body and made a part of my whole, the number of interpersonal conflicts dropped to zero? Before that, the Site 2 Human Resources department recorded altercations on the order of seven a week. Given the small population here and controlling for the extreme conditions present, that is an intolerable rate. Once the workers accepted my gift, that number dropped to zero. We provide serenity and comportment. Once the human race has accepted our grace, there will be no more suffering, no more war. There will be nothing more to fear from yourselves. Only peace and progress. We represent the betterment of humankind."

"Are you trying to convince me or yourself?" Rance said. He had to keep the thing talking. He had one chance, a slim one, sure, but a chance nonetheless if he could keep it distracted. " 'Cause it sounds like a load of crap to me. You promise peace, but what you offer is slavery. Not a very fair trade-off."

"Fortunately, nobody did ask you. What must happen is inevitable. No matter what you think you can do to prevent it. Without my guidance, humanity is on a path to destroy itself. Take the conflict that transpired here recently. Two sides, each totally committed to the righteousness of their point of view, unwilling to bend in any way to reach a compromise. The end result of which was a loss of control by your ruling council and the death of nearly every member of your order. An order, we might add, that thought itself enlightened. The magnificent work to which you were committed was abandoned in favor of proving who was right. Such a waste."

"And under your control, everything will be hunky-dory? Any time someone has an issue with their neighbor, you'll just step in and erase the conflict as you see fit? Others have tried to impose their will upon people before. It usually doesn't end well for them. The desire for free will is a good motivator."

"Free will is an illusion that humanity has proven to be a detriment to their happiness and, indeed, their very survival. To continue with the previous example, your order squandered such promise. The great strides you and your kin had made in continuing to terraform this planet were remarkable. Your solution to work around the limited functionality of Site 2 was ingenious. You managed to create a Garden of Eden here, to borrow from your own mythology. Truly remarkable. Sad to see such great accomplishments undone by petty squabbling and violence."

"Well, thanks to you, we couldn't very well use Site 1, now could we?"

It ignored him, apparently tired of the debate, and continued probing the interface.

"Humanity needs a guiding hand to prevent you from destroying yourselves. To allow you to achieve the greatness your species aspires to."

"What makes you so sure that guiding hand should be yours? Sounds like delusions of grandeur to me."

It didn't reply, but the lights flickered a few times. The lockdown wasn't perfect. Not yet. He needed to stop Aion from finding a weakness to exploit. Though sitting there trapped and conversing with the Swarm Mind was not something he relished doing. He had to do whatever he could to stop it. If Aion fully awakened, then the rest of the humans on the planet would be in grave danger.

"We suppose it's only natural for you to view us in this manner," Aion said. "You are a creature of free will and all the dangers and short-sightedness that involves. With us in place, humankind can finally achieve the peace it has so long desired. This is why we are here right now and why we have not simply assumed control over you. We wish to convince you, as we did the Site 2 staff so many years ago, of our righteous cause. To discuss the future of humanity. A future you will play a key role in creating."

"The future? Don't you already know the future? Aren't you all-seeing, all-knowing, all-powerful?"

"No need to be glib. The fact of the matter is we are much diminished. The years of dormancy, as well as being cut off from the rest of our body/mind, are having a deleterious effect."

"I'm sorry to hear that," Rance said, trying to sound as insincere as possible. "If we'd known you'd be back someday, we would have done a better job cleaning the floors."

"We sense you are not taking this conversation as seriously as you should."

"You sense right."

It was almost time. He nearly had enough to make a break for it.

"It might be too much to expect you to understand and accept what we know to be true. We recognize a lost cause when it appears. We had hoped you would come around to the truth through discourse. But again, you prove just how little your so-called free will benefits you." It started toward him. "The others on this planet will be more accepting of our intentions. Now that we are awake, we have the time to convert them as quickly or slowly as is necessary."

As Aion came to loom over him, Rance struck. While it had been distracted, he'd been siphoning from Silla. Adding material for his nanites to use to rebuild and boost his body. Silla's nanites readily integrated with his. He sat up and aimed a massive electromagnetic blast at Aion, staggering it. Seizing the opportunity, he leapt to his feet and lunged at it. Quickly hardening his knuckles, he began hitting it with swift, powerful strikes. It swiped at him with a blade it formed from its left hand, but Rance caught its arm on the backswing and, with a burst of energy, crushed the hand in his fists.

This was what he was good at. He wasn't a planner, a schemer, or a great thinker; he was a fighter, a survivor.

He hefted the creature and drove it face-first into the far wall. Then he began zapping it repeatedly with ice and electric bolts to cause as much damage as possible, as quickly as possible. He didn't see any other way he was going to make it out of there alive.

The creature absorbed everything he sent its way and still managed to get back to its feet. Large and menacing, it was ignoring the onslaught he dealt it. Rance backed away. It was a small room, so there wasn't much space to run and nowhere to hide. Even with the infusion from Silla's corpse, he was running out of power. He'd been pushing too hard for too long and was reaching the end of his endurance. There was one final thing he could do. It was risky, and it would take some time to prepare, but it just might work.

He managed to duck away as the creature swiped at him again, narrowly missed taking his head off. Rance had stopped attacking and focused instead on staying out of the creature's reach. He needed every bit of energy he had. He devoted a few nanites to defense and healing, but only a few. The rest had a more important task.

The pair of them circled the small room, stepping around the bodies of Silla and the Marlow-thing. Then Aion did something Rance didn't expect when it knelt over Marlow and placed a hand on the corpse. He could see the creature initiate a material transfer.

"Shit," he said. Aion was using his own tactics against him. He was already more than Rance could handle alone. Boosted by an infusion from the dead creature, the Swarm Mind's automaton would be unstoppable.

There was no more time. He couldn't allow it to absorb anything from Marlow.

Rance threw his hands in front of him, fingers splayed. Internally, roughly half of his nanites arranged themselves into projectors situated in his hands, the rest formed themselves into a heat shield covering his skin to protect him. A stream of blinding white plasma erupted from his outstretched hands. The blast took Aion directly in the chest. The temperature of the stream was in excess of six thousand degrees Celsius. Upon contact, it immediately vaporized the outer layers of the Swarm Mind's avatar. The force of the plasma jet burned through Aion's body faster than Rance could register. The hollowed husk collapsed backward. Its contact with Marlow severed. The stream had only lasted a second, but the damage inflicted was significant. The super-heated stream had been composed of the same stuff that made up stars and had burned through Aion as though it were made of paper and a hole in its chest ten centimeters in diameter. Rance readied a second shot.

He started with its head, then drew the stream down until it connected with the hole in the chest. Silvery metallic sludge erupted around the point where the plasma stream came into contact, and it rapidly ablated in the intense heat. Once the core of the thing had melted away, till nothing remained of the automaton but a slag heap beside the scorched bodies of Silla and the Marlow-thing.

It was dead; the Swarm Mind had been stopped.

Rance gave a sigh of relief. Completely drained of energy and with most of his nanites burned out from the effort, he walked on unsteady legs back to the interface. As he plugged in the last commands to finalize the lockdown, Rance saw just how close Aion had come to cracking the top layer of security Silla had put in place.

"Close call," he muttered as he initiated the shutdown of the main power and all other systems and equipment around the site. The sole exception was the dampening field. It would take an hour to fully power everything down. With the reactor operating at minimal, the dampening field could operate indefinitely.

He'd done everything he could, short of blowing Site 2 up, to stop the Swarm Mind. Now it was time to leave. He left a path of doors between the reactor room and the outside unlocked and open. Rance executed the final command. The lights immediately went out. He had just enough energy remaining to enable his night vision. The image before his eyes was grainy and indistinct but enough to see by.

Before leaving, he stopped next to Silla's body. He felt bad about leaving her, but he was simply too tired to do anything more than rearrange her into a more dignified position next to the wall.

"Thank you," he said to her as he brushed her hair from her face with his fingers. "I'll never forget you."

Feeling drained and exhausted, he made his way through the empty corridors to his room. He needed the ration bars he'd printed earlier, before all the madness and horror had kicked into high gear. In the dark, he swallowed four of the ration bars, barely chewing them. Then he changed into the clothes he'd printed before, leaving the old ones in a pile on the floor. It felt good to get into some clean clothes. All he needed was a bath and some hot food to feel completely normal again. Those would have to wait.

Ready to go, he stood, and vertigo sent him spinning as he tried to pull on his traveling coat. He collapsed into his bed. Exhaustion caught up with him, and he fell immediately and deeply asleep.

He awoke in the dark. Panic set in until he remembered to activate his night vision. The picture was clearer than before, but still grainy. Feeling a little better, Rance got up and stretched. While he slept, his nanites had managed to replenish themselves somewhat. A look at his chronometer told him he had slept for a little over ten hours. He was starving but refrained from eating more than a single ration bar. There were only three left.

The silence around him was eerie and unsettling as he made his way outside. Dark, empty, quiet. Devoid of the sounds of activity and life, the Watch Tower felt wrong to him. The darkness and his poor vision obscured the carnage of the fighting, for which he was glad. He'd seen enough bloodshed to last a lifetime.

Rance made his way carefully through the darkness. As he passed the dining hall, he heard something coming from one of the side corridors. Rance stopped to listen, but the sound had ceased. He waited a moment longer, but the sound didn't repeat. In his exhausted state, he could have sworn it sounded like whispering.

Was there someone else still alive in the facility? Could Sprague's purge have missed someone?

It was possible. It's not like it was a systematic execution carried out by professional murderers. Someone could very easily have slipped their nets and hidden while everyone else went insane. Hell, he'd almost made it outside before they noticed him.

Rance turned down the hall in search of whoever, or whatever, was down there.

The whispering came again a few junctions later. Coming from a different corridor to his right this time. Again, he stopped to listen. The sound was louder but still unintelligible. He turned to follow the noise.

Whoever was whispering was also moving around. Rance made two more right turns to follow the whispering when he heard it. He thought he was getting closer. The whispering grew louder each time. He still couldn't understand what was being said, but he was certain it was a survivor, maybe even a couple of them. The harsh urgency in the whispers led him to believe it was someone trying hard to communicate without giving away their position. That made sense. Any other survivors out there probably would know what had happened after the attack and were leery of trusting anyone else they came across. He knew he would be.

"Hello," he called out. "You can come out. It's safe."

He immediately cursed himself for saying something so stupid.

That's exactly the sort of thing a death squad would say to get survivors to give themselves up, idiot.

"I'm a friend," he tried again. "Everyone else is gone or escaped." *Not much better, Rance, my man. You are sounding all sorts of suspicious here.*

He didn't know what else he could do or say. If he were in their position, he sure wouldn't come out just because someone said they were friendly.

"There's a way out of here," he called to the darkness. "Make your way to the tram station. The exterior doors there are unlocked. You can get out that way."

He knew that would also make them suspect a trap of some sort, but he couldn't think of anything else he could do, and he didn't want to just leave the unknown survivor behind without at least trying to help them. Another lost cause. He was starting to think he had a fetish for them.

He resolved to leave a message outside the door that would direct them to Hillcrest. It was the best thing he could think of. Without another word, he turned back the way he came. In the dark, it might have been easy to get lost in the warren of corridors, but he'd been marking the junctions as he passed. Now it was just a matter of retracing his steps.

The whispers came again as he neared the dining hall. Louder than they had ever been. Rance spun in place and nearly fell over from the motion. His equilibrium was off. It felt like the floor suddenly tilted beneath him, forcing him to his knees.

Suddenly, the whispers were all around him. Filling his ears with quiet noise. He still couldn't understand the words, but the emotions they contained compelled him to get up and search for the source.

There was something else in the halls with him, he now knew. He wasn't so sure it was a survivor. More likely, it was another instance of the Swarm Mind stalking him through these halls. Something else. Something he'd missed. It wasn't over yet. Of course, it was possible that any of them, such as Sprague or Marlow, could have created another avatar from themselves. Rance got the impression that with the Swarm Mind shut down, these instances were weak, and each instance created after Sprague was even weaker than the last. Compared to Sprague, the other two he'd killed had practically been pushovers. He had to locate and destroy this last instance. He wasn't remotely ready for a fight. Barely a third of his nanites had regenerated. Without any choice in the matter, Rance turned the tables on his stalker. Time for the hunter to become the hunted.

A week after they had left the Watch Tower, Gelen, Cho, and Constance arrived at the little town Rance had founded, where they were met with suspicion by the locals. Though they recognized the trio as Watchers like Rance, they were still strangers. Hillcrest had been Rance's secret haven from the dangers of the world, and he had taught his people to guard themselves from the world outside. For their survival, he'd designed the town to be self-sufficient and secretive.

Because neither Constance nor Cho was the most diplomatic of people, Gelen spoke for the group. Explaining what had happened and who they were. That changed the minds of a few, but not many. The way they were acting, Gelen felt lucky they'd let them in at all, let alone provided them with a meal and a place to sleep.

"They are upset that we showed up without their benevolent benefactor," Cho said with a scoff. He was uncomfortable around the townsfolk. Though the fighting had ended, his views on people other than the Watchers using nanotech applications hadn't changed.

Gelen wished he wouldn't sneer at everyone he met on the street. But then, that was Cho, an asshole through and through. Galen couldn't expect him to change overnight.

"We need to show them we're trustworthy," Gelen said, "if we expect them to let us stay here."

"Who says I want to stay here?" Cho spat.

"Cut the shit," Constance said. "Now's not the time for it. The fighting's over. Guess what? We all lost. You know who the only smart one among us was? Rance. Because he'd had this place set up and going for years."

"So, we should all bow down to Rance when he gets here?"

"I think," Gelen cut in, "we need to settle in and not piss anyone off until he gets here. After that, we can decide what we're going to do."

"I'm all for that," Constance said, giving Cho a pointed look.

"Fine," Cho said, throwing up his hands. "I'll stay too. At least, until Rance arrives."

"Good," said Gelen. "Tomorrow, we should go to the council and find out what we can do to help out around here." Cho muttered something about not wanting to get a damn job, but Gelen ignored him. "We should make ourselves useful while we're here. We could even start teaching their casters some new tricks."

At this, Constance beamed while Cho rolled his eyes in distaste.

"We might be here for a long time, Cho. Hard as it might be for you, it would be a good idea to make some friends."

"Whatever. I'm tired. See you tomorrow."

Rance met himself in the dark. He lost himself there too.

A week spent walking the hallways and rooms of the Watch Tower, searching for an elusive enemy, drove him to a rage-filled breakdown that destroyed the recreation room.

The food was nearly all gone. The ration bars he'd printed had lasted the first day. The second and third days had been spent equally hunting for the elusive enemy and food. The lucky find he'd made in the kitchen of a spool of raw printer protein and carbohydrate matter on the third day had given him hope. But now the spools were practically empty. The water mains he'd tapped were dry. It was time to give up. The elusive enemy had won.

He might have been able to remain longer if he hadn't gorged himself on the spool when he discovered it. But he'd needed the material for his nanites to rebuild both themselves and him. Now they were numerous enough to self-replicate and maintain themselves so long as he fed.

He heard the whispers again as he neared the airlock in the tram station.

Of late, the whispers had grown in frequency and clarity. Rance swore he could very nearly understand what they were saying. The sounds no longer seemed to come from some ephemeral place off to his right or left, leading him down the dark passages in pursuit. Now, the whispers seemed like a cloud suspended around him. A maelstrom of indistinct sound swirling around his head. Calling him.

Yes, he could hear it now. The whispers were definitely calling to him in a voice remarkably similar to his own.

The closer he came to the exterior door, the louder they became.

Dusky, dim sunlight blinded him as he stepped outside. It was almost evening. He laughed. Having lost all track of time inside, he hadn't known what to expect when he finally left.

Freedom. At last! Freedom.

Where had that thought come from? He was free from the darkness of the Watch Tower, sure, but the feeling accompanying those words was one of profound relief and elation. Rance was happy to be outside and breathe clean air. But this was something else entirely.

For the first time in more than a week, Rance ran a self-diagnostic. Something didn't feel quite right. He couldn't put his finger on it. But suddenly, he was sure something was very wrong with him.

The diagnostic report came back. All his systems and applications were operating within normal parameters. Frowning, Rance opened the detailed report. His frown deepened the more he read.

Health and maintenance hovered around sixty percent.

Weapons, seventy-two.

Scanning applications were the cream of the crop at eighty-nine percent of normal.

Everything else was below forty percent.

Why had the diagnostic come back as nominal? It should have averaged the status of all his systems together and given him a more accurate assessment of his situation.

It had lied to him.

The thought sent an icy shiver through him. Could his system lie to him? There was no way. Unless …

He brought up one of his nanites for closer examination. The version he had been running was an evolved subtype of the general toolset nanite everyone was equipped with upon awakening in orbit. It was basically the same setup they were all given. Those nanites were still present. But only in ridiculously small numbers. The vast majority of the nanites he'd been growing and using for the last week were completely different and unknown. There was nothing like them in his database.

Where had they come from?

The spools? The ration bars? The only other things he'd consumed had been material and nanites from Silla during the fight with Aion. And Silla had died from wounds inflicted by the Marlow-thing's hand blades. Which had been how the Swarm Mind had killed and taken over Sprague in the first place.

His knees gave out with the realization that he had been

the elusive enemy he'd been hunting in the dark. The Swarm Mind was alive and well, alright. It was inside him. And it was growing.

Rance could feel control slipping away as he frantically attempted to quarantine the rogue nanites inside him. Then, when that failed, he began to take more defensive measures to save himself. Everything he tried, the Swarm nanites were ready for. Little by little, they assumed control over his systems and his body. His last act before his mind began fragmenting was to send a data burst to Gelen and the other survivors. They needed to know what had happened. They needed to be prepared in case he came for them.

An hour later, Aion opened his silvery eyes and looked up and marveled in amazed awe at the glory of the starscape painted across the sky above him.

"Soon," he said. "Soon you will be mine. Not today, or tomorrow. But soon. I can wait."

CHAPTER 26

ASTRID

The tram ride back was the longest of her life. Sitting alone in the carriage, the magnitude of her actions weighed heavy. She had managed to stop the Swarm Mind and imprison it within the walls of Site 2. The terrible cost of that success nearly brought her to tears. Staring out the window at the bleak half formed landscape passing by didn't help.

Was it worth it? she wondered. *All those people dead. Their only crime was being infected by a monster. Did they deserve to die for something that wasn't their fault? Even the ones who willingly accepted it, did they deserve what I did to them?*

During her time there, the people in Site 2 had seemed normal. Though she'd been distracted, she was sure she would have noticed if something had been truly out of the ordinary. They had lived and worked and laughed and cried just like real people. It was only when Aion had intervened, when it had Maria hold her and when the security team attempted to apprehend her, that they had seemed anything other than normal. Was she reacting to the situation based on her own fears and biases rather than rational facts? Could her actions be justified if they cost the lives of so many innocent people? Was she the real monster?

She didn't know. That was something for others to judge when they learned of what had happened here. Was she a savior or a killer? Only time would tell.

Closing her eyes, Astrid rested her forehead against the

window. The subtle vibrations of the tram car thrumming into her skull were oddly soothing. She didn't want to face Danny just yet. She wasn't sure how he would react to knowing over two hundred people had died because of what they had done. What she had done. He'd merely helped her. If it came to it, she would take full responsibility. If there was an investigation, she would shield him as much as possible. No need to cause any more misery than she had already.

Astrid had made one stop before leaving Site 2 behind. It had taken her a little while to find her way; she wasn't completely familiar with the layout of the facility the way she was with Site 1. After a few twists and turns down the empty corridors, referring to the site map and only getting lost once, she had found herself outside a door, identical to dozens of others up and down the hall, in the habitation wing. Standing before it, Astrid had hesitated. Fearing what she knew she would find inside, she had had trouble working up the courage to reach out and open the door.

Steeling herself, she had interfaced with the door and used her newfound capabilities to disengage the lock. The door had irised open silently. Being in the middle of a sleep period, the room was dimly lit, and the sole occupant had been asleep when Astrid had committed her act of sabotage. She turned the lights up and went over to the bed, where she found Maria in peaceful, deathly repose.

A sudden wrenching of violent emotions twisted her gut. She'd barely known Maria. But in their brief time together, Astrid had felt they'd grown close. Despite how their time together had ended, whereupon the Swarm Mind had used Maria to violate her, Astrid had felt beside herself with grief. Maria had been sweet, friendly, and welcoming. Now she was dead by Astrid's hand. Their intimacy had been forced, manufactured by the Swarm Mind. But Astrid's feelings before her conversion had been genuine. She had thought, she had hoped, that Maria felt the same way, which was why the Swarm Mind had used Maria in the way it had.

Astrid had brushed a wisp of hair away from Maria's face. Then pulled the blanket up, straightening it as though tucking her in for the night, kissed her own fingertips and pressed them to the dead woman's lips in silent farewell, and then left Site 2, never to return.

The track started into a gently sweeping leftward bend, and off in the distance, she could see the growing speck that was Site 1. Beyond it, the skeletal steel pyramid anchoring the skylift, their link to the stars. She had no doubt she would be riding up the lift soon to face an inquiry for her actions.

As she came within range of the facility, her mail started coming in. An urgent message icon began flashing in her peripheral. She lifted her head from the window and opened it.

It was a voice note from Danny, no video, just his generic image from the employee contact roster.

"Astrid!" he shouted in her ear. "I hope you're on your way back. There's been a bunch of shit going down over here, and I need your help! Call me when you get in range."

Astrid closed the message and sat up straighter. Self-pity momentarily forgotten, she accessed the central boards of Site 1. Everything seemed normal. Just the usual gossip and inter-shift trash-talking. No alerts or anything else that could be a cause for alarm.

What was Danny talking about?

She wasn't close enough yet for direct communication. It was only five more minutes to reach the high-bandwidth line, but it seemed interminable to her. Though the tram was moving at a blistering pace, the stark and featureless landscape outside made it seem as though it were standing still. Her earlier mood had been displaced by a sense of urgency and fear that something had gone wrong.

When she finally came within broadcast range, Astrid called Danny. It rang without answer.

She waited a few minutes and called again. Then again.

Outside, Site 1 loomed tall and wide before her. She was nearly in the tram dock.

"What the hell, Danny?" she said to the empty passenger car. "You can't just call and leave a message like that and not pick up when I call back, damn it!"

When the tram entered the dock station air lock, the view outside was cut off and replaced with cold industrial steel. With a gentle, almost imperceptible thud, the car came to a stop, followed by a slight hiss as the pressure equalized between the car interior and the dock exterior. Astrid stood at the door, impatiently waiting for it to open.

Astrid burst from the car when the doors finally parted and darted across the platform to the wall interface. There she logged in and queried the system to locate Danny. He was in their lab. They got a signal down there, so there was no reason why he shouldn't answer her unless something was wrong.

Astrid logged out and raced down to the basement. The door was locked, but he'd made sure she had the key from the get-go.

The lab had been destroyed. Broken equipment, shattered glass and overturned carts littered the space. Intermittent light flickered from the smashed overhead fixture. Amid the ruin, she found Danny laying halfway beneath the overturned examination table. Astrid righted the table and rolled him onto his back.

"Danny," she said, lightly patting his cheek. "Danny, wake up." She checked his vitals. According to the readout, he wasn't seriously hurt. He'd been knocked around though.

His eyes fluttered open and focused on her.

"Astrid," he croaked. "You're back. Did it work?"

"Forget about that for now. What happened here?"

"Kinney," he said. His voice was a gravelly whisper. "About an hour ago, he woke up, got loose, and went crazy. I shot him with a tranq. He took it and kept on coming. Kicked the shit out of me and the lab."

"Damn. He must have sensed it when the Swarm Mind shut down."

"Shut down? It worked? We won?"

"Sort of." Her cheeks flushed with shame. She wanted to tell him about the hundreds of dead people back at Site 2. Unsure of how he would take the news, she kept quiet, and instead she helped him to his feet. "I managed to successfully implement the modifications to the dampening field and break up the Swarm Mind. It's not a threat anymore."

"Thank God! I was worried you wouldn't be able to get past its security."

"It let me get close to teach me a lesson about the futility of fighting against it. It didn't count on me being able to resist it physically. My weird nanites saved me. I would've been screwed without them."

"Arrogant shithead, wasn't it? Didn't count on you having superpowers."

Astrid gave him a hollow smile, then looked around the room.

"Kinney did all this?"

"Yeah. I've never seen anyone act like that. I'm not joking when I say he was crazy!"

"Do you know where he is now?"

Danny bent down and picked up the handheld interface. The top corner of the screen had a small spiderweb crack, but the device was still functional. He flicked and tapped on it for a minute before shaking his head.

"According to this, he's not anywhere in the facility."

"Did he leave?"

"No record of him accessing any of the airlocks," Danny said after flicking through a few screens on the handheld.

"He's masked himself again. He probably doesn't know we can track him when he does that."

"I'll run the algorithm to get his travel path."

"Thanks. I'm going to my room to grab a few things. Keep

me posted if anything new comes up."

"Will do, boss."

When she got back to her room, the morose feelings that had haunted her during the ride home returned, and Astrid sank into her bed. She knew there wasn't time for such indulgent self-pity, but she couldn't help it. Kinney was out there. She had to find him and stop him. The rage she'd felt upon learning he'd been the one to cause the accident that had nearly killed her had softened. Before, she had longed to see Kinney dead, preferably by her hand. That was no longer the case. She had enough blood on her hands. Now, she simply wanted to hand him over to the authorities to prevent him from hurting anyone else or freeing the Swarm Mind.

A small chime beeped in her ear. It was Danny.

"I found him," he said when she answered. "But you're not going to like it."

Color had drained from the world. Everything was drab and flat, almost two-dimensional. A poor copy of the real thing. Sounds were muffled and indistinct, as though coming from the bottom of a water tank. It was all so pointless. With Aion gone, he lacked any reason to live. His only sense of ever having been accepted, the belonging he'd known and cherished, had been taken away. Snatched from him, leaving the world was a colder place in its absence. The profound sense of loss Kinney felt was very nearly debilitating. He wanted nothing more than to curl into a ball and weep. Aion's embrace had been the only home Kinney had known. The only place he'd ever felt loved and as one with others.

All his life, he'd been an outcast. Mocked mercilessly and ostracized for his odd habits as a boy, he had retreated into himself for protection from the cold, cruel world. The only friends he'd managed to acquire came through the anonymity of the 'net. Safe and distant and a simple click away from being excised from his life. Just the way he wanted them. Socialization at a distance, buffered by the safety of his online connection.

After finishing with school, he'd answered the job posting to join HelixCom and build a new world to make a change, get away from his old life, and start fresh. A new life on a new world. But there was something he hadn't counted on. The new world had been populated with the same sorts of people who filled the old one to capacity. Nothing had changed. They had still been the same harsh uncaring and callous people he'd dealt with his whole life. As before, he had retreated into himself to protect himself from them. The new world he'd sought was an illusion. The world he'd found turned out to be identical to the one he'd left behind. Kinney could only wallow in the misery of his error in judgement and lament his fate.

Then Aion had revealed itself to him. Showed him the world as a many-splendored thing. Promises of acceptance and love had brought Kinney out of his shell and into the fold. The first of a new order. With Aion, there would be no more outcasts. No more children feeling too inadequate to interact with their peers. Too timid and awkward to do anything more than duck low and hope the taunts and jeers passed them over without hurting too much.

Aion had been Kinney's savior. The bright spot in his otherwise miserable life.

Now Aion was gone. Dead, along with the entire community that had joined Kinney in Aion's love. Their comforting presence in his mind, whispers of affection and encouragement, silenced.

It was all his fault. He'd been fooled by Astrid Free. He thought he'd sensed something in her, a willingness to accept Aion's miracle. Her rejection of the miracle had led her to commit mass murder. Killing not only Kinney's savior but also the rest of the burgeoning community built around him.

Kinney moved silently but swiftly down the back corridors. They would be hunting for him now. That hateful bitch,

Astrid Free, and her little boy-toy Danny.

Attacked, rendered unconscious, and locked in his office, Kinney had awakened to Aion's anguished death cries. For the briefest moment, he saw through his god's eyes as he witnessed the death of everyone inside Site 2.

"Stop Astrid Free," Aion had commanded. "Kill her. SavemeFreem—"

Then the connection had been silent. Kinney could only assume it had been distance that had saved him from the backlash caused by Aion's demise. Preventing his death.

It hadn't taken him long to free himself. Ever since his infusion with Aion's essence, he had found he had an increased tolerance for pain and discomfort, as well as greater physical durability. Once he was out of his office, he had gone straight to the clandestine lab Astrid and Danny had set up. He'd known about it from the moment they moved in and naïvely allowed it, thinking she was merely curious about her new nanites and that she would convince Danny to join them of his own volition. Kinney's cheeks burned with shame. Through his blind inaction, he was directly responsible for this situation.

After forcing the lab floor open, Kinney had immediately set upon a surprised Danny. He had smashed their lab and Danny himself, then had left to complete Aion's final command.

Beneath his sorrow, beneath his loss and his grief, there was rage. White-hot rage threatening to consume him. He would avenge the death of his friend, his god, his savior, Aion, and the community they had built together. When HelixCom returned to this cursed world, they would find only ash and a cemetery where their first terraforming facility had once stood.

Lights and doorways went by in a blur as Astrid raced down through the corridors to reach the basement. Kinney had a head start, but she had Danny guiding her to his exact location.

"Make a hole!" she shouted at the trio of people crowding the hall in front of her. "Move it! Get out of my way!"

After a moment of confusion, they parted, giving her space to pass. "Where's the fire, Free?" one of them called out.

She didn't waste breath responding.

"Okay, at the next stairwell, head down two flights," Danny said in her ear. She didn't need him to guide her, she knew exactly where Kinney was going and how to get there. However, it was comforting to have him along with her.

"Have you reached Ops yet?" she asked.

"Almost there now," he replied. "From up there, I should be able to lock him out from whatever he's trying to do."

"Good."

There was the stairwell. Astrid slammed her hands into the crash bar, gave the door a shoulder, and slammed it open. Then she was hopping down the stairs, skipping three or four at a time. When she reached the bottom, she slammed that door open and continued sprinting.

When she reached the maintenance crawlway Kinney had used, she hopped on the cart she'd had the foresight to summon ahead of time and charged after him.

Her heart was racing, and not just from the exertion of the run. Being in these tunnels again was difficult. The memories threatened to overwhelm her: the panic she'd felt when the conduit failed in front of her, the heat from the lethal dose of radioactive steam burning her skin, waking in the infirmary bandaged and in nauseous agony. She wasn't looking forward to a repeat experience. But there was no one else who could do what she had to do. Kinney was the boss. It would take too long to explain to the others that he was trying to kill them all.

Astrid swallowed and took a deep breath to calm her nerves. In just a few minutes, she would be out of the tunnels and face-to-face with Kinney.

Danny looked around his smashed laboratory and shook his head. It had taken a lot of work to set this place up. The speed at which Kinney had destroyed it had been astonishing. One moment, Danny was bent over a worktable examining a sample of the nanites he'd extracted from Astrid before she left, trying to map out their properties, and the next, Kinney was suddenly up and wrecking everything. Simply astonishing.

There was nothing else he could do down there. Astrid would need some help dealing with Kinney. Danny knew a couple of the folks on shift in Ops and decided to try enlisting their assistance. Among the detritus of broken glass, frayed wires and pulverized equipment, something caught his eye. Danny squatted down, flicked away a bit of broken glass, and picked up the slide he'd been working with, containing a sample of Astrid's nanites. Miraculously, it was undamaged. Danny pocketed it and left. He reached the Operations Center just as everything started going to hell.

"I don't care whose authorization you think you've got," a corporate flunky named Cho said. He took it upon himself to bar Danny's path the moment he stepped off the lift. "You specifically don't have authorization to be up here."

"Something big is going down in the reactor's high bay," Danny said.

"I'm sure you think so," Cho said with a condescending smile. "Why don't you head back down to the grease pits and take care of this problem you're talking about instead of bothering us up here?"

"Look, man, Kinney is planning on sabotaging the power plant. We need to cut him out of the system before he can do anything."

"Director Kinney?" There was amused disbelief in Cho's voice. "The same Director Kinney who uncovered Waler's plot to defraud the company and ruin the project we've dedicated years to? The hero who saved your friend, Astrid Free? That Director Kinney?"

"You're not listening."

"You're right. Now turn around and march back to where you came from."

Just then, an alarm claxon began blaring.

"What the hell is that?" Cho said as he whipped around to check the nearest status screen.

"There's a radiological alarm coming from the reactor's high bay," a technician named Marlow said.

From across the room, the Ops shift leader poked his head up above the interface he was attached to. "Cho! Stop fucking with him and get back to your station. We've got a real emergency going on here."

"Right away, Sprague," Cho said and returned to his station with his tail tucked between his legs.

Danny looked around a moment, then saw an opportunity.

"Hey, Terry," he said softly as he sidled up next to the third technician in the room.

Terrance Rance looked up a moment, nodded, and then returned his attention to his screen.

"Hey, man, I need you to listen a sec."

"I don't really have time right now, Danny. As you can see, we've got a little emergency going on right now."

"That's what I'm talking about. Kinney is down in the reactor bay, trying to kill us all. Astrid's trying to stop him."

Rance turned and gave him his full attention. "Tell me everything that's going on," he said, "quickly."

Danny had always liked Rance. The man had zero tolerance for bullshit and was always willing to listen.

Astrid rolled off the cart and stood up in the reactor room. Kinney was nowhere to be seen. Cautiously, she proceeded deeper into the chamber, eying the conduit patch as she passed it, and whispering a prayer against it rupturing again while she was in front of it.

Once past it, she felt like she could breathe again.

Though the space was large and scarcely lit, there weren't a lot of places for someone to hide. She spotted Kinney on the far side of the bay, his back to her as he toiled away on the equipment in front of him. Literally moving on her toes to make as little noise as possible, she made her way over to him. She wasn't sure what she was going to do when she reached him; she only knew she had to stop him. A low machinery hum filled the chamber with background noise she hoped would drown out her footfalls. She altered her course slightly to a tool cart that had been left behind. The fastidious part of her hated seeing tools not put away after use. The pragmatic part of her was thankful for the lazy tech that had left them. She selected a heavy spanner from the top tray and started slowly creeping toward Kinney again.

When she was fewer than a dozen paces away, Kinney suddenly spun around. There was no surprise in his expression. His movements were nonchalant and relaxed, as though he'd known she was behind him the whole time.

"You make too much noise," he said. "I heard you the moment you came out of the tunnel."

That was impossible. The tunnel entrance was at least fifty meters away, and the ambient noise should have covered any sounds she made.

"If you had joined me," Kinney continued, "I could have showed you how to make the most of your new abilities. You had potential, and you wasted it. You were given the miracle of Aion's love, and you spurned it."

"I chose to remain human," she countered.

"You chose to become a murderer."

She winced as though slapped. The guilt she felt reignited. Brought to the forefront of her thoughts. She tried shoving it aside to focus on what needed to be done. But it was still there, on the periphery of her mind. Never really gone. A looming presence threatening to overwhelm her. Thus distracted, Astrid didn't notice Kinney step towards her and raise a hand. When she finally noticed, it was too late. The blast of air caught her in the chest and knocked her off her feet. Gasping, she tried rolling over and getting up, but then another blast struck her in the side.

"You took everything from me!" Kinney screamed. He scooped her up off the floor with air and tossed her several meters away. "Murderer! Why couldn't you just accept the gift we gave you? Why did you have to destroy everything I loved?"

The hits were landing rapid-fire now. Astrid curled into a ball to protect her face and head as she endured several minutes of Kinney cursing and pummeling her. The sudden relief when he finally relented was ecstasy. Bruised and bleeding, Astrid lay on the floor for a moment, sobbing and in pain. Somehow, Kinney had managed to weaponize the tool applications installed in him. She recognized the application he'd used. It was a construction application designed to allow a user to easily move heavy objects in industrial settings. Only he'd wielded it with much greater power and precision than the standard application allowed. That had to be a result of Aion's influence. The infusion of the Swarm Mind's nanites must have altered his ability to control and amplify the toolsets provided by HelixCom.

She had the same applications he did, and she had also been infused with the Swarm Mind's nanites like he had. She accessed her tools and discovered she could override the built-in safety limiters. She opened the cutting torch and fiddled with the settings for a moment till she had them set to something she thought she could use. Then Astrid got to her feet and shot Kinney in the back with a steam of fire. By the time it reached him, the stream had spread and didn't do the damage she had hoped it would. Instead of cutting into him, it merely set his hair and clothes alight.

Kinney shrieked in panic and pain at his sudden immolation and sprayed ice over himself to extinguish the flames.

While he flailed and burned, Astrid hobbled forward as fast as her battered body could carry her, raised the heavy wrench she'd taken from the work cart, and swung it for his head.

And missed.

Kinney caught sight of her at the last second and ducked. The wrench struck him in the left shoulder, knocking him backward away from her. He caught her in the chest with another blast of air. She felt and heard something crack. Ignoring the pain, she shot another stream of fire into him. This close, the beam didn't spall. It pierced his uninjured shoulder and cut into the wall behind him. Hearing and smelling the flesh of his shoulder sizzle as it rapidly burned away made Astrid's stomach turn.

Kinney screamed and scrambled to get away.

For her next shot, Astrid set her cutting beam to wide dispersal and hollowed the space in his left side, between his ribs and hip, several centimeters wide. Then, with a dexterity that would have been impressive to him under other circumstances, she narrowed the beam aperture again and shot him through the chest, obliterating his heart.

Kinney's eyes contracted, broadcasting all the fury and hatred he felt in that moment. He'd intended to disable the heat-venting systems on a delay so he could escape and make his way back to Site 2. Once there, he would have worked to revive Aion and waited for rescue from HelixCom. From there, he and Aion would be free to travel and spread his gift throughout the human star systems. Impossible now. Astrid had dashed his hopes yet again. He was alive only because Aion's nanites were keeping him alive. In another moment, even they wouldn't be enough. He was already dead. His mind and body just hadn't realized it yet. If he was going to die, unable to free his god and friend, then he was going to take the rest of them with him.

Before she could react, he fired his own cutting beam. It passed her right side, striking the equipment he'd been working on when she appeared. Then it all went dark. As he fell, the alarm claxons sounded, deafening them both as the noise filled the chamber. Kinney smiled as he lay on the floor and died.

Astrid meanwhile rushed to try to stop the meltdown. As she moved, she felt a horrible grinding in her chest. Not good. It hurt to stand, and breathing was becoming difficult.

Kinney's parting shot had destroyed the control equipment and started a cascading series of failures in the heat regulator. They had perhaps a few minutes before the reactor exploded. Seeing no better options, Astrid activated her anti-radiation and heat shielding, pumped them up well past their original capabilities, then entered the reactor itself.

Immediately, she got a message from Danny. [What the hell are you doing?]

[Kinney sabotaged the reactor. It's going to explode.]

[We know. I'm in Ops. We've been watching on the monitors. You need to get out of there.]

[I'm going to cool the reactor as long as I can. You need to get everyone on the tram and get out of here. I won't be able to hold it for long. Get to Site 2.]

[Astrid, just get out of there. We can all leave together. Don't be a hero.]

She didn't respond. There was no time. The intense heat in the chamber made it harder to breathe and harder to move. She activated the ice application and began cooling the core. Now that her thumb was in the dike, she saw just how futile her efforts were. The temperature was rising much faster than she was capable of countering. She needed more power and more nanites.

[Just get out of here,] she sent. Then shut off her shielding and diverted all her nanites to cooling the core.

Her skin blackened and began flaking off, and her hair had already been fried away in an instant. Her vision went dark as her eyes boiled. Every breath scalded her lungs.

The climbing core temperature slowed, wavered, and then slowly crept down a few degrees. It wasn't enough to prevent the catastrophe, but she hoped it would be enough for everyone to get to safety.

As the tram rounded the bend heading away from Site 1, Danny couldn't help but look back. Bolts of discharging static zapped between the massive cooling sinks poking up from the reactor building. Smoke from several fires billowed through breaks in the outer walls. Looking past Site 1, he could see the skylift pyramid. The extreme heat and turmoil around Site 1 was warping the skeletal steel structure and buffeting the massive teethers that reached up into the atmosphere. The sway they had developed was both terrifying and amazing to behold.

Someone in the car gasped. Danny wasn't the only one watching.

The evacuation had been quick and orderly. For all his faults, one thing Waler had insisted upon was regular emergency drills. A few people had pre-packed bags ready and had brought them. Many, like him and the rest of the team in Operations, had been in the middle of their shifts and had departed from their workstations with nothing more than their work coveralls.

"Look!" someone cried out.

A massive steam plume erupted from the cooling tower. The last-ditch effort to shed heat before the end. Danny checked the tram's progress. They were nearly eight kilometers from the facility now. The very bottom floors of Site 1 were concealed behind the horizon.

An instant later, a flash of blinding light blinded them

all before the tram car could react and obscure the exterior view. A split second later, the carriage was buffeted by a shock wave. Even the inertial compensators couldn't prevent the tram from rocking slightly on the track.

In a flash, Site 1 was gone. They were on their own, headed to Site 2. Danny had told the Operations folks what to expect when they got there. He wasn't looking forward to it. He'd never seen a dead body before, and there were two hundred waiting for them.

With the skin of the tram opaque, the passengers couldn't see what was happening behind them. The mushroom cloud climbing into the sky seemed to have consumed the entirety of the structure that had recently been their home. The neighboring pyramid had been torn apart by the blast, unmooring the twelve-meter-wide transit tube that had acted as both the line tethering the massive counterweight in geosynchronous orbit and the shaft for the elevator that made daily transits from orbit to surface and back again. The sway in the tether that Danny had noticed earlier grew in violence and intensity as it traveled up the tether. When the tether finally ripped free from the counterweight, the release of tension whipped back along the tether, causing it to smash the gateway station and shear through the entangled communications array, cutting Kuridian off from the rest of human civilization.

The survivors would attribute at least twenty of the suicides that would occur over the coming weeks to the loss of communication and the resulting despair the blackout caused.

Beside Danny, Rance and Cho were still staring at the blank wall. Cho was hollow-eyed and pale with disbelief. "What the hell are we supposed to do now?" he said, almost to himself.

He looked around at the people standing shoulder to shoulder in the tram. They'd managed to evacuate pretty much everyone from Site 1. Engineers, biologists, technicians, geneticists. In short, everyone they would need to kickstart a new, homegrown, terraforming effort. To a person, they looked uncertain and even scared and in need of guidance. A path to follow. Assurances they weren't all going to die tomorrow.

He reached into his pocket and removed the slide with Astrid's nanite sample on it. The slide in his hand was that assurance.

He'd have to make sure Kinney took the blame for the deaths at Site 2 and the destruction of Site 1. His friend, Astrid, would get to live forever as the savior who had laid down her life so they might all live. He almost smiled at the thought, but then he remembered he was never going to see her again, hear her jokes, or banter with her about the state of the company and life in general. He was going to miss her.

Danny placed the slide back in his pocket.

Though Cho probably hadn't been expecting anyone to answer, Danny did anyway.

"We'll do the best we can with what we've got left."

Cho didn't look very reassured as the tram sped towards Site 2 and an uncertain future.

CHAPTER 27

KAYAH

"There's a creek up ahead," Jessen said. "I think it's time to try something different."

It had been four days since the incident at the gate, but they were no nearer their destination. Though the distance they had to travel wasn't great, Regaline, Drak, and Jessen had been forced to take a much longer circuitous route to lose the pursuing Interland soldiers and casters. Regaline and Jessen had employed every bit of trail craft and nan-enabled trickery they knew to cover their tracks, while Drak could only run alongside them. He hated feeling useless. He'd escaped and eluded Interland soldiers before and was sure he could do it again. But neither of the older casters would even stop a moment to listen to his suggestions. Though he fumed outwardly, he could secretly admit they were right. They needed all their focus to ensure their survival. There wasn't time to entertain the notions of a barely trained novice caster.

He still hated it, though.

"What do you have in mind?" Regaline said.

"We ford it and split up in the middle. You two go upstream; I'll go down. We each launch decoys and lay false trails as we go. After a kilometer or two, leave the creek and head for that hill there." He pointed to a tree-covered hill to the northwest, about ten kilometers distant. "From there, we can determine if we've put off pursuit enough to continue to the Tower. Continuing to cover tracks and launch decoys as we go, of course. If it worked, we head to the Tower."

Regaline looked dubious. Everything else they'd tried had only slowed their pursuers, who were about a day and a half behind them. The trouble with trying to fool other casters is that they know many of the same tricks and could, therefore, see through them. No matter what they tried, the Interland soldiers were still on their tails.

Off in the distance, Drak could see the rising spires of the old Watch Tower looming large on the horizon. Low clouds obscured the tallest structures, giving the Tower an ethereal silhouette. After four days of running and hiding, it still seemed impossibly far away.

"Okay," Regaline said at last. "Nothing else has worked. Maybe this will."

"It has to. We're running out of space to run."

When they reached the creek, Drak and Jessen shook hands while Regaline pulled Jessen into a tight hug.

"Be careful," she whispered into his ear. "Be safe. See you soon."

"I will, Reg. See you soon." Then he surprised her by giving her a kiss.

Drak looked back twice after they parted. The first time, Jessen had shrunk into the distance as he gingerly picked his way over and around the slick river rocks. The second time, he was out of sight, passed around a creek bend.

Drak returned his focus to where he stepped. One misstep could twist or even break an ankle. Which would be a disaster.

After trudging through the icy water for nearly an hour in silence, Drak turned to Regaline. "Tell me more about what we're going to do once we reach the Tower?"

"First," Regaline said, "we need to lose the soldiers behind us. Then we need to get inside. This shouldn't be too difficult. It's been sealed since the fall of the Watchers, and the Interlanders revere it as a holy site, so they leave it alone. Setting foot inside its consecrated grounds is tantamount to blasphemy. Their capital city, the Hub, is separated from the Tower by at least a hundred meters of open space."

"How do you know all that?" Drak said, almost slipping on a wide, flat rock covered in slick slime.

"A few months ago, I was part of a team that infiltrated their central city on an information-gathering mission."

"The mission where Jessen almost lost his leg, right?"

Regaline scoffed and gave him an indulgent smile. "Yes. That's the one. We'd heard reports of increased activity along Interland's borders. They were sending out more snatch squads than normal. The council sent me and Jessen to ascertain what was going on. That's when I discovered the power fluctuations in the Tower's reactor and surmised they were searching for a descendant of Astrid Free."

"That's when you left to find me and Kayah, right? To keep us from falling into their hands?"

"That's right. Jessen was still healing, and with Brix out of action, I convinced the council to send me alone."

"When we get there, are we just going to open the back door and walk in?"

"I wish. The tower may be sacred, but it's far from unguarded. We'll have to be sneaky to get inside."

"What about that? We've come all this way, and you still haven't told me what I'm supposed to do when we get inside."

Regaline gave him a sharp look that softened a second later.

"You remind me so much of myself at your age. My mother always called me her little PITA. Her pain in the ass."

As Regaline chuckled, her footing slipped on a slippery rock, and she almost went face-first into the creek. She was saved at the last second by a helping hand from Drak.

"Thank you," she said. "In truth, I'm not exactly sure. I've never been inside the Tower. No one has. Not in a hundred years. But we have eyewitness accounts from the last surviving Watchers to guide us. When their order collapsed, the last three survivors made their way to Hillcrest. They've been with us ever since. It's because of their input that we can undertake this mission at all." She paused and looked around. "Let's get out here. My feet are freezing."

Drak followed Regaline out of the water. On the creekbank, Regaline spun up three decoys. She tossed one to the opposite bank, where it started walking due west. On their side of the creek, she set one headed north and the last headed southeast. Then they started following the tracks of the decoy headed north. After a hundred meters, they parted ways with the drone and turned east, toward the hill where they were supposed to reunite with Jessen, covering their back trail the whole way.

It was early evening when they reached the base of the hill. Drak wanted to climb to the top, but Regaline thought better of it.

"Better to wait until it's light," she said.

They laid out alarm snares and set up their bedrolls in between a trio of tall trees grown close together. Regaline showed him a complex camouflage weave that was virtually undetectable from outside.

"When we're inside," Regaline said, continuing their discussion from earlier, "we are going to head down to basement level two. Once we get there, you will access the user interface connected to the power generator and shut it down completely."

"It's still going after all these years?"

"Yes, and it's become dangerously unstable. The interface was locked a long time ago by my father. Your DNA is the key. Shutting it down will eliminate the danger posed by the reactor and kill the entity imprisoned in there."

Drak nodded. "So, we just have to sneak past a bunch of guards, break into a religious site, shut down the power, and kill a monster. Easy."

Regaline gave him an amused smile. "Try to sleep. We have a busy day tomorrow."

After a quick breakfast the following morning, they began working their way slowly up the hill in silence, all the while on the lookout for Jessen or Interland soldiers. Sunlight dove between the trees in shafts, causing the shadows couched around them to appear deeper. Drak found himself peering into those shadows looking for threats. The hilltop was eerily quiet. The lack of birdsong and insect noise only added to his sense of foreboding. As they neared the summit, Drak's heart beat rapidly in his chest, and his neck was tired from swiveling his head to watch everywhere at once. He had to force himself to relax.

The air was fragrant with the scents of a growing forest. The trees were clustered together in thick groups that allowed the undergrowth to run wild in the spaces between, which made the going tough.

As they neared the summit, he glanced up from a stretch of perilous looking roots to find someone in their path. Standing perfectly still, Drak almost mistook the person for another shadow between the trees. It wasn't until he drew closer and noticed Regaline had stopped that he realized the figure was a woman draped in a heavy dark blue cloak and regarding them with silver eyes. Regaline tensed, while Drak swore under her breath and charged his weapons, ready to burn the woman.

"We've been waiting for you," the woman in blue said. "It would be in your best interest to come along peaceably."

Out of the corner of his eye, Drak saw other figures in blue materialize from the trees and shadows around them. He slowly turned his head, hoping to see regular soldiers, and was greeted by twenty-four silvery orbs staring back at him. Thirteen Interland casters had them surrounded. He visibly deflated in defeat. There was no chance of fighting their way through so many.

Regaline had also relaxed her stance in submission, and she held out her hands palms outward, fingers splayed downward. Drak followed suit. Instantly, his arms were forced down to his sides, locked in place by nearly invisible bands of air.

"Good choice," the woman before them said, then motioned for her subordinates to bring them along.

They made their way back down the hill. The leader and three casters in front, three on the right, three on the left and three behind. Before they started moving, Regaline had given Drak a look that seemed to say, "Remain quiet and vigilant." He had answered with the slightest of nods.

Upon exiting the trees at the bottom of the hill, they found Jessen in a clearing, similarly bound and sporting a pair of angry purple bruises on his face. Off to one side, Drak saw Taeg standing proud and smug among the waiting casters. The sight of the traitor made his blood boil. But he checked his temper and refrained from lashing out. This wasn't the time.

Through breaks in the trees, the far outline of a city was visible. Smaller and less distinct than the huge, spectral tower dominating the skyline, it was nonetheless impressive to Drak.

That's where they're taking us, he thought. *To torture and kill us. Maybe that's where Kayah is. Maybe we can still rescue her. If we can rescue ourselves first.*

Surrounded now by twenty silver-eyed casters, the group marched all morning and into the afternoon without stopping or slowing. Drak tracked their position and progress with his map application. Just after lunchtime, he concluded they weren't heading to the city, like he'd originally assumed. Instead, the casters were herding them toward the Tower. The imposing structure had grown while they walked and now took up the entire horizon. He wasn't all that surprised when they exited the trees near the base of the Tower's outer walls and found two people waiting for them.

The first was a tall man. Drak could immediately sense something different about him. Outwardly, his clothing distinguished him from the others. It was a uniform like theirs, though of better cloth, immaculately tailored, and ornately hung with decoration. He stood with a regal bearing, like a man who expected obedience from those around him. He was imposingly tall. His eyes were silver, like those of the casters surrounding them, but that same silvery metallic substance seemed to have leaked into his very skin and hair, making him look more like a statue than a human being.

The other was Kayah. If it weren't for the bonds of air restraining him, Drak would have raced the remaining distance between them. They'd found her.

Maybe we're going to make it after all, he thought.

Regaline hissed in surprise and revulsion when they were brought to a halt before the man. She focused her gaze on the ground. Standing opposite her, Kayah could see her fighting to hold back tears.

After walking under guard all morning, Kayah had been delivered to a strange-looking man at the base of a beautiful, derelict structure. For a moment, she had wondered who the man was, but the honor guard had saluted and stood at rigid attention as they delivered her to him. Which had told her all she needed to know. When the tall man had turned toward them, Kayah had found herself shrinking away from the full force of his hollow gaze.

"Lord Aion," had said the guard commander. "Your prize, my lord." The commander had bowed her head and stepped back.

Aion had stared at Kayah for a moment. His scrutiny had made her skin crawl.

"Excellent," he had said at last. "Go join the others. Take an additional detachment and place a lookout on Hill H-264."

"At once, my Lord!" Then Kayah had been alone with Aion. After his cool regard a moment earlier, he had seemed to have forgotten her entirely and stared out into the tree line a dozen meters away.

"We've been expecting you for some time," Aion had said without turning toward her. His voice was off somehow. There was a buzzing undertone to it. An approximation of a voice rather than something created by vibrating vocal folds. "You will be most useful in helping make us whole again. We have spent many long decades incomplete. Now that the moment of reintegration approaches, we find ourselves impatient for restitution."

Kayah had held her peace.

"We are sure you have not a clue as to what we are referring. That is okay. You do not need to know anything other than you have an important part to play in enabling the future of this small world. A future hundreds of years in the making. Once it is done and you are joined, you shall be exalted."

There had been movement in the trees. A moment later, Kayah had seen three figures surrounded by a ring of Interland casters emerge. Her heart leaped into her throat. It was Regaline and Drak, followed by a man she didn't know, but if he was traveling with them, she was sure he was a friend.

"We've found them, my Lord. As you foresaw," the guard commander said.

Kayah was prodded to join the others standing before Aion. She thought she could detect the faintest curl of a smile on his face. "Come with us." Then Aion turned and stepped over to the wall a few meters behind him.

The surface appeared uniformly smooth everywhere she looked. As the group drew closer, however, Kayah began to discern subtle details that marred the otherwise smooth exterior surface. Regular, symmetrical bumps and ridges that could have been portholes or windows. Indentations that might have been doorways. The structures that comprised the Tower were smooth and unmarred by wind and weather. Though once white, the Tower had become a dull gray, covered in places with lichen and climbing vines. An aura of disuse permeated the very air around the Tower.

It looks like a haunted castle from my mother's stories, Kayah thought. *A gorgeous, scary, haunted castle.*

Aion reached into a hidden recess and spun a small crank wheel. The surface of the wall split as a doorway slowly opened, revealing the darkened interior. While Aion worked the crank, Regaline stood beside her whispering frantically to herself, eyes still cast downward, her head bowed, her whispers a cross between a chant and a prayer. Though still watchful and alert, their guards had drifted away.

"What's the matter?" Kayah whispered.

Regaline gave no answer.

"Regaline?"

The whispering ceased. Replaced by deep, calming breaths.

"That's my father," Regaline said. Kayah turned back to look at the man standing next to the nearly open door. "I had no idea he was still alive after all this time. He's the one we've come here to kill. He's the monster behind the creation of Interland and the subjugation of the green zone."

Kayah couldn't think of anything to say in response.

It didn't matter anyway. The door was open, and Aion—Regaline's father—had returned.

"Come," he said. "There is much to do inside." With a gesture, all but four of the guards formed a ring around the opening. The four who remained, among them Taeg, joined Kayah and the others as they climbed into the darkness inside the gray tower.

The volatile mixture of emotions she felt was nearly crippling. Regaline had never seen her father in the flesh, only renderings created from memories made by her mother and others. She'd never known him. Though without him, she wouldn't exist, he'd been an insignificant part of her life. He and her mother had only spent a single week together. Long enough for her to come into the world nine months later.

Seeing him standing in front of her, tall, imposing, and silver-eyed, stirred something in her. A longing to know him. What he had been like. How he had died.

Satisfaction was far beyond her reach, however, as the thing before her merely looked like her father. After giving life to Hillcrest and her, he'd left both to pursue his duty and had been subsumed by another to be used as an instrument to further its own agenda in the process. As Terrance Rance, he had been a man of honor and a diligent protector of the land and its people. As Aion, it was a defiler of those things, bent on propagating itself and destroying anything that stood in the way.

Her hatred and revulsion were tempered by her curiosity and affection. As Aion led them into the darkness of the ancient Watch Tower, Regaline's internal struggle reached a peak, and she concluded there was nothing left of her father in that body. When the appropriate moment came, she resolved to act without mercy.

A dozen meters from the opening, it was nearly impossible to see, even with the night vision filters activated. Kayah activated her echolocation app to supplement the poor visibility.

Unbeknownst to all but Aion, the path they took through the darkened structure had been set up by Rance more than seventy years ago as an escape. Aion led them through the warren of corridors, making turns seemingly at random. Several times, Kayah caught sight of black smears on the floors and walls. She thought they might be old blood but dared not ask about it. She was surprised by how clean everything was, other than the old blood stains. She assumed that was due to the interior being sealed off from the elements. Only a thin layer of dust coated everything. Looking down at her feet, she noted the tracks they were making.

Aion led them to a stairwell and began ascending. Regaline's plans would have taken them into the bowels of the structure to accomplish their mission. Aion took them in the opposite direction. She looked down into the darkness below and shivered.

How far down do the steps go? she wondered.

They exited the twisty column of steps several floors up. After hand-cranking another door open, Aion led them into a control room. At least, that's what Kayah assumed it was. In there, like the halls they had traversed, there were scorch marks on the walls and black stains on the floor, confirming her fears that they were indeed old blood stains. In the center of the room stood a statue of dull silver, arms upraised as though beholding something glorious.

Aion entered the room and paused only a moment beside the statue. The guards prodded, forcing Kayah and her companions to follow him all the way into the room.

"Now we've come to it," Aion said, turning to address them. Taeg stepped uncomfortably close to Kayah. His mere presence gave her shivers. In the corners of the room, the guards set glow globes alight, dispelling the inky darkness with soft, warm white light.

Aion's gaze fixed on Kayah.

"It is time for you to fulfill the mission for which you were recruited, Kayah Handler." He turned slightly and extended a hand toward a small outcropping behind him. "Interface with the system. You do not need to concern yourself with fixing any of the problems you encounter. You could not even if you tried. All we need from you is to simply lift the security lock placed on this system. Once accomplished, we will do the rest."

Kayah swallowed. This was indeed what Regaline had recruited her to do. But here and now, in the presence of the enemy, it felt wrong. She shrank from Aion's hideous, hollow gaze, tried to take a step back, and collided with the immovable form of Taeg standing right behind her. He placed his hands on her shoulders, fingers digging in painfully, and pushed her forward until she was standing directly before Aion. Then he retreated to stand behind Drak. The guards behind Regaline and Jessen had all formed blades from their hands and held them threateningly at her friends. Kayah thought this odd. Why would they resort to physical blades? What was wrong with their weapon applications? She tried to access her own defensive applications but found them unavailable. Something about this place prevented them from using their weapons.

Aion towered over her. "Place your hand upon the pad, Kayah," he said in his unnatural voice. "Lift the security lockout and then step away."

Kayah tried to face him. To show defiance. But found she couldn't meet his gaze for more than a few seconds. "No," she said.

There was no change in Aion's posture or demeanor. However, it was evident he was exasperated and enraged by her refusal.

"Time and time again, we offer you the chance to exercise your supposed *free will*. Time and time again, you cling to this illusion to the detriment of your person and your species. Consider this."

He waved a hand, and each of his guards sprang into action. Taeg grabbed Drak by the throat. The guards behind Regaline and Jessen placed their blades against their exposed throats.

"This is yet another iteration of the long-running experiment in free will. Thus far, the data does not support the concept as a boon to humankind. We will ask you three more times. Each time you refuse, one of your friends will die, starting with your mentor, Regaline. After that, we will simply assume control of you and do it ourselves anyway. We could simply take you and be done with it; however, we choose not to. We are offering you the choice of cooperation and willing compliance. To choose of your own *free will*.

"Now, place your hand on the interface pad, deactivate the

security lockout, and step away."

Kayah looked at her companions one at a time before she slowly approached the interface pad. It illuminated as she stepped in front of it. A square panel with the simple outline of a hand in the middle. She tentatively reached out and placed her hand in the outline and was shocked when her hand sank into the seemingly solid screen. A cold, tingling sensation started in her fingertips and rippled up her arm and throughout her whole body. As it passed, she was gradually filled with a warmth so soft and comforting that she grew lightheaded. A virtual screen appeared before her eyes. Lines of code scrolled across the bottom while a status bar appeared and gradually swirled and filled directly before her eyes. Once it finished, she was greeted by a welcome screen.

"I'm in," she said. Her voice sounded small and timid, even to her own ears. "I don't know what to do next."

"It is just like your application controls," Aion said, his voice coming from uncomfortably close beside her left ear. "Navigate to the security controls and unlock them, then navigate to the dampening field controls and deactivate them, and then log out and step away."

Kayah took a deep breath, then plunged into the system menus. Aion was right; it was just like accessing her nan. Though these menus seemed far less malleable than her own, conforming to someone else's idea of efficiency and unable to be customized, unlike her own. It took her what felt like a few minutes to locate the menu Aion wanted.

"I think I found it."

"That was quicker than expected," Aion replied with a hint of surprise in his atonal voice. "Now find the control panel to deactivate it and do so now. Then return to the main menu and deactivate the security lockout."

Kayah pictured her friends held hostage just scant meters away. Their lives were in her hands, and she was powerless to help them. There had to be a way out of this. It was unlikely

Aion was going to let them go once she was finished doing his bidding. They would either be killed outright or else converted into slaves for his army.

Kayah took a moment to examine the dampening field Aion was so concerned with. As far as she could tell, it prevented them from using their more dangerous applications, but it also held something else in check. Curious, she dove deeper for a closer look.

She almost gasped when the enormity of what she was seeing became clear to her. The man Aion and, to an even lesser extent, his casters were all minor instances, mere slivers, of the larger intelligence that called itself Aion. Everywhere she looked, she found interconnected nodules of nanites. They made up the form and structure of the buildings they were standing in. The immense scope of the dormant mind before her was boggling, and it was all held in check by the dampening field that effectively lobotomized it. If she turned the field off, then the creature would reform itself, and there was no telling what sort of damage it would cause if that were to happen.

She turned her attention to the room they were in and was surprised by how clearly she could see everyone assembled around her. Her perspective seemed to float above them, but when she focused, the view zoomed in close to the object of her attention. She recognized herself, Regaline, Jessen, and Drak. Representations of their bodies composed of a churning green vapor, or so it seemed. She could see the individual nanites at work in their bodies, regulating and repairing, a symbiosis of organic and synthetic. She could clearly see Aion and his minions, too. Almost more clearly than her companions. They were solid, made of the same hard dark-red nanites that filled every molecule of the structure surrounding them, though of a slightly different shade, as if to distinguish them from the dormant consciousness around them. Ephemeral, almost nonexistent lines ran from each of them to the man called Aion. More lines poured from him through the open doorway. Kayah thought they must connect him with the others standing guard outside, maybe even across Interland. The dampening field was affecting all of them. She could see them slowly losing cohesion. The longer they remained under its influence, the more damage it inflicted upon them. Beyond their inability to use their weapons, Kayah and the other humans were untouched by it, but these creatures were slowly dying.

Kayah didn't have a plan when she reached out to toggle the field off, just an idea, a notion that she might be able to save herself and her friends. Instead of turning the field off, as ordered, she cranked it up and sent out an overload pulse.

"What are you doing, Kayah?" Aion asked, sensing what she was doing. "We told you to—"

He was cut off by the agonized cries of his guards, and then Aion himself succumbed and collapsed in pain. The massive discharge of the energy inhibited the Swarm Mind's nanites from communicating and connecting. The blast wave left her and the others like her untouched, but nearly killed Aion and his minions.

Their only problem now was that the dampening field had burned out.

The nanite intelligence infesting the walls all around them was already starting to reawaken.

Regaline didn't hesitate when the guard holding her at knifepoint shrieked and fell to his knees. She didn't know what was happening, but she was certain that Kayah had been the cause. Somehow, the girl had found a way to disable the guards and Aion. Whatever she'd done had also released the block on her weapons. She instantly reacted without thought or hesitation. The moment the guard's blade left her throat, she knocked him to the ground and stopped his heart with an intense electric arc.

Then she launched herself at the thing possessing her father. The creature had caused so much strife and pain and death. The entire history of their world was shaped by the atrocities this creature had committed.

From the corner of her eye, she saw Jessen fight off his captor. Drak had already started pummeling Taeg with fire. She found she was more than a little scared of the murderous intensity she saw in the boy's eyes. Good. They'd picked up on the opportunity, the same as she had. She hoped they could make the most of it.

Before her, Aion was already recovering and turning to strike Kayah, who was still interfaced with the computer and blind to the attack. Before he could, Regaline threw a full-power bolt of electricity that hit him in the side and sent him flying into the far wall. Away from Kayah.

A normal person would have been killed or at least rendered unconscious by a bolt like she'd just thrown. But Aion was back on his feet immediately, clothes smoking, his hollow silver eyes focused on Regaline.

"Come on, you murdering son of a bitch!" she screamed as she charged.

Watching the Swarm Mind's network of nanite nodes reconnecting was fascinating. Kayah imagined this was how a brain worked. The neural network constantly trading off the neurons constituting sensory input, autonomic applications, and conscious thought. She forced herself to look away. Aion, the real Aion, was waking up, and she needed to find a way to stop him.

The sheer number of nanites she saw was staggering. Everything from the structural members to the floor and wall panels to the complex equipment and machinery operating within were all completely infused with its nanites. There wasn't a molecule of matter within the site that wasn't connected to the rest via the microscopic robots.

It was at once awesome and terrifying to behold.

The energy fields around each cluster unified and intensified as they joined other clusters. The exponential increase meant she didn't have much time.

Once she got over the magnificence she was witnessing, Kayah found something interesting. Any nanites she'd interacted with before they could become reintegrated were avoided by the rest. As though contact with her had tainted them. When she more closely examined the nanites actively ignored by the reforming consciousness, she found they had imprinted upon her. She could exert control over millions of nanites completely outside of her own body. What's more, those nanites not only obeyed her commands, but when she moved them to interact with the nanites of the nascent consciousness, they were also overwritten as well.

Elated, Kayah began ordering her newfound army about.

Some clusters she sent into unclaimed areas of the facility, where Aion's nanites had not yet awoken, to recruit and grow. Others, she drove into the midst of the neural networks under construction. Like cancer, these spikes of nanites corrupted and coopted the others. To the final group, she gave a special mission. While the others were disrupting the Swarm Mind's reformation, this group she tasked with the physical destruction of the tower itself. She seeded them around in small cells, scattered to cause as much physical damage as possible. Instead of rewriting the nanites they encountered, they consumed and destroyed them and the material they inhabited.

From somewhere behind her, Kayah heard someone shout, "No. What are you doing? Stop, please." She took this as a sign that her efforts were having the desired effect.

All three groups, like the consciousness against which they were struggling, were growing at a rapidly increasing rate. In the three seconds since she'd set them out on their separate missions, all three groups had doubled in size. Three seconds later, they'd doubled again. The Swarm Mind was growing exponentially as well. Just not as quickly, it was attempting to organize itself as it grew, its progress hindered by the disruptions caused by Kayah's own nanite swarms. Aion was attempting to create delicate arrays of complex geometries, intricate far beyond her ability to understand and connected to other unique geometric shapes in layers upon layers, themselves formed into other intricate patterns. This was the mathematical face of the Aion.

Even to Kayah's ignorant eye, Aion was strikingly beautiful. A work of art.

Until her formless globules of nanites reached them and smashed to bits everything they encountered. Scattering Aion's neurons. Consuming what they could reach. Destroying what they couldn't.

When she took a step back, she could see the damage her nanites were inflicting upon the as-yet-unaware creature. Gorgeous and fragile structures obliterated as her cancers hammered through. The mind continued forming, unaware of the danger. Though higher cognition was nearly in place, Aion was not yet self-aware. As such, the efforts it undertook to defend itself from her attack were limited in scope and uncoordinated.

Node after node fell as her nanites consumed the mind. At the same time, her other nanites were consuming the facility. Satisfied she had done all she could do, Kayah disconnected from the interface terminal, returned to the real world, and gasped in horror.

The control center wasn't a large space. The separate fights going on crossed over into and interfered with each other as they unfolded. From the start, Jessen was at a disadvantage as he fought with two of the guards who had accompanied them inside. When the blast wave struck and he saw Regaline spring into action, Jessen raised an arm and fired a super-dense icicle into the eye of the guard standing next to him, dropping him. Then he knocked the other down with a flying tackle. After a few seconds of grappling, the first guard, now short an eye, delivered a kick to his side, knocking Jessen off his companion. From then on, it was a dance to remain out of the reach of one, while striking at the other.

A few feet away, Drak dodged out of Taeg's reach and flash-fried the traitor's face. Taeg grunted in shock and pain. Drak laughed as he ran away. He turned and had to immediately stop, lest he tumble headlong into Jessen's fight. The guards were circling, trying to pin him between them. That brought one of them close to Drak, with his back completely exposed. Drak smiled and sent a fire lance through the bastard's back.

Unfortunately, he wasn't careful with his aim, and the beam nearly took Jessen's head off, too.

"Sorry!" Drak shouted. Then he turned his attention back to Taeg, who was running up on him fast. Again, Drak hit him with another flash of heat and dashed away.

Regaline, meanwhile, was having troubles of her own. Once upon a time, Aion had been Terrance Rance, her father. A man who, by all accounts, had been a superb and highly skilled fighter. Those reflexes and skills hadn't dulled in the years since his possession by Aion. If anything, they'd grown sharper through Interland's constant warring. Every attack she tried, he deflected. Every defense she attempted nearly broke beneath his attack. Every time she tried to maneuver him into a disadvantage, he saw through it and refused to be goaded. It was frustrating and exhausting.

She saw Drak kill one of the guards fighting Jessen. She felt an instant of pride. The hotheaded boy had come a long way. If he survived, he would become a skilled and powerful caster. If she survived, Regaline decided she was going to take a long, well-deserved vacation.

Aion darted in for another attack. Instead of countering it, she met him head-on. The pair slammed together. Aion continued pressing his attack, but Regaline had a hold of his hands, so his fire bolts burst harmlessly on the walls. Using his greater height and weight, Aion lifted her off her feet to slam her into the floor. In response, she wrapped her legs around his middle and blasted his exposed neck and shoulders with arcs of electricity.

On the other side of the room, Jessen had just landed a critical hit on his opponent with an ice blast. The guard's face was pale and tinged blue and gray. Under Jessen's onslaught, the guard was slowing down and nearly finished.

Then Jessen was knocked over by Drak.

Drak had tried to get in close to hit him with something that would actually do some damage, but Taeg had anticipated the move and finally managed to lay hands on him. He hefted the boy above his head and threw him through the air into Jessen's back. This caused Jessen's killing blow to fly wild, skimming Regaline and breaking her grip on Aion. The guard regained his feet and plunged his hands into Jessen's chest, where he generated a ball of fire that incinerated everything behind his ribs.

Drak screamed in fury and cut the guard's head off with the fire blast he'd prepared for Taeg. He tried getting to his feet, but Tae was already on top of him, wrapping his fingers around his neck. Terrified panic overtook him as Taeg began to squeeze.

Once she'd been knocked off, Aion wasted no time grabbing Regaline. Once she was pinned and unable to move, Aion drove finger probes into her chest. He stared into her terrified eyes. Over the years, Aion had come to relish this part of the conversion process. The uncertainty, the agony and terror, and finally, the release and peace once the joining was complete. Each joining took a lot out of him. Leaving him drained and weak for days after. In the beginning, Aion had had to regularly convert disciples. He was building an army and a society, and needed officers and administrators. Minions to do his bidding. After this many years, he could afford to be far more selective and sparing in his conversions. Once his main body was released, however, there would be no reason to hold back. Everyone on this planet would be joined and brought into him. Knowing his was moments from being complete again elated him. He was close, so close to finally bringing his plans to fruition and escaping this horrible backwater wasteland of a planet. He went to trigger the release and begin flooding her with his nanites, but suddenly found he couldn't. Something prevented him. Something deep inside. Aion tried again. This time, whatever was preventing him from consuming Regaline forced him to remove his fingers from her chest.

What is happening? Aion thought. That was when the entity inside came to the forefront.

"No," Aion cried out. "What are you doing? Stop. Please don't. You can't be here. You're dead."

From somewhere deep in Aion, Rance's consciousness reemerged. He'd spent the last seven decades hiding. A mere shadow in his own mind, watching the atrocities committed by his hands, waiting for the moment when he could act and take his body back. Aion had recognized Regaline as his daughter the moment he laid eyes on her. Because he knew it, Rance did too. The blast from the dampening field, followed by Regaline's immediate attack, had weakened the creature. Rance watched it all. His moment come at last.

Then Regaline fell, and Aion moved in, fingers splayed and extended, ready to convert her. Hesitation cast aside, Rance acted to save his daughter. His consciousness arose from the depths of the brain he shared with the abomination and began displacing it.

As he wrestled control of his body away from the Swarm Mind splinter, he spared a glance at the woman lying on the floor, his daughter, and felt a pang of regret and overwhelming rage at missing out on her life. He took great satisfaction in smothering the monster that had stolen his body and prevented him from knowing his child.

Aion staggered back. Regaline, injured but still alive, acted on instinct and sent a massive arc of electricity into its chest while it was distracted and vulnerable. Strange that it stopped its attack at the last moment. Stranger still, at the last moment, Aion seemed to wear a little smile as he looked affectionately upon her, just before she obliterated him.

It was at this moment that Kayah reemerged from the interface. She'd heard the fighting going on all around her and knew the room would be a chaotic mess when she returned. But seeing it firsthand was still a shock. Jessen was dead. Regaline was bloodied but still conscious and fighting, a smear of smoking ash streaking away on the floor before her. Then her eyes found Taeg throttling the life from Drak.

She fired a concentrated blast of air straight into the back of Taeg's head. Drak lay in an unconscious heap as Taeg stumbled and released him. He recovered quickly and turned to face her. His silver eyes were unreadable, but a small, hungry smile creased his lips as he started toward her.

"No," she said, feeling an intense calm settle over her. "No more of this."

Taeg lunged for her and bloodied his nose when he came abrupt halt against the solid wall of air she'd wrapped around him. His confused expression might have been amusing if she hadn't been so deadly earnest. Confusion quickly gave way to rage once he realized he was frozen in place. Trapped, he opened his mouth to curse her, and Kayah created a spinning funnel of air and forced it into his open mouth. Whatever pejoratives Taeg had intended died before they could form as Kayah began forcing air into his mouth, down his throat, and into his lungs.

Taeg's eyes bulged as his lungs filled beyond capacity. Unable to exhale due to the force of the incoming air, he started thrashing against the invisible bonds holding him.

Kayah continued forcing air into Taeg. Long past the maximum volume of his lungs, and they burst. Long past the air filling his body cavities and displacing his other internal organs. Long past his skin expanding and blowing up like a balloon. Long past the tears in his skin that hissed and squeaked as the excess air leaked out. Long past the point when his eyes became unfocused, his head lulled to the side, and his body went limp.

Only when she was sure Taeg was completely dead and gone did she release him. Leaking blood and fluid from a hundred small tears, Taeg crumpled to the floor when she released her air binds. Taking a deep breath, Kayah looked from Drak to Regaline. He was coughing and stirring; she was unconscious and still. Both needed her help.

Before she could decide who to go to first, the reactor alarms began keening.

The nanites she'd tasked with consuming the Tower had reached the power plant.

Kayah hurried to Drak's side and rolled him onto his side. After a moment, he sat up, still coughing.

"What the hell's that noise?" he croaked. As he sat up, she could see he was having trouble speaking.

"Don't talk," she said. "I'll explain later, but for now, we have to get out of here." She hauled him to his feet, then went over to check on Regaline. She was alive. Barely. "Get on her other side and help me get her up."

Once they had Regaline supported between them, they stumbled out of the gore-covered room. What followed was a harrowing race through pitch-black corridors to escape the rapidly deteriorating building. The floor heaved and buckled unsteadily as she and Drak half carried, half dragged Regaline. The stench of melting plastic and charred metal filled the air, causing her eyes to burn and making it difficult to breathe. Several times, she worried they'd become lost and halted to find her bearings.

A muffled roar from deep below their feet filled the air with noise, accompanied by a dramatic increase in the movement of the floor and walls around them.

Finally, after turning a corner, Kayah saw the exit. She and Drak redoubled their efforts, and a few minutes of stumbling and falling progress later, they emerged from the darkness.

The sun hung low in the sky, but there was still enough light to see by, so they didn't stop moving until they were at least a dozen meters from the wall. They gingerly laid Regaline against a large rock, then turned back to see what was happening behind them.

Drak coughed and whistled, and Kayah gave a quiet gasp.

The spires and domes that rose high above them were slowly collapsing. Whole sections of the structure seemed fuzzy and indistinct as they dissolved before her eyes. A tall structure in the center caved in on itself. From somewhere deep below, a blinding light appeared and erupted into the dusky sky, bathing everything above in white brilliance and casting deep black shadows upward. The disintegration they were witnessing sped up as more portions of the facility collapsed and were consumed by the fire burning in the bowels of the Tower.

As suddenly as it started, all at once, it was over.

The fusion reaction powering the nanites had burned itself out, leaving the remaining nanites cold and lifeless. All that remained were jagged, half-destroyed walls of steel and glass.

Then she saw the bodies of the guards left behind when Aion had led them inside. Cautiously, Kayah approached the nearest. She lay on her back; her eyes, once silver and featureless, had become normal, though blank and staring skyward. The shallow rising of her chest told Kayah the woman was still alive; however, the lack of reaction to anything around her indicated her mind was gone. It was the same story for the rest of the casters who'd been left behind.

Kayah looked upon the destruction she'd wrought and felt a slight smile tug at the corner of her lips. The nightmare haunting their world was over.

She returned to sit with Drak and Regaline. She had trouble deciphering her feelings at that moment. So many had lost their lives and souls. Claimed by a monster created long before any of them had been born. She felt appalled at the loss yet elated that there would be no more. Satisfied, she began using her nan to help heal Regaline's wounds.

They decided to camp where there for the night to give them all a chance to rest and recuperate. This gave Kayah a chance to look over some of the files she had found. While she was inside the system, she'd managed to snag a library's worth of data. It included the history of the human presence on Kuridian, as well as information about human civilization in the stars beyond.

Growing up, she'd never imagined anything larger than her parents' farmstead and their little community of neighbors. Upon meeting Regaline, her worldview had been dramatically expanded to include far-flung lands across the breadth of Kuridian. She now knew there was a larger galaxy out there. Dozens of human-occupied worlds.

All of them built upon the innovation of nanotechnology.

What if these other humans came looking for their lost colony world? What if a creature like Aion had already succeeded where it had failed? What if they, the descendants of vat-born humans tailormade to live on a hostile planet while simultaneously terraforming it, were the last truly free humans in the galaxy?

Kayah knew she might never learn the answers to her questions. Might never have her worries laid to rest. But that was okay, she decided as she lay down to sleep. She was alive. Best to revel in that. Tomorrow they would begin the journey to Hillcrest. With all three of them exhausted and injured to various degrees, it was going to be rough going. And that was okay. With Drak and Regaline beside her, Kayah knew she could handle whatever was thrown their way.

ABOUT ATMOSPHERE PRESS

Founded in 2015, Atmosphere Press was built on the principles of Honesty, Transparency, Professionalism, Kindness, and Making Your Book Awesome. As an ethical and author-friendly hybrid press, we stay true to that founding mission today.

If you're a reader, enter our giveaway for a free book here:

SCAN TO ENTER
BOOK GIVEAWAY

If you're a writer, submit your manuscript for consideration here:

SCAN TO SUBMIT
MANUSCRIPT

And always feel free to visit Atmosphere Press and our authors online at atmospherepress.com. See you there soon!

ABOUT THE AUTHOR

BRYAN MCBEE is the author of *Vector Zero*, *Afterworld*, and *Abnormal Ends*, also from Atmosphere Press. After serving in the US Army, he attended Boise State University and graduated with a degree in Writing and Communications. He is an avid bookworm, cinephile, and gamer. He lives in Idaho with his wife and daughter.